THE
DESERTER

by Robert Koch

HERALD PRESS
Scottdale, Pennsylvania
Waterloo, Ontario

Library of Congress Cataloging-in-Publication Data
Koch, Robert, 1943-
    The deserter / by Robert Koch.
        p.   cm.
    ISBN 0-8361-3519-9 :
    1. United States—History—Civil War, 1861-1865—Fiction.
I. Title.
PS3561.029D4   1990
813'.54—dc20
                                                    90-30530
                                                       CIP

THE DESERTER
Copyright © 1990 by Herald Press, Scottdale, Pa. 15683
    Published simultaneously in Canada by Herald Press,
    Waterloo, Ont. N2L 6H7. All rights reserved.
Library of Congress Catalog Card Number: 90-30530
International Standard Book Number: 0-8361-3519-9
Printed in the United States of America
Cover art by Edwin B. Wallace/Book design by Merrill R. Miller

97 96 95 94 93 92 91 90 10 9 8 7 6 5 4 3 2 1

To my parents
Roy Swartz Koch and Martha Horst Koch
for teaching me
the way to peace

PART ONE

THE TELEGRAM

1

A tongue of icy wind licked at his neck, then lifted a strand of his thinning gray hair off his forehead. It went on, traveling down his arm where it riffled the unopened telegram he held in his left hand, away from his thick body like something dirty. He stood rooted to the spot he'd been in since the boy had handed down the message without dismounting his mare. Now messenger and beast were disappearing in a distant cloud of dust. Dust that rose slowly into a sky grown heavy with thunderclouds.

Benjamin King was fifty-five years old, overweight, nearsighted, and sick at heart. He knew he did not need to open the wire he held to learn that his life from this day on would be vastly altered. A mere shadow of its former vitality. The chill in his heart seemed a fitting echo of the mid-September wind which was suddenly unseasonably cold.

"Telegram from Washington, sir!" The boy's four words had been enough. No need to tell this aging citizen what that signified. It could mean only one thing. He shuddered as another gust of wind slid around him, finding his heart somehow.

He thought of Joseph, somewhere in Virginia. Or was it Maryland? It didn't matter, anymore. They would be shipping him home—now he would be useless as cannon fodder. In a box. Would they bill him for the freight, here in far-off Michigan? By the mile? Or by weight? His son was tall, long, and solid.

Grim humor bubbled around his heart, but in an instant it turned into a film of tears on his gray eyes. He brought up his free hand and pinched away the water. His mind spun, striving for balance, for normality. One part of it pushed away the thought of the news that fluttered in his fingertips, another portion of him recalled his son's last letter. From a place in Virginia near the capital, Washington city. Nothing more definite than that, because censorship limited details. It seemed ridiculous to Ben, for letters posted to the West to be considered a possible benefit to the rebels!

But there was never a shadow of doubt where the Army of the Potomac *had* been, Ben thought bitterly. *The New York Tribune* took care of hindsight admirably. Even in distant southern lower Michigan the fire and ire of Horace Greeley left their marks in every local rag-and-scandal sheet till a semiretired farmer and part-time preacher felt like giving up his subscriptions, starved as he might be for fresh reading matter.

He sighed and stared at the sealed telegram. He wiggled a blunt, calloused thumb beneath the envelope flap. Something caught in his throat. Impulsively, he jerked his thumb away again, and stuffed the flimsy paper into a breast pocket of his broadcloth vest. No need to read the actual words. Not yet, anyway. In his mind's eye he already could see the message of sympathy. The personal condolences from Father Abraham. Maybe even in that worthy's own hand, from that great white city which had for over a year now been the seat of the great god of war who ruled the hearts and minds of men. For too long the passions of greed and selfishness had reigned in their souls.

Ben King realized he was trembling. He ran a hand over his balding head. His knees shook. Suddenly, he felt old and he grasped the gatepost to steady himself. He swallowed, took a deep breath, and the movement seemed to cause a door to open into his memory.

Washington city, the District of Columbia, nation's capital. It was a familiar place for Ben King, when he lived just a short buggy ride north, in southern Pennsylvania. That was home, before his father's sudden death and his move to the frontier with his mother and new bride. He had returned there once in the intervening years. It had been back in the late forties and he had taken nine-year-old Joseph with him. The boy had never seen the original family homestead. He had loved it, the trip on horseback, and the paddle-wheel steamboat.

There had been a war on then, too, he recalled. It had been in Mexico, so distant yet so near. Victory was almost a foregone conclusion, and the capital city rang with debate over how to treat slavery in the new territory gained from a prostrate foe.

Many had called the war immoral and beneath the dignity of a democratic republic to wage. Ben and his two brothers had argued with old friends and neighbors one long afternoon, then over the supper hour and into the night. They had marshaled arguments like regiments, slinging barbs and parrying thrusts, recalling how their disagreements had been almost identical before Ben had left. But then, in 1837, there had been no war on, and the arguments were more theoretical.

Benjamin had cited chapter and verse of Holy Scripture to claim that a Christian had a moral duty to renounce war. The old friends and neighbors, good Lutherans to a man, had sat around the fire, back in '37, and stared in consternation. This was treason, their eyes said in judgment. But Ben, spiritual child of Menno Simons and reader of history and the Bible, believed otherwise. For over 150 years, Mennonites had been the apolitical, nonresistant "quiet in the land." War was evil and to be shunned, at all costs. But his non-Mennonite neighbors had commenced to shun *him*, one of the chief reasons he'd moved away.

A decade later, with the spirit of reconciliation strong within him, he and Joseph had come home to Pennsylvania to straighten out a detail of Ben's father's estate. There had still remained too much rancor. Joseph had sat and listened and seemed impressed by the patriotic talk of his father's old neighbors. Reconciliation had failed, but his son's questions on the long ride home were precocious and sincere. Ben had prayed as the frigid hand of fear had gripped his heart: what if a war came when his son was twenty, and not ten years old? But the memory of the neighborly quarrel had faded. Time slid past peacefully. Until this year, 1862.

"The Potomac River!"

His own voice startled him. Hadn't there been something in Joseph's last letter, barely a week ago, about the army moving northwest from the capital city? How Robert Lee's men seemed to be fading toward the mountains after their last big victory? And that General McClellan was taking his own sweet time about chasing him?

Surprising that *that* had passed the censor!

Why had it?

He shook his head, giving up. He knew nothing of the ways of war. Furthermore, he never wanted to become wiser about it.

The telegraph boy's dust had thinned to invisibility. The thunderclouds had melded into a uniform heavy blue-black sky that pressed down on the earth. There was barely room left for the wind to slide between earth and heaven. It smelled of rain and the farmer in Ben King momentarily forgot the heaviness in his soul as he glanced at the cornfield beyond the split-rail fence. It had been a parched summer. Any moisture would be a godsend. As if to second his thought, a stiff gust rattled the prematurely broken stalks on both sides of the dusty road. The rain smell strengthened.

12

He started for the house, pulling shut the gate behind him. As his eyes routinely took in the white clapboard-sided exterior of the two-story building he'd raised with his own hands, he felt a shock. It looked different, suddenly, now that Joseph could no longer come home. Every detail of roof shake, rain gutter, rose trellis, porch railing, climbing ivy, massive stone chimney—features so often viewed they were seldom noticed—all seemed to undergo a change so sudden and deep that Ben was shaken to his roots. Now it would always remain a silent dwelling, bereft of the hoots and shouts of youth. It would stand like a monument, empty of the excitement and promise of the future, of grandchildren. Dead as tradition.

His throat tightened. He peeled off his wire-framed spectacles and brushed the sleeve of his cotton shirt over his eyes. Now there were only the old folks left, and doomed to stay that way. His seventy-eight-year-old mother, Kate. His wife, Lovina, half a dozen years younger than he was, but who looked and acted more like a contemporary of his feisty mother than a daughter-in-law. And himself—a professional tiller of the earth and not-very-successful minister of the gospel—still full of flesh, but already fading, withering and shriveling inside, like the corn in his fields.

He approached his heavy front door with dread. It stood partway open, where he'd left it in his hurry to answer the boy's call beyond the gate. Now came the moment of truth, facing the mother and grandmother with the news. They'd look to lean on his male strength. He almost sobbed out a laugh, but it came out a sigh. He entered, thinking that now he would more than ever have to act the part of the immovable rock. The part of his body that moved seemed to be dead. Seemed to be missing. His heart pounded. Some rock.

The door snicked shut behind him. One part of him felt

the satisfaction of his carpentry skill and another smelled the warm vapors fragrant from the kitchen. It struck him how chilly the outside had become. He peeled off his vest and draped it over the arm of the horsehair sofa, which sat like an ancient gray eminence all along the front wall of the parlor. At its far end loomed the fireplace, dead and cold from the summer's nonuse. Ben's eye caught on the wood basket sitting empty beside the grate. His mind groped for something to fill it, for a way to put off the telling. Could be, he thought, that the coming storm will bring in a cold snap, maybe even first frost. Ought to get some wood, clean out the chimney.

Ben forced his mind to ready itself for breaking the news. Enough of this cowardice. But he knew it was a hopeless struggle. He dreaded too much the saying of the words to his mother and to Lovina. For an instant a foolish hope lit his thoughts, that maybe the telegram was some other matter entirely. But before he had even started to turn toward his vest, to retrieve the paper, his common sense told him to stop his shilly-shallying.

Their voices came from the kitchen, bright and cheery as hope. A ray of sunshine shot in the window and garnished the mantel of the hearth. He felt even colder.

"Who was that?" His wife stood in the kitchen doorway, wiping her floury hands on her apron. Her round, pleasant face was flushed from the stove's radiance. "Why didn't you invite him in, Ben?" She pushed a strand of graying hair behind her ear. "There's plenty of roast for company."

He wanted to turn and flee.

"Benjamin?" His mother's white-haired head came up behind Lovina's. "What's going on?"

"Ah . . . just a neighbor." He licked his lips. "John Schmidt. Wanted to warn me there may be frost tonight." He'd never lied to either of them before. He felt his ears burn.

"Hah!" His mother almost cackled. "Frost out of a cloudy, windy sky! None of us were born during the night, son. Come now, the truth!" She waited, her pale blue eyes accusing.

He swallowed hard. His eyes flicked toward the vest, then dropped to the floor, desperately. "The woodbox," he pointed. "It's near empty. Reckon I'd better collect some more. Getting cold." He bent to pick it up and move toward the door. The women stepped aside, reflexively. Through the kitchen lay the woodshed. Beyond that was the back door, avenue of escape to the woodpile and the barn, always his haven. He strode through the doorway, past his wife and mother like a charging bull, ignoring their startled looks.

He grabbed the double-bitted axe and his ratty gray sweater from where it hung beside the woodshed door. Lovina's voice followed him outside. "You can do that later, dear. Supper's near ready!" He felt her eyes boring into his back as he shrugged into the sweater. But he didn't answer or meet her face, and his agony dug deeper than words. Inside him was a ragged hole, rapidly filling with a silent scream.

Ben stumbled past the woodpile without seeing it, his thoughts in a far-off place. Inside the barn it was already night. His free hand went automatically to his sweater pocket for a match, and just as reflexively found the kerosene lantern on its usual nail inside the door. He set down the wood basket and lit the lamp. In the soft glow of the flame his glance swept across the table, taking in his small herd of holstein milk cows and, at the far end, like a moving shadow, the chestnut stallion in his own pen. The cattle moved restlessly, reminding him it was past milking time as they turned their shining dark eyes toward the sudden light.

It was warm in the low-ceilinged stable, beneath the

beams he'd hewn out by himself a quarter century past. Even in winter the body heat of the beasts warmed the pens and stalls, snug beneath the mows and granary piled deep in the upper reaches of the barn. Being inside this rude structure, among the dumb, predictable animals of God's creation, always gave Ben a sense of peace and prosperity. Now, surrounded by his barn and his stock, his spirit eased.

He moved down the row of stall mangers toward the horse pen. The sacks of feed grain were between mangers and pen for ease in doing chores. He'd quiet the cows with feed before milking them. Ben bent and filled the scoop from the open burlap bag, and almost laughed as Prince swung into his routine. He felt the stallion's velvet nostrils under his sweater back, snorting hot breath up his spine.

"Hello, horse, how you been?" Ben straightened and turned. He set down the lantern and stroked the soft nose.

Prince whickered and nuzzled the man's chest. His tender nostrils beckoned at the brimming scoop. Ben chuckled and held the feed away. "Hunh, that's for the cows, boy! You know that." Prince snorted again, bobbing his head three times. It was his way of giving up. Joseph had labored a whole year teaching the young horse such rudiments of communication.

The memory hit Ben like a blow to the chest. His knees felt watery. He fought the tears and went on stroking Prince's nose. "It's just you and me, now, horse," he said. His voice was tight. His heart clenched and sob broke from him. Prince's ears flicked up, and the eight-year-old arched his graceful neck. His liquid eyes seemed to probe Ben's. He snorted and stamped a forefoot.

"Yes, horsey, Joey went off to war and he's not coming back, I guess." Ben put down the scoop and touched the shiny saddle that sat along the pen wall on its sawhorse. Its beautifully tooled leather was worn and felt like satin to his fingertips. Now its luster was faded by dust. Joseph had been gone for two months and Ben hadn't ridden since his second heart attack, a half year past. He missed the sport, but the seizure had almost finished him. Even now, half a year later, he still felt puffy, slow as a summer day.

A film of tears blurred his sight as he stared, unseeing, at the saddle. Memories flooded over him. Joseph's ecstatic face when on his seventeenth birthday they'd given it to him—both saddle and new colt, only a year old. "Can't go on riding an old bareback plow horse all your life, now can you, son? Eh? 'Sides, if you break in Prince without a saddle, won't you just have to start in all over again when you throw that thing over his withers?"

Ben had dumped the gleaming saddle in Joey's arms and almost dragged him into the barn where Prince was tethered. The boy had been out in the field when they'd brought him into the barn.

Yessirree, that had been one happy boy, that long-ago day, and he'd taken Prince—Joseph gave him the name right then and there—and watched him romp in the near pasture till sundown. He knew he'd have to wait till the yearling had matured before he could mount him, but his joy was already full.

Then another memory followed on the heels of that happy one: the gradual corruption of his son—but he shook his head to stifle that. Not now. Only good thoughts now.

The movement of his head freed a tear, which broke from his eye and rolled down his cheek. His hand moved from the saddle to Prince's silky neck. Ben stroked the quivering flesh and struggled for control. For long minutes he stood, his hand moving idly up and down the stallion's coat without feeling it.

He had forgotten why he came to the barn, that his supper was ready, that his cows needed feeding and milking. He stood and dimly felt walls closing around him, crushing his mind like something out of Poe, as if he were being slowly, horribly buried alive. He shook his head again and felt a scream deep inside his chest. Panicky, he resorted to physical motion. He picked up the lantern, blew it out, then set it down again, surprised at himself for retaining the memory of his usual caution, among dry hay and straw, even while suffering a storm of agony.

Swiftly, he reached for Prince's bridle on its nail, remembering the soothing babble he always mumbled as he prized Prince's teeth over the bit and poked the sweat-stained leather over his ears. The stallion took to the contraption eagerly, a surprise to Benjamin until he realized, with quick shame, that he'd not been giving the horse sufficient exercise.

Ben's hands fell into old practice as he hoisted the saddle from its resting place. But halfway through his swing for the horse's back he remembered the blanket. He broke the smooth arc of his throw and the weight of leather and rivets came down hard on Prince's left haunch. He jumped, thumping into the wall with a whinny.

A cow mooed quizzically.

Benjamin staggered, the off-balance weight pulling hard on his left shoulder. Suddenly, his head cleared and he wondered what he was doing. A sharp pain cut across his ribs and down his arms, as if underlining his surprise. The saddle clattered to the hard, earthen floor.

He steadied himself against the pen wall until his breathing evened out. Fear raced through him, both at the pain and at the fact that he didn't want to try to answer to himself why he was doing this. He denied the dread and settled the old felt saddle blanket across Prince's broad back, pressing out the folds and creases. He took a deep breath, swung the saddle up from the floor, and settled it in place, all in one smooth flowing motion. Pain ripped through his left side again, but he ignored it. In less than a minute, he had the cinches secure and the reins looped over the horn. With his hand hooked through the bridle, he led Prince from the barn.

A plaintive moo followed him outside.

Two pats of rain hit his left hand simultaneously as he grasped the pommel of the saddle. He pulled himself up, but the pain sliced through his chest again, and his toe slipped from the stirrup. He fell in a heap at Prince's feet. Getting up quickly, embarrassed, he stroked the stallion, soothing him with his voice as if the animal had failed him. Carefully, he hauled himself up again, into the saddle. His leg throbbed where he'd come down too hard on it. Half a dozen more large drops hit him, cold on his scalp, as he gathered the reins in his hands. Pain cracked through him again and was gone, but near-panic followed and lay in his gut like mud. For a moment it filled the emptiness he felt.

Ben gritted his teeth, forcing away all feeling, all thought. He slapped leather against Prince's neck. "Giddap!" he cried, simultaneously kicking the animal's flanks. Prince bolted out the lane. Ben's foot throbbed in the stirrup.

Horse and rider shot toward the high road. Ben grabbed tight on the pommel, the reins secure but slack through his fingers. Proper form came back to him like second nature. As he passed the house on his left, his mind was afire with a mix of grief and excitement. He glanced toward the woodshed door and saw his wife's form, outlined in the doorway. She was waving one arm and her mouth was working. A paper fluttered in her outstretched hand, but her words were lost in the clatter of Prince's feet on the gravel and the tearing of the wind in his ears.

And by the sudden crash of thunder.

At the road, without a conscious decision Ben steered his mount eastward, left past the front of the house, the way the messenger boy had gone. He had no plan, except to ride, hard and fast, to fill his body with the deadening pulse of hoofbeats, to kill his awareness. Maybe even to overtake the boy and make him take back the telegram.

Prince seemed to sense the mood of his rider, as if Ben's kicking communicated his agony, and he galloped flat out. Both Joseph and Ben had often turned him this direction, racing along the graveled road toward the St. Joseph River and across the old plank bridge. Then off the highway, at a walk now, taking a bridle path along the wide, lazy river, sometimes for miles.

The clouds had blackened toward night. A brilliant line across the western horizon, under the heavy cloudbank, was all that remained of the day's sunshine. A final ray shot out like a shrill protest against darkness coming, and gilded the puffs of gravel dust kicked up by more raindrops. Prince's feet raised more of the powder, which settled back only slowly, lazily drifting a few inches from where it had lifted. The atmosphere had its own heavy presence. Lightning latticed the wall of sky.

Ben was far away, oblivious to the beauty and the threat of nature around him. His mind was roaming in a world of fantasy. Even the wind over Prince's ears as it parted his graying beard, whistled down his shirt front, and twisted his hair didn't return him to the back of his stallion, thundering down a dusty road beneath a darkening sky.

Time and space became telescoped, warped, and he found himself in another world, a different dimension which was, somehow, familiar and new at the same instant. He saw things: the broken, still form of Joseph. Lying on a brittle, shadowy battlefield. On a muddy riverbank. Deep in a pile of maimed bodies in a bloody ditch.

Then he suddenly found himself in a tangle of dusty hay, high in a mow in his own barn a misty millennium past, his son's sweaty face gleaming through the dust of thrown hay. Now he was transported, magically, to their old, bone-jogging wagon, tugging—Gee! Haw!—at the cracked harness leather and Joseph, lunging and tossing the water-cored turnips to the hogs in the fall field. One meaty globe of the purple vegetable stubbornly clung to the pitchfork's tines. Laughing, Joseph kicked it off and almost tumbled after it into the hogs' wallow!

Then he was in Virginia, as quickly as the lightning unseen by the rider but startling to Prince, who didn't break his stride. Or was it Maryland? Pennsylvania? Hearing the boom—thud of unlimbered cannon, rumbling down corduroy roads. Over countless bridges and through cathedral forests, feeling the pain of the bullet himself, tearing out his lung, bisecting his heart, punctuating his soul.

The echoing, bridge-clatter of Prince's feet stunned him back to Michigan now. He started at their speed and pulled the stallion to a walk. His left hand came up to his chest, checking for the slug. Must be there. The pain. Steam engine whuffing, whistling in his ears. Louder.

He jerked Prince to a dead stop, just beyond the bridge over the St. Joseph River, more than three miles from the farm. It was a brand new span, completed only days ago. The new grading of the approaches had left a foot of soft gravel at either end of the bright raw planks. He could smell the freshness still in the wood.

The pounding in his chest increased, banging like thunder. Spots danced before his eyes. He couldn't breathe! Nothing had ever felt like this before, none of it: the smells, the colors, the sounds. Everything normal in the world seemed to have come violently awake, stunning him with sensations!

Is this what it means to lose someone close, someone as near as one's own blood? Did the nerves react above and beyond the ability of the mind to grasp meaning for itself? He had lost a son, his only son, only *child* (after Lovina had nearly died in childbirth and the doctor had told him she must never bear another)! Did it mean that his own life would never be the same, that his life as he'd known it would stop? Would have to end?

Ben felt an impulsive need to have more space around himself. The earth was too close, the sky too tight down around him! His chest—He clucked Prince to the soft edge of the roadway, where it met the bridge. Perhaps a ride along the bridle path as of yore. Perhaps just to stare down into the moving river in its space under the bridge, the reckless moving brown carpet of water.

But it seemed a long, perilous way down there and the water was already lost in the murk of twilight. He glanced at the sky, then edged Prince forward, until the animal's forelegs slid in the raw gravel. The pommel pushed painfully into Ben's groin.

Another crash of thunder came on top of its lightning and the rain dashed down in earnest. In seconds it was a wall of water soaking him, turning the road to mud and sending rivulets through the graded dirt down the steep slope to join the river. The forlorn farmer stood in his stirrups to stare down toward the current, thinking of shelter beneath the trestle. His movement echoed through his left side at another sharp pang, but his mind stayed on the stream under the bridge.

Suddenly, the river bore a weird fascination for him. The storm would give it broader life, pouring its celestial torrents down into the earthly flow till it would flood its banks, wash away all that stood in its way—violently, irrevocably, drowning even a horse and a rider who felt too tight a pinching in his soul.

It had only been a notion, as quick as lightning, but he stopped the thought and turned it around in his head. It had a startling appeal to him. He suddenly realized he was already *so* tired of grief. It was less than an hour since the wire had come, but the agony was already like an overflexed muscle. He just wanted to let go. He didn't have time to wait for the wound of losing his only son even to begin to heal. How much easier just to fall into the water, let it roll him and wash him away into oblivion.

Just as quickly as the thought had come he forced it down; there was no divine forgiveness for those who deliberately took their own lives. He felt a twinge of shame because that thought brought with it the words of comfort he'd used more than once, from the pulpit: "O death, where is thy sting? O grave, where is thy victory?" How pious he must have sounded. Now the words had a special ache of their own for him, yet paradoxically they gave him the first ray of comfort he'd felt since the telegram. In spite of himself, and the thundering rain, a small smile started to push its way across his lips. He knew where that seeping balm came from! He bent his knees to settle himself in the saddle again.

The smile was arrested. Ben's mouth froze open. His body went rigid; his eyes bulged. Prince felt the stiffness and tossed his head, pawing the muddy road edge. It was just enough movement to tip Ben's unresponding body off balance. Racked with pain beyond belief, he was barely aware he was falling. It felt more like floating. Then he hit the streaming shoulder with a grunt, teetered a moment and rolled swiftly, awkwardly down the steep slope.

Prince's ears snapped forward. He snorted and tossed his head three times. The man's limp body fetched up hard against a large boulder less than two yards from the already swollen river. It didn't move. In the last gray of day the stallion looked down at the man, then he let out a short, shrill whinny. He pawed at the roadside, nickering in puzzlement.

2

"Seems odd goings-on for a full-grown man, I'd say," Kate King muttered to herself. Ben's mother turned from the kitchen window where she'd watched him hurtle past on Prince. She was tall and lean, her spine ramrod straight. If her luxurious pile of hair hadn't been snow-white, she'd easily have passed for a woman twenty years younger than her seventy-eight years. Her blue eyes were as clear as a girl's if not as sharp or innocent anymore. Only her vanity kept her from using the gold-rimmed spectacles she needed. Let anyone suggest she wear them, for greater safety or pleasure in life, and she'd snap back as soon as give the time of day. There was nothing or no one in her world she feared. Having been a pioneering widow for some two dozen years gave her a leg up in the self-confidence department, she always said. If anyone was bold enough to doubt her.

Her daughter-in-law came inside through the woodshed. "He didn't hear me, Mother," she sighed. She was a heavy-set woman of medium height. Like her husband and mother-in-law, she also needed glasses. And she wasn't too proud to wear them, even if they were always halfway down her broad nose. Her fleshy face wore a perpetually harried look that rarely broke even for a moment into any expression other than a reflection of the silent worry that seemed to be her natural condition. Yet no one among her acquaintances in southern Michigan had ever known her to be anything less than utterly tireless and dependable. "A perfect saint" were frequently the words people used to describe her.

But tonight her careworn face looked much older than her forty-nine years and wore an exaggerated expression of concern. "I'll wager he believes this has a different message than what it does," she said. She held up the opened telegram she'd been waving at Ben. "It fell from his vest pocket when I went to hang it up. Hadn't even been opened." She handed it to Kate. "You know what telegrams most always signify."

The old woman glared at Lovina as she took the paper. She squinted at the lettering, holding it at arm's length. "Says it's from Washington, D.C., I think." She moved the telegram closer, then farther away again. "Oh pshaw, Lovina, the printing's too jiggly. Here, you read it, girl!"

Lovina took it and laid it on the table. "I'll just tell you." Her voice was quiet. But she looked away, then crossed to the stove and lifted the roaster lid. She'd just pulled it from the oven before Ben had galloped off. The meat looked done.

"Well?" Kate's voice was demanding.

"It's from General Halleck. At the War Department. He says that Joseph has been charged with desertion and giving aid and comfort to the enemy—something like that." She picked up a fork. It trembled in her hand. Quickly she poked it into the roast. The pork was crumbly tender.

"Desertion?"

"Yes." Lovina's pale gray eyes met Kate's. "They're holding him in a prison in the capital city. It's called Old Capitol Prison, I think." She picked up the telegram again and peered at it. "Yes. The general says they haven't yet set a trial date, but there's no bail." She abruptly crumpled the paper, lifted a burner, and tossed it into the flames.

"What is this . . . this 'desertion'?" Kate almost barked. "What does that mean? What did he do *this* time?" She sounded cross, but Lovina wondered whether the irritation was at Washington city, or with her grandson. Joseph had always been impulsive, frequently careless, and so much like Kate that Lovina suspected he often felt he had to compete with his grandmother, ridiculous as that seemed to his parents. She had been impatient with his impetuousness, as if not recognizing its mirror image of her own. Now she assumed this latest news was just the logical outcome of another "scrape" his nature had gotten him into.

"It says only that he 'laid down his weapon and marched to the rear in the face of enemy fire.' " She could recall the exact wording because it had struck her as odd that anyone would march—not run or sneak away—from any battle. It was too much to understand, and suddenly she felt like weeping. She felt her face twisting and she struggled for control.

"Well of all the—" Kate hesitated at the expression on Lovina's face. "What is it, child?" Her voice softened and she moved to lay her arm around her daughter-in-law's ample shoulders. "There, there," she cooed. "There has to be a logical explanation for all this. Everything will be all right."

Lovina flickered a smile. "I'm sorry, I know that's true. But it's not Joseph I'm most worried about right now, Mother." Her smile disappeared. "Do you suppose Ben's odd behavior comes from that telegram? Saying he's going for wood, then taking off on a ride with a storm coming on? When he knows supper's near ready?" She paused thoughtfully, tapping the meat fork against the roast pan. "I just have this strange feeling that he didn't open it because he was afraid he would find that Joseph had been—"

A violent crash of thunder drowned out her words. The two women stared at each other, startled. Lovina glanced at the window above the sink, still open a few inches for relief from the afternoon's heat. A gust of wind suddenly came in, cold and laced with rain. She laid the fork on the counter and stepped to close the sash. A premonition shot through her and she hesitated, hands poised above the potted geranium on the sill. Then she quickly recovered, set the plant aside, and slammed down the window. An instant later a blast of rain-filled wind slapped hard drops against the glass. Lovina shivered.

"Quickly, Kate, the parlor!" Lovina headed for the stairs. "I'll get the upstairs windows." She puffed up the worn wooden steps, pausing for breath on the landing where the staircase made a turn back on itself before climbing to the next floor. She slammed down the sash of the window there, then hurried on up.

The second story contained only two small bedrooms. Joseph had slept in a lean-to beside the woodshed. Lovina tended first to the windows in their room on the west side, the direction of the storm. Then she rushed across the narrow, plank hallway to Kate's bedroom on the east end of the house. She secured the windowpane, then strained to see through the sudden weather into the murk of twilight for sight of her husband. As if to help her, a final shaft of sunshine beamed out and lanced itself through the rain, but all she could see of Ben, in the golden glow, was a rapidly disappearing cloud of dust. It hung vaguely off toward the St. Joseph River bridge.

In all their twenty-six wedded years she had never known her instincts to fail, when it came to sensing trouble. And just a moment ago, at the kitchen window, she had felt it as solidly as touching wood: Benjamin was in trouble.

Her stomach did a slow, sickening turn, her throat went dry. She sank to her knees and rested her forehead against the pane. Its damp coolness was soothing. Her attitude was prayerful, from long habit, but no words came to her. Only memories, and a groaning of her spirit. Ben was far from a healthy man. Even before the first heart attack, on the day he turned fifty, she had tried to get him to cut down on his exertion. He must realize, she said, again and again, that he was middle-aged and hefty, not twenty-five and thin. His 220 pounds were more than his bones were meant to carry, even if it was mostly muscle. It was aging muscle.

That first attack had not been really serious, but it had scared them both, her more than him, she soon realized. It had laid him out on his bed for a few days, and Doc Adams had watched him closely for a month or so. Yet soon he was back into his old habits. He'd gone on as if she were nothing more than a familiar fact of nature, always there and to be taken notice of no more than a ray of sunshine or a windy day. And he'd kept pitching hay, forking manure, tossing heavy sacks of feed—working from sunup to dark. Then he'd sit by the fire reading, thinking, and writing his sermons until all but the owls had sought the surcease of slumber. Her scolding he would only ignore. At most, he gave her a tired, patronizing smile.

How that had cut her! Yet she would never let him know it. And when Joseph had up and gone off to war, she'd kept that inside too, even though it nearly killed her. There'd been some small satisfaction in that, however, for it had really gotten to Ben, too. If she hadn't been so filled with her own private agony at her son's enlisting, she might almost have laughed in her husband's face, at the sudden change it brought in him. Instead, she forced herself, characteristically, to try to imagine how it must have been, for him. How shocked Ben must have been to learn that his lifelong testimony to the evils of violence and war was as chaff to his son.

She had managed the jolt of Joseph gone off to war. Her heart perceived a parent's terror of the battlefield where a child's life is worthless. She sensed the added burden in Ben's soul, the horrifying prospect that his only son might die in sin. What a load of guilt must be added to her husband's deathly fear! And her heart went out to him. But he sat like a stone.

She knew, of course, that he lived in dread of the coming of the telegraph boy. He'd never said he worried, but she'd seen him tense up whenever the boy galloped by, bearing important—maybe cruel—news to others along their road. And now it had come, she thought, with a sigh that immediately fogged the glass. The time had come when the boy had stopped to deliver the wire from Washington, to Ben himself. Yet its news was not the worst, was not without hope. If only Ben had known that, if only he'd taken time to open the wire! But she knew what he believed was written there, and her stomach did another slow turn.

She rubbed the steam of her breath from the pane, but the darkness had swallowed him and gave back only her own reflection. She struggled to her feet with a sigh and sat heavily on the bed. Since it was Kate's room, it was neat as a pin, and unconsciously she was careful not to wrinkle the spread. She sat and stared at the streaked window, not knowing what to do next. What *could* she do? If Ben didn't return soon, in this weather, she would have to try to get the neighbors for help. But the nearest one was a mile away, in the opposite direction. Their own plow horses were out in the pasture somewhere. Even if they'd been in the barn she doubted she could get one hitched to the buggy or outfitted to ride anyhow. And bareback riding wasn't her specialty.

The thought almost made her laugh. She looked down at her ample body, her thick arms and legs only whitish blurs in the dim lamplight that filtered up the staircase. Me, riding a horse, on a cold wet night! She shook her head. Any notion of humor died.

"What would I do if Ben were gone?" The question

struck her so vividly that at first she thought she had spoken it. She sighed, remembering that she wasn't the sweet young thing she had been on her wedding day, over two dozen years ago. Probably stay a widow till I die, she thought. Maybe I am already! Again that shocking clarity, as if the notion were announced as truth revealed from Beyond.

It had not been easy being married to Benjamin King. That was no small truth! He didn't make it easy. There were times when the resentment between them was as thick as the maple taffy they used to pull by the fire at Christmas when Joseph was a boy. She'd never understood where the tightness came from, between her husband and herself, but it had always been there, literally from their wedding night when she had felt both fright and pain.

She had always loved him in the only ways she knew. Hadn't she been a good cook and seamstress? Not to mention caring for the livestock, milking, gathering the eggs, making sausage, canning fruits and vegetables? Giving him a son? Wanting to give him another, maybe many more? Except that he stopped coming to her as a husband, after the birth of Joseph. Was it her fault he found more solace in his books and his Bible than she could ever seem to give him?

Lovina felt the unseasonal chill of the damp evening seeping into her body. She rubbed her bare upper arms vigorously, fleetingly irritated at the way the excess flesh seemed to slap back at her fingers. The chill brought with it another memory, still achingly fresh, when a terrifying coldness had worked its way out from her heart until it had nearly paralyzed her. It had come on that awful Sunday noon, the twenty-first of March this year, 1862. Almost six months it was now, but it seemed like yesterday. The date was etched forever in her memory because her husband's mortality, and with it her own, had become real for the first time in her life. As if on the first day of spring her being had been plunged into a winter of the soul.

She, Ben, and Joseph had just emerged from church into a bright day which had turned frosty. Her heart was light because their son had attended services with them for the first time in many months. Her husband, too, was exuberant and loving, full of the presence of heaven in his soul, as he always was after rendering a powerful sermon. (No matter what the climate between them, she always loved to hear him preach.) They had found the mud around the carriage wheels had frozen and Ben cheerfully leaned into the job of helping their horse break it loose. All so unnecessary. What horse couldn't do the work of ten men!

She would never live long enough to forget the stricken look on her husband's face when his heart gave out for him again. She could tell from his expression it was far worse this time. The surprise, fading into anger. She'd been stricken herself, uncomprehending at first. Then she knew, and when dismay and disappointment followed the anger across his features, and perspiration stood out on his skin, she knew she was staring death in the face.

Never would she cease to give thanks to a merciful, loving God that Ben's attack had come at the church and not when he was alone in the barn or out in the field. There had been men's arms and strong backs to help Joseph lift him into the buggy and rush him to Dr. Adams' house less than a mile away. Even so, it had been nearly a week before it was known whether he would live or die.

"Lovina?" Her mother-in-law's voice came up the stairs. There was concern in it.

"I'm coming," she called. She hoisted herself to her feet and descended the steps. Kate stood at the bottom of the staircase.

"Did you see anything?" the old woman asked. She peered at her daughter-in-law's face.

Lovina shook her head. "Just a cloud of dust by the bridge. Before it got too dark."

Kate shrugged, breaking off her scrutiny. "Well, everything will be all right. You'll see." Her voice sounded sure. As if her words ended the discussion, she turned and walked into the kitchen. Lovina followed her.

While Kate set the table, she honed the long knife blade. Suddenly she felt famished and realized it was far past suppertime. It surprised her how long she had been upstairs and she wondered why Kate hadn't called up to her sooner.

She uncovered the roast (Kate must have put the lid back over the meat), glad to see it still gave off steam. She watched the slices of brown meat curl over and lie like the spring earth behind Ben's plow. Then, for no apparent reason, Joseph appeared in her mind, and for an instant she saw a bloody bayonet in place of her kitchen knife. The roast was her son's chest. Outside, the rain's drumming was transformed into the rattle of musket fire. A crash of thunder shook the house, like the discharge of artillery. Things all she'd never witnessed but which appeared in her dreams almost nightly.

Another blast of thunder followed, rattled the windowpanes, vibrating in her abdomen. Joseph's face dissolved in a tableau of violence, his mouth gaping in agony. She screamed, jumped away from the roast pan. Her knife clattered to the floor.

"What is it?" Kate nearly dropped the plates she was carrying to the table.

Lovina quickly recovered. She brushed back a wisp of hair. "Nothing," she said. "I just burned my hand." She sucked the thumb of her left hand, one part of her mind surprised at the ease of her duplicity. Her heart was beating wildly. Kate stood watching her.

Shaking, Lovina picked up the knife, wiped it on the

apron at her waist, then finished carving the meat. It struck her, how absurd this situation had become, sitting down to eat a big meal, with her sick husband (that's how she thought of him ever since the second attack) out in the storm somewhere, on horseback. And her only child in some cold, dark prison a million miles from home.

She put the incongruity from her mind by sheer force of will. She forked several slices of pork onto the ironstone meat platter Kate had set on the counter, then carried it to the table. It shook in her hand.

"Here, let me help. Sit down, child." Lovina obeyed as the old woman took the dish from her. Her eyes bore into Lovina's. "Worry never mended a thing!" It was a litany in this house, almost a singsong admonition that rarely worked—for long anyway. Lovina tried, though, and flashed Kate a tremulous smile.

Her mother-in-law's voice became solicitous. "Everything will be just fine." She dumped the steaming potatoes into a bowl on the oilcloth-topped table. "I reckon we'll hear Prince gallop up any minute now." She smiled. "You just relax, now!"

As if on cue, the sound of trotting hooves grew out of the hissing rain. The women stared at each other, comically, then Lovina's face broke into a grin as she leaped to her feet and ran to the woodshed. She flung open the door, ignoring the rain. Her eyes probed the night. It was Prince. She'd recognize his gait anywhere. Her heart leaped.

"Hurry, Ben!" she called out. "Supper's getting cold." She could hear the relief in her own voice, felt it smoothing out the bunched nerves in her abdomen. "Shame on you for running off like that, in the rain and all!"

There was no answer from the dark except a whinny and a noisy exhalation from flapping nostrils. Hardly a human sound.

"Benjamin?"

Prince's hoofbeats had slowed nearly to a stop on the cobbles by the barn. When she spoke they started up again, toward her. It was fully dark now and she could not see the stallion until his head came into the dim swath of light from the kitchen windows. His coal-black eyes were wide. He tossed his shapely head and his mane flapped, soggily. Sputtering snorts issued from him, as if he were trying to speak. He moved another two paces toward Lovina. The light fell across his back.

The saddle was empty.

3

Great, fat drops of rain plopped loudly on the buggy's dusty roof, leaving scattered blotches of shiny black where they had hit. To the two shadowy figures inside the moving carriage, the promise of moisture was welcome, as it was to nearly all residents of the valley this drought-stricken summer.

One of the figures, tall, cadaverous, and dressed in black from heavy boots to broadcloth coat and wide-brimmed hat, leaned forward to lower the weather flap across the front opening of the horse-drawn vehicle.

He struggled briefly with the cumbersome square yard of old cracked leather, letting it drape down across the front of the buggy. When tied down with straps to the foot rail, it severely limited visibility, for the only sight possible was through a scratched glass pane he had jerry-rigged across a two-foot square hole cut from the tired material of the flap. But it kept out the weather.

Isaac Miller had mixed feelings about the storm that was obviously coming. He'd seen it brewing before setting out with his daughter Rachel and it made the farmer in him glad. But the buggy horse he typically used, a frisky two-year-old filly, was temperamental and given to catching cold. So he'd hitched up his fourteen-year-old mare when it looked like chilly wet weather was on the way. That substitution took half the pleasure out of a carriage ride.

Even though the imminent rain was desperately needed, and he was happy to see it come, he cursed the ache that was already spreading through his hips and shoulder joints. At fifty-eight, he seemed never to have a day completely free of pain anymore, and rain always made it worse. So much for forty-odd years of unremitting toil on the seventy-five-acre spread he'd homesteaded when Michigan was still a wilderness. If only God in his infinite wisdom had given him sons instead of a litter of daughters, four of them! A lot of good they were. Mouths to feed but hands and arms too weak to help with the heavy work of farming.

Isaac threaded the reins carefully through the slit he'd cut in the flap for driving in bad weather and took both in his right hand. With his free hand, he pulled the old buffalo robe from the compartment behind the seat, narrowly missing the girl's head with it. He tossed it over their knees, tucking one end of it behind his right hip. He glanced at his daughter as she adjusted her side of the woolly robe. She was barely visible in the dim light.

"Warm enough, Rachel?"

The frail-looking girl gave him a quick smile. "Yes, Father, I'm glad you keep the robe in the buggy." She wore a thin cotton dress, its bright yellow flower pattern slightly luminous in the dusk. It had been hot and humid all day. All month, for that matter. "The cold has surely come quickly and unexpectedly, hasn't it?"

"You can say that again," he replied. His grizzled beard hinted good humor. "Who'd of thought the middle of September would get so chilly?"

Despite her earlier assurance to the contrary, the girl—she didn't look a day over sixteen, yet she was past her twentieth birthday—shivered, drew a black knit shawl from a pouch attached to the inside of the buggy-wall, and wrapped it around her shoulders.

"Reckon it's worth the trip, Rachel-daughter?" Isaac Miller squinted at her under the brim of his Quaker hat. His eyes stayed on her face. He could never get accustomed to this child-woman he'd sired. Her three sisters, all older and "married off," as the folks in the valley put it, were tall and buxom, with light brown hair and blue eyes full of merriment, yet otherwise stolid as the pillars of Hercules. Or milch cows, if you wanted an uncharitable comparison. In appearance, if not in personality, they took after their mother, for better or worse.

Rachel, on the other hand, put him in mind of a—well, of a gypsy. An undernourished-looking creature of the mysterious East, sometimes sunny of disposition, sometimes morose. No, that wasn't the right word . . . contemplative. Yes, that was better.

She looked at him. "Yes it is, Father." Her green eyes drilled into his, then fell to her primly folded tiny hands in her lap. "I simply must find out something about Joseph." Her voice was low but intense. "He hasn't written me and I must know if Lovina's heard anything from him!" She abruptly lifted her miniature oval face. Her luminous gaze held his again. In the dimness her eyes seemed to have their own inner fire.

He looked away, feeling awkward. It was so often that way with her. She seemed weak, in need of his grown-up strength and protection. Then that dark force came out of her. It made him feel like a boy, inexperienced, almost shamed by a mother for being obtuse about the mysteries of life. Yet he could never arouse the boldness of boyhood enough to demand to know how he was supposed to be privy to these "mysteries" of life which women always seemed to understand, if no one ever *explained* them! There were times when Rachel's resemblance to his departed mother was uncanny.

"You know that Ben won't be overjoyed to see us," he said, "or the old lady either, for that matter." To his own ear he sounded petulant, but he was determined to *act* the part of the father at least.

"Hah—that's an understatement." Rachel's laugh was short, almost bitter. "But my business doesn't concern those two." Her manner evened out again, softened by a thought for poor Lovina.

"So why make me and poor Bess take this ten-mile journey over roads that'll soon be mud to drop in uninvited at a house where I'm about as welcome as boils?" His tone came out sharper than he'd intended. "I'm sorry," he said. He laid his calloused hand on his daughter's arm. "Didn't mean to bark."

Her bright laughter startled him. "Father, you know perfectly well that Joey isn't the only reason we're making this trip! You were too easy to talk into hitching up the buggy to make me believe otherwise. I know as clear as daylight how you've got your heart set on talking Ben King into selling you Prince. And trading him Bess and a couple of porkers for him!" She laughed again, like a schoolgirl with the right answer.

"Come now, Rach, you know that would not be a fair trade!" He felt chagrin at how easily she saw through him.

"Sure, I know it and you know it. But would Mr. King, before it's too late?"

A brilliant shaft from the setting sun shot through the dirty glass and decorated her face in gold. Her eyes sparkled with teasing humor. He was struck by her beauty, as he was so often. Small wonder the boys all over the county found her irresistible.

Her mood was contagious. He assumed a hurt tone, in jest. "Well, of course, I was planning to sweeten the pot a bit, Rachel. Ever since Ben had his second attack, and the boy left, he's not been able to keep up with his work, so I—"

"So you thought you'd offer him your help?" Surprise erased her teasing. "When's the last time you two little, grown-up boys exchanged civil words? Besides, you're not in much better shape yourself."

She had meant it solicitously, he told himself, but it cut him, nonetheless. He forced a grin to cover the hurt. "In a business transaction, civil words are not absolutely necessary, and . . . and I figured I could rent him the labor of Rufus."

His daughter made no response. She stared ahead, the sunshine gilding her delicate features.

"He's got my corn all in. I can spare him a few days." He studied her face in the sunbeams. Then the brightness was gone, as quickly as it had come. The planes of her face receded abruptly into the gloom. The sudden evaporation of light made the dimness seem thicker.

"That's good," she said, in a flat voice. "Rufe's a good worker."

Fury boiled up in him. "And that's not all he is!" He felt the urge to shout. But he bit his lip, forcing his attention back to his driving. Through the rain-flecked glass he could just make out Bess's ears bobbing up and down against the last bar of golden light left between the horizon and the night. The sprinkle was fast becoming a shower. He felt pity for the old mare, and that emotion dulled the edge of his anger.

"Rufus been leaving you alone—"

"He never did a thing wrong, Father," she cut in. "You know it perfectly well!"

His rage surged back. It was accompanied by a pulse of lightning that cast an eerie paleness over the landscape. "What I cannot fathom is how you can give that boy those calf's eyes, and claimin' to be Joseph's girl—"

Isaac's words were swallowed in a crash of thunder. It came so close and loud that Bess jumped in her traces and commenced to galloping. "Whoa, girl. Take it easy," Isaac directed, pulling on the reins. The mare gradually settled back to a walk. He glanced at his daughter. In the dusk her face was little more now than a whitish blur. He saw her reach quickly to brush at her cheeks, first one, then the other, with her right hand.

His heart clenched. "Didn't mean anything by that, child." His voice was plaintive. It surprised him and he bit his lip in self-disgust. "Only, what's a man to think, when he comes on his daughter unawares, she staring at a naked-chested man, watching him with his full knowledge while he pitches hay?" Isaac cleared his throat. "With a look in her eyes like a man shouldn't see, except on her wedding night." His voice made it a statement, but he paused, as if expecting a reply.

Rachel was silent, her pale face staring at the new night.

"And here I thought you and Joseph were as thick as thieves." He reached down to pull the buffalo robe back up over their laps. "Joseph's maybe a little wild, but down deep he's a good boy, daughter. You could do a lot worse." He was warming to his subject. "Yes, sir, if I had me a son, I wouldn't complain if he were mighty similar to that boy. Matter of fact, he seems more like a son of mine than of that pacifist-spoutin' preacher pa of his!" He chuckled, already forgetful of Rachel's wet cheeks. "And when he gets back, maybe that's what he'll become, huh, girl? My son?" Isaac nudged her with his elbow.

The heavens let go with another horrific blast of thunder, right smack on the heels of a blaze of lightning. It was so unexpected and loud it pulverized thought. Bess bolted with an alacrity belying her age. Almost simultaneously the skies opened in a deluge.

Isaac Miller tugged on the reins, uttering curses, yet knowing the poor beast was out of earshot and out of control. Father and daughter bounced around in the close, narrow buggy like a pair of rag dolls. St. Joseph County roads were washboards at best. No one in his right mind took a wheeled conveyance at more than a slow trot. Such a downpour as had come upon them would soon turn it into a river of mud.

Rachel's ears burned at her father's profanity. "How far yet, Father?" It was suddenly too close in the vehicle.

"How could I know?" he shouted too loud even for the clatter and hiss that echoed in the box on wheels. He released one hand from the reins and tugged at a watch fob in his vest. "We been riding some forty minutes now. Shouldn't be but ten more." He peered sightlessly through the now-black square of glass. "Unless Bess kills herself first." He dragged hard on the reins again, slowing the poor animal still more.

Rachel Miller blessed the ruckus caused by the lightning and thunder. It seemed to have taken her father's mind off Joseph. At least he didn't return to it when he got Bess steadied. That was a good thing, she thought. She had no idea how to respond to questions put to her by her father, or anyone else for that matter, on the subject of Joseph. And she had no desire at all to talk about Rufe.

There was too much pain inside her, and not just a little confusion. It was not a sharp, tearing storm of pain, just a dull ache, which maybe was worse in a way because it was persistent. Sometimes the ache was present simply because Joseph was not. She loved him with utter helplessness. No more could she control her desire to be his wife than she could stretch out her hand to stop the rain in a moment. And though she always stamped it down before it could grow large in her mind, she was always at least dimly aware of the realization that she did not know the true nature of his feelings for her.

That realization increased the ache manyfold and seemed to cause her desire for him to burn even brighter. And sometimes she felt an agony of a different, more physical, sort. Then it came like a clump of smoldering coals deep in her loins, giving heat that spread outward through her body, setting up a shivery craving for a male form tight against her own. That ache left her numb with unspent energy.

And guilt.

She knew well enough, from long chats with her sister Ruth, who was only two years older and already the mother of three, that what happened inside her was nothing abnormal. Not at all! What tore her apart was that it was Joseph whose manly body she wanted to cling to. But it was Rufe who was there.

What her father had seen he had indeed seen. More than once she had surreptitiously followed Isaac's hired man with her burning eyes, wondering, imagining. Grafting Joseph's deep-set blue eyes, his sandy hair, and firm, goateed chin onto Rufe's vigorous physique.

Rufus Jones was only a boy. He was not quite eighteen, whereas Joseph would be twenty-four before the year was out. But he was built much like Joseph and sometimes Rachel, concealed by a wide-trunked tree, or a whitewashed stable corner, would squeeze her eyelids down to the place where things went blurry, and Rufe's head and wide shoulders and tapering chest and rippling muscles became Joseph's.

Then a fever would sweep over her. She'd turn and slip away, run for nowhere. Or just somewhere else. After a while, a recklessness within her no longer cared whether Rufe witnessed her tense flight. She almost hoped he would, for reasons she never tried to understand. When her body cooled, she was always consumed by shame. Tears would come, and she would find a quiet place and Joseph's name would be on her lips. And she would let pictures come to her: memories of that one, chaste kiss after a summer swim, years ago; dreams of that sweet moment when one day they would entwine, as one. (She shut from her mind the possibility he might never want that.) And it would be the first time in her life, when she would give the best she had to give. It was too precious not so to vow.

"Whoa—hup!" Isaac's exclamation followed hard on a lingering flash of lightning. "What's that?" He pulled up hard on the reins.

"What's wrong?" Rachel snapped alert as the buggy squished to a stop, dead center in the roadway. The rain crackled like popping corn on the taut rubberized fabric of the roof.

"Thought I saw something on the road," Isaac whispered. "Right in front of Bess!"

Lightning flickered again. "It's a horse, just standing there." Then it was dark again. "Looked like someone's a settin' on it."

Rachel saw the bizarre spectacle in the next flash. "Land's sakes, it's Lovina King!"

Isaac let go the reins with his right hand and fumbled under the seat. He'd built a drawer there, but in the dampness it wouldn't budge. Cursing, he shoved the leather straps at Rachel and winched his long lean frame half around, to reach down with both arms. In a moment he produced a battered tin lantern.

He handed it up to Rachel. "Here—hold it!" She grasped the bent wire handle while her father crouched and groped deeper into the drawer. In another moment he resumed his seat, grunting with exertion and pain. In his hand he gripped a small bundle wrapped in waxed cheesecloth, tied around snugly by a thong of rawhide. Hurriedly, he undid the packet and took out a wooden match, then handed the unused ones to Rachel. Her hands were getting full.

"All right, give me the lantern."

He took it from her and lifted it to his ear. He shook it gently. "Ah, excellent! Still some kerosene left."

Presently a soft glow filled the buggy, transforming it into a cozy nest. But Isaac lost no time contemplating the aesthetics of the moment. Carrying the lantern high, he flung aside the side flap and stepped down into the road.

43

Rachel heard the squish of his boot in the mud an instant before his voice called out: "Lovina? Lovina King? It's Isaac Miller. You all right?"

Rachel remained in the carriage. She could hear the woman's response only faintly. It was still raining steadily. At this rate, she mused, there won't be any bridge left when we get to the river. In the darkness she didn't realize they were practically on top of it.

After his first words, Isaac's voice had faded into the drone of the downpour. The lantern's dim light moved past Bess and stopped where they'd seen Lovina astride a horse. She felt herself growing impatient at the delay despite her curiosity about the apparition out there on the road. Nothing mattered quite as much as having some word of Joseph. Then she felt the sting of shame at her selfishness, but that emotion was immediately followed by excitement. It was no longer necessary to drive clear to the King place. Lovina was right here!

Then her excitement dissolved into anxiety and perplexity. Only an emergency would bring Joseph's mother out on a night like this. And on horseback. The girl tried to recollect ever having seen Lovina ride. The wife of Ben King might have the complexion of a girl, and straight teeth, but not even the most charitable observer would term her slender or agile enough to ride a horse. Let alone mount up.

Any humor Rachel might have started to feel at the notion quickly became alarm. Maybe Lovina had heard from Joseph something so portentous she had impulsively headed for Rachel's place to tell her, without a moment to lose! Not even waiting for Ben to come in from choring, or whatever. Her hands flew to her mouth.

"Joseph!" She said his name breathlessly, and felt her stomach turn. "Oh no!"

She threw the robe off her lap. "I've got to know!" she whispered, and reached for the flap. Just then it burst in on her. Isaac's arm pushed it back, holding the lantern.

44

"Take it!" he barked, "while I help Mrs. King into the buggy."

Rachel quickly obeyed. She hung the lantern wire on the whip rack, ready to lend a hand. Lovina's rain-plastered head poked inside. In the dim, flickering light her face seemed ghoulish.

"Here, let me help you." Rachel stuck out her hand. It was almost pulled off as the heavyset woman grabbed hold and hoisted her bulk upward. Isaac was too much of a gentleman to assist from the rear.

Nor did he follow her in out of the weather. The carriage was designed for two adults. For Isaac to join them would have called for greater intimacy than the situation seemed to warrant.

Lovina slumped into the thinly padded seat, her breath coming in shuddering gasps. Isaac stood with only his head thrust inside; the flap draped down past his hat gave him a disembodied appearance rendered almost sinister in the pale lamp glow. Rachel had to bite her tongue to repress her fearful curiosity while Lovina caught her breath.

"Prince came back empty," she said at length, enigmatically. She breathed hard for a moment. Her fingers fidgeted, fooled with the ropes of gray hair snaking from beneath her kerchief. "Benjamin galloped away just before dark. Prince came back alone. About a half hour later." She took a corner of her home-knitted shawl and wrung it out. Rainwater dripped on the buffalo robe and rolled to the buggy floor.

"Oh, then it's not Joseph!" Rachel's words were barely a whisper. She felt weak with relief.

The lantern flame flickered. Isaac sneezed. Lovina threw a guarded look at the girl. "Not exactly," she said.

"Listen!" Isaac hissed. He jerked his head outside. A second later, he reappeared. "Thought I heard a song, from down by the river," he said. He shrugged, dismissing it as too unbelievable.

"As I was saying," Lovina went on, too wilted to notice Isaac, "Benjamin's out there, somewhere. Close by." Her arm came up and described an arc, lazy and despairing. "Prince came back alone." She sniffed and picked at her shawl, seeking a dry spot. "Please help me find him," she pleaded, looking at Isaac. She appeared ready to seize him in desperation, but all of him that showed was his somber, lean face under his dripping hat brim.

"Of course, Lovina," he said, "but where to start?"

"Before you came, Prince had stopped here." Lovina pointed through the window. "Right at the bridge."

Isaac studied her face for a moment, then his wet arm snaked inside. "Rachel, the lantern!" She handed it to him, quickly, and he was gone, leaving the women in the damp darkness.

Through the glass they watched the rain-distorted light as it moved, slowly and jerkily along the shoulder of the road. First away from the buggy, then back toward them, then away again. Suddenly it disappeared from their field of vision as abruptly and completely as if the earth had opened beneath Isaac's feet.

Rachel extracted another lucifer from the waterproof packet, assuming the lantern had gone out and her father would be back directly. But minutes passed and the only sound was the unceasing rain. She decided her father, for some good reason, she hoped, must have gone down the bank to search for Ben. She put the match back.

Lightning flickered again. Rachel braced herself for the thunder, then realized she had not heard loud thunder since before they'd seen Prince and stopped. When the thunder came, it was only a distant rumble, and she felt more at ease than she had for quite a spell. The storm was passing. She let herself relax, even after the sweet relief she'd felt when Lovina had said "not exactly."

Now that gnawing curiosity rushed back over her again.

She just had to know more! She opened her mouth to quiz Lovina, but a second thought, one of compassion for the poor wife, shut her up. She wasn't a child. She could wait until Lovina was more composed.

The steady drumbeat of the rain continued, unabated. She felt the jerky shivers of the big woman beside her. "Here, Lovina," she said, pulling the shawl from her own shoulders, "put this on, or you'll catch your death."

"Thank you, child." She gratefully lifted her own sopping shawl from her neck and clasped Rachel's around her shoulders and throat. Her own she let drop in a heap to the floor. "That feels oh so much better," she sighed.

"What made Ben ride out this way, on such a night?" Rachel asked. She was dying to talk about Joseph, but she intuitively grasped how much greater, right now, was Lovina's crisis. "Since his attack I thought he stayed close to home and didn't ride."

Lovina shivered. In the dark, Rachel felt Lovina's trembling, and heard her teeth chattering. "He got pretty upset, just got quiet," she said. "A telegram came from Washington city. He didn't tell us he was going for a ride. Just got up on Prince and tore out the lane like there was no tomorrow." Her voice was flat. "And mother and me having supper all ready—"

She sneezed so loud and sudden in the closed carriage that Rachel jumped.

"A telegram?" Rachel asked. She hadn't heard a word after Lovina's first sentence. "What did it say?" Her heart was beating louder than the rain.

"Ben didn't even open it," Lovina continued, as if she hadn't heard the question. "He just went out to the barn in a hurry, as if nothing mattered more than getting wood for the fireplace." She hesitated. Rachel felt like screaming. "Then ten minutes later he came racing out the lane on Prince. He didn't have on a coat or a hat, only his old sweater," she said. "He'd taken off his vest. That's how come I found the telegram. It was sticking out of the pocket."

Rachel's eyes pierced the darkness where Lovina's face would be, could she see it. "The telegram!" she almost hissed, "What did it say? Is Joseph—"

"He's not dead." Lovina might have been reading a grocery list.

Rachel's heart sang. Her breath exploded. "Thank God!"

"But it's what Ben must have thought." The older women seemed not to be aware of the girl's agitation. "He hadn't even opened it. But everyone always assumes the worst, when they get a wire. Especially in wartime. And from General Halleck himself. Everyone thinks it must be a death announcement." Lovina's voice stopped.

Lightning lit up the sky again. There was no thunder at all this time. But the rain continued, as steady and careless as life.

Rachel took a deep breath and held it to still her pulse. She let it out slowly. "Do you suppose Ben was headed for the Martins' place?" Rachel asked. After her sudden relief had tempered itself, she realized with shame that for Lovina the crisis was not over. "They're less than a mile from here. Maybe he's there now, warm and safe, waiting for the storm to end."

She knew as soon as she'd said the words that they had no meaning, were just sounds to make up for her selfish jubilation. Why would a father—probably reckless with grief, no less real for being misplaced—leave his home and ride wildly to a neighbor's, only to sit out a storm likely brewing when he'd mounted?

"Prince came back by himself," Lovina said. That was answer enough.

It was growing colder in the buggy. Lovina's teeth chattered like castenets. "You should go home and get out of those wet clothes, Mrs. King. I can drive," Rachel said, remembering how she had tried to get Isaac to let her go on this trip by herself. "I'll take you home."

"What about Ben? And your father?"

If Ben's anywhere around here, Rachel thought. Or still alive. But she held her tongue.

"It's less than fifteen minutes to your place, Lovina. We could be back here in no time at all with umbrellas. Help with the search."

There was no sound now but the older women's breathless shivering, and the castenets. Then she spoke, her voice expressionless. "All right, Rachel, if you say so. No sense in both of us passing on."Rachel knew Lovina did not mean her, Rachel Miller.

"I'll drive you home," she said. Uncurling the reins from the whip post, she rippled them through the buggy front and toward the invisible Bess. The mare responded with a start that snapped their necks. She moved a dozen yards before Rachel pulled her up. She leaned across Lovina and pushed aside the flap. Rain pelted her face. She called out into the darkness, hoping her father was close enough to hear. "Father, I'm taking Mrs. King home for dry clothes!" she shouted. "We'll be right back!" She waited, but only the rain hiss answered. She let the flap fall back and clapped the reins across Bess's rump.

As if from relief at moving again, Lovina's tongue started to work. Her spirits seemed to rise with each rod of distance rolled off. "Kate will be furious with me. She hates to have anything disrupt our supper. She thought me mad to leave a dry warm house, with roast and potatoes all ready to eat, to mount up on a wild horse and ride out into the rain!"

She gave a laugh that rattled away into a cough. Then she went on. "Well, Prince just stood there, and when I saw Ben wasn't on him, I just froze, Rachel. It felt like the end of the world! Then Prince slowly came up close, until his nose was nearly in my face. And would you believe it, Rachel, he whinnied in a way that sounded like he was trying to tell me something!"

She paused, and in the lull Rachel heard a new sound outside the buggy. There was the sound of another horse, trotting along the muddy road! Apprehensive, she peeked from the flap on her side. The invisible animal was less than five yards away. "Look!" Rachel exclaimed. She leaned back in her seat, holding the flap open wider, which was pointless. Nothing was visible in the night. "Who is it?" Rachel called out.

Lovina leaned across Rachel's lap. "Prince?"

An answering nicker came out of the damp darkness.

Lovina laughed. "Isn't that just the limit! He's just like an old faithful lapdog. I suppose he thinks we've got Ben in here."

The spoken thought must have sobered her, for she remained silent from then on, squinting ahead, searching for light. It could not be much further to the King farm buildings, Rachel thought.

Lovina sneezed. Rachel heard her rubbing her upper arms vigorously. Then they saw it, a pinprick of light up ahead. Rachel slapped the lines across Bess's backside, but the old mare apparently had seen the light, too, and knew what it meant. She needed no encouragement.

Five minutes later they pulled into the barnyard. Kate's white head framed itself in the kitchen window.

"Come inside while I change, Rachel," Lovina urged. "I'll be quick and we can head right back." She pushed aside the flap and awkwardly climbed out. Once safely on the cobblestones, she turned to face the girl. "Come in and have a hot drink while I get out of this dress. Get warm. Then we'll take some coffee and blankets back out there, and a raincoat for your father and—" She cut herself off and stood motionless for a moment. Her face was part of the streaming night, her form only a silhouette against the window. Without another word, she turned and ran for the shelter of the woodshed door.

Rachel sat in the buggy for a moment, reluctant to get out into the rain, even for the short run to the warm, dry kitchen. She was worried about her father. Now that she had come on this errand of mercy, she was suddenly anxious to be back at the bridge. Isaac was not a healthy man, she knew. This cold and wet will do him no good at all, she thought, grimly. But the anticipation of a hot drink, not to mention getting out and stretching her stiff, cold legs, edged out much of the reality of the past half hour. Besides, her sitting out here would not shorten the time until Lovina returned. She winched herself out of the buggy and ran for the woodshed, nearly slipping on the wet stones when she jumped down from the vehicle.

"Sorry, Bess!" she cried over her shoulder. "Just give us a tiny bit more time!"

Inside, Lovina had already disappeared into the depths of the house. Kate King stood near the stove, in her hand a brightly colored pot holder. She watched Rachel wipe her feet on the kitchen mat just inside the door sill. Disapproval lined her craggy face.

"No sign of Benjamin, Lovina says." It was an accusation.

"Not yet," Rachel admitted. The delicious fragrance of roasted meat made her suddenly ravenous. "But Father is searching—I think."

"What do you mean, 'you think'?"

Rachel felt a dagger of resentment. "I mean that I think Father went down the riverbank right where Prince was standing. By the bridge." She struggled to keep her voice even. A droplet of water slid along her scalp and ran over her ear, causing her to shiver. She hadn't run fast enough to get between the rain drops.

"Humph!" Kate's face was stony.

The girl's resentment burned hot. Why was it always like this with the old woman? Ever since Joseph had started courting her, with their frequent comings and goings at both the Millers' and Kings' homesteads, his grandmother had treated Rachel like a naughty pet and never had a good word for her. From that Sunday when Joseph had first come calling nearly a year ago, initiating their formal courtship, Kate had regarded Rachel as something to be guarded against. (It had been in early October and the maples, oaks, and beeches had been dressed in clouds of color.) It was as if she might bring some strange plague upon the house if not constantly watched.

When they were children, it had been different. But now that Joseph had begun to treat her like a woman and caused her to imagine that she might someday be more than just a neighbor and a friend, Kate had grown cold toward her. And all they had done on that Sunday afternoon was to come to the King house after a long buggy ride to sit side by side in the parlor and eat fudge.

To this day Kate hadn't changed, only now Rachel had the uneasy feeling that Kate somehow blamed *her* for Joseph's enlisting in the army. But who could ever tell what she was thinking! As they stood and looked at each other, Rachel felt a sob take form deep in her throat. If only she knew how desperately I wanted to keep him here, she thought, suddenly miserable all over, again, at the memory of their last day together, over two months ago.

Lovina breezed in, looking considerably more comfortable. She had changed into a gray woolen dress and her feet were shod in a pair of huge scuffed brogans—no doubt her husband's—that reduced her already debatable femininity by a notch or two, yet simultaneously lent her an air of rock-ribbed stability. The only outward sign of her recent physical discomfort was her still-damp hair. However, she covered her head snugly in a plaid flannel kerchief, which gave promise of shelter from the dangerous night airs.

She rubbed her hands together. "Have the coffee ready, Mother?"

Kate turned to the stove and, adroitly manipulating the pot holder, lifted the heavy iron kettle and deftly poured a stream of the steaming black liquid into a galvanized bucket after first lifting its lid with her free hand.

"That should stay hot till you get back to the bridge," she said, her voice expressionless. She let the lid fall back into place with a bang, laid down the bucket and pot holder, and strode into the back bedroom. A moment later she returned carrying a foot-high stack of dark green, woolen blankets. She handed them to Lovina, then she opened a cupboard door and took out a small pile of white flannel cloths, folded neatly, and placed them on top of the armload of blankets. "Take these things along!" Her voice was brusque. "You'll need them—they are very absorbent." She didn't hand the coffee to Rachel, but bustled from the kitchen without another word.

"Rachel?" Lovina's eyes followed her mother-in-law's exit. "Would you be so kind as to carry the coffee? And there are mugs in that cupboard there," she added, gesturing with her chin. Then she gave Rachel a tired, sad smile. "Oh, well, it's hard on her too." She sighed, then exploded in a violent sneeze. "Let's go." She led the way, sniffling as she went.

The girl followed her out into the weather again. The rain was as incessant as doom.

4

Consciousness returned to Ben as a finger of frigid wetness along his neck. His eyes blinked open, but he saw nothing in the darkness. He blinked again, uncomprehending. There was no meaning in his mind. It seemed to Ben King that he had no body, that he had become a disembodied spirit, that he had ceased to exist. It occurred to him that he had died.

Unmeasured time passed and his swirling mind came to a gradual stasis. He figured out that he was lying down and the steady beat of cold needles on his face was rain. He decided that his time had, after all, not yet come. The sensation brought him back to life. Images came into his awareness. Like a slowly opening scroll, his memory brought back the recent events in a series of pictures that slowly acquired meaning. Standing in the stirrups, the daggerlike pain, his foot slipping, his body falling, rolling. Before that, riding along the road on Prince, speeding through the falling night, the storm. Seeing his wife waving her arms, her open mouth, calling. The fluttering telegram—

Of course—the telegram! It all came back like a slap in the face, the scroll of unrolling memory slapped shut. His mind was left clear and resolute. He had to get back to comfort his wife and his mother. What was he doing here, anyway?

Reflexively, he started to sit up. A bolt of pain shot through his chest and down his left arm. His breath caught in his throat and he fell back again, startled even in his agony at the splashing sound. Where *was* he?

The pain evened out but it didn't go away. Instead, it flowed out through his body until it seemed to reach the ends of every nerve he had. Star-shot darkness fluttered at the edge of his consciousness and he quickly took another breath. But that only seemed to sharpen the suffering again. He let it out quickly, then continued to breathe in shallow puffs. Panic nibbled at him like an icy counterpoint to the scorching pain.

He'd had another heart attack!

His panic grew, and with it another stab of pain, incredibly sharp. He tried to get a grip on his fear, to force himself to relax. The shock to his body ebbed slightly and he felt his pulse slacken. He lay completely still, focusing on the steady rain and the violent cold that seemed to chain his back to a bed of ice. He remembered the splash when he'd lain back and wondered whether he was in a puddle somewhere in the flats, or at the margin of the river itself. His panic started to mount, but he exerted his will again. At the same moment it occurred to him that the frigid water might be exactly the needed antidote to the pain.

Another thought immediately displaced that more comforting one. If he was actually almost in the river, would the water level rise rapidly enough to endanger him if he didn't quickly get out of this situation? The falling rain tickled his nose. Instinctively, he reached up to rub it, and his elbow encountered a sudden, hard surface. Gingerly, so as not to stir up the demons of pain again, he felt around the hardness. It started practically at his left shoulder and extended as far as he could reach before his chest pain flared again. A flash of lightning came to his aid, revealing a huge boulder looming high over him. He remembered it now, from his many trips down to the bridle path along the St. Joseph. Inches beyond it, in the momentary flash, he saw the river's inky liquid. He was amazed. The ancient rock was normally at least six feet from the river. Since the earth had been so dry for so long, how could the water level rise so fast? He shivered as he realized the boulder had saved his life. If it had not been there, to stop his tumbling descent as it so obviously had, he likely would have awakened in another world.

Carefully, with infinite patience, he tried moving again. He managed to get his right elbow under him without the keen agony returning. He ventured another small movement, drawing his knees up, preparatory to getting into a crouch. Done. He got the balls of his feet solidly beneath his haunches, his boots squishing the sodden grass down into pools of mud. Deliberately splaying the palms of his hands against the rock, he pushed himself to a standing position.

He'd risen just past a halfway crouch when the bolt of pain returned like lightning itself. The white fireball exploded in his brain. His legs gave and he fell, scraping his face roughly along the stone as he collapsed. He managed to twist away from the lip of the river as he fell, at the last instant. The movement caused a fresh twinge to shoot up his back, but he quickly had more urgent matters to occupy his mind. His left shoulder splashed into the rapid current, and for a breathless second it tugged at him, threatening to swirl him away. He fought it more with his will than with his pain-racked body. Then, unaccountably, the current weakened, momentarily, and he flopped onto his back, against the rock again. His damaged heart thudded violently in his rib cage. Every breath felt as if someone were reaching into his chest and tearing his lungs apart. Yet a part of his awareness noted that the pain he'd just felt in his back had subsided to a welcome numbness.

Ben lay still as the bright, tearing chest spasms began to ebb. He caught his breath again and gradually, as the torment receded, he became aware that his changed position might very well bring death sooner than his original one.

He realized with a start that the water was running over his left shoulder and arm, lapping intermittently along his jawline. He didn't know where the energy or the will to move again would come from. But if he did not move, he would drown.

He suddenly felt inexpressibly weary. And then he noticed, for the first time, that the pain had been replaced by a spot of heat which seemed to be growing from deep inside him. All of a sudden it was just there, incredibly, spreading out like the rays of a summer sunburst. He closed his eyes, tired of staring into the pouring blackness above, and concentrated on the knot of warmth. He tried to ignore the line of icy water along his throat. He shivered, at the same time realizing, with an almost idle detachment, that there was no longer any discomfort along his shoulder or upper arm. Or in his back, or his legs. This was it, he thought.

Not from the heart attack, not directly at least. The attack brought me to this place, this "rock of ages." But now my old ticker is becoming entombed in numb flesh. The thing that will take me is the water, the rising river. Black, silent, raging, unfeeling river.

It seemed as good a time as any to consider one's life, he thought. But he wouldn't have much time, with the rain never ceasing, the river still rising. He had often wondered what comes to the mind in the last moments of earthly life. He had always hoped for peace, for a sense of work well done. Now the things that were coming were not bringing him peace.

Up until two months ago, when Joseph had enlisted, he might have had that peace. No, maybe that was too recent. It had been in the days and weeks after the war began, some sixteen, seventeen months ago. That's when strife had reared its divisive spirit in the brotherhood, and peace had fled from their church as well as from the nation's hearths and halls of government. When his own peace had left. When Ben had remained true to his Mennonite heritage and had preached against the bearing of arms, against the orgy of violence that had been unleashed at Fort Sumter in the harbor of Charleston, South Carolina.

Preaching the historic message of nonresistance and peace had not been unanimously admired, Ben remembered sadly. None of the members of the little church they had started up on a song and a prayer back in thirty-eight were Mennonites except himself, Lovina, and Kate. Although the three Kings had come by themselves, not in a migrating group, other pioneers had ventured from the East to put down new roots in the St. Joseph Valley and try their plows in a brand-new state. All were willing to leave behind most of their old civilization—except for their churches. When they'd learned that Ben King was educated beyond the norm, and pious as well, they unanimously drafted him as their minister.

These settlers were members of other denominations, and few had ever heard of a Mennonite. Some of them put the flag right up there with the Holy Bible. And when Ben got wound up about refusing to have anything to do with the war, several families had quit their small fellowship, holding the notion that Ben was a copperhead South-lover, if not actually saying it. With the Millers, the Martins, and the Stephensons gone from the congregation, it was a small group Ben King addressed each Sunday morning. That wasn't so bad, but the hard feelings that remained, especially in Isaac Miller and his wife, had really complicated the relations between their two families now that Joseph and Rachel—

The thought of Joseph brought Ben's remembering up short. His eyes misted over with tears from the heart, not from the sky. There was the true measure of his failure as a minister of the gospel and as a father. A son who'd gone wild and in effect thumbed his nose at everything his father had stood for. Ben felt the tears roll down his cheeks and he thought how odd it was to cry in a rainstorm, while gradually sinking beneath a flash flood, and still feel one's own tears on the cheeks.

Maybe it was the extremity of his situation, or maybe just his native sense of humor, irrepressible as ever, even in the face of imminent death, but Ben smiled at the thought of crying in the rain. The smile became a laugh. And then Ben King was thinking of God.

It wasn't the God of pulpits, Sunday dinner grace, and sunny summer sunsets. It was a God he'd never thought of before. It was a God who was a loving presence standing as close as his next heartbeat, one whom he, Benjamin King, would be meeting on his own ground in about five more minutes.

A rush of ecstatic peace suddenly swept through him, so palpable, so warm, so real, that for a moment he felt the beat of his heart as if his whole being was caught up in its pulse. Slowly in the blackness, feeling better than he could remember ever feeling, he opened his eyes to the invisible dome of heaven. From somewhere inside came to his mind the words of an old hymn, his favorite: "Faith of our fathers, living still. . . ."

The frigid water lapped over his throat, spread across his chest. He was completely without feeling now, except for his head. His brain was an island. He knew he was going to die, and his mouth gave song to the words in his mind.

"In spite of dungeon, fire and sword." His voice grew in volume. It seemed to him that the invisible skies were opening to him, ready to receive him. The warmth spread inside his numb body. He felt light, floating. . . .

After what seemed an age, he became aware of a light growing, off on the edge of his vision. It was a sign he knew; it was his salvation. His burden was lifted. The light came closer, brighter. He shivered, whether from the cold or from the thrill of the moment he didn't even try to decide. His eyes closed. His mind was spinning, as if into a bliss unknown to human beings.

He felt his tired, worn-out body being lifted. The light was so bright. Then the hands under his shoulders set off a blaze of brilliant pain in his head. He was puzzled. Why pain now, at this wonderful instant? Then the light went out and he went spinning down, down into impenetrable blackness. His awareness ceased.

PART TWO

THE DESERTION

5

Joseph King pushed aside the tent flap and quietly stepped outside. There was enough of a bite in the September predawn air to brush the sleep from his brain. Clear of the tent where his fellow soldier was still deep in slumber, he stretched until his joints popped. The crescent moon hung inches off the western horizon, above the invisible crest of South Mountain. Even now he could make out a handful of early lights in the houses of Frederick, Maryland, a short distance below him as he faced eastward. All around him lay the quiet tents of his regiment, the Seventeenth Michigan Volunteers, just visible as pale blobs in the almost imperceptible lightening along the horizon.

He stretched again, feeling the tone of his muscles like new rope. He was just under six feet tall, wide across the shoulders, and lean as an antelope. His sandy hair was clipped short and it curled tightly against his head. His calm eyes were pale blue, as if he'd spent his youth staring into the sky until its color had leached into them. He had a wide mouth and generous lips, which laughed easily, yet suggested determined strength when in repose. Surrounding his mouth like a frame was a neatly clipped moustache and goatee, surprisingly thick for a youth of Joseph's age. He was twenty-four, and it would not be an exaggeration to say that many who encountered this striking young man with his erect posture and self-assured manner expected he would make fine officer material, once he got a bit of seasoning.

He walked a dozen or so yards along the dusty street between the rows of shadowy tents and turned off to relieve himself near the stream bank. From across the narrow run came the gentle lowing of a cow, its sleep disturbed by his sounds. A pair of crickets scraped out their protest at his presence. He finished his chore, moved a few feet along the bank, and sat down in the soft grass. Its crushed dampness gave off a sweet fragrance that made him suddenly homesick. Overhead in the branches of a huge oak, a first breeze of the dawn set the leaves to gentle whispering, unseen and unfelt below.

Joseph drew up his knees and rested his chin on them, savoring what he suspected might be his last morning of a peacetime life. Even though he had been a duly sworn-in U.S.A. soldier for nearly two months, he had yet to fire a gun in anger. Or be fired at. But today, or tomorrow, or the next day, the war would most probably come to him. The war. The war that was over a year old and so far had been kept in the South, where it belonged. The war that was not going well for the Union.

He smiled at the quiet dark. We've heard plenty about that—us new boys just up from Washington. When the Seventeenth Michigan arrived in camp a couple of days ago, it had found an army that was in a strange, even paradoxical, mood. It had been outfought and outmarched by Ol' Stonewall just a short time before. Shame and anger filled the breast of every red-blooded Northern boy. Yet these baser feelings had been cauterized and molded into a new hope. The general responsible for the defeat was dumped and replaced by the Army of the Potomac's hero, good ol' General McClellan. Now the humiliated boys had their spirits up again. They were good and ready for Bobbie Lee *this* time. And the Seventeenth Michigan Volunteer Regiment, fresh from Detroit via Washington, had arrived just in time to be part of it.

A thin finger of cloud poked across the slice of moon. The crickets stilled their sound. Joseph shivered as another breeze rustled the leaves overhead. War, he thought. What is it like, when you are actually in it? Why is it so exciting? Why is it attractive? What strange pull is this thing called war, that drags me away from the pleasures of life, from the warmth of home? From the comfort of a peaceable life of farming? From a lifetime of antiwar teaching? From Rachel?

He shook his head, almost painfully, to dispel the thoughts that had come to him over and over since the day when he had first arrived in Detroit, back in mid-July. He'd refused to work out the answers then, and ever since. The thoughts and questions came to him with barbs of guilt, even shame. And he always had something to do—orders to obey, drill routines to memorize, men to converse with— that helped him still the unquiet these thoughts and feelings brought. In their stead he had always substituted the words, phrases, and events which prompted his enlistment in the first place.

Now, in his memory's ear, he could still hear them: the speeches in Washington city that found their way into the Kalamazoo *Gazette;* the harangues by the petty politicians in Vicksburg and Schoolcraft, the villages where the Kings bought their nails and notions; the two-month-old news of Shiloh that still excited him. He had the freshest remembrance of the monologues of Rachel's father, poor old half-crippled Isaac Miller. Even now it brought a grin to his face when he recalled the disgust and anger in Isaac's expression when the middle-aged farmer remarked on what *he* would do, were he young and strong and free of the farm and his brood of women. Joseph snorted, the sound unnaturally loud in the quiet morning. It was no wonder he left the church when Pop started spouting his pacifism.

He felt the humor vanish. He also recalled the look

which always came over Rachel's face when her father spoke like that, the look which always had as its main feature a penetrating search of his own face. It made him uncomfortable, seeing again the luminous intensity in those beautiful eyes. He knew what it meant. He always saw the fear and the revulsion toward her father's meanings. And, always, there was the unmistakable love for him, Joseph (the Playboy) King.

Joseph squeezed his eyes shut. With an almost physical effort, he pushed the thoughts from his mind. In their place he let pictures come, pictures he had seen through the train windows between Kalamazoo and Detroit. Of the first sight he had had of the city and the river beyond it. The men he'd been mustered in with, almost all of them middle-aged and dandified, which had surprised him in no small degree. He let the sights and sounds and feelings return to him of those first days of marching, carrying a gun, taking orders—

As if his thought had given a cue, the predawn stillness was shattered by the bugle-blast of reveille.

"Time to roll out, Red!" Back in the tent, Joseph prodded his friend's shoulder with his boot. "Rebs're waiting to get whipped."

A groan escaped from the blanket, then silence. From outside came the sounds of men yawning and cursing.

"Listen to them," Joseph said to the lumpy, unmoving blanket. "The whole passel of 'em is a bunch of slickers used to loafing in bed half the day." He laughed. It had a rich love-of-life sound. "Not like us young farm boys, huh?"

A tousled head of ocher-hued hair emerged from the gray folds of blanket, followed by a face as full of freckles as Michigan has trees.

"Sheep dung!" muttered the face. "Farm boy I may be, but this ain't no hour of the morning to get up." Blue eyes crinkled into a grin, revealing startlingly yellow teeth. "Milkin' cows is one thing. Gettin' up to *walk* all day leaves me colder 'n—yawhhhnn!" The comparison disappeared in a gigantic open mouth.

"If we're lucky, Red," Joseph said, quietly. His humor had fled at Red's reminder of their business. "You know what comes at the end of all that walking."

Red's eyes held his a long moment. "Don't I though," he finally said. "Don't I sure enough."

They finished dressing hurriedly, in silence. They both slept in their socks and trousers, and Joseph had donned his boots and shirt earlier, when he'd risen to walk outside. He rolled up his blanket, sat on it, and watched as his partner finished his toilet. He felt sorry for Red, whose Christian name was John Milton, sheerly out of coincidence. His parents were as ignorant of classic literature as they were of the far side of Saturn. Red was a twenty-six-year-old, more boy than man. Though raised on a farm in southern Michigan like Joseph, Red looked soft and vulnerable. At least that was the impression he gave to the casual observer. Barely five-and-a-half feet tall, his weight seemed to hang on him in rolls of flab where young flesh should have been firm and flat. Hardly the type of man to go soldiering, Joseph had thought when they first met at the station in Kalamazoo.

When they arrived in camp in Detroit, however, Joseph found that he himself, at twenty-four and in excellent physical condition, was more the exception than the rule. Most of the recruits who made up what became the Seventeenth Michigan were a dozen years older than he was. At least. Fully three-fourths were also bodily unfit for anything more strenuous than climbing a flight of steps on an empty stomach. And John, quickly dubbed "Red" by his messmates for obvious reasons, had soon revealed qualities of character which in Joseph's opinion more than made up for his physical softness.

A tousled head thrust between the tent flaps. "Hey, you loafers, rise and shine! General Willcox's ordered us on the march in half an hour." The corporal's head disappeared before either man could muster breath for the ritual groan.

"I'll start the fire," Joseph said. "You got the matches?"

"Yeah," grunted Red. He bent over to pick up his boots and fished inside one of them. His hand came out with a match in it. Characteristics like this endeared Red to the men.

"Pee—you!" Joseph cried, holding his nose. "Strike that and the whole tent'll go up!"

"Hah, you should talk! Leastways I changed my socks this week."

They laughed together in the camaraderie they had developed in the two months since they had met. Joseph took the match and left the tent. He struck the match and held it to the little structure of twigs and dried leaves they had built up between two green logs last night before retiring. After it had caught, he fed in several larger cuts of stump, then set the coffee pot on the logs to boil. After he'd tossed in a handful of ground coffee, he flipped a couple hunks of hardtack into the skillet, added some lard from a small tin can, and sat back to wait for the aroma of boiling coffee. He let his eyes sweep around their "village," noticing how normal everything appeared: chaos. At least that's the way it would have appeared to the uninitiated observer, had there been any such animal thereabouts.

It was true that with a bare smattering of the rudimentary drill needed for soldiering, the Seventeenth Michigan could justifiably be called uninitiated. But they certainly were not observers! To some, indeed, to most of them, this fact was the tragedy. They were participants without a doubt or reservation, and if they reaped their crop of battle before the sun set, it would be because they had sown it in anticipation, even eagerness. Back in July they couldn't wait to enlist, but how changed was their perspective here, Joseph thought, with a wry smile.

As if to underscore this fact for all the greenhorns as well as for Joseph, their sergeant some yards away began to bawl out his displeasure at some idiocy going on near him. He grinned, in spite of himself, when he saw the object of the noncommissioned officer's frustration.

Of all one thousand men, give or take a couple dozen, who had been mustered in mid-July in Detroit, Poor Claude caught most hell from the noncoms. Even the officers, including the colonel himself, didn't try much to hide their irritation, often tinged with scornful amusement, when they had any dealings with "P.C.," as he came to be called.

"Roll that rusty ol' hide out o' that blanket, P.C.," the sergeant bawled, "or I'll tan it and wrap Jeb Stuart's carcass in it, come nightfall!"

Joseph's eyes followed those of the men near the sergeant and he saw the mound of ratty army blanket close to the oak he had sat beneath a short while ago. He saw a tentative movement at one end of the blanket. Then the sergeant launched a swift kick at the other end. As if their leader's act were tacit permission, half a dozen of the partially clad soldiers standing around laughing, grabbed the blanket in several places and rolled it about to secure their load. They stumbled the few paces toward the run and with a "Yo heave ho!" tossed the blanket's occupant far out into the brown water. The loud guffaws of the men nearly drowned out the splash.

Red emerged from the tent, buttoning his fly. "Hey, what's going on out here?"

Joseph pointed, his grin wide. "They got ol' P.C. again," he chuckled. "Sanders booted him to roust him and then half the company dumped him in the stream. Poor guy."

Red glared at Joseph. "Yeah. Poor guy all right." His

glance flicked to the water, where Poor Claude had surfaced amid much spluttering and blowing. Then they returned to Joseph's face and bored into his eyes. "You all should be ashamed of yerselves. Claude can't help it if he's fat, forty, and bald."

"And rich," Joseph added. "Family-rich. From slaves."

"He's a human being, friend," Red said. His voice was quiet and gentle, but his eyes pierced into Joseph's like ice picks.

Uncomfortable, Joseph looked back at the run. All the men had turned away and were walking back to their tents. There was no point left to the tableau now. P.C. was trying to pull himself out of the muddy water, clutching awkwardly at the long, dry grass on the high bank. His eyes met Joseph's for a moment, then his handful of stalks tore loose and the bedraggled man fell back with a splash.

The sound prompted Sergeant Sanders to turn around on the way to his tent. "Come on, private!" he yelled. "Take your bath when the fightin's over. That's an order!" He spun and walked away. All trace of amusement had left his voice. It was hard and cold.

Joseph felt a small shiver ripple through him. That was the hardest thing he'd had to get used to in the army, the downright meanness in many of the men in charge. And he wasn't really used to it yet. He could not remember even once being yelled at while he was growing up. His father had rarely even raised his voice, even at the farm animals. Certainly, Joseph could understand, with his mind anyway, the logic behind the soldier's creed of discipline: "Obey promptly and stay alive." But the head-knowledge did not dispel the quick rage and the burning shame of being ordered about, like a dog. Early on he had determined to use his brain and learn what was expected of him, and do it quickly and thoroughly.

For some reason or other Claude Fournier, however, was

habitually either wrong or slow in his response to orders, and so had become the butt of jokes and growls from both noncoms and officers. Not to mention outright physical punishment as in the scene just acted out.

Joseph stared at Poor Claude still trying to claw his messy way up the bank. A finger of contempt tickled him, then gave way almost immediately to shame. He glanced around at the busy breakfast activity. Red, in the middle of tending to their own morning meal, looked up at him with a quizzical expression. Then Joseph went to P.C. and extended his hand. In a moment the soaked man was on dry ground, sputtering his thanks. He quickly began to shiver in the early morning chill. He was even chubbier than Red, and with his cotton shirt clinging to every wrinkle and bulge of his body, he looked older than his reputed forty.

"You can use my tent to change," Joseph said quietly. There had not been enough camp tents to go around. It came as no surprise to anyone when P.C. turned out to be one of those left out in the cold. His family's Louisiana roots determined that. Little did it matter that Claude's branch of the family tree had migrated to Detroit a generation ago.

"Thanks, Joseph," the short, fat man said, his teeth chattering. Looking ridiculous, he padded to his camping place, retrieved his rucksack and blanket, then disappeared into the tent.

"You got too much heart for a killin' machine, Josy," Red said, handing Joseph a steaming tin cup and leaving space on the handle so neither would burn his fingers. He chuckled. "But he is a human being, right?"

Joseph took the cup and said nothing, letting Red have his moral victory. He sipped the scalding black coffee. They grinned at each other over the rims, sobering, feeling the weight of the day's expectations settle over them like a shroud.

"Men like ol' P.C.'re going to have a rough time of things," Red said. "He ain't accustomed to marching, let alone fightin'. Them two weeks of squeezin' his innards out drained off what strength he might of had before."

"You could say that for all of us," Joseph added. "I'd still like to get my hands on that storekeeper who unloaded that spoiled meat on us. I'd personally escort him to the rebel lines!"

"Ha!" Red laughed. "You kin say that again! Down from a thousand to barely half that many men, in two weeks' time." He took a sip of rapidly cooling coffee and wrapped his hands around the cup to warm them. "Can't imagine any battle that'd do that much damage!"

The mention of that word *battle* reminded both of them of who they were, where they were. They fell silent and let their eyes roam over the scores of tents of their regiment. Beyond them, camped further west along the creek, sat the tents of the Forty-fifth Pennsylvania, reportedly as green as their own motley group of Michigan private citizens turned soldiers. Some of the men in both regiments were already striking their tents, home for all of them for the past few days, since they'd arrived by train from the capital. How many of them would still be alive, a day from now? Two days? Next year? Joseph wondered. Then he made himself stop wondering.

When P.C. came out, Red and Joseph invited him to join them for breakfast. Claude and Red were on closer terms than Joseph was with Claude, but Joseph got on well enough with the man, face to face. He generally managed to put down his contempt for the fat man's physical ineptitude, but he made no effort to get to know the Detroiter better. He felt sympathy for P.C. when the latter was victimized. The moral upbringing Joseph had had wouldn't let him participate in the hazing. On the contrary, his rearing even prompted Joseph at times, against his superficial preferences, to come to the assistance of this beleaguered man old enough to be his father, as in the blanket-tossing incident.

Besides the coffee, which Joseph had started, Red had rustled up a decent gravy from wheat flour in water, salt added, with fried bacon broken into it. Spread over the ubiquitous, rocklike hardtack, it was almost possible to enjoy a meal, if one had a good imagination! They ate in silence, feeling the prodding of time and circumstance.

By now most of the men were packed up and crouched on their haunches waiting for the marching to commence. Word had come that their march would start shortly after sunup, which could be anytime now. The scuttlebutt was that a stroke of luck had fallen on headquarters in the form of some soldier finding a copy of Lee's orders that one of his men must have dropped. True or not, all the Yanks knew combat probably wasn't far off. Maybe today. For the volunteers of the Seventeenth Michigan and the Forty-fifth Pennsylvania, it would be the first bloodletting, the first time they would point their guns at live human beings. The realization turned off speech and filled heads with private thoughts.

As he sopped up the last of the tasty gravy, Joseph stared into the dying flames of the cooking fire and thought about Rachel. His memory's eye clearly saw her insistent, worried expression on the day he'd left. He was glad he'd taken the time to write to her yesterday, as well as to his family, but—

"Hey, you there, get to it!" Sergeant Sanders' shout broke into Joseph's thoughts like a clap of thunder.

"Yes sir. Sorry, sir!" Joseph said, rising so fast his head swam. The others stood up, too.

"Private, how many times I got to tell ya? I ain't no officer, so none of this 'sir' stuff!" Sanders strode up and glared at Joseph. He seemed ready to bite off his head, even though Joseph was half a foot taller and about fifty pounds heavier, all muscle. Then his manner softened. "King, you and this whole crowd. I pity youse guys." He shook his head sorrowfully. "Cannon fodder. Yessirree, that is what you poor bastards are: cannon fodder. Least they coulda done is give me another month to put some steel in your backs and know-how behind those triggers."

He turned to walk away, then stopped and looked back reflectively at the three of them. Even though he could not have been more than two or three years older than Red, and younger by ten than P.C., his expression was almost fatherly. "Get packed up, men. General wants us on the road by sunrise. We're late already." His voice softened further. "And pray to God that Lee's men are as sick as you all were, when you meet up with 'em." Abruptly he spun and walked away. His voice was loud and gruff again when he ordered all his men to fall in.

Joseph and Red hurriedly struck their tent, rolled it with their beds into a neat sausage that wrapped around their necks, rested on the shoulders, and could be tied with dangling guy lines in front. The odds and ends of their gear, and their spare clothing, went into their haversacks. Claude, with no tent to deal with, wiped out the skillet, tin plate, and cups, and kicked dirt over the embers while the others finished up their tasks. Minutes later the three privates fell in at the tail end of the column. It had already moved out and they became separated from the rest of their company. Rapidly, the line of men swung into marching formation and headed west along the National Road out of Frederick, toward South Mountain. Toward destiny.

6

The fresh sun seemed to hang just above the horizon behind them, red and moonlike as it rose through the humid
atmosphere. Joseph could already feel its warmth on his
back as he strode along. He glanced at P.C., marching in
front of Red, who was on Joseph's right. The fat man's
shivering had stopped and what was left of his matted hair
was nearly dry. Joseph knew that within an hour, at the
most two, the transplanted Louisianan would be sweating
and puffing with the effort of a sustained trek.

It had been that way all during training and drill, Joseph
recalled. He still could not understand what prompted men
like Claude Fournier to enlist in the army. And P.C. hadn't
been the only one of his ilk who had signed on, in Detroit.
Joseph had never known much about armies and fighting
and such, but the pictures he'd carried in his head had always been of trim young men, hard-muscled and energetic,
with determined set faces, marching or riding heroically
into battle. He'd always assumed others of his generation
saw similar imaginary images.

Yet nearly all of the hundreds of volunteers in Detroit a
few weeks ago were middle-aged, established individuals,
many in outfits that were characteristic of bank or board
room. Most of them were married and prosperous-looking,
an impression vouchsafed as much by their paunches as by
the cut of their cravats. Joseph had felt almost conspicuous
by his comparative youth, his tall, muscular build, and his
bachelorhood. There actually were more men in this regi-

ment who resembled old P.C. than Joseph. Yet most of them had avoided becoming the butt of jokes and horse-play, probably because they either almost died of diarrhea the first few weeks or toughened up quickly.

The sun climbed higher and the dew-sparkle disap-peared from the fields of grain stubble and dried-out clover as they passed. The steady rhythm of marching feet began to lull Joseph's brain. He was not really aware of the roll-ing country, or of the gradually increasing pitch of the road as they approached a height of land, still a mile or two ahead. Since marching formation consisted of the classic two-abreast column, and because he was at the extreme tail of it, the only other men he could see directly and entirely were Red, Claude, and the soldier immediately in front of him.

Joseph had studied this soldier with interest, when they first started out, thinking he remembered him from the train ride to Detroit. From his youth and clean-cut appear-ance, Joseph guessed he belonged to E Company. This was a unit which had idiosyncrasies totally different from the rather bizarre uniqueness of his own company. E Company was made up almost exclusively of youthful future teachers from the Normal School at Ypsilanti. Even to Joseph, youn-gest man in his own company, these men seemed mere boys, wet behind their trigger guards.

Now and then a mounted officer galloped past on one or another errand, acting important. Joseph assumed they were keeping in touch with headquarters and the main part of the army back in Frederick. He did not recognize most of them, knowing only from their insignia whether they were staff officers, lieutenants, captains, or majors. The boss of their regiment he knew on sight. Same for the gen-eral of their division, Major General Orlando Willcox, who was visible from time to time while they camped. Their corps commander, however, Major General Jesse Reno, he had seen only once, the day the regiment had arrived in Washington city not more than a couple of weeks ago. And McClellan, the Big One, Joseph of course had heard much about, but had never seen, except in pictures.

So much brass, he thought with a sigh. So many with bars and stars on shoulders and collars and hats, with so much responsibility. He smiled a tight smile. And with the privilege to *ride* everywhere. He felt a rush of nostalgia as he remembered Prince, his beloved stallion. How fine it would be, to be prancing along on him right now, ignoring the jealous glares of the officers. Why, Prince would put 90 percent of the mounts of the officers of this Army of the Potomac to shame.

He sighed again, brushing his brow where sweat had already formed. The band of his forage cap seemed glued to his forehead. When he took it off, the line of wet across his hairline instantly turned refreshingly cool in the breeze from their pace. He took out a bandanna and wiped his face. For mid-September, it was going to be a hot one, he could tell already.

"Whatsa matter, King, tired so soon?" Red's voice broke in on his thoughts. "Big, healthy-looking specimen like you?"

Joseph laughed. "No, just thinking about my horse. And how good it'd be to have him now."

"Haw! Just be glad you don't," Claude put in, with a glance over his shoulder, "or you'd be in the cavalry, up against the likes of Jeb Stuart!"

"Or an officer in the infantry!" Red cried. "Would you like that, Joseph? Gettin' to order us poor foot slobs around?"

Joseph chuckled. "Sure, with me hardly knowing how to execute a simple marching maneuver, you think I could even order a column into fighting formation?"

They all laughed at that, even the boy from E Company

marching in front of Joseph. He half turned and spoke past his shoulder. "Such as the maneuver of falling in with the wrong company?" The sting of his meaning was blunted by his friendly tone. They all laughed again.

They lapsed into silence, concentrating on their marching feet, on how the gear was riding. Joseph had to grin as he studied the contrast between the three of them from his own company and the sartorial splendor of the boys from Ypsilanti. He'd noticed it when the youth in front of him half turned. Now he let his gaze travel further forward and noticed that every one of the individuals he could see had his coat on. From the way they fit snugly across shoulders and around necks, he guessed the top button on every tunic was done up. Each wore a high-crowned black hat, with a feather stuck jauntily in the band. He felt a stab of wicked glee as he wagered with himself that each future teacher probably had his dress-parade gloves carefully folded and stuffed into his breast pocket.

His amusement rapidly gave way, however, to boredom. His mind groped for something on which to fasten. His own paraphernalia, for example. It could get to be irritating, actually. How a canteen, hooked to a belt on a hip, would creep around and bump on thigh muscle, impeding the stride. The bed roll and tent would have to be shifted a mite to let the air touch a sweating neck. The haversack shifted for the same reason. Then a musket would be humped from one shoulder to another to ease the weight—strictly taboo in parade drill. There were advantages to bringing up the rear, unless an officer, or sergeant, took a notion to ride behind, and saw all the out-of-place gear.

As the long line of men angled upward and the sun climbed up the sky, Joseph's attention was drawn back to their surroundings. He naturally surveyed the fields with a farmer's eye to make judgments about agricultural techniques and crops, here in the South. True enough, Maryland was loyal Union, but everyone in the army knew it was a slaveholding area. And there wasn't a soldier among them who did not recall the fracas in Baltimore, in this "loyal" state over a year ago. Lincoln had to use force in that city so it would allow Northern soldiers through on the railroad to the capital city. That was back in the days when everyone reckoned the war would be over in weeks, even days. Before Lee and company had made fools out of the army.

Joseph felt a quick surge of anger, akin to his emotion when he had first heard about Second Bull Run of just two weeks ago. It was the defeat of the Army of the Potomac under John Pope which had brought McClellan back to top command, and the Seventeenth Michigan to the war. Joseph had enlisted out of patriotic ardor, fanned by Fourth of July rhetoric. He'd lost much of that ardor after a couple weeks of mind-numbing military life. But the humiliation dealt out by Jackson, Longstreet, and Lee had effectively restored his desire to fight for his country against the slavers of the South.

His thinking of the Independence Day speeches again, and his subsequent passion to enlist, called up to his memory the face of Rachel. He hadn't really thought about her much since he'd enlisted and he only partly understood why. Now, as the bone-jarring, mind-deadening march up the long hill went on, he pushed the memory around inside himself. Guilt twinged him as he recalled the day of his leaving. He had not treated her the way she'd wanted to be treated. He might not be the world's most sensitive man, but he would have had to be downright obtuse to miss her meanings, and her feelings.

It had been barely a week after his final decision to enlist that his train had left the station at Kalamazoo, bound for Detroit on the Michigan Central Railroad. Only at the station had his zeal faltered, if just for a moment. Rachel had gone with him, to take home the horse and buggy. And certainly to give her farewells. He had stopped in at the Millers to say good-bye to her parents. He'd been puzzled by the bemused look in Isabel Miller's eyes. Since the beginning of the formal courtship between Rachel and Joseph, she had been less open, more reserved with him, frequently studying him with an enigmatic expression.

But he could easily read in Rachel's face, in those darkly luminous green eyes, the pain his going brought to her. There were not many words exchanged, at the station. They had been said earlier, when he had first told her he was considering joining up. At first she had tried to talk him out of it, using more than one argument. The one about his father's weakness still troubled him, and even now he shut the thought away. He hadn't really had good answers for her arguments, good to her anyway. It was his patriotic duty to go, he'd said, and he believed it and felt it. He must help his country. When she threw that pacifist garbage at him—that he'd been hearing from his father—he saw red. It did not even bear thinking about.

Yet a deep feeling of discomfort remained inside him, after his explanations. Then as the eastbound chuffed into the station, she had impulsively thrown her arms around his neck and clung to him so tightly he had felt her trembling. Her last words, whispered in their intensity, were brief: "What will become of us, Joey?" Breathed into his ear, they seemed to linger there so that even now, two months later, they were as clear and present as if she were still with him. He hadn't answered her, and he had boarded the train without a backward glance. His discomfort had still been undefinable, but it was stronger than ever. He'd left as a patriotic but miserable man.

"Reckon we'll be stopping for chow directly?" It was the boy in front of him, glancing back.

"We just got started, man!" Red cried. "Don't you want to hurry and get there? Do some real-live fightin'?"

Just then a sound like distant thunder rumbled out of the southwest. But it was like no heavenly electrical storm the men had ever heard, for it continued longer than any natural thunder. It grew louder, and Joseph felt the earth tremble beneath his feet.

"Hey!" the boy cried, losing his foot rhythm as he half turned toward Joseph and Red. "That's artillery, isn't it?" His eyes were huge. "Do you suppose it's theirs or ours?"

All along the line, the men started jabbering and pointing off in the direction of the sounds. Marching discipline disintegrated. Within seconds a muddled bunch of schoolboys had replaced the disciplined blue line. Joseph felt the excitement. Glancing wordlessly at Red, he was startled to see a new and strange light in his friend's eyes.

"I hope the bastards leave some of the fightin' for us!" Red growled. He brought his musket half off his shoulder, and Joseph saw his fingers tighten around the trigger. "Yes sir," he muttered. "I been waitin' for this for weeks!"

Joseph gave a laugh that came out sounding more nervous than he liked. "Relax, Red. From the sound of it, the guns must still be miles away." He gestured up the slope. "And from the looks of it, this crew will never get there!"

By now the men of the Forty-fifth Pennsy, who had been marching ahead of the Seventeenth Michigan, had completely halted their forward movement. They were milling about, each man squinting in the direction of the firing, pointing and talking animatedly with his nearest comrade. Nothing could be seen because the guns were obviously beyond the summit of the ridge they had not yet topped.

Suddenly they became aware of sounds other than the guns, sounds a lot more immediately threatening than distant artillery. Galloping straight toward them, tearing into the shapeless formation from the direction of the head of their regiment, came their colonel, Robert Mulligan. His mount was dragging a roiling plume of dust and from his open mouth issued a torrent of words which became clearer as the man neared them. The nature of his vocabulary bore no resemblance to the language Joseph had heard from the church pulpit all his life.

Joseph watched the officer whipping his horse and spurring it like a rider possessed, and he felt a flash of anger at the treatment of the poor beast.

He nudged Red. "Here comes trouble," he said between pursed lips.

Red nodded, a grim expression now on his face. The boy was standing stock-still, staring at the onrushing officer with his mouth open. His face was ashen. Joseph reached out to push him into step again, but P.C. beat him to it.

"Get marching, boy!" he hissed, just as the colonel reined up at their end of the line in a billow of dust. He had ceased his swearing and his mouth remained closed, but his gray eyes and livid countenance spoke volumes.

Ahead of them, up the line of men, Joseph saw in a quick glance that Mulligan's verbal lashing had been effective. The order of the column was restored. The troops had started to march again, much subdued. They marched, that is, until the colonel rose in his stirrups, half turned, and bellowed "Halt!" in a voice that could no doubt be heard back in Frederick.

All movement ceased immediately. No one opened a mouth or moved a boot. Even the distant bombardment chose that moment to cease.

The colonel relaxed and sat his saddle again. He ran his hard eyes along the tail of the column, starting with the four men now standing at attention beneath his horse's flared nostrils. He had a stocky build and wavy black hair stuck out from beneath his gray hat, which sat at a jaunty tilt on his head. The ends of a luxuriant moustache drooped down past the ends of his thin lips, enhancing the scowling appearance of his whole face. He appeared to be in his early forties and the habit of command rested easily in his manner.

He stared long and hard at Joseph, then at each of the other privates along the last fifty yards of the line, where the disorders had been greatest. Gradually, the hard fire in his eyes faded, only to be replaced by contempt. When his glare came back to the end of the line again and met Joseph's eyes, he felt the blood creep up his neck and his ears start to burn. The officer's expression showed more clearly than any words, what he thought of his Seventeenth Michigan Volunteers.

Joseph felt sudden anger, a quiet but intense rage, boil up inside his gut as the colonel's eyes swept them again. Mulligan then jerked his horse's head around and walked it along the silent, waiting ranks, glaring at each soldier as he passed.

It was the same hot fury he had felt when he had heard of McClellan's losses outside Richmond last spring, and when Pope had made such a fool of himself, just two weeks ago. Only now the passion was sharply focused. For the first time in his life he was mad enough—and that was truly the word, mad—to kill. Not the Rebs, but his own superior officer! How ironic!

Practically any verbal reprimand for their admittedly unsoldierly behavior would have been easier to take than that glare of silent, cold contempt. Joseph had expected a blast of vitriolic speechmaking to follow up and consolidate, so to speak, the torrent of cussing the officer had unleashed as he galloped back down the line. That would have been understandable and in order. Instead, Mulligan evidently had decided that more words would be a waste. Joseph had never felt so insulted.

When he reached the head of their regiment, the colonel

83

raised his arm then brought it down and forward, hard and vicious, as if he had an executioner's sword in hand. The column began to move. Subdued, the troops swung into their rhythm again. If the rest of the men had thoughts and emotions like Joseph's, it would have been hard to find anyone in the ranks who could tell which was worse: the chastisement from their commander or the new awareness that marching to battle was no Sunday school picnic.

None would have admitted it, but yes, each man was at least slightly ashamed of his behavior and glad their disorganization had been out of direct view of the other regiment in their division. Far ahead of them, as they topped a slight rise in the otherwise gradual slope, they could see the other brigades. The veterans. Between them and their own brigade yawned a gap of some two hundred yards, mute testimony of their greenness and unsoldierly behavior.

As the morning aged and the sun's heat warmed the endless dust cloud raised by their tired feet, their chagrin gradually dissolved. Into its place crept a degree of sobriety most of the men had never before experienced. Climbing helped wonderfully to focus their minds.

About halfway between Frederick and South Mountain stood the spine of the valley, so to speak, that they had been ascending all morning. It had appeared low, from back at camp. After all, the distant blue line of the mountain had towered over everything else in sight. But now that they were in the last few hundred yards to this intermediate ridge, the grade abruptly steepened, laying a load that dusty boots and tired legs protested against. Joseph took a pull on his canteen then shook it, computing the supply remaining. Yesterday afternoon orders had come down to pack a three-day supply of rations, giving them the first hint they would be marching and time to write letters. Now he felt a stab of anxiety that one canteen might run out fast, unless a man saved it for emergencies.

He threw a glance at P.C. and the boy. The latter was gulping at his canteen, and Joseph recalled noticing Claude frequently upending his.

"Better ease up on the water," Joseph said. "We're not even half through the first day."

The boy jerked his canteen away from his mouth as if he'd been slapped. P.C. only threw Joseph a dark look. Then he startled them all by tearing off his forage cap, upending his canteen, and letting water cascade over his bare head.

"Hey, man!" Red yelled. "Wanna die o' thirst?" He grabbed at P.C.'s hand holding the canteen.

"We are all going to die anyway, and you know it," P.C. said in a voice so low it was nearly lost in the rattle and tramp of their marching. "Besides," he added, anticlimactically, "there's bound to be a river or a stream somewhere up ahead."

No one spoke. Joseph felt coldness like an icy glove close over his heart. He started to whistle. Red gave him an odd look, then his freckled face broke into a grin. He winked at Joseph and started whistling an accompaniment, trying to follow the other's tune. However, because the tall soldier's tune was being composed as he went along, the effect was less than harmonious. They broke into laughter. The boy ahead of them joined in. Even Poor Claude's face eased.

Minutes later they went over the summit of Catoctin Ridge.

A breathtaking panorama met their eyes, along with a welcome sight. The valley between their position and the bulwark of South Mountain stretched out before them like a brown-and-green plaid carpet about five miles across. A clump of trees in the hollow at the bottom of the valley signified a creek and likely a hamlet. Otherwise, the landscape was bare of all growing life higher than dried grass and corn stubble. Almost at their feet lay the veteran regiments, stretched out for a midday break.

"Wow," Red breathed. "Ye buzzards! Did you ever see anything like it!" He laughed. "Back in Michigan we got no views like this."

"You're right about that," Joseph agreed. "Wouldn't you like to farm such a valley?"

P.C. chimed in, sounding happier than he had since his early-morning splash: "I don't know about the farming, but I see a nice shady spot where I'm going to rest these aching feet and belt down some chow!" He veered off the road toward a tall maple, one of only three or four trees between the hilltop where they were and the copse at the lowest level of the bowl-shaped valley.

They laughed, watching him go.

"Sounds like a great idea," Red said. "Think I'll join him." But before he'd moved a foot the boy grabbed their attention.

"Look," he cried, pointing to the distant southwest.

"What is it?" Joseph asked, shading his eyes. The glare of the sun in an almost cloudless sky was painful.

"Looks like a string of blue ants!" the boy went on, "climbing that road way off toward that gap in the mountain."

As if it had waited for their undivided attention in order to start its show, the pass in the long mountain suddenly erupted in smoke. An instant later, the thunder of artillery shook the earth beneath their feet. The row of ants they had been watching disappeared from the road into the nearby trees in less time than it took for the resting men around the summit to scramble to their feet and crane their necks to the southwest.

"Holy Moses!" the boy breathed.

Without warning, another burst of cannon fire and

smoke shattered the last vestige of their peaceful rest stop. This barrage was closer, directly west across the valley from them, in another pass through the long mountain.

Red let out a long low whistle. "Hey, I'll bet that's where we're headed for!"

"Sure would seem so," P.C. said. "This here road 'pears to head straight across the country to that gap." He started to giggle.

The boy glanced sharply at Claude. "Do you suppose that means we will be marching there straightaway?" He bit his lip and fingered his musket stock. He had unslung his weapon and was holding it awkwardly across his chest.

"Watch where you're pointin' that thing!" Red cried. "I aim to stay away from the business end of one o' them things at least till we get to the mountain!"

"Here comes the colonel," Joseph said. Their heads pivoted down the slope to the west, taking in the steady progress of their leader as he rode slowly in their direction. Every few yards he paused to talk to a group of men, clustered around their tiny fires. He was smiling.

"Looks about as peaceful as a parson comin' to pay a Sunday afternoon call," Red snorted.

"Sure, and why shouldn't he?" Claude spoke up, his voice bitter. "He's probably happy, now that the fightin's about to commence."

"Aw, knock it off," Red said. "At least the waitin's done with. And once we get there, the marchin'll be over."

"Then we'll prob'ly wish we was back marchin' again," Claude retorted.

"Shut up, you guys," the boy hissed. "Here he comes."

Colonel Mulligan reined up his horse and dismounted. "Afternoon, men. Getting your feet rested?" His voice was hearty. "Whew!" he breathed, grinning like a small boy. "Hotter'n hell for September, no?" He tipped back his hat and wiped the sleeve of his tunic across his forehead. A lock of hair fell across his skin and he brushed it away. "But in another couple of hours we'll know what hell is, huh men?" He tipped back his strong-jawed face and laughed uproariously. "Or maybe we'll send Lee's miserables there first!" His gray eyes flashed.

"Sir? Are those Lee's men there in the gap?" The boy pointed to the cloud of smoke floating into the sky straight in front of them, although miles away.

"You bet, soldier, and in about five more minutes our regiment is going to head toward that den of iniquity and twist the tiger's tail!"

"All by ourselves, sir?" Joseph asked.

The colonel barked out a laugh. It was not a pleasant sound. "It would take a lot more than just us! No, the rest of Willcox's division will be going in, too. There will be about three thousand of us." He jerked his head in the direction they'd just come from. "And General Reno will be bringing up the rest of the corps soon. Matter o' fact"—he took a few steps to the top of the rise they had just crossed —"here they come now, not more than an hour or two back." He turned and walked back to them with a bounce in his step, as if it were an everyday affair for a high-ranking field officer to confide in tenderfoot enlisted men.

It occurred to Joseph that maybe Claude was right. Maybe the colonel only felt expansive and jolly when battle was imminent. Which would not be such a silly notion when one took to mind that soldiering was, after all, his trade. When the Seventeenth Michigan had formed, back in Detroit, they had elected their own colonel—not an uncommon practice in this war between citizen-soldiers. He had been a real lemon, however, hadn't known a certain part of his anatomy from the business end of a musket, as Red had delicately phrased it. After one week he had quit and gone home.

When the regiment had arrived in Washington city, army

headquarters had assigned them Robert Mulligan, fresh from commanding a regiment that had been virtually wiped out by Jackson's troops at Bull Run. He was regular army, West Point class of '41. Few of the men in the regiment had gotten to know him well, so far. The gossip was that he was a real hard case, spoiling for a comeback fight to avenge the "murder" of his troops, as he put it. It wasn't hard to see the perfect naturalness of that, Joseph thought, as he watched the man remount and carefully adjust his hat over his thick hair. Maybe a lowly private should reserve judgment on the man, until later.

"As I have been telling all the troops, gentlemen," the officer said, expertly holding the reins of his prancing black, "our objective is to create a diversion on the south side of Turner's Gap." He pointed to the low cut in the mountain straight ahead of them. "General Reno will support us as soon as he comes up, and McClellan intends to clear the Rebs off South Mountain and chase them all the way back into Virginia." His eyes probed into theirs, by turn, seeming to rest for long moments on each of their faces as if to reassure himself about these unpredictable tenderfeet.

Then he went on, choosing his words carefully. "Let me observe and be proud of what the Seventeenth Michigan Volunteers are capable of. I want you to kill and kill and kill! And do it with dispatch and efficiency! We will teach that turkey over the mountain there that he *dare not* make fools out of the armies of the United States!" With that, he jerked his mount's head around and spurred toward the head of the column.

7

Minutes later the sergeant's orders to move out were bawled down the line. The men groaned and grumbled themselves into formation, with much shuffling of booted feet and adjusting of gear. Fires were kicked out and coffee cups drained and tossed into back packs. Once under way there was no small talk or even complaining. To a man, this group of soldiers, hardly more than a civilian rabble, knew they were at last within close reach of their initiation as real soldiers—as killers of other men.

"As murderers," Joseph thought to himself as he stared at the growing cloud of spent gunpowder pouring from the big guns on the mountain. His stomach tightened and he had trouble swallowing. In spite of the heat of the sun, which was now just past its apex, coldness filled him. The sweat along his neck and under his cap brim turned icy. He shivered.

" 'Spect they'll quit shootin' long enough for us to get information?" Red asked. He said it like a joke.

P.C. snorted.

"What'll we do if they don't?" the boy asked, in earnest.

"I guess we'll just have to trust God to protect us," Joseph said. He was surprised at himself as soon as the words had passed his lips.

Red looked at him quizzically.

"I'm counting on it," the boy said over his shoulder. He was completely sincere.

P.C. said, "I reckon God'll be pretty close by. After all,

he knows there'll be a whole mess o' judgin' to be done in a short time!"

"Watch your tongue, man!" Joseph's voice was sharp. "Or you'll be dead before we get there."

"Struck down, you suppose?" P.C. laughed bitterly.

Joseph shuddered.

They marched on, silent again, the only sounds once again the clump of their boots, the jangle and thump of guns, bayonets, and haversacks against warm, soft flesh. It was an appropriate occasion for a man to think private thoughts. Important thoughts. Joseph was surprised by the erratic behavior of his mind: one moment full of excitement and anticipation, the next almost paralyzed by fear. And regret. Pictures floated in and out of his head. He was amazed at the sudden and arbitrary series of memories that streamed through his consciousness. Yet they all had a common theme—the Mennonite doctrine of nonresistance.

There were his father, uncles, and neighbors arguing till the cows came home over the Mexican War. There were his father and Isaac Miller arguing about the present war. There were the speeches, the sermons, the endless arguments against war until it seemed to him that there were nothing but negatives about his family's faith! It had seemed to him then, and it still did, that there was no difference between Mennonites and "the world" other than that Mennonites would rather die than take up the sword. Yes, it had seemed so backward, so against human nature, which wants to fight every bit as much as it wants to feed, drink, and procreate.

To his young mind the arguments had seemed to be conducted more by vehemence and noise than by logic. It had disturbed him, too, that strife between members in his father's church, when the war started, had seemed sometimes to be the only result of the debate over war and nonresistance. Rachel's parents had dropped out of church over the matter and Isaac was now a cynical, faultfinding man. The irony of that sad fate had not been lost on Joseph, who by then had long ceased to attend his father's church regularly.

Joseph's attention was brought back to the present by a sudden awareness of the silence. The artillery fire had ceased.

"Thank God for small favors," Red said to Joseph. His voice was unnaturally loud. Joseph was startled at the absence of his earlier belligerence.

"Yeah," chimed in P.C., "but look how close we're gettin' to where we'll have to start shootin' back!"

It was true.

Joseph half turned in midstride, glanced back up the way they had come, then looked to the front again, up the mountain. He was surprised. They had marched about halfway through the valley. Where had the time gone? A short distance ahead could be seen the clump of trees and, as expected, a small village nestled in their shade, along a small creek. He was sure he wasn't the only one who looked forward to refilling his canteen and standing beneath a leafy tree for a minute. He looked behind him again, wondering where the rest of Reno's command was. No one had yet appeared over Catoctin Ridge.

Sergeant Sanders' stentorian voice reached them from far forward. "Double-time, men. Let's move it out!"

Immediately the pace quickened. Joseph heard a groan from P.C. Complaints from more of the marchers drifted back to him like chimney smoke on a stiff breeze. But the additional effort soon silenced them.

"Sarge must've picked up a load of ants in his britches," grumbled Red. "Either that or the colonel's finger is a-gettin' itchy."

Joseph only grunted for response.

Two minutes later the reason for their speed-up became

clearer. They became conscious of a sound no one had noticed for a while, even after first hearing it. It resembled nothing more remarkable than a few million grasshoppers kicking up their heels in unison in the corn stubble and dried vegetation on either side of the road. As they kept on, the noise took on a new, sinister meaning.

"What is that?" the boy asked. "Firecrackers going off?"

They all cocked their ears to the southwest, off to their left. "Sounds more like musket fire," Red suggested.

Immediately they all recognized that he was right. As they squinted off toward the sound, the voice of Sergeant Sanders boomed out again, confirming it. "General Cox is in hot water, men. Let's pick it up." And the already stiff pace was accelerated again. Joseph and Red glanced at each other. Red's eyes were wise in wonder and fear. Joseph had no doubt that the same expression was reflected in his.

Suddenly, several hundred yards in front of them, they saw the head of their column veer off to the left, toward the sound of battle. The troops, a brigade of their division they hardly knew, seemed to be marching into an empty field. But within minutes, when they got there themselves, Joseph and the others saw it was another road, stretching off in a dusty straight line directly toward the sounds of firing. Now Turner's Gap sat slightly off to their right. What the colonel had said was true. They would be aiming at the pass from the flank, evidently to cover the approach, and then the attack, by the bulk of the army.

Joseph felt like asking Red what he thought about their apparent destination and likely assignment. He didn't expect Red or anyone below the rank of major to know, but it would be good to talk about the onrushing events. He was not getting any happier about the idea of fighting just because it was rapidly approaching. But the stiff pace took all the breath he had. It even emptied his mind of all but the matters at hand. There was no longer any leisure to daydream about home or the past. Or even about the "conscience" his father had said would severely trouble him when he raised his gun to point at another human being.

Instead, his eyes and his thoughts were glued to the rapidly approaching wall of South Mountain. It climbed farther and farther into the bluish-white, cloudless sky. Perhaps Lee had drafted the mound of inanimate earth, granite, and wood into service for the Confederacy, even though it was on loyal soil. Off to the south and to the north the long mountain—really more a range than a single peak—seemed to be stretching arms out in slow, sinister curves, as if to reach around the tiny contingent and trap it before McClellan could arrive. Another thousand yards and as Joseph looked up again, he felt something crawl along his neck. No, the mountain's "arms" were easily huge enough to encircle the whole Army of the Potomac!

He gave his head a sudden shake and blinked his eyes rapidly a few times. Knock it off, King, he told himself. Watch out for straight ahead; *that's* where the danger lies.

But it didn't seem to. The general of their division, Orlando Willcox, somewhere ahead, kept up the double-time until it seemed these several brigades would be swallowed by the mountain, or that it would fall over and crush the men. Each step was heavier than the last, each yard covered was a reckless rushing toward doom. Or at least it felt so. He guessed this feeling was shared by the three thousand or so soldiers. Joseph fully expected the big guns to open up again at any moment, at point-blank range. He was convinced that every tree and boulder and windfall on the looming slope concealed a veteran Reb, gleefully biding his time. Then he'd be in range and could let loose with a volley of balls that would cut the Yanks down in windrows like a scythe.

There had been a small reprieve a few hundred rods back, when their column had veered off this new road, to the right this time, taking them away from the fight still raging to their left. Now they were again approaching the gap more directly, but from its southern side. But Joseph saw no reason not to expect the left flank of the Reb brigade firing at Cox's boys on their own left to be facing the Seventeenth Michigan straight on. Waiting for the blue-clad suckers to walk right into it. Like babes in the woods.

Woods. There was one small consolation. The long marching column had been trudging along under a hot sun all afternoon in the comparative openness of the valley. Presently they saw the fields give way gradually to a covering of oaks, maples, and beech trees as they reached the base of the slopes.

As they approached the cover of the trees, still wearing their summer green, Joseph could feel the tension mounting in the ranks. Each man, he felt, knew instinctively that any attack to come must start before they reached the comparative concealment of the thick foliage. It only made sense, Joseph thought, as he tried in vain to stem the rapid beating of his heart. Johnny would be crazy to let us get into the forest, he thought. It can't be more than a hundred yards now to the nearest trees.

"Leastways we're safe from the artillery," Red said, his voice a breathy squeak.

Joseph glanced at him. "Why?"

"Can't depress 'em down this close."

His words weren't intended as a joke, but with the next beat of their hearts the irony almost killed them. With a mighty thwuuummpp! the heavens split apart in a crash of sound, followed immediately by a drawn-out, arching shriek straight out of hell and coming closer by the half second!

"Look out!" P.C. screamed.

The warning came too late. In another split second Joseph felt as well as heard a sickening thud behind him. Simultaneously a violent pressure slammed into his back, lifting him off his feet then tossing him down many yards away. He was nearly buried by flying earth.

For what seemed a short moment, he lay face down in the dirt, stunned. Slowly, disgustedly, he grew aware of the soil in his mouth. He raised himself to spit it out, shaking his head. Trembling almost uncontrollably, he got to his feet, testing his body for damage. Everything seemed to be all right.

He looked around, expecting a hideous scene of carnage. There was no one in sight, neither a living nor a dead body. He spun to look east. Not a soul behind him, either. Wait—what was that? He squinted in the direction they had just come. Unless the blast had scrambled his brains, those were Union guns on the ridge where the division had paused for a breather just a short while ago.

At least a half-dozen big, rifled Parrotts were lined up, wheel to wheel on either side of the road, allowing only enough space for the rest of the army to stream through toward the action. A smudge of black smoke drifted lazily upward from the muzzles which were pointing at the gap. For a moment Joseph stared, open-mouthed, then it hit him: he had almost been cashiered by his own side's artillery! Rage swept through him. He raised his fist and shook it at the distant hill, even though he knew the tiny figures moving around the guns could not see him. Feeling more frustrated and insignificant than he ever had in his life, he suddenly saw red. He reached for his gun strap on his shoulder. He'd show those treacherous bastards!

His weapon was gone. He swore, looking wildly about, then he saw it. It was lying twenty yards from him, toward the trees. With a sob of fury, he ran for it. "Wait'll I get my hands on that gun!" he cried, aloud.

As if laughing at his impotence, the cannon behind him spoke again. With reflex action Joseph fell flat on his stomach. He covered his head with his arms. His heart stood between his teeth. He dug his face into the rich soil of the valley, and waited. As he listened to the growing, eerie whine of the missiles, he felt a bitter amusement. "So this is how I'm to die," flashed through his head. "By the hand of my own country!" He groped frantically for an appropriate "last thought." None came.

There was no violent eruption of the earth, as last time. No blast of dirt-filled wind against his back. Instead, from what seemed a world away, came a crashing thud, followed by an inhuman scream which rent the hot afternoon like a knife, then whimpered off into nothingness. Silence reigned. Joseph jerked his head up. He stared at the woods in front of him.

There were men moving around among the trees. Men in blue. Joseph was on his feet, running. In a flash he understood. Clutching his musket, he put his head down and raced for cover. For the first time he realized that was what everyone else had done when that first shell had almost got him. Of course. His own army's artillery gunners had been seeking their range. All his fellows had lit out, assuming he was dead. Or, more likely, not having any room in their thoughts for anything but finding cover in the trees.

He was still a number of yards from the first trees when the mountainside above him erupted in flame and smoke and thunder. He nearly flew the last few feet to reach the cover of foliage and wood. Then he was among the trees, but he continued running as his eyes searched for the blue line.

He heard them before he saw them, shouting to each other over the rumble and rage of the enemy's guns overhead. Sergeant Sanders' voice sounded hysterical. Joseph could hear it coming from a leafy glade nearby. In the opposite direction, off to the right, the colonel's voice roared from a hundred yards away. Obviously the blue was a line no more.

Joseph started in the direction of the sergeant's voice. Something wild in it, though, made him reconsider, and he turned to head toward the commanding officer. Then, abruptly, he stopped in his tracks, and broke into laughter. The comedy of the chaos suddenly met head-on the rush of relief he felt from his recent brush with death. He laughed until his sides ached and he sagged to a sitting position against a huge oak tree. He was still sitting there, wiping the mirth from his eyes, when Sanders broke from the undergrowth directly in front of him at a dead run.

He slid to a stop when he saw Joseph and his mouth dropped open. "King!" he cried. "What in God's name are you doing here? I thought you were dead!" There was something furtive in the man's face.

Joseph sobered immediately. His eyes narrowed. "That's why you left me for the buzzards, right?"

"Uh—naw!" Sanders said, too sincerely, Joseph decided. "We had to take cover, get into the trees. . . ."

"And you'd have come back later to retrieve the body, right." Joseph made it a flat statement. He didn't know how he knew it, but something was fishy. Something in the sergeant's manner said clearer than a signpost that his path when he'd come upon Joseph would have carried him straight to the rear. Away from the fighting.

"Yes, sir, we sure would've!" the sergeant said. His tone of command had returned. Joseph decided the man might be a fair-to-middlin' poker player. "But now that you're fine and healthy let's be getting back to the regiment. On your feet, King."

Joseph obliged, but with deliberation. He felt gratified, without really understanding why, at the noncom's refusal to meet his eyes. "Yes, sir!" he said, emphasizing the "sir."

The sergeant said nothing. He just waved the muzzle of his gun in the direction he was to head—which came too close to Joseph's position to suit him.

"Only I'd appreciate it if you would keep that thing aimed somewhere else," Joseph said. His voice was cold. "Sure would hate to have anyone figure things backward."

Sanders acted as if he'd been slapped. A look of naked fear came to his eyes. In an instant it was gone, replaced by the anger of authority wronged. But he dropped the gun barrel to his side. The two men started off in the direction of the colonel's voice, which had been sounding off loudly throughout the entire scene between Joseph and the sergeant.

They hadn't gone more than five steps when the whisper of musket fire flared up, directly ahead of them up the slope. Sanders stopped dead in his tracks and stared at Joseph. His face had gone white, and the expression on it spoke louder than words of the panic in the soul of this strict disciplinarian. He licked his lips and held Joseph's gaze a moment longer, then his eyes dropped to the ground.

"Let's go," Joseph said quietly. "They'll be needing every man."

The sergeant's head snapped up. His gun came up, too, its muzzle bearing directly on Joseph's chest. Panic and anger mingled in his look. "You can go, King!" he snarled. "I ain't gettin' myself killed over some godforsaken mountainside!" He glared at Joseph a moment longer, fingering the trigger as if daring him to make a move. Then he began to back away, half crouching until he'd gone about twenty yards. He threw a glance over his shoulder, then looked back at Joseph.

Joseph felt the curious urge to shout "Boo!" at the man, and a half smile tugged at his lips. He held his tongue, though, and forced the smile away. This was ridiculous, but he didn't know whether he should feel fright or scorn. He'd had no drill to prepare him for such behavior, and from the very man who'd hammered correct military procedure into him. Sanders' eyes held his for a second longer, then the man turned and ran. Ran as if the bullet with his name on it were already headed his way.

The last look in the noncom's eyes would stay with Joseph for the rest of his life, he knew.

He followed the sergeant with his gaze until the man disappeared into the trees, then he shrugged and moved away in the direction of the fight. He made his way carefully, sure not to stumble and maybe shoot himself out of lack of caution. Fear lay like a coat of fresh paint over his heart. He was going into battle. For the first time in his life he would face men trying to kill him.

It was a powerfully sobering thought to deal with. For a moment he wanted to turn and run for his life, like the sergeant had just done. Joseph suddenly envied the man, even though everything he had been taught told him the soldier's behavior was wrong. No, not because they'd said he should stand and fight like a man. That, of course, was totally un-Mennonite. But they had always insisted that a man who has put his hand to the plow should not look back. And had he not put his hand to the task of helping to save his country from those evil ones who sought to dismember it, a nation conceived under the benevolent hand of Providence?

Sunshine flickered through the trees up ahead. Must be some kind of clearing, Joseph thought. It was. Soon he could see, through the thinning forest, a meadow stretching away for some hundred yards. As he approached, looking for his regiment, the noise of musket fire grew to the steady rattle of hail on a tin roof. At shorter and shorter intervals came the sound of things flying low and fast through the leaves. It didn't dawn on Joseph just what the sounds meant until he heard, not two feet away, the thwunnk of a solid object embedding itself in a nearby tree trunk. A bullet.

His body dropped to the grass before his mind had finished dealing with his perception. Smells of crushed fern and moss wafted before his face. Ever so slowly, he raised his head to peer over the tops of the dried grass stalks. Through the few trees remaining between him and the meadow he could make out a partly wrecked rail fence. It ran its zigzag path along the edge of the woods, some farmer's line between field and forest. A heavy growth of weeds among the rails made the cover look more substantial than it was.

From time to time Joseph detected a bare head raise itself from behind the rails, sight along the barrel of a musket, fire, then quickly drop out of sight. Splinters off the rails steadily flew away at all angles, marking the hits of Confederate lead. Obviously the balls came from an invisible army, across the clearing. Too often for Joseph's comfort those bullets missed fence and soldier completely to come ripping into the trees all around him. While he watched, one tore a furrow and died less than six inches from his right elbow.

He took a deep breath and rose to his hands and knees. "I belong up with those men," he muttered between clenched teeth, rapidly closing the distance to the fence. Bullets whined past his ears. He was scared to death.

From behind the last fat trunk before the open field, he peered up and down along the fence, now less than ten yards from his position. The soldiers of his regiment were dug in behind the rails, spaced about four or five feet apart. Each man hugged the earth, staring across the field of corn stubble. Joseph followed their looks. And he gazed upon his first enemy line. Or where he knew it to be. Running along the far side of the meadow was a stone fence some three feet high. Greenish-brown vines and moss stained the grayness of it, and along the uneven top of its length, like a row of Christmas candles, twinkled the muzzles of Rebel guns.

Joseph shivered. There must be ten thousand of them, he thought. He would have given twenty years of his life at that moment to be at least a hundred miles away. Suddenly he couldn't move. Goliath himself would be required to drag him from behind the two-foot oak trunk that was protecting his life. He squeezed his eyes shut, feeling dizzy. Against his left cheek the rough bark ground painfully. It wasn't enough of a protection.

"Hey, King, over here!" Red's voice cut through the din of musket fire. "Where ya bin? We thought you'd bought it!"

Joseph peeked around the wooden pillar toward the sound of his friend's voice. Red was crouched behind an old stump that had been incorporated into the fence line. He half rose as Joseph's face turned toward him, and waved Joseph over. He cupped a hand to his mouth. "We got a hot spot saved fer ya!" He had a wild and glowing look on his features.

And suddenly his face was gone, replaced by a shapeless, ragged stump of gore. The hand that seconds before had been raised to his mouth clawed at the gelatinous mass of red, then stiffened and dropped. A lucky cannon shell had found a mark. Red's body slumped over the old tree stump, twitched once, and was still.

Joseph vomited. The strength left his legs. He had been bunching his muscles to race for the fence, but now he sagged to his knees. His stomach was trying to get into his throat. He gagged and retched until there was nothing left to come up, and still his gut heaved.

"Oh, God," he moaned. "No, no. Not Red. He didn't deserve it! Why? Why!" His voice gave way and all the sound that came from him was pathetic sobbing. Still behind the tree, his forehead touched his knees, in an attitude of earnest prayer. All around him guns cracked and bullets whined and whispered of death. He wanted to die.

No, he did not, he suddenly realized. As abruptly as the missile that had taken Red's life, a blind hatred seized him. His head jerked up. The trembling in his legs ceased. He sprang to his feet and glanced at his weapon, reflexively, to check its readiness. It wasn't loaded.

"Can't take time for loading it now," he muttered. He jerked out his bayonet and clapped it into place, one part of his mind surprised at how the motion had become second nature. He was shaking again, now, but not from fear and shock. He wanted to kill. No one was going to kill a friend of his and live to crow about it.

The thought was actually only a half-formed one, because he was already in motion. He leaped from the shelter of the tree with a yell. He had no plan. Safety was forgotten. In three long strides he reached the rail fence, still bellowing. Wordless, it was a scream from a mysterious, unknown place inside him. One foot up, then the other, he scrambled to the top of the fence.

Then he was over it, down in the meadow, running. His mouth was wide, words coming out without thought, meaningless. Dimly he heard shouts behind him, the colonel's distinctive voice, the boy. The boy from E Company, screaming at him to get down or he'd be killed.

He shut out the cries. There were no more sounds in his world except the pounding of his breath past his ears as he ran. Tears streamed from his eyes but he didn't notice them. A fury possessed him, a rage he knew would be mollified only when he felt the thrusting of sharp cold bayonet metal deep into the warm, living flesh behind that stone wall. His mind was a vacuum.

Gradually, as if from a different dimension, he became aware that someone was coming up hard behind him. The sound of running feet and tearing breath cut through his red fog.

"Joseph! For God's sake!" It was the boy. He was rapidly

overtaking Joseph. "Get down, you fool!" The boy's voice was a scream as he came alongside. Joseph glanced over at him. The future teacher's eyes were wide with terror. He closed on Joseph and reached out for his arm.

Joseph's rage suddenly focused on the boy. He was trying to stop him. "No!" he shrieked, jerking away from him. The boy was faster. He gave an extra sprint and his fingers clawed at Joseph's tunic. He jerked and Joseph pulled away. The motion threw him off stride. "Blast you!" he sobbed as he felt himself falling. The toe of his boot kicked his other heel and down he went. His musket was torn from his grasp as he rolled over and over, coming at last to a stop with a jagged butt of cornstalk pushing into his back.

An instant later a body crashed to the earth beside him, a face inches from his, legs across his own. It was the boy. A bloody hole marked where his left eye had been. His right eye was open, but sightless.

* * *

From somewhere far away, yet terribly near, came the noise of screaming. High-pitched, maniacal screaming like no sound from a human throat. Only when his breath failed did Joseph realize the screaming came from him. He averted his gaze from the horrible sight of the boy's still face and wide, sightless eye. He felt as if he were emerging from a dream. For the first time he realized just where he was, what he had done in vaulting the fence. It was a miracle he had not been shot dead.

His frenzy gave way to a feeling of tragedy, deeper than tears or screams. His friend Red, and now this young student-turned-soldier. Joseph realized with a shock that he had never learned the boy's name. Within minutes, both Red and the boy were no more. Two human beings who had worked, eaten, loved, and lived for a span of years. Children of mothers who loved them, and did not yet know, but would know grief as they had never known it because to them these men were unique. Gone. Existing no more on this planet.

Bullets whisked over his head. Suddenly he was deathly afraid. He hugged the torn earth as if beseeching it to swallow him up. The insane bravado which had brought him this far across the open space was totally and irreplaceably gone. Tears began now. He glanced again at the innocent young face. He had killed this boy, because the boy had cared about him and tried to save him from his own folly. He, Joseph King, was a killer. It was what had been in his heart when he had stormed across the field. But it wasn't supposed to be this way. His own compatriot.

The hatred melted from his soul like snow in spring sunshine. A flood of compassion engulfed him and he raised his head to stare at the stone wall. Muzzle flashes still decorated the top row of rocks, but the boys there were just like ours. Like the one who lay still in death, half beside him, half across him. It was wrong. Oh, God, it was so wrong! It had to be stopped; that was all there was to it. No more living human beings, children of the Creator, must be killed—not one. He must stop it. Now.

Joseph gently pushed the boy's body off his legs. Gradually he raised himself to his hands and knees. The fear was gone now, but it was not like earlier, when he had charged like a maniac. It was a grim confidence now. There was no murder in his heart. He got to his feet and slowly raised his arms, high above his head.

"Stop!" he yelled, facing the stone wall. "This is insanity. Nothing will be solved by more killing. Stop!" He took a step toward the concealed Confederates.

"Get down, you fool!" A voice roared from behind him. It was his colonel. "You'll be killed!"

Joseph ignored him and took another step in the direction of the enemy, his arms pushing at the invisible men. "No more, you Southerners. We are all Americans!" he shouted.

A half-dozen heads poked up from the stones. Joseph was too far away to see their faces distinctly, but he took their interest as encouragement. He spun to face his own men. "See?" he yelled, "They'll quit if only we—"

The blow felt like a sledgehammer swung full against his right shoulder. It spun him around and knocked him to the earth before he knew what had happened. His eyes stared in shock at the pearly blue sky, seeing but not comprehending the crow flapping in leisurely fashion high above the noise and fury of the earth. Then the blue faded to black in his vision, and the crow disappeared. A roaring sounded in Joseph's brain and suddenly he was falling, spinning as he went. Abruptly all sound and motion ceased. He knew no more.

8

Slowly Joseph became aware of vibrations along his back, even before the cacophony surrounding him broke into his consciousness. He opened his eyes. All around him was a sea of motion: blue legs and arms swinging and sweeping against a whitish sky. Fearful of being trampled, he moved to get up. Instantly the blue and white exploded into a pain-filled smear of red. With a groan he fell back to the ground, squeezing his eyelids tight against the agony.

"Ye alive, soldier?"

He opened his eyes again. A kind but worried face filled the sky above him.

"Yes," Joseph grunted, between teeth clamped against his pain.

"Tsk, tsk, looks bad," the man said. He looked to be about Joseph's father's age, but no gold or silver bars showed on his uniform. He must be a professional private, Joseph thought, amused in spite of his agony. "That was a crazy fool thing ye done, charging the whole Reb line by yourself." His mouth broke into a toothless cackle. "Boy, but ye sure got 'em going, though. They're chargin' that ol' wall like a passel o' dumb banshees!"

"That's fine," Joseph said, forcing a grin which quickly turned into a grimace. "But my main concern right now is whether I still have a right arm."

The face stopped grinning and disappeared from the sky. "Hey!" the man's voice bawled, "stretcher—over here!" Then it was back, commiseration written all over the expressive features. "We'll git ye to a doc directly, son." Joseph felt a hand patting his where it lay in the dirt. "Good luck to ye, soldier. Time fer me to go get my licks in agin them naughty Rebs!" He was gone.

When he was lifted to the stretcher, Joseph passed out from the pain. The next thing he saw, when his consciousness returned, was the gently swaying leaves of a maple above him. A throbbing, pounding pain was where his right shoulder should have been. "No. Oh, God!" he moaned. "They've amputated it!"

He lifted his head to look and a fresh, new pain nearly tore him apart. It was the first he realized he had a head wound, too. But it was enough to see the swaths of white cloth wrapped tightly around his shoulder and arm as far down as his elbow. "Thank God!" he breathed. He took a deep breath and let it out slowly. As an afterthought, almost, he tried to wiggle his fingers. They responded, but painfully, and the attempt sent a searing new stab of pain shooting up his arm.

"Take it easy, soldier." A gray-haired man in a blood-splattered white smock leaned into his field of vision. His eyes were tired. "We managed to save your arm, but you'll not be using it in a long spell." The doctor smiled briefly. "Maybe never like normal again. Best just lie still now. I'll be back later," he said, and moved off like a man in a trance.

Joseph sighed and closed his eyes. Too much had happened too fast. Too much to absorb. From the edge of awareness came the din of battle, sounding far off, almost harmless from where he lay.

When he woke again his head was pounding with the thunder of a thousand bombardments. He tried to raise it and the shooting pain brought a groan to his lips. He reached up to touch his wound and his fingers came in contact with a strip of rough cloth, tightly wound around it.

He let his arm fall back to his side, closed his eyes, and lay as still as he could. Gradually he became aware of the silence all around him, like a shroud.

Or was it only that the roaring in his ears covered all outside sounds? Gingerly, ever so carefully, he swiveled his head to look toward the meadow. It took an effort to focus, then he saw the blue uniforms, far away near the stone wall. He blinked, trying to steady his vision. They were coming back, dragging their muskets or leaning on them like crutches. Some of the soldiers were assisting others to walk, some were being carried. Joseph closed his eyes wearily and let a long sigh escape.

It was over. The charge he had apparently triggered, inadvertently, had succeeded. He looked again. Mingled with the dusty blue uniforms were a handful of gray-clad men, their eyes on the ground, stumbling along with the boys of his own regiment and the Forty-fifth Pennsy. Joseph swallowed and felt tears burn his eyes. So few prisoners. So many must have died, likely fleeing from the wall's safety. And he, son of a preacher, had tried to warn them, to end the violence before all this could happen. A great weight seemed to settle down over him, like a haystack falling, toppling slowly but inexorably. It seemed to shorten his breath. He choked out a cough. His voice came as a hoarse whisper. "Oh, God, God! I'll never shoot a gun again!" He coughed again, then again. His head was splitting.

"You awake, Joseph?" There came a rustling of dry grass. A moon face rose beside him. It was P.C. A blood-stained, filthy rag circled his plump features, diagonally covering his left eye. "I been worried about you, boy."

Joseph gave him a tired smile. "I'm okay, Claude. Good to see you. It hurts powerfully, but the doc said my head was just grazed by a ball. Should be all right by morning," he said. He turned his bandaged head further, carefully, until he could look full on P.C.'s face. "What happened to you?"

"I wasn't so lucky," Claude answered. He sounded lost, far away. "From now on I'll be doing with 'monocular vision,' doc told me." He sighed as he reached up and touched the dressing on his invisible eye.

"You mean you got it shot out?" Joseph suddenly felt ashamed of his own hurts, minuscule in their significance next to Claude's misfortune.

"Hardly," the man said with a short, mirthless laugh. "I don't reckon I would have much of a brain left in that case! "No," he said, "meet the king of freakish mishaps. My left eye met up with a wooden missile launched from a fence rail by a meandering musket ball." He winced as if the memory had its own, corporeal form. "That's what I get for hunching down behind supposed shelter like a coward!"

Appalled, Joseph turned away and stared at the meadow. So much violence and destruction, he thought bitterly. The troops were nearly back to the trees now with their gaggle of prisoners. Could it be that just a couple of hours had gone by since the four of them had been marching together? And now there were only two left, and only he himself remaining to carry on the fight, in reasonably normal health? But he couldn't and *not* only because his gun shoulder was sore. He knew that as certain as he knew that it was day.

Daylight. For the first time he became aware that the sun had nearly gone. This day was mostly over, and what a day! What a change had come over him. It was too soon to tote up the good and the bad, to tell whether he was a better man now with his experience. Or damaged beyond repair.

From far away to the north came the strident, steady sounds of war. It was still going on, somewhere higher up where no doubt the sun's rays still lit the hellish tableaux of man butchering man.

"Don't reckon I'll be much for sighting a gun now." P.C.'s plaintive voice broke into Joseph's thoughts.

Joseph moved his head to look again at his comrade. This time the movement brought less pain. "Consider yourself lucky," he said. "You'll likely get sent to the rear, maybe even home."

P.C. swore with passion. "Over my dead body! Just when I've gotten me a real good reason to blow some Rebs away?" He started to shake his head, then thought better of it. "So long as I got me one good peeper, I'll gladly take on that whole blasted pile of Johnnies!"

"But what about what you just said?" Joseph asked. "How are you going to sight your weapon, with one eye?"

P.C. snorted. "Why, I'll—I'll—" His voice broke. A tear squeezed from his good eye and traveled halfway down his round cheek before he savagely wiped it away.

Joseph laid a hand on P.C.'s shoulder. "Take it easy, Claude," he murmured. "Take it easy."

P.C. jerked away from Joseph's touch. He took a half-dozen steps into the deepening shadows beneath the trees and stayed there.

Joseph sighed and lay back. He stared up into the patch of sky between the treetops. It was a deep dark blue. He could just make out the first star of night. What of tomorrow? he asked himself. What of that moment—tomorrow, the next day, or the day after that—when I once again face the gray coats? He remembered his hoarse vow of only a short while earlier, and it troubled him.

For now, though, all that mattered was to sleep so the last of the pain could leave his head and get reduced a notch or two in his shoulder and arm before he had to get up and move again. He tried not to think of what would come after that. Maybe the colonel would roust all of them out to march toward the still-booming cannon, or maybe the shooting would begin again from behind the wall, from a fresh army of Rebs.

Suddenly he didn't care, not a whit. Sleep pressed on his eyelids. He didn't fight it.

He woke to the sounds of men moving about, talking, and folding tents. A moment later the doctor appeared at his side. The sky over the treetops was gray, the sun still a long way from breaking over the world.

"How's the head, son?" The gray-haired man looked as tired as before.

"Morning already?" Joseph asked with a groan. He cautiously touched the bandage, but forgot to use his good arm. Pain shot simultaneously through arm, shoulder, and temples. "Ow!" he squeaked.

"Here, let me change those dressings," the doctor smiled. He set about the task with a deft speed that was surprisingly gentle. Five minutes later Joseph felt a hundred percent better.

"Try sitting up." It was an order.

Joseph obeyed. His head swam and spots danced before his eyes, but the pain was minimal. He managed a wry smile at the doctor. "It's okay, doc. I'll manage."

"Good," the man said. He clapped Joseph lightly across the shoulders. "Better get your gear together. Colonel's ordered us to start immediately, if not sooner." He turned and moved to another wounded soldier.

Joseph found his haversack lying at the foot of his blanket roll. Suddenly ravenous, he fished inside for a couple "rounds" of hardtack. Munching on one, he swung the pack carefully over his left shoulder. Before rising slowly to his feet he reached for his gun and slid it over the strap of his haversack. He wondered who had retrieved his gear for him. P.C., no doubt, he thought.

He got to his feet again, surprised at how rested he felt, now that he was fully awake. A good thing too, he thought. There's no telling when I'll sleep again. Somewhere inside of him he felt a premonition that yesterday's fighting was just a preliminary. He shuddered and did not try to figure out why he felt that foreboding.

He managed somehow to secure his backpack, by running a strap across his back, through his belt near his right hip, then up across his chest to his left shoulder again. It wasn't comfortable, having the weight of his pack riding unevenly, pushing into his left shoulder blade and bobbing against his elbow. But any tension of a leather strap across his right shoulder would have been far worse than mere discomfort. Anyway, he didn't figure it would be long before they dug in to fight again. Till then, he'd carry his gun in his left hand and worry about bracing the stock in his wounded armpit when the time came. Then, like a vulture to carrion, came again his vow of yesterday, and he asked himself, Would he use a gun again? Something felt like undigested matter, deep inside him. He was confused, then angry. His appetite fled and he tossed away his food.

He had just gotten himself all set to march when Colonel Mulligan came galloping through the trees. His face was open in a wide smile. "General McClellan says to congratulate all of you on a great and glorious victory!" he said as he pulled his horse up near Joseph. There were a dozen odd men standing about, ready to move out.

A voice called out, "That mean we're through fightin', sir?" There was a distinct note of disappointment in the tone.

"Hah!" snorted the officer. "Not on your life! We are ordered to form up with the rest of the army on the other side of the mountain, along some creek by the name of Antietam." He whipped off his hat and wiped a big hand across his forehead. It was obvious to Joseph the man had ridden a long way, and without dawdling. "Yes, boys, we got Lee on the run. I just been up the road. It's full of troops, guns, and supply wagons. The works!" He broke off to flash a wide grin, his splendid white teeth gleaming in the dimness of early morning in the woods. "Yessirree, men, looks like we're gonna get some *more* revenge for Pope!"

His smile faded to a businesslike expression. "So hop to it. Let's get moving!" He slapped his hat against his big black's rump and was gone.

"What's he so all-fired cheerful about?" It was P.C. He had suddenly appeared at Joseph's side.

"You heard him yesterday, on the road," Joseph replied. "He's still smarting from getting beat by Lee and Jackson at Second Bull Run."

"And that ain't all. He figures maybe he'll be making brigadier before the day's through." Their captain, Lawrence Zook, had come up while Mulligan was talking. "Now that Reno's bought it, maybe he will, too," he continued. "Likely Willcox'll get promoted, so Colonel Bob will get *his* job."

"General Reno is dead?" Joseph stared at the captain, a small, self-important West Pointer whom they rarely saw. He had been brought over from another regiment in a different brigade, after Second Bull Run, two weeks ago. His fine-featured face was pale and heavily freckled, his hair as red as blood. His ice-blue eyes could stare down a general, it was said.

"Yep," the captain said. "He was tryin' to put some spine in the Fifty-first Pennsylvania last night and up hops a swarm of Rebs and blasted him right off his horse." Zook grinned. "They said he was dead before he hit the ground!"

Joseph and P.C. stared at the captain. Joseph opened his mouth to ask what that would mean for the future of their corps, but Zook cut him off.

"You seen Sergeant Sanders this morning?" He quartered the slowly brightening woods with accusing eyes. "I been looking high and low for him since first light."

Joseph swallowed. "Yes, sir, I—I saw him—" Suddenly, he wished he'd kept quiet. Something about Zook frightened him.

"Well?" the captain barked. "Speak up, boy!" He was all of two years younger than Joseph himself. When Joseph continued his hesitation, the blue eyes became gimlets.

"I think he deserted, sir," Joseph said quietly.

"He *what?*" The blue gimlets bulged. The normally pasty-white face went livid. "Deserted? Explain yourself, soldier!"

Joseph quickly recounted the scene in the woods on the previous afternoon. Zook seemed on the verge of a seizure and Joseph grew increasingly uneasy. It didn't pay to occupy the attention of a martinet like this miniature officer, especially when one was the bearer of bad tidings. But he also felt a growing anger as he spoke, feeling the rank injustice of being grilled for another's offense. That was definitely the feeling the captain's eyes gave him—being slowly and deliberately rotated on a spit over a bed of glowing hot coals. P.C. was watching Joseph's face with a look on his own of bewilderment.

The captain's anger, however, was clearly not for Joseph. When the latter finished, Zook in his rage viciously kicked his boot against a stump: "Desertion!" he shrieked. He was almost beside himself. "If I ever get my hands on that yellow-backed coward, I'll—" But words suddenly failed him and he appeared to be on the point of sputtering. The dozen or so men standing around didn't know where to look.

Zook took a deep breath and glared at Joseph and P.C. and the others, suddenly self-conscious, it seemed. He began to mumble, then quickly checked himself. He leveled a finger at Joseph's nose. "If you ever see him again, *you* let me know! That is an order!"

He spun and began to stomp away, then he stopped. His

back became ramrod straight, and he wheeled and faced them again. "You heard the colonel. Let's be on our way. We got a good way to go to our rendezvous." His voice grew mean. "All uphill!"

Ten minutes later the troops were marching, or as close to it as was possible as the grade steepened. Somehow the lieutenants and sergeants got their units organized and moving, heading north and west for the road climbing the eastern slope of the pass. Joseph was surprised to see that their regiment appeared almost intact. In the tumult of yesterday, he had assumed that at least eight out of every ten men must have fallen. Bitterly he realized that it must have been only in his immediate vicinity that men had died so profusely—and because of him!

"Have I become a Jonah?" he asked himself. In his stinging self-castigation he unknowingly spoke aloud.

P.C. was walking beside him and glanced his way quizzically. Joseph grinned at him, but his face felt like that of a corpse.

He forced his mind shut on the grim, grisly memory of Red and the boy. Instead, he did an inventory of his aches and pains. His right arm, from the shoulder to the wrist, throbbed with each beat of his heart. It was a manageable pain, though, but it would be many days, likely weeks, before he could accurately aim a gun and pull a trigger. The soreness in his head was hardly noticeable anymore.

"Hunh!" he grunted. "A lot of good I'll be as a fighting machine, Claude," he said. P.C. glanced at him again. Joseph barked a laugh and half raised his bandaged upper arm.

P.C.'s face broke into a sweet smile of insight. "Hey!" he said, "how's about me holding the gun and you sightin' it? Between the two of us maybe we can get in a few licks for the Union!"

Joseph laughed. "Maybe you've got something here, friend."

"Silence back there!" their lieutenant bawled. "Save your breath for the climb."

* * *

They continued marching for hours without a pause. The sun beat down without regard for life or season. Joseph found it hard to believe it was the 15th of September, not the middle of July, and felt pity for Poor Claude who had lost his forage cap in yesterday's battle. The middle-aged, overweight man was sweating profusely. Joseph feared he might come down with sunstroke any minute, what with his unprotected bald pate getting no shade once their division reached the road. As if his thinking had prompted some evil spirit to make P.C.'s life even harder, Joseph saw Claude stagger, then stumble and fall to the dusty road.

Joseph started to move to P.C.'s aid, but just then Captain Zook rode up from the rear. "Let him be, soldier!" he snapped. "He can catch up with us when we camp." He glared down at the fat private. "Get into some shade and rest up, *soldier.* If I don't see you in camp by midnight you'll be shot. Is that clear?"

P.C., whose face had begun to smooth into incredulous delight at Zook's words to let him be, seemed to go into shock when the captain had finished. He swallowed hard, then his mouth fell open. He stared up at the mounted officer.

"I asked, is that clear, private!" Zook's blue eyes blazed.

"Y—yes, sir," P.C. managed to answer. His eyes moved to Joseph's, desperate and pleading. Then he staggered off the road to a shady spot and lowered himself at the base of a spreading chestnut. The last Joseph ever saw of him, P.C. was tipping up his canteen and letting the water run down over his head and face. Then Captain Zook fastened his cruel eyes on Joseph and ordered him back into line. "Men like that have no place in the army," the captain muttered, half to himself. "If I had my way, I'd march all the old fat ones till they either shaped up or fell dead!" Grim humor flickered in those eyes as they bored into Joseph's, as if he recognized, and admitted, the contradiction between his words and his treatment of P.C.

He was about to spur his mount down the line when he seemed to have another notion. His amusement reached his thin lips. "Seen any more runaway sergeants, private?"

"No, sir!" Joseph answered. Why couldn't this man move on? he thought. A shiver seemed to be starting at the base of his spine.

"Well, if you do, just remember where to report them!" Then Zook threw back his head and roared with laughter.

The shiver made it all the way to Joseph's neck.

9

Five minutes later all hell broke loose. A pocket of Confederate soldiers had apparently been left behind last night by their retreating army. They waited until Joseph's division was opposite their position in a clump of roadside bushes, then blasted them with muskets, pistols, and even a howitzer. It didn't surprise Joseph that the heaviest blow fell precisely on the Seventeenth Michigan Volunteer Regiment. He'd come to the conclusion, after the horrible deaths of Red and the boy, that he *was* a jinx, a Jonah. He had no business here in this army and that's why everyone near him was doomed.

These thoughts were only half formed up to the moment the ambush was unleashed. They finished forming in his mind as he raced for cover along with several dozen other men in the direct line of fire. They instinctively dove for the ditch, bushes, rocks, and tree trunks on the other side of the road. As soon as they reached their respective bits of shelter, they turned and gave as good as they got. At least the ones who'd survived the initial barrage.

Joseph was one of these survivors—miraculously, he was ready to admit—and he even managed to keep hold of his gun. But his clumsy landing in the ditch was anything but comfortable. When he turned to view the roadway, all he saw were the stars and shooting lights from the pain in his jarred head and shoulder. When his vision cleared and he took in the human wreckage that moments before had been living, marching men, he felt a wave of nausea.

But this time it was different. This time he didn't feel the frenzy of rage sweep through him, as he had when Red was killed. Only disgust. He physically could not handle his weapon, but even had he been hale and hearty, he knew he could never again aim it at a fellow human being and pull the trigger. It was criminally and barbarically wrong, no matter what the politicians and leaders might say. He felt soul-sick of the whole murderous business of war. It had to be about the most evil sin in creation.

Behind his shelter of the roadside, crouched low in the dry ditch, Joseph bowed his head. He leaned his forehead against the cool earth and gasped for air. His disgust deepened, and then suddenly it turned to anger. Anything but a killing anger, however. It was an anger that brought him to a decision which would brook no argument. All he had to do, he knew, was take a step, a simple first step, but one to remove the conflict which he'd felt in his breast from time to time and was now making him so sick and angry. There would be peace, then, he knew. He could desert, just up and leave.

Suddenly he was terrified. What if he stood up and started to act out his father's teachings now, in the thick of battle? He might die, right here and now! Or, if he lived, what would happen if they caught him? Captain Zook's icy eyes appeared in his memory, and he shivered. But he couldn't stay any longer, knowing like a sudden revelation that war was hell. Literally. He had to go. No, he daren't. He must decide—

He started as the man who'd been firing next to him suddenly relaxed against him, pushing his injured shoulder painfully. Joseph looked at the soldier, prepared to yell at him. His words died on his lips. The man's lower jaw was gone and his tongue dangled grotesquely down Joseph's tunic front. The eyes were blank and staring.

Joseph screamed. Something inside him seemed to burst.

He could not take any more of this! That was the un-adorned truth of it. He simply had had enough of the struggle and he was leaving. Not only the fight raging all around him: the cannon fire, the minié balls, the screams, the cursing. Boys falling dead, some with barely a whimper, just sagging lifeless to the Maryland soil. Some with an arm or a leg blown away, expressions of amazement and puzzlement on their faces as death stole away their lives without so much as a by-your-leave.

No, the battle raging was bad, but the conflict that precipitated Joseph King's actual leave-taking was the turmoil of disgust, anger, and fright tearing him in his gut. Suddenly, as if these things were a trigger in his memory, he recalled with shocking clarity all the words he had ever heard his father preach and speak and pray, even sing, on the subject of loving one's neighbor and turning the other cheek. They all came together and he knew they were truth. In that moment the words became his own beliefs. He knew as sure as the sun was hot that it would be a sin for him to partake an instant longer in the savage feast of slaughter. No more could he remain an agent of death to others, or risk that in life's last instant he would smell the fire of hell.

So he ran.

He had no plan. He only turned, scrambled out of the ditch, and faded into the trees away from the tumult, expecting at any moment to feel a bullet strike home as he went. There was no furtiveness in his movement, no attempt to conceal his flight, no thought of what he would say if he got caught. He did not think that far ahead. He knew only that the solemn stillness of the trees and the green fields away beyond the blue lines of troops represented a peace his soul hadn't felt since his feet had carried him toward the stone wall which was spouting star-flashes of musket fire.

Had it been so recent—just yesterday?

It felt like a lifetime since his comrades had died so suddenly and violently: one moment beside him with the warmth of human life making them his brothers, the next second as innocent of breath as the stone wall that sent them to their deaths. He, Joseph, was not the twenty-four-year-old boy he had been then, less than a full rotation of the earth ago. Now he was old, older than pain and memory. Life seemed like a river rushing past, having cast him high up its bank where he would shrivel and die slowly and miserably, envying the vital flow, but incapable ever of joining it again.

His feet crunched in the brittle September grass, jolting his aching arm. He looked down at his gun, surprised that he was carrying it in his right hand anyway, then stared at it thoughtfully, pausing in his rapid walk. Abruptly, symbolically, he flung it away, far out into the underbrush. Then, as if a sudden resolve had come to him, he undid the haversack strap from his shoulder and belt, shrugged it off, and let the bulky burden fall to the ground.

Feeling light and free, he went on his way in the same direction as before, running now. Presently he stopped. He had started out with no plan, but it occurred to him that if his decision to leave had validity, then it would be foolish to be apprehended only to be returned to duty. He had better have a goal to run for and take pains to see that no one saw him.

Glancing around like a man waking from a dream, he hurriedly stepped into the shadow of a grove of oaks. Crouching down to his haunches to reduce his presence even more, he called up a mental picture of the country he was in. He decided he would head north for home—of course—keeping in the woods along the slopes of South Mountain, praying he'd see or hear other troops before they spotted him. The flatter lands were nearly bare of trees up here in the panhandle of Maryland, so once he left the forested slopes, he would keep close to fencerows and wooded stream valleys, if there were any. He'd certainly stay clear of farmhouses and towns, at least until he was well into Pennsylvania and away from probable Union cavalry patrols and provost guards. If he found railroad tracks heading in a generally northern direction, he'd follow that, ready in a second to leap into the brush for cover if trains, troops, or other signs of humanity came along.

Joseph had never found geography his strong suit in school, but he knew he had a good chunk of Pennsylvania and all of Ohio to cross before he got anywhere near home. Not to mention the wide Ohio River. With good weather, though, sufficient food, and a bit of luck, he should make it to St. Joseph County within two or three weeks.

Food. He stopped in his tracks. He had just discarded his pack and his gun. Without them, how would he eat? The haversack still held nearly all of the three days' rations they'd been issued yesterday morning. He had always been a good shot and an avid hunter, but without his gun he'd have to chase rabbits and squirrels on foot!

His heart dropped to his stomach. "I'd better return and get my things," he said, aloud. Then for the first time real fear of capture seized him. Facing it down, he began to retrace his steps. He was disgusted with himself as he crept back through the crushed grass, easily spotting his footprints. How could I have been so foolish, he wondered? Suddenly each tree, every clump of grass, was the hiding place for a provost guard, a military policeman. Back the way he'd come, the rattle of musketry faded out and all that broke the threatening silence was the cry of a distant crow.

And the loud snap of a dead stick.

Joseph fell to his belly in the grass. His heart thudded painfully in his wounds. Minutes passed. There was no other sound.

He struggled to his feet and put one foot in front of the other. The dry grass rasped loudly. Then he saw it—his pack, half hidden behind a rotting log. Another three steps and his fingers closed around the strap. He dropped to the earth again, behind the log. He was shaking all over.

After what felt like hours, he slowly levered himself to a standing position. His pulse raced and his shoulder burned as if freshly branded.

Nothing happened. Only the birds and the breeze broke the silence. He took a step in the direction he'd thrown his musket, then another. A half dozen more, and he had it in his hand, clutched tight in the same grip with his pack. He took a deep breath and let it out slowly, then he took off, forcing himself to march as if on an assigned errand in the direction of his original flight.

But he'd taken only three strides when he heard the loud flapping of a horse's nostrils, off to his left in a small copse of birch.

Joseph slid to a stop and spun around. He found himself staring up the barrel of a Colt revolver. He felt his bowels turn over, as he let his eyes travel up the arm holding the gun—and looked into the icy gaze of Captain Lawrence Zook. He was mounted on a chestnut gelding.

"Going somewhere, soldier?" The smile was angelic, the voice gentle. "The Rebs are off thataway." Zook jabbed his handgun in the opposite direction from which Joseph had just been traveling. The officer's eyes flashed in sadistic delight.

Joseph swallowed. The atmosphere of menace was palpable. He vividly recalled his earlier conversation with this martinet. Zook had never found Sergeant Sanders, but somehow he had found him, Joseph. Suddenly desperate, he hitched his weapon up a few degrees, unthinkingly.

Zook's smile vanished. His thumb clicked back the Colt's hammer. "Hold'er right there, private!" His teeth clipped off the words. "Throw down the musket!"

Joseph obeyed. His knees felt as if they'd give out in another minute.

"Back off!" The captain swung down from his horse, at the same time managing to keep his revolver steadily on Joseph. "Hold out your arms."

He did as he was told. The officer, without taking his eyes off Joseph, flipped up his saddlebag flap, reached in with the hand that wasn't holding the gun, and pulled out a pair of manacles, connected by a thick steel chain. He tossed them at Joseph. "Put these on, soldier," he snapped.

Joseph's ears burned with humiliation. For an instant, as he reflexively caught the flying metal with his good hand, he considered throwing them back at the officer, hard, straight for his gun hand. But Zook seemed to anticipate the notion. He quickly raised his gun barrel until it pointed directly at Joseph's forehead. A glinty smile crossed his face. Joseph shivered, and something inside him wilted. He remembered why he had fled. To resist now with violence—even if it was unsuccessful, as it likely would be—would invalidate the choice, the moral decision, he had made by leaving the war. He submitted meekly as the captain warily stepped up and snapped the cuffs locked around Joseph's wrists.

Now his hands were prisoners of each other, tethered together with a foot of oiled chain. He stood with his head bowed, suddenly alone in a new world of submission and resignation, only dimly aware of the dull throb in his injured shoulder and arm. To the dismounted officer, he was the perfect picture of humiliation and failure.

* * *

"Taking a page of Sanders' book, right, private?" Zook gave an ugly laugh. "Only you're still around to be made an example of!" He gave another, unpleasant chuckle. Then his face lost its mirth. "Now git going. I'm taking you in and I'll see to it you never desert again." He moved his horse alongside and gave Joseph a push with his boot, square in the middle of his back.

Joseph half stumbled forward. An icy trickle of fear ran along his spine. Then, suddenly, he felt a sense of peace expanding within his chest. It was as if someone had reached into his soul and touched the pain and fright, removing it and leaving in its place a calm assurance that all would be well. The sensation was so unexpected and so delightful that a smile crept over his lips. He was hardly aware when the mounted officer cuffed him across the side of his head.

"Wipe that smile off your face, deserter!" Zook growled. "You'll soon learn that no one lights out from any part of an army that Lawrence Zook has anything to do with, and lives to laugh about it!" For good measure, he gave Joseph another shove with his foot.

Joseph said nothing, and he let the smile fade. Something about the new feeling of peace made him feel sadness for the officer. He was amazed.

The mounted man dropped back a few paces, keeping his revolver trained on Joseph. From time to time, as they moved through the swishing grass, he made a remark about the intellectual deficiencies of men who preferred to hightail it for the rear, and got caught. Joseph ignored him, except to pick up his pace slightly when he felt Zook's horse begin to breathe in his ear.

He continued to marvel at his lack of panic, and the peace that seemed to explain the lack. Yet there was not really anything to fear greatly, except that in his case his captor for some reason was clearly a fanatic about desertion. Desertion was high in the Army of the Potomac, especially this spring and summer of '62, when every major clash with Lee's army seemed to bring on a humiliating defeat for the Federals.

Joseph supposed that running away was a fact of life in any army and likely always had been since men first organized to fight battles away from their homes. Such a conclusion would never have entered his head before his own service began, but he now knew, from simple listening in camp, that much of the "taking of French leave" arose from relatively harmless causes like needing to go home to plant the crops, seeing if the wife and young ones are making out fine, or from simply having sore feet. Or from fear.

There was a lot of that, he'd learned. "Cowardice," the boys he fought with always called it—until it came to them. Running for the rear was a lot more common than the average hometown sweetheart or Sunday-morning reverend would reckon. But what made the difference between these boys and himself, was that he'd had no intention of returning.

Give someone enough time and he'd likely come back to fight another day. That's why so-called desertion was taken fairly lightly, Joseph knew, unless you had some burr-under-the-saddle like Captain Zook after you. Even so, he thought, probably all I'll get is a haversack full of rocks to wear around camp for a day, or on the next march. Or maybe they'll make me walk the platform or tie me to the spare wheel for a while. At least they have never *shot* a deserter. Not yet anyway.

That last notion made him nearly lose a step. He knew about the deserter they had lined up to be shot by a firing squad not long ago; then Lincoln had pardoned him at the last minute. The president had taken a lot of abuse for that, Joseph remembered. It had been the talk of the army for several days. Desertions had increased, not so surprisingly.

They were approaching the road where the ambush had occurred. The fighting was over and through the thinning trees Joseph could see men moving about in a casual way, preparing camp, it appeared. He guessed the Rebs' attack had been beaten back, once their advantage of position and surprise was lost, and that the men were being allowed to rest up, as a reward.

For a moment his arrival felt almost like a homecoming. That surprised him. Was it, he asked himself, because there was greater safety in numbers when you were in the hands of a fanatic like Zook? Or was this feeling simply another unexpected effect of the curious peace that had come to him? He didn't know yet, but he was beginning to believe the tranquillity came from the knowledge that he'd made a correct decision and nothing Zook or Lincoln was able to do could touch him. Or spoil the moral choice he had made in leaving the hell of war.

* * *

A half-dozen soldiers in the immediate vicinity turned mildly curious stares on Joseph as their little parade came into the camp which the men were setting up. A few tents had already been pitched, but it was obvious that hunger came first for the regiment because scores of cooking fires were already burning brightly. An officer returning a "runner" was fairly common. They turned their eyes back to their tasks.

"Sergeant Hawkins!" Zook bellowed. "Get your butt over here, on the double!" In a voice only slightly quieter, he ordered Joseph to step up to a large oak, several paces to his left.

Joseph did as ordered, curious. Several of his fellow soldiers looked up again, interest showing in their faces. Others began to gather around. Was something about to break the routine of army life? Something besides just indigestion and death?

A big, middle-aged man appeared from behind a clump of willows off to Joseph's right. It was Sergeant Wilfred Hawkins of A Company. "Yes, sir!" he said. "You called, Cap'n?" He snapped a salute to his battered forage cap. "What'll it be, sir?"

Joseph studied the gray-haired, pot-bellied man with interest. Sergeant Sanders had spoken of this kind and gentle man who'd gone to West Point and graduated as an officer in the engineers, but then signed on as an enlisted man when the war broke out. It was an amazing thing, everyone agreed, especially when your old friend was now your corps commander.

Joseph had seen Hawkins from time to time, when their own company had camped near A Company. He knew that the sergeant's manner was bluff and hearty, matching the eternal twinkle in his gray eyes. He was nearly fifty and was like a father to his men. They all loved him.

Zook detested him. On the first day of his active duty, six months ago, Captain Lawrence Zook had had to ask for help from this experienced, paternal noncom, and the young, proud officer would never forgive Hawkins for that.

Today Hawkins's manner was not his normal hale-fellow-well-met, for his good friend Jesse Reno was dead, since yesterday afternoon. When he answered Captain Zook's peremptory summons, his gray eyes looked lifeless and the flesh of his face and barrel chest seemed to hang on his jowls and belly like a tired burden.

"Sergeant Hawkins, I want you to tie this deserter to that tree there." He gestured toward the huge trunk near Joseph." "And flog him." A glint came into Zook's blue eyes. "Twenty lashes with the cat-o'-nines!" He tossed a key to the sergeant.

The lifeless quality in Hawkins's eyes fled. Shock and disgust replaced it. "Twenty lashes, sir? Isn't that rather severe? He's obviously been in some action and has wounds to prove—"

"Silence!" Zook hissed. "I gave you an order, sergeant, and I'm used to having my orders obeyed. Immediately!"

Joseph watched the sergeant's face, feeling oddly detached, more interested in the play of emotions in his eyes than the pain soon to be visited on his own flesh. He knew from what he'd heard about Hawkins that the man detested unnecessary brutality. That was one of the qualities that made his men willing to walk the second mile for him. But he also had the reputation for following orders promptly and thoroughly, as one would expect from a professional soldier.

"Yes, sir. Right away, sir," Hawkins said, his voice like a sigh. He looked intently and curiously at Joseph in a way that reminded Joseph of his father. He felt a pang.

Hawkins stepped up and removed the manacles. "Take off your tunic and shirt, son," he said in a quiet voice.

Joseph did as he was told, first dropping his haversack. His injured shoulder gave him a twinge when he removed his garments. For the first time, the fear of pain, pain enough to make his battle wounds feel like no more than hangnails, coursed through him.

"Wrap your arms around the tree trunk." Hawkins's voice was almost a caress. His eyes still held Joseph's. "Cross your wrists, soldier." Then he disappeared behind the tree. Captain Zook moved his horse to a position from which he could watch Joseph's face. He looked like a small boy at an amusement park.

A second later Joseph almost cried out as he felt the sergeant jerk his arms and tie his wrists tightly together, out of sight around the wood. Hawkins came into his line of vision again, but Joseph could see him only at the corner of his eye. His upper body was tight against the tree.

"Open your mouth," Hawkins ordered.

Joseph obeyed, curious.

The sergeant placed a smooth-barked stick of wood between Joseph's jaws. "Bite down," Then he glanced into the boy's eyes and away quickly again. "If you're a praying man, now's the time, soldier." His voice fell to a whisper. "Forgive me, son." Then he disappeared from Joseph's field of vision.

He caught his breath and tried to brace himself, but nothing happened. An eternity passed. Joseph's senses seemed to sharpen themselves to an unbelievable pitch of expectancy. His ears strained for the slightest sound of activity behind his back, for the noises that would signify the trickle and clatter of the jagged pieces of bone tied into the twisted rawhide as they swung together at the ends of their lengths. He had witnessed a flogging once. It had also been under the baleful eye of Captain Zook, he realized with sudden horror. That time the recipient had died!

His legs gave way in panic. The tree bark tore at his chest as he slid down until his tied arms caught him. Pain raced through his wounded shoulder and he quickly pushed himself up on quivering legs until they took his weight again. He would never forget how Zook had urged on the flogger that other time—it hadn't been Sergeant Hawkins, he was sure—with glazed eyes. And, yes—how weird—he'd seen foam on Zook's lips, in the corners of his mouth. Before he had quickly wiped it.

There had been a reprimand, he remembered. After all, floggings were supposedly illegal—

"Ahhh—" Joseph shrieked. The stick fell from his mouth. "Oh, my God—no, no! Ahhh—" He'd been sliced in two, across his back. Fire, liquid fire, raged like a frothing river from his right shoulder clear down to his left hip.

"Uhhh!" There it was, again. Oh no, I can't take this. "Oh God!" Then again, and again. And again. Joseph's head swam. Dizziness nibbled at his balance. He fell against the tree trunk again, but now the rough bark on his chest and the wrenching pull of his injured shoulder were no more than mosquito bites. His back—oh, God—the back! Had there ever been such agony, since the beginning of time?

Again the straps, the rawhide-and-bone, switched across his flesh. He knew it was lacerating the skin, deep. He thought he could sense the rush of cold air on his ribs. Oh, God—how many was it? Were they becoming lighter? Was that a sob? A maniacal laugh? That one—ohhh!—was number eight, wasn't it, please, God? Wasn't it—please? Only twelve more? Yes, that was a sob! Sergeant Hawkins?

"Stop it—I can't take it!" Joseph felt rather than heard his scream bounce back off the wood only inches from his face. His head swam. There was a roaring in his ears that was trying to penetrate into the very center of his brain, his being. Then, suddenly and miraculously, the noise died. All sounds faded to nothing. He smelled the sweet, cool scent of crushed grass, of bleeding bark. To his thrumming eyeballs there came a great, white light. Was that a shadow standing on it?

All became darkness and silence. Joseph's last sensation was of falling. Then nothing.

10

Joseph's awareness came back like a knife in the back, suddenly and piercingly. He was no longer lashed to the oak. Now he could feel the cool grass beneath his ribs. There was no weight on his sore arm, which was a mercy, but the torn, angry rawness that had taken the place of his back was trumpeting enough misery to make up for ten sore limbs. And it was being bathed, which somehow made it hurt worse!

"It doesn't look good, sir," Sergeant Hawkins's voice said, from above him.

"Well it shouldn't, Sergeant, else what's a punishment for?" It was Captain Zook's satisfied voice.

Joseph lifted his cheek from the grass and turned his head to look up at the mounted officer. All he could see was a silhouette. The sun was setting over the man's shoulder. He realized, with detached surprise, that at least two hours must have elapsed since he'd turned and run. Several other shadows stood about, in various attitudes of watching and waiting. He suddenly felt like a sideshow freak.

Zook continued addressing the sergeant in his smug tone: "Soon as you get that deserter wrapped up and on his feet, I want you to march him down to Frederick and put him on the next train to Washington city." His voice became shrill. "I am sick to death of desertion and it's time we made an example of someone! Send a wire from the station to Colonel Lafayette Baker and tell him—"

"Sir!" Hawkins interrupted. "*March* him, did you say?"

His anger was manifest. "Why, this poor man can barely stand, let alone—"

"That will be enough, sergeant!" Zook's voice dropped, menacingly. "As I said, it's about time these *traitors* are taught a lesson! And I know my good friend Lafe will be delighted I've found one. That'll be all." Abruptly, Captain Lawrence Zook wheeled his mount and trotted off into the twilight.

Joseph had laid his head back on the grass and closed his eyes. The pain was nearly too much for toleration. Whoever was bathing his torn flesh was gentle, he'd give them that much, but a feather touching his back would have felt like fire. He thought, with a sinking heart, of the hours the trek out from Frederick had consumed. Just the notion of returning there on foot, now with darkness coming on and his body racked by mortal pain, made him almost sorry a bullet hadn't found his heart today.

He felt the gentle hands leave his back. "This will hurt a mite, soldier," Hawkins said. Joseph realized for the first time it had been the sergeant himself who had bathed him. He marveled at the irony of it.

A tearing noise came to his ears and a moment later his shoulders were lifted, gently, and a strip of cloth passed beneath him, around his chest.

"Here, you two, give a hand!" Hawkins barked. Presently strong hands lifted Joseph's upper body higher while the sergeant quickly and efficiently wound the strips of bandage repeatedly around him. Then they assisted him to a sitting position. Sergeant Hawkins tossed Joseph's shirt to him. "Put it on," he ordered. "We'd better be going. Frederick's some ten to twelve miles off."

Joseph stared at the middle-aged noncom as he gingerly donned the garment. With the bandages securely in place, the cloth did not rub too painfully against his skin. The men gave him a quizzical glance, then he turned to the two soldiers who had helped with the doctoring. "Keep an eye on him," Hawkins ordered. "I'll be right back." He walked away briskly.

Joseph finished dressing and got to his feet. Sudden weakness caused his head to spin. He started to fall. One of his guardians quickly grabbed his arm and held him up.

On his feet, unsteady at first, he looked around. Besides the two privates who had helped Hawkins there were at least a half-dozen soldiers standing and staring at him. They were silent, their expressions touched with pity. He looked from face to face, not recognizing a single one. He wondered what had become of P.C.

He opened his mouth to inquire what company they belonged to, but one of the two helpers spoke first.

"Yer lucky 'twas Sergeant Hawkins what done whupped ya," he said. "If'n it'd been Zook hisself, ye'd be daid now." He spoke matter-of-factly, but Joseph studied the long bony face for a sign of friendliness. There was only the same pity as in all the others. "But ya mought as well be daid, if'n he be sendin' ya to Lafe Baker."

"Now that is a fact truer'n Christmas, soldier," said one of the bystanders. Two or three others nodded, sagely. "They stick you in Ol' Capitol 'mongst them other deserters 'n traitors," he went on, "you'd best be aready for glory."

One of the men laughed, a high-pitched titter that faded quickly away into silence. Then, in clumps of twos and threes, they drifted away, some shaking their heads as if at the incomprehensibility of a child's behavior. Only Long Face and the other private remained, as ordered.

Fear closed around Joseph's heart. "Who is this Baker I keep hearing about?" he asked. "What does he do?"

Long Face only smiled sadly, then leaned against a tree trunk and slowly slid to a sitting position at its base. The other soldier copied his action. He plucked a spike of grass and stuck it in his mouth. Both men rested their heads against the bark and let their eyelids close.

Joseph stood with his left arm braced against a tree trunk. A wave of passionate anger engulfed him as he looked down at his relaxed guards. Whole and free, they sure had every reason to be easygoing, while he—

His thoughts suddenly jumped at an unexpected notion. Guards! Why, they weren't guarding him at all. What if he just up and trotted off into the trees? Might be a mile away before they raised their lazy heads again! There was really nothing to prevent his lighting out for freedom again. He took a step, tiptoe, toward the freedom of the North. Another, carefully. His foot came down crooked on a clump of grass. The momentary uneven distribution of his weight pulled the fabric of his shirt across the mangled flesh so it felt as though the bandage wasn't there. He bit off a scream and the step turned into a stumble. He brought himself up against the tree with his wounded right arm. This fresh grief was too much. His head spun. Nausea wallowed in his gut. He slipped to his knees and gently leaned his head against the rough bark of the tree.

There was no comfort in his soul.

He remained in this attitude, trembling with pain, until Hawkins returned. He was riding one horse and leading another. He dismissed the two soldiers, who walked away without a backward glance.

"Save your praying for later, soldier," he said. "You'll need it far more after riding one of these for a few hours!"

Joseph looked up and rose to his feet, using the tree trunk for support. He took in the horses. They were a pair of grays, looking as if they'd just been unhitched from a plow.

"I thought Captain Zook said I was to march," he said, but his heart leaped at the prospect of riding.

Hawkins snorted. "Hah—in your condition I'd end up

carrying you after ten minutes! Besides, this child'll never see forty-eight again and I'll be blasted if I am going to march any dozen miles to Frederick, in the dead of night!" He swung down off his mount and picked up Joseph's gear. "Now mount up, boy. Take the other horse, there, the one without a saddle."

Joseph obeyed, but carefully. The gray indicated by the sergeant was a gelding that appeared to be at least twelve years old. He somehow managed to hoist himself to the bare back without passing out from the fresh hurt. By the time the wave of agony cleared itself from his head, the sergeant was astride the other horse, in a saddle.

"Hope you don't mind not having a saddle," Hawkins apologized, "but I'm not much of a rider. Grew up in the city. Boston."

"No problem," Joseph said. He leaned forward and took in his left hand the knotted rope which draped across the gray's withers. He noticed that Hawkins had hung Joseph's pack across the saddle horn, along with his own. He wondered, idly, what had become of his musket. The sergeant had apparently left his behind, for the only weapon Joseph could see on the man was his pistol, which he wore in a leather holster on his belt.

"I'm ready," Joseph said. He tried to ignore the pounding in his temples which traced itself all the way down through his neck, right shoulder, arm. As long as he sat still his back was tolerable.

Sergeant Hawkins led the way, guiding them through the gathering dusk in the trees. They reached the road and turned left, downhill toward the valley. The dead and wounded had all been removed from the highway and the guns on the mountain had wrapped silence around themselves for the coming night. When Joseph let his eye follow the long, straight road stretching down and away before them, it was hard for him to believe a war was going on.

The track was devoid of a single human soul and the last ray of summer sunshine gilded the very tip of Catoctin Ridge, some five or six miles across the valley. Nearby a cricket scraped out its song to the dark.

Hawkins dropped back to ride alongside Joseph. "Peaceful, isn't it?" His voice was tinged with sadness.

"Yes, it is," Joseph agreed.

They rode on in silence for a while. Joseph realized that his pain was gradually lessening, at least so long as he remained still on the horse's back. He didn't mind riding bareback. It took him back to his boyhood and he preferred it to saddle-riding. He felt more a part of the animal and the ride was smoother when horse and rider were in direct contact.

As his pain seemed to lessen, his awareness was free to wander off on its own, and he suddenly was ravenous. He thought of the rations in his haversack and was on the verge of asking the sergeant to hand it to him when Hawkins spoke.

"I'm going to stop in Middletown, up ahead," he announced. He pointed to the twinkling lights in the village at the bottom of the valley. "I reckon McClellan might be thereabouts and I've got to see him about something."

Joseph's hunger vanished. He was going to see Little Mac! Then he abruptly remembered what he was, now, and his empty stomach flipped over. General McClellan was the last person from whom he wanted attention and scrutiny.

"Do we have to?" he asked, in a small voice.

Hawkins looked at him, his expression unreadable in the thickening gloom. Then he laughed. "It doesn't directly affect you, although it may mean I'll be your escort all the way to Washington instead of only to the train." His voice grew heavy. "No, I'm going to ask George if I may personally carry the news of Jesse to his widow."

"Oh," said Joseph, and they both fell silent again. Only

the sounds of horses' feet and cricket chirpings, and the creak of Hawkins's saddle leather disturbed the coming of the darkness. As the dew came down, the aroma of growing things reached Joseph's nostrils. He inhaled deeply and felt the welcome return of the peace that had come to him earlier, before the lashing, before the pain and fear. He let the feeling build in him as they peeled off the miles. The slope of the mountain seemed less than it had yesterday evening and this morning, when he'd done it on foot, with the threat of instantaneous death and dismemberment hanging over his head.

The twinkle of the Middletown lights evened out into a steady, brighter glow as they approached the village. It began just a few hundred yards on the other side of the creek where they'd slaked their thirst, on yesterday's march. When they clumped across the narrow wooden bridge, Joseph thought again of his hunger, and now he realized he was, also, very thirsty. He had no idea what had happened to his canteen. Likely lying beside my whipping tree, he thought. Suddenly, he was frightened again. He kept forgetting he was a deserter, on his way to punishment.

As Hawkins led the way into a yard where officers and horses were milling about, his anxiety increased. There was a small house in the yard and its front door was wide open. A bar of yellow lamplight streamed out into the young night. Men came and went through the doorway in numbers and with an urgency fully in keeping with the importance of an army's headquarters. This had to be McClellan's command center. Joseph swallowed hard and wished he could become a fly on the wall, in a dark corner.

As if perceiving Joseph's nervousness, the sergeant walked his mount around the spill of light and drew it up to a hitching bar near a closed door at the back of the house. Joseph followed. Hawkins dismounted and wrapped the reins around the rail.

"Wait here," he said. "I'll be right back." He took a step back toward the open door when suddenly his way was blocked by a corporal leading a squad of men who in turn were herding a group of prisoners. The young corporal was heading for the closed door, not six feet from where Joseph sat on his horse.

The corporal reached the door and turned to address his men. "Wait here while I ask the provost marshal what we should do with these Rebs." Then he turned back to the door, gave a swift knock, opened it, and took a step inside.

Joseph could see that the officer sitting inside behind a brightly lit desk was in his middle thirties, handsome, and debonair-looking, and right now quite irritated. "What is it? Can't you see I'm busy?" he rasped out, without looking up.

The corporal just stood there, his lower jar doing pushups. Joseph realized the truth at the same moment as the boy did, and almost fell off his horse. It was General McClellan himself!

The great man looked up. "What do you want?"

The corporal gulped and explained that he and his men had some prisoners to deliver and he had opened the wrong door by mistake.

McClellan's face relaxed, and he asked the corporal for his name and regiment. When he was told, his eyes brightened. "Oh, you belong to Gibbon's brigade. You men had some heavy action up there today."

"Yes we did, sir," the boy said. "But we gave them as good as they gave us!"

"Indeed you did, son. Indeed you did." He laughed happily. "You made a splendid fight."

The corporal hesitated, and Joseph wondered what was coming next. Already he was starting to feel sick. Just what he needed—to have Little Mac see him, as a deserter, after a happy little scene like this! Then he heard the boyish noncom say, in saccharine tones, "Well, General, that's the way we boys calculate to fight under a general like you!"

McClellan got up, came around the desk, and gripped the corporal by the hand. "If I can get that kind of feeling amongst the men of this army," said the general, "I can whip Lee without any trouble at all!"

Only his plunging despair kept Joseph from making a loud, kissing noise into the air. That, and a not-quite-dead instinct of self-preservation.

McClellan clapped the corporal heartily on his shoulders and ushered the boy out, apparently oblivious to the smug look on the noncom's face. The general stood in the doorway, a wide smile on his features as the corporal and his charges marched away. Then he noticed Joseph for the first time and his face reverted to its businesslike attitude. He nodded at Joseph, who was doing his best to look nonchalant. (Joseph mentally blessed Hawkins for not putting the irons back on his wrists after the beating.) Then the general's gaze moved to Hawkins, still standing where he'd dismounted. He squinted and stood aside to let the light fall on the sergeant.

"Bless my soul, it's Wilfred Hawkins!" He took several agile steps through the door and toward the sergeant and clapped him on both shoulders at once. His grin was boyish. "How are you, man? It's been too long, too long. What brings you here now, anyway?" McClellan's eyes moved from Hawkins to Joseph, sprouting question marks. "You two together?"

Hawkins ignored the question. "It's about Jesse, George." He also had beamed at the general when they'd met, but now he sobered abruptly. "I'd like to request permission to go personally to inform his widow and take her his personals. If I may, sir."

McClellan's face immediately sobered also. "Of course, Wilfred, certainly." He threw Joseph another quizzical look, then put an arm around Hawkins's shoulder. "Come on inside, Will. Let's work out the details. I'd like to send a message, too."

The general ushered the sergeant into the house, then closed the door. Joseph was left outside, in the company of only his fears. And they were considerable. He knew that behind that door his fate would be decided. They didn't come any higher in military rank in the army than McClellan, the Young Napoleon, and the general could probably have Joseph executed right then and there, if the inclination hit him.

Joseph suddenly felt very sick. He sensed that he was starting to slide off the horse's back and was dizzy enough to fall. Yet somehow he managed to grab a handful of mane and hang on until the vertigo passed. His heart thudded painfully in his empty stomach as well as in his wounds. His mouth was dry and his whole body suddenly felt feverish. He desperately plumbed his soul for the peace so recently there, but it was gone. Tears lurked behind his eyes.

Then a fresh surge of dizziness went through him. He quickly lay forward and struggled to wrap his arms around the gray's neck. Just then the gelding, probably alarmed at the antics of its unfamiliar rider, tossed its head back and met Joseph's face with a sickening crunch. He went limp and sagged off the beast's flank into an ungainly pile at its feet.

Joseph felt his consciousness slipping in and out of focus as he lay there. No one seemed to have noticed his fall, but he suddenly felt foolish and tried to get up. It was no use. He couldn't get his limbs organized and a far-off corner of his mind shrieked in panic. What was going wrong with him? What had happened to him? Could all this have come just from a gaggle of healing wounds and an empty stomach? Or weren't the injuries mending? The panic mounted and usurped a bigger piece of his awareness.

Light shafted across him, as abruptly as an insight. Hawkins stood in the open doorway, McClellan just behind him. "What the—" Hawkins said, springing forward and helping Joseph to his feet. "Can you help me, George?"

The smaller man, the commanding general of the Army of the Potomac, helped Sergeant Hawkins lift the deserter back onto the horse's back, carefully, as if he were a precious burden. From what seemed miles away, Joseph heard the concern in Mac's voice. "Will he be all right, Wilfred? Until you get him to Old Capitol?"

There was a long pause and Joseph, even in his world of fog, wondered at it.

"You sure, sir, that's where you want him?"

"No doubt of it, sergeant." The iron of command was back in the voice. "We can't let deserters escape retribution for their mistakes, now, can we?"

Joseph was aware of the sounds of a large man hoisting himself up into a saddle, nearby. "No, George," Hawkins sighed, half from sadness, half from the exertion of mounting his horse. "But I do have your permission to have him treated, don't I?"

At that instant, Joseph heard a loud noise in his head. The combination of buzzing and ringing covered the reply of General McClellan. Then Joseph became aware that his horse was moving, past the well-lit doorway where the staffers were still coming and going, past the house, and again onto the National Road, into the night. He was aware that Hawkins was riding on his left. Close enough to catch me if I start to fall, Joseph thought. Which will probably be in ten seconds, he speculated, with a grimace. He didn't recall ever feeling so poorly in his whole life.

11

The remainder of the trek to Frederick was only a blur to Joseph. He supposed, later, when he was clearer in the head again, that the snowball of pain and vertigo had finally got too big to control. It had rolled down across his consciousness, flattening his awareness of night and day, of thirst and hunger. Without Sergeant Hawkins's aid he probably would have died along the way, even though just a couple hours earlier he'd thought he was mending.

When he regained some awareness, he found himself in a bed with crisp white sheets. He lay belly-down on the top sheet, the side of his face nose-deep in a clean-smelling white pillowcase. His eyes had no sooner popped open, discovering these startling details of his surroundings, than they closed again in a sensation of bliss.

Natural curiosity soon asserted itself, however, and he opened his eyes again. Less than a foot away, on a small table near the bed, stood a burning lamp. Joseph unthinkingly lifted his head to look around him. Before a bolt of pain clattered through his head, he took in the fact that he was in a large hospital ward full of beds in two rows with an aisle down the middle of the room. It was too dark to tell whether the other beds had occupants, but he assumed they did. Then the hurt hit him. He dropped back to the pillow and lay there throbbing like doom itself. He felt himself spinning off into oblivion, the questions in his mind fading as if answered.

Suddenly his nose was bombarded with a heavenly fragrance—food! His eyes shot open, yet he had the presence of mind not to raise his head again. Through the corner of his vision he saw a long-fingered hand set a steaming bowl on the table beside the lamp. A spoon handle stuck out over the edge of the dish. His mouth watered.

"Just lie still, soldier. You have had a lot for one body to put up with." It was a female voice, and gentle.

"When's he going to be able to continue on, nurse?" That was a stronger voice and not female. Sergeant Hawkins.

"Don't be silly, sergeant! This boy's wounds will keep him in bed for at least three or four days." A no-nonsense voice.

"I'm afraid not, ma'am." Sergeant Hawkins meant business. "You feed him and get him bandaged up and he may sleep until morning. I want him ready to move before sunup. He's a deserter and my prisoner. All your medicine and loving care would better be spent on a real—"

"Sergeant, you listen to me!" The nurse interrupted. She was sounding more military by the minute and Joseph was glad she was on his side. He almost grinned into the pillow. "As long as I am in charge of this hospital ward," she went on, "any boy gets the care he needs. And I don't care if he is a murderer!"

There was silence after that, a long pause. The throbbing receded in his head. Joseph felt himself falling into a long, dark place again, but it was only sleepiness this time. Just two inches from oblivion he heard the sergeant's voice. The words were a blur, but he caught the threat in the tone. Then heavy footsteps were going away.

Cool fingers touched his neck. "Are you awake, soldier?" the voice was mild again. He swept back up into awareness. "I'm going to put more salve on your back and rewrap it. It will hurt a bit when I remove the bandage." He heard a smile in her voice. "Then we'll get some of this soup into you, all right?"

He braced himself for the pain, but as the gentle hands peeled away the now-crusty bandage, her touch itself felt like balm. In spite of the promise of food, his mind floated in and out of sleepiness as she covered his sores with cool ointment. When she wrapped his back in clean strips, he hardly felt it.

"Soldier, you awake?"

"Yes, ma'am!" Joseph's mind came abruptly to heel.

"Please sit up, if you feel able, so I can finish my bandaging." It was a firm order, gently given.

He obeyed, twisting his legs around to sit on them. His head reeled, but not enough to make him dizzy. For the first time he saw his benefactress. She was sixtyish and had a lean, lined face. Her ample body, incongruous with the thin cheeks, was soft and motherly, as he'd guessed. Her hands echoed the appearance of her face, thin and efficient-looking. She looked haggard, though, and when she smiled at him, Joseph recalled the exhausted doctor. He suddenly realized that those of the medical profession might be the true, but unsung, heroes of this war.

Her strong fingers nimbly wrapped the linen strips several times around his chest and the wound in his right armpit, then rewrapped his head wound. As she worked her tired eyes repeatedly came back to his. He saw, besides the exhaustion, the mix of speculation and compassion.

"A deserter—is that what your friend said?" A twinkle belied the severe tone. "You don't look the type, I must say."

"Not exactly, ma'am, but—"

"Call me Hannah—Hannah Campbell, and I'd be honored."

"All right, Hannah," Joseph went on. "I suppose to anyone else, I'd seem a deserter, but. . . ." He paused, suddenly struck by the insight that it might be hard, if not impossible, to explain his deed of that afternoon. He hadn't, up to now anyway, really *felt* like a deserter.

"Well?" Hannah had finished with her bandaging. Her busy hands now lay idle in her lap. She sat on the rickety wooden chair at the bedside, ready to help him eat. "Then why did that man call you a deserter, if you don't think you are one?" The twinkle stayed in her eyes. It gave Joseph courage.

"You see, ma'am—I mean, Hannah. . . ." He swallowed and looked down at his hands, lying in his lap. He was still sitting cross-legged on the bed like a Buddhist monk. "I believe it is wrong to kill."

"Pssh—I should say it is!"

"But a soldier can't say that, Hannah!" Joseph almost laughed aloud at her apparent ignorance of the irony.

"Hey, pipe down over there!" A disembodied voice came out of the gloom, halfway down the ward. Hannah looked guilty and touched her index finger to her pursed lips.

Joseph went on, in a loud whisper. "I mean, a soldier's job, his profession, is to destroy the enemy. But, all of a sudden, I just could not point my gun at another human being. I just turned and walked away. It suddenly was not important what might happen to me, except that I didn't go on killing, or trying to kill." He stopped. It felt odd to be putting actual words to his feelings.

"Go on," she prompted. In the lamp glow Joseph could see her eyes had lost their twinkle.

"It was the way my father reared me, I suppose," Joseph said. "It was different from most fellows, I'd wager." He paused, unexpectedly shy. But he presently realized that he wanted—no, "needed" was the word—to unburden himself. He was beginning to comprehend, ever so slowly, that the outcome of his decision to turn and leave the carnage of war was going to affect his future, possibly quite significantly.

"What is your name, young man?" Hannah asked as she handed him the bowl. A thin skin had formed on the surface of the soup. "Here, you'd better eat this before it's cold."

"Thank you," he said. "King. Joseph King is my name." He took the bowl and spoon and slurped down half a dozen spoonfuls of the creamy potatoes before he could control himself enough be sociable again.

Hannah was grinning at him. "Where are your people from, Joseph?"

"Michigan, the Kalamazoo area." He spooned down several more mouthfuls. "But before that, my family lived in southern Pennsylvania. Not far from here, as a matter of fact." He finished the soup and handed the bowl and spoon to the nurse. He felt like a new man.

She took the bowl and set it down on the nightstand beside her without looking. Her eyes held his, showing interest.

"How *were* you reared?" she asked. Her interest seemed to be like something he was saying being measured against something else she knew.

"My family is Mennonite," he answered, then he paused. Only rarely did he meet persons who had heard of this minor sect, even though the religious group had been in the New World since the 1680s. But the light of recognition shone in her face.

"Is that right? Well, I declare! I grew up in Lancaster County in Pennsylvania." She laughed, then quickly shushed herself, glancing around at the sleeping forms. "I didn't know there were any of your group in Michigan."

"There aren't many of us," Joseph said. "Actually, in my father's church there's just our family." He stared at his hands. "And I guess I strayed away from it and don't really practice the faith anymore." Guilt stabbed him as he realized that he, Joseph, the preacher's kid, had become more of a backslider than a member in recent years.

"Oh, so you are the son of a minister?" Hannah sounded surprised.

"Yes," he said, his whisper falling almost to nothing. To his mind and his heart came a wave of remorse and repentance as he told her of his last conversation with his father, who had pleaded with him to change his mind about going off to war. And as he talked, it came to him that the decision made on the field, in the ditch during the ambush, the moral choice that had made him a deserter, would forever after remain with him. It would affect his day-to-day living, his approach to his fellows, to his father. To Rachel.

When his memory lit on her, his remorse slid away and left him with a warm feeling. Suddenly he craved her in his arms. It startled him, because it was a sentimental thing and he'd always tried to avoid sentimentality, thinking it somehow immature, undignified.

Yet, as his mind explored the change in his feelings toward the loved ones back home in Michigan, he began to realize that a vast change had taken place in him, or at least was starting to occur. Since that moment of truth in the woods, when he had turned his back on war, something had sprouted in him that now made him want to be back there with them, face to face with his father. He would tell him that now he, Joseph, saw clearly the rightness of everything his dad had always taught and preached. Now he knew it was true.

A puzzling notion hit him. How had his father known all about these truths? How had he understood the evil of war, without ever having participated in a battle? How—

"Joseph?" Hannah's kind eyes searched his face. There was a look of amusement in them. "There are some strange thoughts going round and round in that head of yours, aren't there?"

He chuckled. "Yes, I think you're right." He shook his head in wonder, not even realizing it hurt only a tad. "I believe that I have learned a little something new over the past day or two."

Her features showed understanding. "All the Mennonites I ever knew, back in Pennsylvania, would have moved to Canada before they'd of let themselves be put into a military uniform."

She pushed herself to her feet and prepared to leave. A gentle chuckle issued from her, and the twinkle returned to her eyes. "I'd wager my best petticoat that I may be talking with someone who, in the last minute or two, has decided maybe he's returned to the fold."

She glowed down at him, then suddenly she was all business again. "Now, young man," she said, smoothing out her skirt and apron with gentle sweeps of her hands, "you just lie there easy and let those wounds heal. There's been a lot of shock done to your system and it's only because you're young and strong that the damage isn't worse. But it still could be bad. The best medicine for you is several days of bed rest."

Joseph smiled. "Thank you, Hannah. Thank you for everything. Thanks for listening. I feel much better." He couldn't find the words to express the lightness in his heart. It made his bodily ailments seem trivial.

"Now you just get some sleep, young man! I have others to see to as well, you know." Her smile was tired, as if her duties made her sad.

Joseph suddenly felt wonder at this woman. It seemed incredible to him that she apparently understood him, even better than he did himself. His answering smile felt like a boyish grin.

"I'll be back in the morning to look in on you," she said. She gave his shoulder—his left one, of course—a motherly pat, then picked up the lamp and made her way down the long aisle. She stopped here and there, solicitously, to check on wounded soldiers. Joseph watched her go, marveling at her, reflecting on how her spirit was the opposite of warlike. Yet it was the gods of war which called out the benevolence of her spirit.

A moment after the nurse had disappeared through the doorway at the far end of the ward, Joseph remembered Hawkins's terse order to have him bandaged and ready to move before dawn. An arrow of cold fear shafted through him. Hannah hadn't seemed to take the words seriously, but what if the sergeant did come around to collect him, before the nurse came back? Or after, for that matter? There wasn't a whole lot the nurse could do to stop him if the big sergeant decided to spirit Joseph away to prison, by force.

Why would he, anyway? Joseph asked of the darkness around him. What was all the hurry? You'd think a friend of the widow would want to go slow on his way to tell her of the death of her husband. Drag his feet even. And what was the hurry to get a prisoner to his prison? Because he might escape? When the captive was hurting in countless ways, and so tired he could croak?

Joseph would have grinned at that, except that a jaw-popping yawn took him then, reminding him it was night and that he had had a full day. Weariness flooded his consciousness, putting Hawkins out of his mind. Just before sleep triumphed, he reveled in the newfound peace again. It seemed always to be there, just outside his awareness like a guardian angel. With it came the quiet assurance that his "desertion" had been right, no matter what the laws of men. Nothing the sergeant could do—or this infamous Lafe Baker, for that matter—could alter the fact that Joseph was now at peace with the teachings of his youth.

* * *

It seemed only minutes later that rough hands were shaking him awake. It was still dark.

"Get up, King. Time to get back on the road." It was Hawkins. His breath smelled of whiskey.

"But the nurse said—" Joseph began.

"I don't care if she's the holy virgin herself!" Hawkins cut him off. His voice was fierce. "The train's leaving for Washington in twenty minutes and we are going to be on it. Now get up and get dressed. Hurry!"

Joseph obeyed, with as much speed as his sleep-stupor permitted. He pondered the odor of the brew which hovered about the big sergeant. He was beginning to suspect General Reno's death might have been harder on Hawkins than the latter had let on. The sergeant just didn't seem the type to overindulge for no good reason. Then the soreness of his back and arm and shoulder as he got into his clothes precluded further pondering. Suffice it to say, he thought as he buttoned up his tunic, that the sergeant was turning out to be a more complex person than his manner, so far, would have suggested. Else why the booze and the hurry? Surely there were other trains to catch, if they missed this one.

When Joseph was all laced up, the two of them made for the door of the hospital ward, the sergeant slightly in the lead. Although Joseph's multiple wounds gave him no bright, stabbing pains this morning, as he walked he felt sudden dizziness. Unthinkingly, he reached out to grasp Hawkins's elbow. At the same moment as he reached, a flickering light appeared around the corner of the hall directly in front of them.

It was Hannah Campbell, bearing a candle aloft.

The simultaneous grabbing of his elbow and the appearing of the nurse had a curious and drastic effect on the sergeant. He leaped backward and to his left, jerking his pistol from its holster. He fell into a half crouch and waved the weapon back and forth between Hannah and Joseph. His eyes, even in the dim candlelight, had the look of an animal at bay. Fear, cunning, and defiance somehow all managed to find room in his glare.

His support unexpectedly gone, Joseph followed the man to the floor, stopping only when he had toppled into an ungainly heap. He instinctively tried to catch himself with his wounded arm. His shout of pain echoed through the sleeping room.

Nurse Campbell stood in the doorway with her mouth agape, still holding the light high. She stared in disbelief at the tableau before her, frozen in the flickering shadows.

"Hey, what's going on?" came a sleepy voice from the dark ward.

Hannah's mouth clapped shut. "Put that pistol away, you fool! It might go off and hurt someone." Without waiting to see whether she was obeyed, she stooped to help Joseph regain his feet. At the same time she shouted over her shoulder at the curious patient. "Go back to sleep!"

Hawkins seemed to come out of a trance. He looked stupidly at the gun in his hand. Then he put it away and came up out of his crouch. In the dim light his expression changed to sheepish. "Sorry," he muttered. "You startled me."

"I should think you *would* be apologetic!" Hannah bit off the words. "Abducting this poor boy in the middle of the night, like some thief! I told you he needs several *days,* not hours, of bed rest, at least!"

Her anger acted like a tonic to Hawkins. "And I told you, lady, that it isn't possible! He's coming with me. Now!" He seemed to regain his authority along with his feet.

"What is so urgent," Hannah asked, "that requires he be taken to Washington this minute? He is only going to be shoved into prison as soon as he arrives, anyhow. God only knows what kind of medical attention he will get there!" She shook her finger at the big man. "And I must tell you, sergeant, that Private King is still a very sick young man."

"Seems like you got him bandaged up pretty fine, nurse," Hawkins said. "Now step aside. We have a train to catch!" His voice was full of irritation.

Hannah Campbell did not move aside. Instead, she moved the candle so its light shone full on Joseph's face. She said nothing, only stared at his eyes. He could see compassion there. But he also detected anxiety, and that worried him. Maybe his wounds were more dangerous to him than he knew. They *felt* better, but—a shiver of fear rippled down his spine.

He was opening his mouth to ask Hannah what was wrong, what was the cause of her anxiety, when Sergeant Hawkins rather rudely ended the conversation. "Let's go, private," he said, jerking on Joseph's good arm. He strode past the nurse and out the door. Joseph had no choice but to follow.

"God go with you, son!" she called after him.

Outside, it was still night except for a thin blush of pink along the eastern horizon. The air was chilly. "Horses tethered this way," Hawkins grunted, tugging lightly on Joseph's arm again. Even out in the fresh air the aroma of distilled spirits clung to him. Joseph made a mental note not to stir up the man's ire. He himself had experienced enough hangovers to know the morning after was no bed of roses. The thought struck him with a feeling of shame, which in turn surprised him. He pondered this as they stumbled through the dark.

Was there something about his change of heart on the battlefield, his conviction that war was wrong, that was going to affect his habits too? He toyed with the notion some more as Hawkins steered him along. Have I experienced more of a conversion than I originally imagined? he asked himself silently. As if in answer, the feeling of peace swept through him again. It was exciting and it banished his anxiety, like a miracle. Yet almost immediately the worm of another worry came to him, as though the exorcism of one fear left the way open for others: How will I tolerate prison? How long will I have to be there? Will there be a trial?

He decided to give voice to at least one of these concerns: "Will I be given a trial, Sergeant Hawkins?" he asked, hoping it was a safe-enough question.

No answer.

"Why is it so urgent for me to get there, sir?" Maybe he was pressing his luck. "Like the nurse said, I'm only going to prison."

The sergeant stopped and Joseph could feel rather than see the man turn his face toward Joseph. But he did not utter a word.

"I really don't feel very good, sir," Joseph said to the dark between them. "Not sure I'll be able to stay on the horse. Sort of dizzy."

"You'll do all right," Hawkins grunted. There was a trace of returning goodwill in his voice. Then he turned away again and led Joseph another rod or two before stopping again. "Here's the horses." He placed Joseph's left hand on the reins. It was still pitch dark, despite the fingernail moon. The gelding nickered at Joseph's touch. He wondered how Hawkins had found the invisible animals so surely in the dark.

"Mount up," Hawkins ordered. "And no more malingering." Joseph heard the big man climb into his saddle and cluck his mount into motion. He mounted and kicked his own horse to follow. Hawkins apparently trusted Joseph's wounds to keep him from jumping down and running away. He hadn't bound Joseph's wrists or made any other provisions to restrict his liberty. He simply assumes, Joseph mused, that my horse will follow his, and if he hears the hooves go off on a tangent, why he'll just pivot in his saddle, point that hog-leg of his in the direction of the noises, and blast away!

Joseph was not in a spirit to try to escape, anyway. Part of the reason was simple: he was still groggy with sleep and the stiffness of his aches and pains. In a way he was a spectator of himself and his actions. So much had happened in the past forty-eight hours or so that he was somewhat overwhelmed, he decided, as the gelding clumped along the cobble street behind the sergeant.

He smiled. How could something be partly overwhelming? Well, it was all a bit much, anyhow. Less than two days ago he had been an average, ordinary boy dressed up as a soldier in the Union's main army, fighting patriotically for his native country. Now he was aching with the hurts of battle and of punishment, an official deserter and coward, being dragged to a prison in his nation's capital. In chains, with a cloud of ignominy hanging over him.

He sighed. It all seemed a bit unreal—maybe a better word than overwhelming.

The peace of the predawn was shattered suddenly by three staccato bursts from a train whistle. Almost at the same moment, Hawkins steered them around the corner of a building and along another street of the still-sleeping town. Less than three blocks in front of them was the B&O station, where a locomotive stood on its tracks, its brilliant headlamp glaring straight into their faces, its rotund iron belly whooshing up a head of steam.

Joseph's heart beat faster. He had always loved the sight of these huge metal machines, which seemed more alive than mechanical. One of the never-to-be-forgotten delights of his young boyhood had been his first ride on one of the new steam engines. A member of his father's church had shipped a load of cattle to Detroit and Joseph had been invited to ride along. He'd even been permitted to ride on the engine itself!

A wistful smile crossed his lips as they guided their mounts over the remaining distance. Now he was about to take his *last* train ride.

He sat bolt upright on the horse's back. Where had that thought come from? He gave a sharp, nervous laugh.

"What's so funny back there?" Hawkins called out. It was now just light enough to make out his form in the saddle. He was turned to look back.

"Nothing, sir," Joseph said. "Just daydreaming."

Yet it was like a premonition, and it stayed with him. It sat on his shoulders like a visitation from another world. He shivered.

Hawkins led the way up onto the wooden platform that fronted on the tracks. Joseph followed, and they rode past the chuffing locomotive and pulled to a stop beside a boxcar slightly beyond the station house. Its door was slid wide open and a stock ramp angled down to the platform. In the rapidly brightening dawn, Joseph could see approximately a dozen more such cars stretching away toward the rear, all with their ramps and open doors, looking like a line up of square-headed citizens having their tongues examined. He guessed this was a load of beef heading to the markets of the capital, and he wondered where all the cattle were. Then as he watched he saw two men jump out of the rearmost car, slide the ramp inside, and slam the door shut. They proceeded toward him, performing the same task on each boxcar as they came.

"Looks like we just made it," Hawkins said. "You take my horse and get into this first car." He gestured up the ramp directly before the feet of their horses. "I'll show my pass to the stationmaster and be right back."

He handed his reins to Joseph and dismounted. He gave his horse a slap on the rump and it readily clumped up the ramp, as if it had done so before. The other mount unquestioningly followed as Joseph ducked to protect his head. Inside the boxcar, he painfully dismounted and lowered himself into the fresh straw with a sigh of relaxation. In two minutes Sergeant Hawkins was back, waving his paper with

McClellan's signature in the face of the attendant, whose manner instantly changed from resentment at the intrusion to fawning respect.

The sergeant climbed up the ramp, the attendant scooted it in, and, still grinning like a toady, slid the door to. Hawkins reopened it about a foot to give them air and sunshine. A moment later, with much slamming and clanking of heavy metal, the train pulled out of Frederick.

12

Joseph quickly became aware of the presence of cattle all around them. The sudden invasion of horses and humans must have startled them, he decided, because they had pushed as far away into the corners as space allowed. Now they ambled forward inquisitively, their puffing breath and shuffling feet barely audible over the chuffing of the engine. Joseph felt oddly comforted by their presence, as if he were abruptly transported back to a cozy childhood barn. He sighed and scrunched down into the fresh straw. His eyelids drooped.

"Sit up, private," Hawkins's voice was gruff. "I'm gonna get some sleep."

Joseph obeyed and the sergeant shackled him to the metal frame of the boxcar. "You don't have to do that, sir. I don't feel much like moving a muscle."

Hawkins only grunted, gave a tug on the chains, then moved away through the milling beasts to the opposite side of the car. The two horses had already joined the cattle in their nosing of the loose hay mixed with the straw all over the floor. He sagged to the floor and laid his head against the car wall. "Maybe you won't, King," he said, raising his voice over the lowing of the cattle, "but this way I don't have to worry." A bar of light from a passing street lamp momentarily illuminated his face. It looked haggard and drawn. His eyes were closed.

Joseph's heart went out to the man. "I'm sorry, Sergeant Hawkins, about the loss of General Reno."

"Consider yourself fortunate that you don't have to face his widow," Hawkins said. There was a long pause, but Joseph sensed more was coming. He was right. "She already lost a son in this bloody war. Died at Shiloh. Same day and same place as my boy." The sergeant's voice was strained.

Joseph felt ashamed. "I'm sorry, sir. I didn't realize—"

"No, soldier," Hawkins cut in. For the first time since they'd left McClellan, he seemed more his old self. His voice seemed to regain some civility. "There's nothing for you to be sorry about. It's the fortunes of war. I almost wish now that John—that's my son—had done what you—" But he didn't finish.

Joseph waited in the gloom of the car. The animals had subsided and the swaying and clattering of the train blended into a muffled background. But the man didn't speak again. Joseph withdrew into his own heart, appalled. A son had been killed, and now a friend, General Reno. Who was he, Joseph, anyway—youthful, summertime soldier-civilian—to judge harshly? It was more a wonder that Wilfred Hawkins had a measure of compassion in the way he treated Joseph than that he had yielded to a nighttime bottle. Yet he, a noncommissioned officer in the United States Army, had not turned and marched away in disgust. As he had a perfect reason to do, now that those close to him had been sacrificed.

Joseph rested his head against the hard wall of the boxcar, aware of new complexities, new doubts. He began to wonder whether he had, maybe, been too hasty, in his decision to desert.

"Desert." There was that nasty word again. It described him to all others, even if it felt too glib and simple to his own self-estimation. It was a word to mark a crime, but to him the motivation must be taken into account. Just as "patriotism" was only a word, yet it embodied a lot that was wrong to a Mennonite, he now realized.

A deep sigh overcame him, and suddenly all he wanted was sleep. He became aware of his pains again, and simultaneously of Hawkins's deep breathing. Or was it a cow? In the growing gray light of morning he looked at the sergeant. The man's eyes were closed and his chest rose and fell rhythmically, as he lay propped against the far wall.

Joseph sighed again and closed his own eyes. The click and clack of iron wheels against rails soothed him to sleep.

* * *

The train's lurching woke him. The sun was streaming through the partly opened boxcar doorway. As the train stopped, jerkily, he became aware of the staggering of heavy bodies all around him. Alarmed, he quickly sat up and drew his knees to his chin. A moment later, Sergeant Hawkins appeared at his side, crouched, and unlocked his cuffs.

"Get up, King. We have to change trains for Washington."

Joseph struggled to his feet. His joints had stiffened and shooting pains stitched across his vision. His tongue felt dry and swollen. With his head spinning, he followed the noncom down the ramp when the train had come to a full stop. Hawkins led both horses.

"No need to mount up," he said. "Other train's right over there." He pointed and Joseph staggered after him. Two attendants, coming to their car to handle the stock, gave the pair of them strange looks, then shrugged and went about their business as if anything was plausible in war-torn America.

In minutes they were ensconced in another boxcar, identical to the one they'd just left, except that it had neither cattle nor clean straw on the floor. Hawkins shackled Joseph to the frame again, then slid to the floor, as before, his back to the wall. "Shouldn't be more than an hour till we're in the capital," he said, then promptly went back to sleep.

He had left the sliding door slightly ajar, as in the first car, and Joseph could tell that it was midmorning by the angle of the sun's rays. It was already growing hot, especially here inside this car, as though it had sat on its siding since sunrise, soaking up heat. He felt groggy and miserable and he yearned to sleep, too, but his body must have had enough. All it left him now was growing hunger pangs and, of course, the steady pulse of his pains. He shifted, using the length of the chain to secure a more comfortable resting place for his back.

Gradually, almost imperceptibly, as if Joseph had been the special cargo now delivered, the train slid out of the station. Southward instead of east, this time, along the trunk line from Baltimore to the capital. To Washington city, where his destiny awaited. In a cell.

Joseph deliberately emptied his mind and stared out at the passing countryside. He refused to think or to let his fears grow. He had never felt so alone, yet at the same time he was confident of being right. He concentrated on sensations only, letting his anxiety and pain subside as he watched the sun-dappled trees and fields of Maryland race past. He smelled the sun-warmed air that breezed in the open door. He even contrived, in some irrational corner of his brain, to enjoy the gentle sway and swing of the train instead of dwelling on the pain which the same movements cost him.

From time to time the train slowed, then went on at greater speed again, or stopped completely. He could not see the causes of these delays, nor did anyone come to their boxcar. Hawkins stirred restlessly each time the rhythm of the car changed, and finally, after what felt like about three-quarters of an hour, he stretched and got to his feet. When he came over to unlock Joseph's chains, his eyes looked clear and the whiskey smell was partly washed away in the warm wind. He even managed a half smile.

"Should be at the station in ten minutes." He took a step to the door and looked out in the direction they were heading. "Yup, here's Washington. Get up."

Joseph looked outside as he rose. In spite of the circumstances of his arrival, he had to admit to a growing excitement as the first buildings of the capital city came into view. He stood beside the sergeant, gripping the iron-and-wood post of the doorway with his good hand. Standing up had caused dots to dance before his eyes, but they soon vanished.

Then, without prologue, the sight of the unfinished Capitol dome slid into the frame of the open door. Simultaneously, the train began to slow. Mounted soldiers, wagons, and heavy guns appeared, lining the tracks like a sinister decoration. Hardly anyone even glanced at the arriving train. Life was cut and dried here in Washington city. One more prisoner with escort was hardly the excuse to stop moving and hauling to watch.

Another five hundred yards went by and the train ground to a shuddering, crashing halt. Their car just overlapped the end of the wooden platform, so there was no need for the ramp. Hawkins got their horses in tow while Joseph worked his arms and legs to restore feeling and use. Pain shot through his right side and back and exploded in his head. He staggered and fell against the car wall. For a long moment, until his head cleared, Joseph braced himself there. Meanwhile, Hawkins coaxed the two grays across the gap to the worn, greasy planks outside the boxcar and on down to ground level. Then he turned and watched Joseph. There seemed to be a shade of sympathy in his look, but the bright, noon sunshine beaming down over his forage cap cast his eyes into deep shadow, so Joseph couldn't be sure.

"Mount up, soldier," he said. His voice seemed falsely gruff. "We've got a twenty-minute ride to Old Capitol." He stood as if to grab Joseph if he should stumble. But the private managed to get aboard the bareback beast without passing out. Hawkins had left Joseph's mount close enough to the end of the platform without making his kindness obvious, yet the fresh agony of the exertion caused Joseph a dizzy moment after he'd climbed on. He took a fistful of ragged mane in his left hand until the sensation subsided.

"Okay," he said. He managed a small smile.

Hawkins swung into his saddle and made a kissing sound. His horse moved off along the dock and Joseph followed. He was grateful the sergeant hadn't chained his hands together. Must be obvious I'm in no shape to cut and run, he thought, with a grim, inward smile.

They paused at the gate only long enough for Hawkins to show the guard his pass, signed by McClellan. The uniformed sentry, one of a half dozen scattered about the station house, stepped back and saluted smartly when he'd seen the signature. As Joseph passed, the man looked up at Joseph with an expression of surprise mingled with contempt. Then their mounts tramped down into a sea of mud. Obviously, there had been rain before this day's sunshine. A lot of it.

Joseph looked up at the sky as the gelding followed leisurely after Hawkins. He felt a profound thankfulness for the brilliance of today. He was on the last leg of his trip to prison, there to remain for God only knew how long. To have traveled the last mile in foul weather would have plunged his mood into bleakness, he knew. As they sloshed through the slop, he felt bleak enough already. He closed his eyes, swallowed hard, and tried to concentrate only upon the glow of sun on his head, shoulders, and back. He tried to forget his destination, his destiny.

"Why did you desert, soldier?" Hawkins's voice startled

him, coming at his right shoulder. His eyes flew open. The sergeant had let his horse drop back beside Joseph's. His eyes were kind.

Joseph swallowed again. It was a question he wasn't sure he was able to put into words yet, at least to a sergeant. With Hannah Campbell it had been almost natural. But to try to explain to a soldier? He stared at Hawkins. His expression must have looked startled, for the noncom's smile grew into a chuckle.

"Go on, tell me," Hawkins said. "You don't have to worry what *I* think. I'll be gone in a few minutes and any answer you give to me doesn't count. I'm only a delivery boy."

Joseph suddenly felt the familiar peace, and he smiled at the man. With the peace came boldness to answer without guile. "Because in my heart and soul, I suddenly realized there is no law under heaven that allows one man to take the life of another." His eyes bored into the sergeant's. "For whatever reason, or whatever the circumstances."

Hawkins studied Joseph as their mounts churned a path along the street. Something in their look made Joseph feel like a specimen, like a thing to be examined even if not understood. But he thought he also detected sympathy in the face of the sergeant.

"Well, I can't agree with you, of course," Hawkins said. "Else I'd give the lie to half my life." The big man chuckled and the sound warmed Joseph. He began to wonder whether he should hope for reasonable treatment, after all, in prison. "But I dare say at the Old Capitol *their* disagreement with your philosophy will bring down on your head a trifle more pain than I have caused you, to date. Even with my rousting you out of your sickbed."

Hawkins shook his head. At his words, Joseph's hope died. "Yes, sir, Mr. King, there you will not find a whole lot of sympathy from the likes of Lafayette Baker. If you ever see the man, that is. He's often gone for weeks at a time." He turned and looked at Joseph again while their horses plodded miserably along. "But I think I have lived long enough to distinguish folly and cowardice." It hung in the air like a *non sequitur.*

"Are you saying—" Joseph began.

"No, I am not calling you either a fool or a coward, King," Hawkins's severe voice cut him off. "In fact, I think you have a lot of courage, if maybe tinged with naïveté." He looked to the front again, then pointed to an intersection coming up. "We turn right there." He looked back at Joseph. "Indeed, I think there are qualities in you that are lacking in too many of our nation's young men." His eyes were sad. They had turned into the new street before he spoke again. He preceded his next words with a shrug. "Unfortunately, most of my generation were taught a morality which seems to have gone out the window with the cannonade on Fort Sumter. It won't be me who decides what to do with you."

Hawkins quit speaking and they rode on in silence for several moments. Soon they came to another junction of streets. Mud-splattered signposts indicated they were at First and A streets. They passed a pair of large trees still wearing their full summer green. Then Hawkins pointed beyond them to a building that had been hidden behind the foliage.

"That's it," he said. "Your new home." His voice was abruptly noncommittal.

Joseph's eyes followed the pointing finger. "That's a prison?" It was a square, two-story edifice with mullioned windows on the two sides visible to them. White paint, although dirtied by the dust of several years, was still in good trim. There were no high, pointed fences, no guard towers, no sense of desolation. The smallish trees along the structure's sides seemed to have been planted in decorative patterns. "It looks more like someone's residence, or even a government building," Joseph said.

"It used to be," Hawkins said. He spurred his horse forward. "Let's get cracking, private. Enjoy your last minutes of fresh air and sunshine." Now he was strictly business, as if he were aware of faces that might be watching from windows for any sign of softness.

Joseph followed, curiosity momentarily overcoming his fear of the unknown. "Used to be which?" he called out. "Residence or government building?" He kicked his own mount to catch up.

"Both," the older man said as Joseph came up. "Back in the 1812 war when the British burned the Capitol, Congress met in this building. Most recently, I believe, some German family lived here. Raising hogs." Hawkins snorted. "Start of this war, I guess they commenced putting other kinds of swine here: Confederate spies, traitors. Even some famous newspaper editor, I heard."

Joseph watched the building over the bobbing head of his horse. So this is Old Capitol Prison, he thought. "No, it doesn't really look much like a prison," he said, half to himself. His spirits were rising. At least it didn't appear to have deep, dank dungeons, fields of mud and worse, as in some of the prisons he'd heard tell about, down South. Or that he'd read about in novels.

"Don't let appearances fool you, King," Hawkins put in. "From what I've heard Captain Zook report, it's hardly a mansion with servants." Distaste flickered across his face, immediately followed by furtive guilt. It was clear, to Joseph at least if not to any possible watchers, that Hawkins detested the dirty business of incarceration. "Anyway, even a palace would become a prison if you were never allowed out." He grinned suddenly, wolfishly, as if overcoming his weakness. "Or if you had to live on water and bread while everyone around you was feasting on roast pork and potatoes."

They reached the front of the building adjacent to the muddy street and the sergeant dismounted. "Stay on your horse," he ordered. He tied both the animals to the hitching rail, then stood back and pulled his pistol out of its holster. He brandished it ostentatiously at Joseph.

"Dismount, Private King!" he called out, loud enough to be heard through closed doors.

Joseph obeyed, stiffly. Hawkins' tone brought back reality and he felt his optimism fading fast. He forgot to favor his wounds and his shirt and tunic rubbing across his back gave him a sudden burning, followed by a wave of nausea. As his left boot touched the earth, his leg almost gave way. He grabbed the horse's mane with his good hand.

"Get your haversack off my saddle and follow me!" Hawkins hadn't noticed Joseph's momentary infirmity. He was in a hurry. Joseph pinched his eyes shut and shook his head. The wave of weakness passed. He opened his eyes, went to Hawkins's gelding, and peeled his pack off the saddle.

"Up there." The man gestured at the closed door with his weapon.

Joseph obeyed, almost stumbling on the one step up. Then he was standing before the door, studying its finely carved ornamentation, the delicately wrought sidelights, the polished brass knobs. He felt like a caller at some high-society fandango, instead of a prisoner.

Hawkins reached past his head and knocked with the butt of his gun. The illusion of a social call fled. Yet Joseph wondered why there were no guards.

The door opened, almost before Hawkins had stopped knocking. Joseph's wonder ceased. An armed sentry, in the crisp uniform of a private in the United States Army, stepped into the doorway. He barred the way, his musket held diagonally across his chest.

"I have a prisoner here, from McClellan's army," Sergeant Hawkins announced. He reached into his tunic with his free hand and produced the pass. He shook it open and handed it to the sentry. "He's a deserter."

The guard reached for the document and glanced over it. "Wait here," he said, then turned on his heel and disappeared into the gloom at the end of a long corridor. Halfway along the same hallway stood another sentry, stiffly at attention. Now he brought up his weapon and held it as his cohort had done.

Hawkins glanced at Joseph. Mingled in his expression were pity and resignation. He was clearly glad to be done with his responsibility, yet he obviously felt concern for Joseph, as a fellow human being.

Embarrassed, Joseph looked away and began to study his new home. For the first time he became aware of the muffled din of many voices, and he noticed a door directly across from where the second sentry stood. He guessed, by the sounds emanating from it, that the room beyond was large, probably a former parlor or ballroom, now full of men. A new fear came to him: what if he were placed in a large room with many other prisoners? How would they treat him, when they learned the nature of his offense? The reason for it?

He did not have long to let that worry grow, for presently the first guard returned, followed by another man in uniform, with officer's insignia on his collar. This individual had about him an air of authority and Joseph immediately wondered whether he was at last setting eyes on the infamous Lafe Baker. But then he remembered Zook calling Baker "Colonel." He breathed a sigh of relief as he noted the man's rank was only major.

The soldier was of medium height, fortyish, with neatly trimmed hair and beard of dark color. His soft black hat was set at a rakish angle on his head. His expression, as he came up to them, was businesslike, but not hostile. In his right hand he held Hawkins's pass.

"It says here you've got a deserter, sergeant." A flat statement in a strangely musical voice. Intense dark eyes moved from Hawkins to Joseph's face. "Name of Joseph . . ."—his eyes flicked to the paper—"King. Moving to the rear at height of battle."

His gaze fastened on Joseph like a predator's, studying him intently. A ghost of puzzlement flitted across his face, then was gone. Only blank professionalism remained. With his eyes still on Joseph, he said, "Thank you, sergeant. You may report back to General McClellan's army. Tell him your charge has been left with Major William Wood."

"Yes, sir!" Hawkins smartly saluted and pivoted to go. "Oh—" He suddenly dropped his arm and reached into his tunic. "Almost forgot. Here's the special orders on Private King. From his captain. Endorsed by General McClellan." Hawkins turned back to face the officer and handed over two sheets of paper neatly folded but rather rumpled. Joseph felt a shock of surprise and apprehension.

The major's eyes registered his surprise too. "Special orders?" he asked. "We need no help in dealing with deserters, sergeant." But he reached for the sheets.

Hawkins shrugged. "Don't know, sir. Just following orders."

"Very well, I'll have a look."

"Thank you, sir!" Hawkins's boot heels gave a slight click as he saluted again. Then he turned and was gone, without another glance at Joseph.

Joseph half turned to watch Hawkins go. His heart felt a surprising softness as he watched the middle-aged man untie the two horses. The guard closed the front door before Joseph saw Hawkins mount up. He didn't envy the sergeant his next duty and suddenly Joseph felt a furious rage at the fates that had brought on this war. It was an odd sort of fury, though, different from the fierceness that had caused his mindless charge on the field of battle. Instead, this was a sentiment that was more like the frustrated sadness of an ancient man, an emotion born of a line of disappointments and disillusionments stretching back over a lifetime of observation of human foibles and weakness. He felt the sudden awareness of insight.

He became aware, too, that Major Wood was speaking to him: "... *Mister* King, if you are quite ready!" The biting voice dripped of sarcasm. Joseph's mind snapped back to the present.

"Follow me, *please!*" The major pivoted and strode along the corridor toward a door at the rear. There was no choice but to follow, especially since both the guards had their alert eyes fixed on him, and their rifles braced across their chests, at the ready.

Joseph's final illusion that this building was a residence or a government office died when he passed through that doorway behind the officer. The brightness of the September noon, even its faded version of the entry hall, was gone in an instant with the click of the door behind him. The only light in the windowless room came from a coal-oil lamp, turned low, set on a small table in the center of the room. As he glanced around him he could see that in two of the walls had been windows, now boarded up completely. Cut into the wall directly beyond the lamp from where he stood was another door, now closed.

The table bearing the light had a hard-looking, straight-backed chair behind it. Another chair, looking even less comfortable, sat directly across the table in front of it, so close that anyone sitting on it would have a bit of a time deciding where his knees might belong.

On the table lay an old-fashioned quill pen, a bottle of ink, open-topped, and a blank sheet of paper. There were two other chairs in the room, one on either side of the door, their backs to the wall. No one else was in the room.

The officer walked behind the table and sat down. He turned up the lamp. It cast weird shadows over his face. A chill ran through Joseph.

"Sit down, King."

Joseph obeyed, deciding the tone of voice was merely severe in a professional way. He relaxed, slightly, and let his haversack slide to the floor. He discovered that the chair was nailed to the floor and that there was just enough room for his knees snug under the table. This puzzled him until he realized any occupant of the chair would be in a poor position to try any sudden moves. It began to dawn on him that he must be in some sort of interrogation room. His relaxation gave way to apprehension.

The officer across from him unfolded the special orders, tilting them the better to see the script in the light of the flame. He was silent awhile, reading, occasionally putting a note on the sheet of paper. Finally he laid down the orders and the quill. He folded his hands over them and looked at Joseph. In the lamplight his eyes gleamed darkly. For an irrelevant moment Joseph was reminded of the glistening orbs of the occasional doe he used to watch come down to the river to drink. It seemed years ago. Erratically, the thought came to him that any similarity of character traits between doe and man was highly unlikely. A smile tugged at his lips.

"Something amuse you, soldier?" An undoelike glint was suddenly in the brown eyes. The voice was cold.

"No, sir!" Joseph's smile fled.

There was a pause. Now the officer's eyes had a look of curiosity. "King, in this note to me from your Captain Zook it seems that yours is a special kind of desertion. One he thinks requires the severest kind of punishment."

It was Joseph's turn to be curious. Interest even banished anxiety, for the moment. "What was special about it, if I may ask?" Joseph queried. His mind raced, trying to recall every detail of his encounter with Captain Lawrence Zook. "What punishment?"

The major studied his face. His fingers began to rap the wooden tabletop, slowly but rhythmically. The sound was loud in the silence. Then he shook his head. "Didn't really say. Only that he saw something in your facial expression, in the set of your shoulders, or your gait, when he apprehended you, that expressed gross insubordination."

Joseph searched his memory, remembering the pain from simply walking which his wounded armpit had given. But surely a stiffness in movement couldn't be so misinterpreted. It came to him that he had felt a sensation of relief, or release, when he had dropped his pack and cast off his weapon. Would such an emotion register noticeably on his face and bearing? Had it? Or was this just the rabid imagination of an unbalanced officer? He gave his head a quick shake, in confusion.

The officer was studying him. He went on. "Zook says he can spot a fanatic a state away and he wants us to make sure you don't infect anyone else." He cleared his throat. "Also, he says, and I quote"—he glanced down at the papers—" 'I want this deserter to be handed over specifically to Colonel Baker.' " He looked at Joseph again, as if in pity.

"Who is this Colonel Baker?" Joseph asked. "Sergeant Hawkins mentioned him, too."

" 'Colonel' is his honorary title," the officer replied, not quite managing to keep the scorn completely hidden in his voice. Then a shiver seemed to go through his shoulders, and his dark eyes went past Joseph, as if searching the shadows. "He's the government's head traitor-catcher." His eyes snapped back to Joseph's. "He detests military deserters, even more than spies and seditionists. Can't say I would want to trade places with you." He laughed. It was the first time he had done so, but to Joseph it sounded melancholy.

"Will I have a trial?" Joseph asked. He suddenly felt as if a crow had walked on his grave.

The officer pushed back his chair and stood up. "That remains to be seen, private." His voice became strictly business. "Come along. Have to lock you up now." He picked up the lamp by its ornate glass base and crossed to the door between the chairs. Opening it, he held the lamp high and stepped aside. He motioned for Joseph to go ahead. When he moved to pick up his haversack, Wood snapped, "Leave it." But immediately his voice softened. "I'll go through it. Maybe we'll give it to you, later. Now go. Watch your step. Turn right and descend the staircase. There is a door at the bottom."

Joseph felt his way down the dim steps, careful not to lose his footing and plunge into an abyss that might add a broken bone to his already existing aches and pains. With each step the air seemed to grow both stuffier and cooler. In the gloom he could hear the sounds of small feet, scratching and hurrying. Then he was at the bottom. As the major came behind him he could see from the light that the door was a heavy one. It was constructed of thick oak planks with iron slats crossed over them and bolted to the wood with rusty rivets at least an inch in diameter. It looked as solid as a cliff.

Joseph's heart sank. "When will Colonel Baker be here, to see me?"

The officer dug into his tunic pocket and withdrew a huge, old skeleton key. Before replying, he inserted it in the lock and gave it a turn. "No one knows where or when he'll show up. Maybe today, or six weeks from today. He's like the wind, which bloweth where it listeth." He cleared his throat noisily as the heavy door swung open on protesting hinges. "Please enter, Private King." His voice was strained. "I'm sorry, but General McClellan's orders are to confine you to solitary. This is the only empty space in the building."

Joseph stood on the threshold and stared into the dim cellar. The man behind him gave his shoulders a gentle shove. Joseph swallowed hard. "Will I have a trial, sir?" He didn't remember until the words were already out that he'd just asked that question.

"That will be Colonel Baker's decision," the major said. His voice was firmer now, and patient. "But I would expect there to be one."

Joseph took a few steps into the damp, dark room, then he turned to face the officer. "Do I get any light, or something to read, or write on?" He made a valiant effort to conceal his sudden panic, the kind he had felt when his mother had tucked him in for the night, then stood in the doorway with the lamp, ready to leave. But he could hear the trembling in his voice. His mouth was dry.

The officer started to shake his head, then he stopped and stared at the lamp in his hand. His eyes came up and met Joseph's. Impulsively, he handed the lamp to Joseph and dug in his tunic pockets. "Here are some lucifers," he said, handing a half-dozen matches to him. "Use the light sparingly, for I doubt there'll be any more oil for you. As for reading and writing materials, ask Colonel Baker, when he comes."

As if embarrassed by his charity, the man turned brusque. "Try to prepare yourself for the worst, private. Colonel Baker will not bend over backwards to prove you innocent."

Then suddenly he was gone, pulling the heavy door shut behind him. The click of the lock was loud in the dank silence. Joseph heard the officer's boots thudding up the steps, then the solid thunk of the door at the top of the stairs, as it was closed.

Silence reigned.

13

Joseph took a long breath and let it out slowly. He held the lamp just inches above his head, as high as it would go in the low-ceilinged cellar, careful not to smash the glass chimney on the broad, massive beams the light revealed. There was no need to plan a tour of his new home. It was small enough for the lamplight to illuminate from where he stood just inside the door. Four stone walls, an earthen floor, a pervading smell of old mustiness, and a rickety old wine rack along the far wall.

Curious, he walked over to the structure to see whether there might be any bottles still in the latticework of wood slats. By moving the light about, he could just make out the deeper recesses of the yard-wide storage frame. He did not really expect to find any bottles and even if he did, he didn't figure they'd add much sunshine to the dingy cell. The drinking of alcohol was a practice heartily scorned at the King home. Although Joseph had developed a taste for beer in the past two years, he had never found wine particularly appealing. Then he noticed a dull red gleam from near the back of the rack, close to the wall.

He moved the lamp to change the angle of the light. The reddish glow didn't change. He set the lamp on the floor, his heart thumping in excitement. Eagerly, he reached with his left arm and pulled out the bottle. A cloud of dust assaulted his face and he sneezed, nearly dropping the grimy, ancient flask. From directly behind its place on the rack issued a brighter gleam, still red but with more of the color of the distilled grape. Trembling with anticipation, he reached again, and came away with another dusty bottle. Where it had been was only a patch of brilliant daylight.

A window! Joseph quickly set down the second bottle beside the first. Suddenly he just had to know about that window, how big it was, whether it could be opened. He grasped the two-by-four uprights and pulled, but gently, favoring his sores. He did not want to bring down the ancient wooden structure in pieces all around him.

The rack didn't budge. He picked up the lamp again and investigated the anchor points of the struts. They were bolted securely into both ceiling beams and thick wooden plates on the floor. Built-in, they were likely to last until rot took them, a century or two hence.

A sigh escaped him and he turned back toward the door. He yearned to sit down and observed for the first time that there was nothing in his cell even distantly suggesting a table or a chair. Despondent, he turned toward the shaft of daylight again, and now noticed that the wine rack did not cover the entire wall it stood against. There was a two-foot gap between its last tier and the far wall. He crossed to where the light could fall into that back corner.

His heart leaped. Stacked into the dim recess were several ancient and filthy kegs. He approached them carefully. There was something brittle-looking about them, as if by staring at them too long or hard he might cause their staves to collapse. He nudged the foremost barrel with his toe. Immediately, the stirring of small feet sounded out, startlingly loud. He jumped back, his heart beating a rhythm.

Joseph laughed nervously and moved forward again. This time he confidently leaned down, set the lamp on the floor, and lifted the top keg from the small pile stacked like cordwood. It came away easily, apparently empty. He lifted it to his ear and shook it. No sounds of sloshing or scraping, but a vague whiskey smell floated up and assaulted his nostrils.

Stepping back, he set the keg down near the light and thumped the top with his knuckles. He could see gnaw marks around the edge of the staves, but the container sounded solider than it looked. He set it down on end and lowered himself onto it. It held his weight.

Hurriedly now, with a spirit of optimism like salve to his spirit, he carried the drum to the middle of the cellar, then went back and got another one. That done, he set the lamp on one and sat again on the other. Like a king on his throne, Joseph gazed possessively around his domain. Only then did he notice the pile of rags crumpled into the angle of floor and wall, directly in front of him.

Curious again, he stood, walked to the pile, and probed it with his boot. He lifted the filthy-looking bundle and presently realized he was looking at an ancient pallet, his new bed. He sighed and gently shook the dirty rag. Dust cascaded into the lamplight, causing Joseph to sneeze again.

Then he was laughing. Suddenly and uncontrollably, mirth flowed out of him, like blood. It was all so sad and ridiculous. It couldn't be real, this situation he found himself in. Any moment now, they would come and get him. They'd release him with handshakes and apologetic smiles and confess it had all been a mistake. He should rejoin his regiment as soon as possible and get back to the job they were paying him for. Killing.

His laughter ended abruptly. Embarrassed, he held his breath to listen. Such an unlikely noise would bring his jailer quicker than anything. Angry this time, not compassionate. But he heard nothing except the occasional scrape and clump from overhead, where probably some other prisoner was moving about, searching for greater comfort.

He felt alone. More alone than he would have believed

possible until fifteen minutes ago. The glow of the lamp on the keg beside him did not bring any warmth to his soul. Rather, its flame cast his shadow large and ominous against the wall beside the door. He put his face in his hands and didn't even try to stifle the groan that came up from his chest like a cry. And then he was thinking of Rachel.

She would hear of this, and bring help. His parents —they would not let him sit and molder in a dark cellar for long! His spirits began to rise, but immediately they plummeted again. What could they do? What good would a preacher and a farmer's daughter be able to do when faced with the anonymous might of the modern state?

He felt a finger of despair poke at his heart. Into his mind's eye came Rachel's face as he remembered her at the station in Kalamazoo. As clearly as if they were still together, he could see the naked love in her eyes. And he could see his own face, as if with her vision, showing his impatience, his eagerness to be gone.

The finger touching his heart multiplied itself and became a fist, gripping tightly with an icy grasp. He felt weak and he tottered over to the keg and sat down again. Self-pity swept over him. He stared straight ahead at the stone wall. His mind went slack. He felt like crying. Fear rose in him like a flood, sweeping every other consideration before it. How could anyone exist like this? How could a human being go on living in a dark, subterranean hole, without fresh air, sunshine?

How long until he broke and went crazy?

And then the tears did come. In a daze Joseph got up and stumbled to the limp rags that were his bed. He fell to his knees and smoothed out the filthy material, as well as possible with his shaking fingers. He lowered himself to the makeshift bed face down, cradling his face in his arms. He let the tears soak into his tunic material. He didn't care anymore, about anything.

More than any conscious willing of himself back into control, pain brought him back. His shirt and coat tightened across his torn back as he folded his arms for a pillow. The hurt forced him to take steps to focus on his physical condition.

He pushed himself up to arm's length and struggled to a sitting position. His fingers rapidly undid the buttons of his tunic, then he carefully peeled off the coat. Immediately his back felt better and he wondered why he hadn't thought of removing it sooner.

The improvement to his physical well-being caused his spirits to brighten perceptibly and suddenly he was ashamed of his lapse into self-pity. Fear was still present, of course, but he determined to deal with it in a manly fashion. He almost smiled. Amazing what positive results in one's mood could follow from even a slight reduction in bodily pain.

He folded his tunic neatly and, crouching, laid it at one end of the bed. "If it doesn't get too cold in here at night," he said aloud, "at least I'll have a pillow."

The sound of his voice startled him. It also comforted his spirit. He chuckled. "Well, Joseph King, if you are the only company I've got, then I don't doubt you'll be hearing more of my voice!" He laughed. "Or should I say *your* voice?" Again he chuckled. And suddenly his cell seemed cozy, the lamplight a warm glow, his cask seat an easy chair.

A key rattled in the lock and the heavy door creaked open. Startled, Joseph leaped to his feet. Major Wood entered, carrying a tray. Behind him, holding a lamp, stood a man Joseph hadn't seen before.

"Chow time, King," Wood said. On the tray sat a bowl and a mug, each issuing a head of steam. There was also a lump of hardtack. Joseph's nostrils fairly twitched at the aroma of coffee. His empty stomach did a little jig. "I see you've already found yourself some furniture," Wood said, with a wry smile. He carried the tray and set it on the keg Joseph had been using as a chair. The lamp-bearer remained in the doorway.

"Thanks," Joseph said. He'd forgotten how many hours it had been since he'd eaten, and Hannah's soup had not satisfied him for long. He reached out for the bowl. A battered pewter spoon lay beside it.

"Ye'd better wait to bestow yer gratitude till ya done partook of it. I've met some hawgs what'd turn their snouts up at that swill. Hee hee." It came from the man in the doorway. His voice sounded like gravel being swished in a pan.

Joseph looked at him closely for the first time. He saw a tall, cadaverous man in his late twenties or early thirties, with black hair hanging in oily strings down past cheeks that seemed hollowed by illness or want. In the lamplight his complexion was sallow—what could be seen of it—for he had a thicket of a moustache on his lip, and several days' growth of scraggly beard covering his face. His eyes were set deep but huge and darkly gleaming in the lamp glow, like a bird of prey. When he laughed Joseph saw that several of his front teeth were missing.

"Shut up, Zack," Wood said, without looking back at him. His voice was petulant.

Zack's slack lips closed in a sneer and Joseph saw the gimlet eyes flicker with hatred. He shivered, involuntarily.

"Cold, King?" Wood asked. His mouth curved in a wry smile again. "It's only noon, now. Wait until nighttime, when the damp and the rats come out." He said it not unkindly, but Zack's few teeth glinted through his moustache again.

Joseph said nothing. He took the bowl and spoon in his left hand and went into the crouch characteristic of the soldier around his campfire. If he was careful, he could use his right hand to manipulate the spoon. The two men stood and watched him. He tasted the contents of the bowl. It was soup from salted pork, fairly brackish, but he'd tasted worse. He picked up the rocklike piece of hardtack, tapped it the obligatory several times on the tray—all soldiers soon learned how to dispense with weevils—and dipped it in the broth. His eyes met Zack's as he bit into the bread. The man's mouth was hanging open, his eyes wide in the lamplight.

Wood laughed. "You must be famished, King. Not many prisoners take to Zack's cooking so quickly." He glanced over his shoulder at Zack, then back at Joseph. "Nosirree. I reckon you are an exception." He laughed again. "But I'll wager you'll find the coffee all right. Zack makes that for all of us, and if he wasn't a better coffee cooker than he is a chef, why he'd soon be back out on the battlefield again!" Still laughing, he spoke over his shoulder. "Isn't that right, Private Zachary Winfield Washington?"

"Yessir," grated Zack, "I reckon that's right, sir." It was said obsequiously, but again Joseph saw the hate glinting in the man's eyes.

"Well," Wood said, dusting his palms together. "You just finish off that swill and Zack'll pick up the dishes when he brings you supper." He turned and walked back to the cell door, where he turned to face Joseph again. "If it's any comfort to you, King, I've reported your incarceration to the War Office. They said they'll be wiring your family in the next day or two." He smiled, but it suddenly seemed to Joseph—for no reason he could put his finger on—that there was something weak about the man. He glanced at Zack once before the two men left. Wood was already out, and Zack turned and looked over his shoulder at Joseph. In his brooding eyes was a speculative look. Then his mouth twisted around the yellow teeth in a smirk that made a cold finger slide down Joseph's spine.

* * *

Joseph was almost glad to see Zack again when he brought his evening meal, in spite of the sinister aspect of the man. It had been a long afternoon. Very long. The broth and coffee had warmed him, cheering his soul through his stomach. Sunshine, too, had brightened his spirits when it penetrated his dank cell through the small grimy windowpane as the sun rotated into the west. He had even initiated a project, trying to reach the glass with a long piece of splintered wood he had twisted from the wine rack. He'd hoped to be able to push the window open, for fresh air. It hadn't been too difficult to reach the glass through the slates, but it hadn't budged. He was careful not to smash it. There was no telling whether the nights got cold, especially if he were to be confined here, perish the thought, into winter. He did not need a draft from a window he'd not be able to close again.

After eating, drinking, working on the window, beating his bed to get out as much of the residual dust and vermin as possible, there had still been many hours to pass. He battled with the goblin of self-pity again. And the faces: Rachel. His parents. Grandma King. Red. The sightless gaze of the boy, with the bloody eye socket. . . .

His thoughts were disjointed. He lacked the will to force his mind into orderly channels. And there was the fear, and the pain. Then the fear *of* the pain. The anxiety that nurse Hannah's medication would eventually go corrupt, and infection would take him. That fear had worked on him more than any other notion for most of the interminable afternoon.

He'd heard the horror tales of boys dying from slight wounds because they hadn't been treated properly or soon enough. But he hadn't seen any of it himself, not having been in combat before. True, he'd had good care, himself.

183

God bless the overworked, battlefield doctor, and sweet, selfless Hannah Campbell! If it hadn't been for them, what shape would he be in by now?

Even so, as the day wore on, and the westering sun shot its first rays into his dungeon, thin as fork tines, he had felt the soreness of his body multiply itself. Shooting pains up and down his back. Hollow aches in his armpit. Throbbing in his head.

Or was it only his imagination? If so, did it matter whether it was? He'd read once, some new theory or ancient one resurrected as modern medicine, that one could *will* oneself better, or worse. The notion had caused him to rotate his right arm experimentally, telling himself the agony was not really as bad as it *felt*. But afterward his right hand hadn't stopped trembling for at least fifteen minutes. It made him realize he wouldn't be able to use it for a long time, even for something as minor as wielding a pen.

That notion had caused the faces of his family, and Rachel, to swim into his consciousness again. He must write to them. But how could he? The wire the War Department would send (*if* they sent it; in wartime such little things could easily get overlooked) would doubtless cause more worry at home than reassurance. Joseph vowed he would demand paper and pen when his jailers next showed up.

There had still been more hours to endure, after he had made that vow. He had lain down, on his back this time, to watch the slow progress of the sunbeam. Carefully, to be sure, but he had ordered his body not to feel the pain of his lacerated back. And once he'd gotten flat and stopped inching around for better comfort, it had not gone too badly. He mentally blessed Hannah again.

He'd thought of how he would spend the hours, if his stay lengthened. It was still beyond his imagination that he'd remain confined here for more than several days, at the most a week or two. He wouldn't let his mind push that far ahead. It was like trying to imagine the everlasting life his father always talked about. Your mind could only handle so much timelessness, then it would feel as if it were bending out of shape, like a bow being stretched too far.

He had just gotten up and begun to pace his cell when Zack brought supper. There was no Major Wood this time. Zack opened the door just a crack, cautiously, as if he expected Joseph to be waiting behind it with an axe or sledgehammer. It wasn't a foolish precaution, Joseph decided. He'd blown out his lamp when the sun light had come to visit, but to someone from outside, the cell would seem quite dark.

"Stand in the middle 'o the room, deserter!" Zack called out. His voice made Joseph's skin crawl. "Out whar I kin see ya!"

When Joseph had complied with the order, Zack entered, the supper tray in one hand, lamp in the other. Warily, his luminous eyes hard on Joseph, he moved to the keg and set down the tray, then quickly stepped back a couple of yards. His free hand immediately dropped to rest on the holstered pistol.

"Dig in, reb," he rasped. "It's my 'welcome-to-O.C.-meal!' " He threw back his head and guffawed. Joseph saw his hairy Adam's apple bob up and down in the scrawny neck.

"What is it?" Joseph asked, as he stepped closer to the steaming plate.

"Why roast rat, o' course!" The Adam's apple bobbed again.

Joseph felt his stomach do a swan dive toward his bowels. "Ah—ah, no, thanks, I—" He swallowed.

Zack was promptly sober. "My cookin' ain't good enough fer ya, hunh?" He took a quick step toward Joseph, at the same time raising his lamp so its light fell on his face. For the first time, Joseph noticed a long, jagged scar, tracing a whitish-purple path from his chin and around the mouth to the corner of his left eye. It gave him an even more sinister aspect than his eyes had, when Joseph first saw Zack. "Ya think yer too good fer this prison, that it? Hunh?" He cackled loudly and took another step forward. "Well, I don't! Yer just a deserter—that's what ya be! Ya don't deserve to *live*!" He punctuated his final sentence with a swift kick at the keg the tray was sitting on. Whiskey keg, tray, and its steaming plate, mug, and spoon went flying. They landed directly on top of Joseph's rag bed.

"Why you—" Joseph bellowed, springing for Zack with his hands curled into claws.

Zack was quicker. He threw the lamp at Joseph and, in the same instant, grabbed at his pistol and flung himself backward toward the door.

Joseph dodged the lamp, lost his balance, and fell heavily against the wall. From reflex he used his right arm to catch himself. Instantly, as his body crushed his arm against the rough stones, a galaxy of bright stars exploded in his brain. With a whimper, he sagged to the dirt floor. There was a roaring in his ears louder than cannon fire. His head spun, and he started to cradle his face in his hands, but he could barely move his right one up to his face. It was shaking violently.

Gradually, as the thunder in his ears subsided, he became aware that Zack was yelling at him.

"Ya ever try that again, reb, 'n ye'll be deader'n a mackerel!"

Joseph raised his eyes, slowly, agonizingly, and stared into the vast tunnel of Zack's pistol, inches from his face. The man's face, sighting down the barrel just beyond the yawning muzzle, looked ghoulish in the greater gloom that had abruptly descended with the breaking of the lamp.

"And so yer really a fighter, after all?" Zack's lips curled in a sneer. "Mebbe the major'll want to know that." He laughed tauntingly. "He said yer a passafist!"

Joseph felt sick with shame. He dropped his eyes. The waves of pain were receding, but inside his gut he felt like a traitor.

Zack released the hammer of his pistol and stood up straight. "Waal, I reckon ya'll be a-goin' to bed tonight without yer supper." Joseph heard the sound of the gun sliding into a leather holster. "Serve ya right if'n ya had to miss a few more meals!"

Joseph looked up quickly as Zack moved toward the door again. The thin beam of sunshine momentarily caught and held the holstered pistol, glinting malevolently in the golden glow. Then Zack turned to pull the door wider and step through it. But he paused and spoke once more.

"An' here I was going to tell you, if'n you was a good boy, all about your trial. . . ." There was a steely glint in his eye, just visible in the gloom of the doorway.

Joseph's breath caught in his throat. "My trial?"

Then Zack pulled the heavy door to with a loud slam. Joseph could thinly hear his loud, rusty laughter as he clumped up the steps.

* * *

The rest of his first day in prison was a torment for Joseph, in his bouncing to and fro between anxiety, hope, then near despair. For long minutes after his jailer left, with his last words hanging like a garland of promise in the dark, dank cell, Joseph's heart pounded in a crazy tattoo of pain and hope. "My trial!" he said, aloud, finally.

His mind raced. When? How soon? Will I be able to get out of here? What all is involved? Will Captain Zook be present? Sergeant Hawkins? Colonel Baker? He'd never been to a trial and didn't really know how trials went.

Mennonites tried to avoid going to a court of law, so he had largely ignored trials and lawyers and such.

Lawyers. He knew enough, from school days, to realize that the accused were always supposed to have a lawyer to defend their rights. Would he be given a lawyer? And witnesses? Didn't the person charged with a crime usually have persons to speak up for him in court? Who would be mine?

A chill went through him as he asked himself that last question. There wasn't anyone left from his regiment who'd known him closely. He, Joseph, felt as if he had personally disposed of one of them, the boy, who hadn't really known Joseph anyhow. And Red. He'd had his life snuffed out because he'd raised his head to call to Joseph. And P.C. What had become of him by now? Fat chance Zook would let him come to a trial, anyhow.

The raw feeling deepened. Joseph stared at the door. The sunbeam had climbed off the dusty floor and was halfway up the scarred oaken planks. It wouldn't be long until the sun set. He shook his head, gently. Must've been sitting here longer than I realized, he mused. Gotta light my lamp.

He struggled to his feet. The effort started up the tortuous tattoo again. He leaned against the wall to let his head clear. Working his right shoulder, ever so gently, he felt stickiness under his arm. He probed carefully inside his shirt with the fingers of his left hand. They came away with an ugly mix of pus and blood.

Frantic, he tore off his shirt to check the damage. He stumbled into the sunbeam for better vision. No, the bandage Hannah Campbell had skillfully applied was still secure and neat, but messy fluids had soaked through. For a panicky second, Joseph was on the point of ripping off the dressing—for what purpose he couldn't have said—but better sense prevailed. He knew he had no clean bandage to replace it with.

While his shirt was off he reached with his left arm to investigate his back. His fingers encountered no stickiness or wetness there. "At least I'm still in one piece in my rear," he said, aloud.

A bubble of humor rose to the surface of his mind, at that. It didn't quite burst into a smile, but it dispelled his panic. He shrugged into his shirt again, wrinkling his nose at the unpleasant smell of it. As he buttoned it, he noticed the last of the sunlight was climbing over the crack at the top of the door. He knew its path across the ceiling and back to its source would be rapid. Already he felt the chill of coming night. For a moment he debated whether to save his tunic as a pillow, or wear it for greater warmth. He decided on the latter course.

Until he picked it off the bed. Whatever had been on the plate Zack had brought, as well as the coffee, had now thoroughly soaked his raggy bed, his coat, as well as the dust for a foot or two around the cloth. Joseph almost laughed, in his dismay. "Probably doused my matches, too!" he said, bitterly.

Fortunately, he had laid them beside the lamp on the other keg. Zack's kick had not disturbed Joseph's own lamp. Now he struck a match and lit the lamp Wood had left him. The soft yellow flame added more light than Joseph expected. He realized the sunbeam was nearly gone.

In the fresh illumination, Joseph felt better. He decided to ignore his fear over his wound, just force it out of his mind. He did not know whether he would be able to control his thinking as time went by, but he'd make a valiant beginning at least. He would start by taking stock, by making his head rule his heart, by applying a bit of that commodity so valued and preached by his father: self-discipline.

He picked up the articles kicked over by Zack. The keg had withstood the booted assault without caving in. This

Joseph set upright again, then retrieved the tray, plate, and mug. His stomach did a slow turn when he thought of roasted rat, but there was no denying he was getting quite hungry. And his regret over the wasted coffee was sharp. Worry flickered through him as he remembered Zack's crack about missing a few more meals. But there was his just-made vow to put head over heart. Put "stomach" along with "heart," he thought. And laughed.

The sound of it startled him, yet cheered him too. "I'll have to remember to laugh regularly," he said to himself. "Maybe even work out a schedule: laugh once every hour on the hour." He practiced it again, and kept chuckling as he bent to pick up the bits of broken lamp chimney, sparkling like stars where they reflected the light of his glowing lamp.

"Hullo, what's this!" he exclaimed softly as he stooped to retrieve a larger shining piece near the wine rack. It was the glass reservoir of Zack's lamp, largely whole yet and still containing most of its oil. It had fallen in such a way as to minimize breakage. "Thank heaven for small favors," Joseph whispered, almost reverently.

Carefully, he picked up the globe and tilted it upright. About three inches of kerosene remained. He set it down next to the keg his lamp sat on, making sure it didn't leak.

There was nothing left to do now so Joseph sat on his keg and fell to his new task with purpose, using his will to keep his mind on an even keel. He sat with his back as straight as was allowed by the rubbing of bandage against rawness. He decided he would begin his taking stock by simply listing the pros and cons of his situation.

First there was the hope of the trial, for that definitely was a positive. Without a trial all he could look forward to was rotting. Then there was the fact that his back seemed to be healing. At least its discomfort was not horribly painful anymore. Add to these two that he had a lamp, a fresh supply of oil, some lucifers, and don't forget a window that gave him afternoon sunshine. Tack on to the growing list that he had been assured that his loved ones would receive a telegram so they wouldn't have to worry as much. Don't forget that there's not been any cruelty here, that Wood seems a decent chap, and Zack—well, Zack is still a puzzle. Put him down in a separate column: "to be decided."

Joseph smiled to himself when he came to his last so-called plus. It was the best one, the one that sustained all the other "goods," and reduced the impact of the negatives. He had not thought of it much because he'd been too busy. Hah! That sounded odd. Busy, in this place! But his consciousness had been too busy at least. It was his decision. His desertion on the grounds that he must object, by conscience, to the horrible carnage that war brought to the mind and body of mankind.

Yes, the greatest positive of his being here was that it was the logical result of his moral choice. His decision to eschew violence and rejoin the fold of nonresistant Mennonitism gave his life a new meaning. It gave his present circumstances a slant far different, at least in his own eyes, than if he had merely been a criminal, jailed for giving in to greed or lust or dishonesty.

Joseph was beginning to feel good. It was easy, now, to ignore pain and fear, all those baser emotions and feelings. His father was right. Self-discipline, self-control, that was the best pol—

And then his neat little card-house of vanity came crashing down as he remembered his attack on Zack. He remembered Zack's words, and the accompanying, taunting laugh: ". . . you're a pacifist!" Mortification swept through him like a storm of fire in a dried-out pasture. What kind of an example was that, a physical attack on a man who obviously held him in contempt already? A fine specimen of Mennonite Christianity he was, Joseph King, the preacher' son, who deserted for conscience' sake!

Once again he felt sick in his soul. His good intentions fell aside and he realized as he never had in his life how weak he was. How undeserving of any good thing he would be, if somehow he got out of this mess by dint of lawyers or intercession by family. He would deserve it if he were convicted of treason and executed, or left to rot in this cell.

With a sigh that seemed to echo despair, Joseph rose and straightened out his bed. Wet as it might be, he would lie in it, force his body to suffer. He blew out the lamp. He didn't want to see anymore. There was just enough of pale sunset left to find his way onto his damp pallet. He lay down with another sigh. As he settled himself, there came into his mind, like a magical string of moving pictures, the faces of his family, of the members of his father's church, of Rachel.

He felt, suddenly, as if he were already in hell. It was the place for weakness. It was just deserts for people who took a stand one day only to betray it the next. The faces were seen from afar, across an abyss. They smiled at him. Rachel smiled, in his mind's eye, and it was like a hopelessly beautiful sunrise, or a blooming flower. In that moment, when he knew it was too late, he realized that he loved her. That he always had.

Joseph King hoped to God for one last thing, even as he knew that prison was the name for the death of hope. He hoped that God would grant him one more thing—to listen to a wretched soul. And he prayed.

14

Joseph came awake gradually, not knowing or caring the exact moment when consciousness returned. That was normal now. Over the past weeks his dreams had begun to occur even when he was awake, so there was no clear break between slumber and wakefulness. Even the frequent squeaking of rodents did not serve as his alarm clock because that high-pitched sound came in his dreams, too, and it was only when a rat crept boldly over his arm or his leg in the dark that he knew for certain whether he was awake. Then he would jerk the insulted limb to his chest, his heart thumping.

At other times he would be pulled from his sleep by the bar of sunshine, striking his face from outside the cage of his window. He would know for sure that was no dream. In his dreams there was mostly darkness, or uniform dreary gray. But because the window faced the west, the sunshine never woke him in the morning.

It was the sun that woke him now. As awareness seeped through his brain, he felt the warmth against his chest, creeping along his throat, up over his stubbled cheek as if to add to the fever that now was always like a poorly tended furnace beneath his skin. Seconds before he knew the beam would hit his eyelids, his eyes came open. Reluctantly, for it had been the first good dream in many sleeps. No bullets or bayonets. No blood or screams.

Only Rachel. As she'd been on that afternoon at the Kalamazoo station a hundred years ago.

He swallowed hard. The effort of forcing saliva down his inflamed throat made his eyes close again. He rolled out of the sunshine and pulled up into a sitting position, gripping his knees, his seat in the dust. Uninterrupted now, the sunbeam shot true and straight across the floor, jutting off at a weird angle against the closed door. Particles he'd disturbed danced wildly in the bar of light before gradually settling back to the universe of their fellows on the floor.

Joseph sneezed. Any moment now they'd be feeding him, he thought. Like an animal in the zoo. He studied the distance from the center door hinge to the outside edge of the sunshaft. It must be about six. Without a clock, he had grown accustomed to telling the hour by the angle of the sunshine. It had changed, slightly, since the first days, showing the advancing of the season. Or was it just that they didn't always bring him his meals at the exact hour of each day?

It didn't really matter, yet it mattered a great deal. Both at the same time. Every day was exactly the same as the day before it, yet it maddened him that he didn't know the date. He hadn't started to keep count of the passing days until a week had passed. Or had it been two? What difference did it make? Except that one morning he suddenly had a compulsion to keep track of the march of time. He had begun his calendar, simple finger strokes in the loose dirt back in the corner where he'd found his kegs. But by then an uncounted number of days had elapsed, so he had no idea whether he had been taking up cell space for two weeks, four weeks, or more. There were now sixteen marks in the dust. Or was it twenty-six?

What did it matter?

He heard heavy footsteps descending the steps outside his door. He hoisted himself to his feet, brushing the dust from his trousers, gripping the stones to steady himself. The dizziness came again, as it did after every quick movement.

The key rattled in the lock. The heavy door groaned open. Zack came in with the tin plate and the cup on the tray. Steam curled from both. All was the same. Habit was king.

"Chow time, deserter," called the gravel voice. The gimlet eyes drilled into Joseph's. "Beefsteak 'n mushrooms agin, with a hot toddy ta chase it down!" The hair-covered lip lifted off the yellow teeth in the familiar smirk.

Joseph took the dishes from the man. "Thanks, Zack," he said, in a monotone. "Much obliged."

Joseph stepped back and sat on the wooden cask, the tray across his knees. It had become the standard procedure since the beginning, when Zack's boot had hurled the precious chow off the cask. And Joseph had gone through three days with little water and no food. It hadn't made a particle of difference in the treatment he got that he had apologized to Zack, three days later. The tattered, vulgar man had simply taken the apology as his due. The smirk never left his face.

Joseph took a sip of the steaming coffee. It burned in his raw throat like acid. Yet somehow it felt good. Tears came to his eyes. His hand shaking, he set the cup down on the tray.

"Hee hee," his jailer chuckled. "Reckon it be a mite hot, ain't it?" He made no move either to withdraw or advance further into the cell. It was a ritual Joseph had come to expect.

He raised the tin dish to his lips and scooped the contents into his mouth, with his fingers. He never knew what became of the pewter spoon, but he surmised Zack preferred to watch Joseph use his fingers. The meat was as far from beefsteak as Washington city was from victory, but Joseph had learned not to debate the merits of Zack's nomenclature. He didn't care anymore. He closed his eyes as the food rasped down his gullet. Funny, he thought, how a person doesn't really get used to pain.

He opened his eyes and stared in surprise. Zack had moved to within a yard of him. In reaction Joseph rose and took a half step backward. Such a move on Zack's part broke the routine, the pattern. What was going on?

The keg tipped over as his foot caught it. He fell heavily, on his right arm of course, the tray clattering to the ground. Pain danced behind his eyes as his tender arm crushed behind him.

"Sorta clumsy, ain't ya?" Zack's face moved into the sunbeam. Joseph saw the leathery skin around the man's eyes scrunch into lines of mirth. "Ain't no reason to be afeared, King. Come a tad more time, and they'll be atakin' ya to trial!"

His long, skinny arm shot out and retrieved the fallen mug and reached for the plate. He didn't even bother to watch the prisoner.

Joseph came to his feet shakily. He'd dumped the mug and now he stared at the finger of steam that curled from a wet spot in the dust where the coffee had soaked away. He licked his lips and swallowed, wincing, trying not to think of the agonizing comfort of the hot drink.

All the while he kept a tight rein on his heart. It was just some more of the same. Zack had been spouting "trial" for so long now all it showed was his lack of imagination. A creative jailer would have devised a new torture by now.

Joseph couldn't risk it, though. "Trial? When?" He cleared his throat. He couldn't risk it. Maybe *this* time Zack wasn't crying wolf.

"Oh, soon enough, I reckon." Zack cackled and backed toward the open door, hoisting the tray to one shoulder. "Any day now, I 'spect." Then he stepped outside and slammed the door.

Joseph's shoulders drooped, along with his spirit. No use, he thought. There'll never be a trial. He stood for a long moment, then turned and walked back to his calendar.

His head felt light and his throat hurt. Under his right shoulder something wet trickled out and ran slowly down his rib cage. The bandage which had wrapped his chest had long since been torn up and stuffed into the hole under his arm that never fully healed. The scabs on his back were gone but the armpit was a cauldron of fire and slipperiness. It reached its tentacles out into Joseph's body, weakening him, causing his will to sag even further.

He knelt and let his fingers trace the shallow furrows that marked his days. His eyes were dry, his lips slack. His heart pounded in his head. He rose again and went to his bed.

It was a day like all the others. Joseph lay on his pallet and slept, most of the time. He'd never have believed a body could sleep so much. It left him numb and acted like a narcotic to his pain. A small part of his mind told him he should devise some sort of project to keep himself busy. An even smaller portion of his consciousness scolded him, then made him feel guilty for not working out the meaning of his incarceration. And sometimes when he'd been awake several hours or was having trouble falling back to sleep at night, he worked over his choice that had caused him to flee from the battlefield. But he didn't have enough energy anymore even to think that through systematically. He guessed it was his lingering embarrassment about waxing violent towards Zack that kept him from trying harder.

It was easy, too, to make excuses. Easier just about every day. He didn't have a Bible, so he couldn't be expected to come up with chapter and verse to put down some solid foundation beneath his impulsive stand, back there at South Mountain. Also, there wasn't anybody to talk with, or should he say to talk against? Joseph's mind had always been better able to build arguments when there was someone to argue back. Sort of like pushing weights to build muscle. Without resistance, life gets flabby.

Mostly, he knew, he was just coasting and he blamed it on the sickness. The sore that would get a scab and feel like healing would then pop open and drain for a day or two. Every time. He'd given up asking Zack for a doctor, or at least a nurse. Wood never came back, after that first day, so there was no appeal there. It left Joseph feeling low, and he wouldn't have wanted anyone to see him, or smell him for that matter, the way he'd become. He even tried hard not to think about his loved ones anymore. It made him want to cry, in weakness and in shame. And when he prayed to God, it really did make him cry.

And then one day, with neither a by-your-leave nor advance word, Rachel came. It was a rainy afternoon, full of the scents of approaching autumn. Joseph was lying on his bed, staring at the gray light lurking in the wine rack, and feeling some better than he had in a while. Two or three days earlier he'd suddenly had a memory come to him about the disinfectant properties of wine. He had long ago stashed the two bottles he'd found back in the rack, but now he had excitedly opened one of them, lay down, and poured half of the contents over his armpit. It had burned but he'd been hilarious. If the boys back at the Vicksburg Saloon could have seen such waste of a good beverage!

It must have worked because when he woke that morning, earlier than usual—another plus—he seemed better than he had since he'd been left without victuals those three days. He had used up one whole bottle and reduced the second to less than half full, but his fever seemed to be down.

So he was alert when the sound of two sets of footsteps came down the steps. He froze, then came slowly to his feet. Was it Colonel Baker, at long last? He'd almost forgotten about the promised villain, but now suddenly as the key rattled in the lock, his heart raced.

Then the door swung open, slowly, creakingly, and she

was standing there, looking at him. Behind her was Zack, his eyes glowing like a cat's in the reflection from his shoulder-high lamp.

"Rachel?. . ." He took a step forward, his left arm coming up. Then his illness swept back in a rush of dizziness. He felt himself falling.

"Oh—Joseph!" She rushed to him, dropping her bundle and reaching for him.

His last sensation was of the sweet, familiar fragrance of her as her arms went round his head and shoulders. She caught him, sagging to the keg with his weight. She straightened his crumpled legs on the floor as best she could, then hugged him tightly to her bosom. Her trembling fingers stroked his hair, passed down his cheek, unfamiliar in its new, full beard. A wracking sob escaped her lips. She turned and glared at Zack.

"Please leave us," she almost hissed. Even in the dim lamp light her green eyes flashed.

Zack stood immobile. The smirk faltered on his lips.

"Get out! We'll not be going anywhere!" This time her voice was clear and intense.

Zack stared at her, his mouth working. Abruptly, he set the lamp on the dirt floor, as if its handle were suddenly burning his hand. He tore off his cloth cap and crumpled it in one hand, somehow managing a combination of bow and salute with the other. "Yes'm, miz. Pardon me, miss!"

He nearly ran out, and pulled the door shut behind him.

A second later, it opened again. He stuck his head in. "Be right outside, miss."

Rachel barely heard. A tear slid unheeded down her cheek, tickling her nose, but with no response. Her hands held and stroked. Her heart felt too big for her chest.

For a long time she sat, holding and caressing the man she had come to realize meant more to her than life itself. For a long time she felt only happiness, the hugeness of joy swelling her like a balloon, filling with hot air beneath her ribs.

He was alive!

As if waiting to feel the words in her heart next to his ear, Joseph stirred. He gathered his limbs to sit up straight, then she felt him flinch.

Fear shot through her. She pushed his face back, to meet her eyes. "Joseph—are you hurt?"

The fog of pain slowly cleared from his eyes. He gave her a crooked smile. "Nothing that'll make any difference in fifty years."

"Oh, Joseph!" Then she was crying. Not just a tear now, but a flood of feeling. Her arms tightened about his shoulders, but she felt herself crumbling. She was hardly aware of him moving, but presently he was the one holding her, pulling her up as he stood, until she was virtually hanging from him with her arms around his neck. Sobs racked her body.

Joseph only held her tighter, burying his face in her hair. After what seemed to be half a lifetime, he pushed her gently to arm's length. "Let me look at you, Rachey." His voice was like warm honey. Her heart raced wildly, in new beautiful knowledge. "You are quite a sight for starved eyes you know."

"Oh pish!" Embarrassed, she pulled away from him and patted her hair. Her dress was mud-spattered from her ride. "I must look a sight!"

"Yes, that you do, my dear friend." He laughed and was startled at the sound of it. "But the best sight I have had since Zack started combing his beard." He glanced around. "Where is he, anyway?"

"I sent him out."

"You *what*?"

"I told him to leave us alone."

Joseph laughed again, a long flowing chuckle. He was

sounding stronger by the minute. It felt mighty good. "I've been here I don't know how many weeks and if I'd ever tried that, they'd have had my head examined, with me still alive!"

He sobered abruptly. "What happened, Rache? The last thing I remember was you stepping—"

"You were so glad to see me, you swooned." Her eyes were glowing and her voice was bright. But now that she was slowly descending to the plane of normal human existence, his question chilled her. What *had* they done to him? She would never in a hundred years expect someone like her Joseph to *faint*!

As she looked hungrily up at him, he reached with his right hand to brush at his eyes, as if pushing away cobwebs. She saw him wince, and quickly drop his arm to his side. She noticed what seemed to be a tattered, filthy bandage, for the first time.

"Your arm—what is wrong, Joseph?" She reached for it. Her touch brought a sharp intake of breath from him. "Oh my darling!"

"Gunshot," he whispered. "Only flares up once in a while now." But the familiar, feverish dizziness swept over him. He lurched toward the keg. She grabbed for him, but he sat down heavily and laid his head on his good arm, resting it on his knees.

"Here, let me see it." Efficiently but gently, Rachel loosened his shirt buttons and peeled the rotting garment from his chest and shoulders. She almost fainted at the sight of his pallor and the emaciation of his body.

She gingerly touched the skin around his right shoulder, surprised to find it hot and dry. Her exploring fingers brushed the rawness under his shoulder. He shivered, then his whole body began to shake.

"Oh, Joseph," she cried. She bit her lip to control her tears. "Hasn't this wound been attended to?"

He shook his head. "Not since I got here."

Rachel turned away, struggling for control. Her pulse throbbed. She covered her agitation by reaching under the hem of her dress, lifting it, and tearing off a long strip of petticoat.

"Here," she said. "Let me bandage that."

She went about the task with the utmost gentleness mingled with a deftness that surprised her, although she felt all thumbs. She heard Joseph's sharp inhalation when her hands touched him and was aware of his holding his breath until she had finished. But with his exhalation came the flicker of a grin. His eyes locked on hers.

In that look was the memory of the togetherness of other places, other times. Suddenly she knew she'd been right to come. Right in her journeying to her man, even when there had been no formal understanding between them.

Joseph's grin widened. "Feels better, nurse." He worked his shoulder carefully. "Best I've felt since Johnny's bullet first made its mark." He started to rise.

"No." She pushed him back, careful to touch only his left shoulder. "You stay put, young man! You have a fever and Lord knows what you have been keeping your strength up with."

She came around to face him squarely. "Now, if you feel up to it, I want to hear all that's happened to you." She backed off a couple of paces so he didn't have to look up. "Start from the day you left me—I mean, uh, from the time you left Michigan."

He grinned at her catching herself. "You don't want to hear all that, all the boring nonsense we had to put up with the first weeks." He glanced at the closed door. "Besides," he went on, his smile dying, "I doubt that Zack will leave us alone much longer."

At that moment, as if on cue, the jailer opened the door and poked his head inside.

"Just five minutes more. Please!" Rachel's voice was sharp and petulant. Zack disappeared like a scolded puppy, slamming the door.

"Wow—remind me never to get you mad at me!" Joseph chuckled.

Rachel made a face at him. She stepped close to him again and her touch was like butterfly wings on his cheeks. He saw the tenderness in her eyes, and he knew she would never address him in that tone.

She tilted his chin up with her delicate finger. "Tell me why you are in here, Joseph King."

She remembered the notion that had come to her, back in Michigan, and how she'd let it grow and blossom into a scheme on the train. When the days following the arrival of the telegram had grown into weeks with no word from or about Joseph, she had decided finally, in desperation, to jump on the train and go to be with him. She knew her mother had kin in Washington city. They had come to visit in Michigan, years ago. Rachel had practically forced Isabel to "warn" them that she was coming to the district. Mrs. Miller had been adamantly opposed, saying Rachel was better off by far forgetting any jailbird of a beau. She'd always known he'd never amount to much, with a father like Ben.

But Rachel had dug in her heels, and given her mother so little rest, that Isabel finally had promised to write her cousin in the capital. She had peevishly informed Rachel that her cousin's husband had recently become a close adviser to the president. Joseph's being a deserter, and in prison, would just get the whole family in hot water with Mr. Lincoln, so she was doing it against her better judgment.

Rachel had been amazed and delighted to learn that she had relatives who knew the president. She was a little hurt that her mother had never told her before. And that was when Rachel hatched a scheme. She'd had sense enough to keep it from her mother. It was too soon to tell Joseph, most likely she'd raise hopes that would then be dashed, for herself and for him. It was also unlikely Mr. Lincoln would even listen to her, let alone give her an audience.

Her eyes fastened on his, expectantly, and he began, in a low voice, speaking quickly. He skipped lightly over the details of the march from Frederick, the fight in the gap, the hell at the meadow and on the road. Since his abrupt exit from the field of battle, with all its meaning, the events that had preceded his decision felt buried in some distant, deep place in his mind, deeper now than his conscious memory wanted to probe. In the telling of it, to Rachel, he felt he was becoming a different person. This new man was the only one he wanted to be when he was with her, for now and in the remainder of his days.

He wasn't sure how to describe that leaving experience, the insight which had made him turn his back on war. Yet he knew it was from that point in his life that he must spell out the words as deliberately and painstakingly as he could. The new creature he was becoming, through the cauldron of decision and imprisonment, was a man that Rachel would not know. But one she would want to know, he hoped. Oh, God, how suddenly and prayerfully he hoped!

His voice stopped when he reached the moment in his story where he'd deserted. Zack's lamp burned steadily, casting its light from its resting place near the door. It threw one side of Rachel's face in shadow, yet both her eyes burned brightly into his.

"You just dropped your gun and left the battle?"

He nodded.

"Why?"

There it was, again. The question that had come to him so often, in his thirst and hunger and nightmares. And never yet had his mind and his heart answered that query to his soul's content. His conversation with Hannah seemed a decade ago, and he seemed to be a different person. Yet he still hadn't found the *words* that would give the choice its meaning.

He stared at her. Then his eyes strayed past her, coming to rest on the wall behind her. "I don't know how to say it . . ." he began.

She waited, her eyes studying his face in wonder. She had never heard him talk in such a voice.

"Something came to me," he finally said, his eyes meeting hers again. He smiled. "Or should I say some *One* came to me? All I know is that all the words, all the examples that had ever been set for me or said to me, from the time I was a boy, came rolling down over me like a heavenly flood." A look of anguish came into his eyes. "I knew I couldn't bear a weapon anymore. I couldn't shoot at another human being again. Ever again." A heavy sigh lifted his shoulders. He looked away. "I just couldn't remain a soldier."

A strange expression stole across Rachel's face. "But the telegram said. . . ." She hesitated, willing his eyes to return to her face. Her hands gripped her skirt tightly. "The telegram had the word 'traitor' in it, I think." Suddenly she couldn't trust her memory. This man in front of her was no criminal, but the telegram had said—

"I wouldn't doubt it!" Joseph laughed bitterly. "To General McClellan and to the government, what else would my action look like?"

"Why didn't you answer anyone's letters?" Rachel's agitation made her voice startlingly sharp. His eyes came up to fasten on hers again. Hers glistened with unshed tears.

"With this wing?" Joseph half lifted his sore arm.

"Ohhh—" Rachel's hands flew to her mouth. "I'm sorry, I didn't think—" A tear broke free and rolled down her cheek. "I was so afraid that you had done some terrible crime, that I. . . ." Her voice died. They just looked at each other.

"I didn't receive any letters, Rachel," Joseph said quietly. "At first I thought it was because no one knew where I was. Then I figured everyone at home might be embarrassed, you know, ashamed at having a member of the family in jail charged with desertion, or treason, as you say. I was pretty sure they would so charge me." He paused and laughed, with more weariness than bitterness.

"The funny thing is, I have never been formally charged, here at Washington city, at least not that I've heard of it. I tried to tell myself at first when Hawkins was bringing me here that what I had done, the reason I had deserted, would make Pa glad when he heard about it. But then I began to wonder, especially when I never got served any papers myself, if the authorities would even bother to report to Pa more than just that I'd deserted and been arrested. And then the more I got used to the way they treat prisoners here the more I figured the reason I was getting no mail was simply because they didn't want me to have any." He grinned vaguely. "They don't care much about prisoners' feelings in this place, you know."

Rachel's mind was wandering. Her face grew pale with the realization that she hadn't yet given Joseph news from home. He had no way of knowing that his father had almost died and was still laid up with his third heart attack.

"Then you hadn't heard," she whispered.

"Heard what?"

"About Ben—about your father."

"What about him?" Joseph's good arm snaked out and his fingers gripped Rachel's arm tightly. "Is he—"

"No, he's not dead."

Joseph's grip relaxed.

"But he had another heart attack."

Joseph's mouth fell open. "No!" he groaned. "Not again. Not just when I. . . ." He put his face in his hands.

"He received that telegram, about you," Rachel explained. "It came just after the Antietam battle. I guess that was a day or two after you had—had done what you did. He didn't even open it. He was so sure it announced your death, he told us later, that he just stuck it unopened into his vest pocket, then went out to the stable, saddled up Prince, and rode away."

Joseph looked up, surprised. "Rode away? On Prince?" The look on his face was so comical Rachel almost hooted. "Where was he riding for?"

"Just riding, he said, later. He had to *do* something, move fast, expend energy or he'd go crazy. It started to rain. Real heavy. Not just an ordinary shower, but one of those electric storms where you can barely see, it comes down in rivers. Well, Prince missed his footing at the bridge near your farm and fell. Your father was thrown down the riverbank. He fell hard against that big rock and if Father and I hadn't come along right then, he might have drowned in the flood. His heart attack happened just before he fell from the horse, he said."

Joseph's eyes had probed Rachel's during the whole tale. He asked, with visible effort: "How is he now?"

Rachel smiled and reached out to touch Joseph's arm. "Oh, he's much better. In fact, when I last saw him, he was still in bed, but he was laughing and threatening to get on the train and personally come to get you released! But I told him I'd already bought *my* ticket."

Joseph relaxed and grinned. "I was going to ask you about this surprise appearance. I didn't know you were such a bold, young—"

At that moment the door burst open, and not one but two men stood in the gloom behind the lamp. Major Wood stepped into the light, an enigmatic smile on his lips. Zack lurked in the doorway with the familiar smirk once again set on his features.

"I must say, young lady," Wood chuckled, "you certainly

have a different conception of five minutes than most peo-ple." Deliberately, with exaggerated motions, he pulled a gold watch from his tunic pocket. Its chain shimmered in the lamplight. "According to my chronometer you have been consorting with the prisoner for nearly half an hour since I admitted you." He jerked his head toward Zack. "My jailer here says you ordered him about like a school-boy. Ha ha, no doubt that'll do him good!" His smile was wide, but Rachel didn't miss the glint of coldness in his eyes.

"Har har, captain," Zack croaked, "it's like I said—"

"Silence," barked Wood sternly.

Zack looked as if he'd swallowed a large bird.

"Now, young lady," the officer went on. His grin was back, only now it looked forced. "If you will please come with me. We don't want to tire the prisoner." His eyes swept over Joseph, lingering only a moment on the petti-coat bandage. The smile faltered, then returned as the cold eyes went back to Rachel.

"May I return to visit him, tomorrow?" Rachel asked. There was none of the impatience or authority she had used on Zack.

"Well, now, we'll just have to see," Wood said, geniality almost oozing from his voice. But Joseph detected the flash of something else in the officer's expression, as the man's eyes swept over Rachel's body. His blood ran cold.

"We'll just have to see," Wood repeated. With a hearty laugh he touched Rachel's back, to usher her out with a firmness that brooked no second thought, let alone a senti-mental farewell.

Zack took a step and retrieved his lamp. With his free hand on the door handle he turned and leered at Joseph. "Hee hee," he mocked, and his tongue snaked between his yellow teeth and traced the perimeter of his lips.

He slammed the door behind him.

15

Their shadows wavered eerily on the stone walls as Major Wood led the way up the steps. Holding up her skirts Rachel followed hesitantly, for the steps were rough and uneven. Zack brought up the rear, lamp held high. Through the interrogation room they went, then into the long corridor, the day's grayness through the fanlight bright in Rachel's eyes after the murk of Joseph's cell.

"Come along with me, Miss Miller," Wood said, opening the front door and stepping out. "Zack, go back to your rounds." The two sentries snapped to attention, one on either side of the door.

She followed him. Zack disappeared down the foyer, the burning lamp still clutched in one hand. Wood turned to look toward the street.

"Is there someone to pick you up, Miss Miller?" He asked.

"Yes," she replied. She pointed to a carriage parked along the street about fifty yards away where it had dropped her a half hour ago.

"Fine." Wood turned back to the open door. The guards still stood around ramrod straight.

"But, sir . . .," Rachel began.

"Yes?" The officer paused with his hand on the doorpost. He turned to look at her over his shoulder.

"May I see Joseph again tomorrow?" Her pulse was pounding. A half hour ago, he'd been polite, formal, and accommodating. Now he seemed to be toying with her. She didn't know whether to be furious or frightened.

"Well now, that depends." He turned fully to face her and crossed his arms. "*Why* should I let you?"

"Well . . ." she began, but suddenly couldn't find the words. Why did she have to state a reason? Wasn't it obvious to this man? Surely he was human! "It's his wound. I'll bring some ointment."

"Don't you know that, on repeat calls, visitors need a pass, signed by the Secretary of War?" It was a flat lie, but Major William Wood had just decided to have himself a bit of fun. The monotony of this place could drive a man mad. There was absolutely no reason not to let King have a visitor, twice or twenty times. In fact, he'd begun to wonder why no one had come to see the poor stiff in the month or so since he'd been brought in.

"I'll get one!" Rachel's tone of eager hope belied the despair she suddenly felt at Wood's words. How would she ever get in to see the secretary? She wasn't even sure who he was!

"That's all right, dearie." Wood grinned. He stepped forward and laid a hand on her shoulder. "Just a little joke. Just a little joke." Then he laughed boisterously. The two sentries grinned. "All you need to do is come tomorrow ready to show some appreciation to your boyfriend's jailers!" He roared again, then he winked at the sentries.

Rachel spun on her heel, almost catching her boot in the rough slats of the boardwalk. Wood's hand slipped off her shoulder, but seemed to linger against her hip as it fell. She walked briskly toward the street, her heels clopping on the wood, her head held high.

Wood's raucous guffaws followed her, joined by titters from the guards. There was a quality in their mirth that caused her ears and cheeks to burn. She thought of the way the officer's eyes had swept down over her, back in the cell. She remembered his touch just now, and the fire spread down her neck.

Rain started to fall as she reached the covered buggy. Her mother's cousin's servant, who'd introduced himself as Willie, stuck his face around the corner as her foot pressed down on the stepping plate. Agile as a deer in spite of the gray in his kinky hair, he leaped down to help her into the conveyance. Disapproval etched lines around his mouth. "Missus Carey, she gonna be mighty worried, Miz Rachel! She done tol' me to hurry right on home from the station cuz Washington ain't no place for a young lady to be out on the street these days!"

She gave him a tired smile as he tucked the wool lap robe around her knees. Fatigue was settling over her like a fog. "I'm sorry, but being so close to Joseph finally, I just had to see him right away."

Willie's kindly black face melted. "Yessum, Miss Rachel, I unnerstand." He gave her a huge grin. "I'll jus' get ol' Sally to skedaddle on home." He gave a quick bow, climbed to the high seat in front, and clucked his tongue. The gray mare pulled away into the mud of First Street as the rain began to come down in earnest.

Rachel sank back into the center of the padded seat. She pulled the blanket up around her shoulders. The carriage had no side flaps like the ones on her father's buggy, and the chill October dampness seeped into her like a cold bath. She felt a rush of sympathy for poor Willie, sitting too close to the front of the roof to derive much shelter from it. Their speed increased as much as it could in the inches-deep mud.

She laid her head against the seatback and closed her eyes, grateful for the buggy and driver that had awaited her train. Just as if she hadn't totally forgotten the practical details of her trip, such as taking time to telegraph her mother's cousin with her arrival time so she'd be met at the station. She had remembered before the train had even left the outskirts of Kalamazoo, but of course there was not a thing she could do about it until the first stop, an hour later. Then she had telegraphed her mother because she didn't even remember her relatives' last name!

Isabel Miller's reply had been waiting when the train stopped later in Detroit. It had been brief and to the point. "HAVE WIRED CAREYS STOP WAITING STATION FORTY-EIGHT HOURS STOP LOVE MOTHER."

The memory warmed Rachel. Leave it to efficient mothers to think of everything. There was no way to know all that Isabel may have put in her message to her cousin. But Rachel doubted her mother would have spent a bucketful of cash giving the Careys all the lowdown on Joseph's situation. Especially since Joseph wasn't exactly her mother's favorite person. Regret dampened Rachel's spirit.

And the carriage had been there, with the beaming middle-aged black man sitting astride its high seat holding a neatly lettered sign identifying the conveyance as belonging to "Dr. Randall Carey, Esq." The train had been delayed several times over two days. Rachel wondered for how many hours or how many trains the poor man had sat and waited for the young woman from distant Michigan to alight.

And then she had selfishly insisted on being taken straight to the prison. She didn't think an extra few minutes one way or the other could possibly matter to her relatives. But it meant everything for her to see her beloved right away. How could she have mustered the social graces to meet and renew acquaintances with her scarce-remembered kinfolk when Joseph sat in a horrible jail only minutes away?

She sighed deeply. She was too weary even to know her feelings, whether she was elated or worried, or just craving of a good sleep. Her body was exhausted. On the train she had had no place either to change her clothes or stretch out prone. Sleep on the crowded, overheated coach had been patchy at best. The seats were poorly padded and dusty, a sure sign that railroad operators had more on their wartime minds than civilian passenger comfort.

With her physical weariness came now a mental grogginess. It was a reaction to the high pitch of excitement her mind had maintained for so long in anticipation of seeing Joseph and learning whether he was all right, even still alive.

Now that she had seen him, the greater part of her mind was resting easier, but she was by no means totally at rest. He was alive and although he hadn't put it into definite words—there had not been time!—she knew in her heart of hearts that he cared deeply for her. But he was ill and he was different. Oh, why hadn't she been allowed more time with him! Tomorrow was an eternity away. And maybe she would have trouble getting past that horrible man, Major Wood. She shuddered and tried to put his eyes out of her consciousness.

What had Joseph experienced that made him desert? There hadn't been enough time to learn about that, either. He was a different person now, more sensitive. He certainly did not behave like a person labeled a traitor. If there was anything about him that marked him as a criminal, she certainly hadn't been able to see it. So if he were a monster in the eyes of the government, but a better man in her own eyes, what was she to make of that? She didn't feel she could defend his decision to anyone, if she'd be called upon to do so. But was that an intellectual disagreement? She didn't understand him now, yet she felt closer to him, she suddenly realized. She had loved this man for so long. Even though there was something about him that was unknown to her, she loved him still.

Did that make her a fool?

For an uncomfortable moment the thought dug into her. In her fatigued state she couldn't push the notion away. "A fool's errand." That's what her mother had said, even while blessing her and wishing her Godspeed. She pushed the memory away vigorously. She could not think that about her trip. Instead, she must wait to draw conclusions until she had more time to talk with Joseph. Tomorrow. Then she would hear him out. In the meantime she would put a leash on her worries and bury her fears.

A clap of thunder came like a punctuation mark. With it, the rain sluiced down like a solid fog.

A minute later Willie steered the horse into a driveway which climbed a light knoll and stopped beneath a roofed arch connecting a large house to a smaller outbuilding. Rachel had hardly been aware of their progress. She was startled to realize she'd reached her destination already. Suddenly embarrassed at what she knew must be an unkempt appearance, she brushed at her skirts and adjusted her bonnet.

Willie helped her down. He looked miserable and wet, but he grinned politely.

"Jez follow, Miz Rachel," he said as he took Rachel's bag and led the way beneath the roof to the door at the rear of the house. The window in the top half of that door was filled with the beaming grin of a large, moon-faced woman. Willie stepped aside as the door swept inward and the big woman filled the space with her wide-flung arms. Willie bowed, set down the bag, then returned to the horse and buggy.

"Well, I do declare, it's finally Rachel!" Large, fleshy hands clasped her shoulders. "Come in, come in!" The huge smile and warm, crinkled eyes almost made up for the wretched weather, as the woman practically dragged her into the kitchen. It was warm, dry, and brightly lit by two reflector lamps mounted high on opposite walls.

"Rachel, I'm your mama's cousin, Rose, as you must remember." She indicated a younger woman standing near the sink, "And you recollect your second cousin, Hetty, I suppose?"

Rachel glowed at them both. "It's been a long time, cousin. You look much the same, but Hetty, you were just a little girl!" Rachel did a quick calculation. She thought she remembered her cousin as being about two or three years her junior.

"Ha ha!" burst out Rose. "As were you, too, Rachel!" And she went on laughing as if it were a cherished habit. Hetty only smiled briefly, then looked out the window above the sink. Rachel was surprised. She remembered the girl as bright and vivacious, always cheerful.

"Well, dear Rachel, please sit down," Rose boomed. She practically pushed her onto a brightly painted yellow kitchen chair. "You must be tired, and being out in this poor weather—my, my." She snapped her fingers. "Let me fix a cup of tea to warm you up a bit. And here, let me take your bag and your wraps!" She did so, disappearing into an adjoining room with them, then returning like a small storm.

She swept to the cast-iron cookstove, struck a match, lowered it into the already-laid pile of kindling, then replaced the lid and set a copper kettle on it. "Hetty, don't just stand and stare. Sit down, sit down!"

Hetty obeyed, but she moved mechanically. Rachel thought she seemed pale and weak. When she looked back at Rose, Rachel detected a glimmer of pain in the soft brown eyes of the big woman before her merriment returned.

"Now tell me, young lady," Rose thundered, her round, pink face wreathed in a wide smile, "how was your trip? Your mother wired us to say you were on your way, to visit your betrothed in the Old Capitol Prison. Needless to say, we were delighted to have you, but very curious as well." She paused, then went on. "Isabel never was one to throw money around, so her wire was too short to tell us how your man got captured." A frown momentarily creased her abundant face. "In this weather Willie should have been more in a hurry. Or was the train late?" She gave a small "tsk tsk" and shook her head. "I suppose in wartime that is a normal thing to expect, right?"

Rachel's head was spinning. She hardly heard Rose's monologue after the word "betrothed." Her mother had used *that* word? She was stunned. Then mystified. Then happy. Suddenly, goldenly happy. And she loved her mother almost to the point of tears. Her mother was blessing her choice of man after all! It seemed everyone was, now. All that was left was to get Joseph to realize it—the silly bum! Amusement tugged at her lips.

"Rachel? Oo-hoo?" Rose was grinning at her. Hetty was looking at her with a spark of interest.

"Uh—no, my train ride was fine. It was almost on time, Mrs. Carey." Rachel felt the woman's friendly scrutiny bring the blood to her cheeks. She could hardly restrain the impulse to burst out in glee at awareness of her mother's approval. "I told Willie—"

"Please, call me Rose! We're family."

"I asked your driver, Cousin Rose, to take me straight to see Joseph. I—I wanted to see if he's all right."

"You went to Old Capitol? All by yourself?"

"Yes," Rachel said. "I had to see him. There hadn't been any letters, and—"

"Of course, my child." Question marks sprouted in Rose's eyes.

A shiver raced through Rachel's body as a drop of water fell from her hair and dripped down her neck.

Rose noticed. "What is the matter with me?" She almost shouted. "There you sit in your damp traveling clothes, all chilly and tired, and I stand here and chatter like some old biddy! Now you just strip down to your petticoats and,

Hetty, go get a blanket for your cousin to wrap in! Get the dark green one. It's warmest." Hetty wordlessly obeyed and departed. "Now don't you be embarrassed, child. It's just us women here in the house!"

Rose added several pieces of wood to the stove while Rachel stripped off her outer garment. Then she moved closer to Rachel and said, in a low voice, "Don't mind Hetty's behavior. She's usually full of sunshine and cheer, but she lost her sweetheart in this war. It's been past six months, now—happened at Shiloh—but they were supposed to be married in June. Poor thing. She's taking it hard."

Rachel gave her cousin warm thanks when she returned with the blanket, but as she wrapped the warm wool around her shoulders she was speechless. She remembered the soul-killing agony she had endured when she knew horrible battles were being fought and Joseph might be in them. After going so long without any word, she had found out that he was alive. Just thinking of how she would be now, if he'd been killed as Hetty's beau had been, she shuddered. And she and Joseph had not even had an "understanding," let alone been engaged to be married!

"Here now, I think the water's hot." Rose had been fussing at the stove and then got a dainty white cup and saucer with gold trim from the cupboard. She took a pinch of tea leaves from a canister on the sideboard, dropped them into a tea ball, and set the ball in the cup. She wrapped a hot pad around the teakettle handle and gripped it firmly as she poured the steaming water directly into Rachel's cup. She set the cup and saucer before Rachel.

"Aren't you both going to have some, too?" Rachel asked.

Hetty shook her head. She'd resumed her station by the sink, staring out the window, toward the south.

"Maybe I will," Rose answered. "Thank you." She got

out another cup and saucer, repeated her operations at the stove, then sat down across the table from Rachel. While she was making her tea, Rachel studied her, thinking how different Rose was from her cousin, Isabel Miller. How warm and wanted and welcome Rose made a body feel. Then she was ashamed as she remembered what she had just guessed about her mother's acceptance of Joseph. She felt a warm breeze of affection for her mother.

"Now, Cousin Rachel," Rose exhaled, as she lowered her bulk into the chair and leaned on her elbows, "tell us about your Joseph." She beamed, compassion reaching out from her expressive eyes. Isabel's wire didn't tell us much, only that Joseph—is that his name?—only that he's at the Old Capitol Prison here in the district." She arched her eyebrows and seemed to be reluctant to ask her next question. "We thought maybe your mother got the name confused. Old Capitol's really only for deserters and traitors to the Union and for Confederate prisoners of war. So we were a mite puzzled. Isn't your Joseph a Union man?"

The question hung in the air. It wasn't asked in an unkind way or with anything but simple curiosity attached to it, but suddenly Rachel was reluctant to begin the story she had to tell. Not because she was ashamed of Joseph. Certainly not. But because she had not been given time to hear him out, she didn't know the whole story, so she couldn't give it to her relatives. And she didn't want to *sound* the fool, to them. She hardly knew them, and even persons at home who knew her well had thought her trip a fool's errand. Or some of them had. Like her mother.

She felt rather than saw Hetty turn from the window to stare at her. And suddenly she did not ever want to tell these two women what she knew, already. She could fib, tell a white lie, save the truth for when she knew it more fully herself, after talking more with Joseph tomorrow. Then she would explain.

Meanwhile, though, what could she say? How could she respond to her mother's cousin's innocent and logical question? They sat there watching her quizzically, a questioning look on Rose's broad face, simple attention on Hetty's.

She breathed a sigh to herself and tried to smile. It felt quavery and weak. "There was a misunderstanding. A mistake—"

She was interrupted by the sudden stamping of loud boots on the front porch. Then came the sounds through the length of the big house, of a large, heavy door opening. Rose's face cracked into an expectant grin.

"Anybody home?" A clear, hearty male voice echoed through the building. "Ah, I see lights in yonder kitchen where I trust a spot o' tea doth wait!" The ringing voice came closer, partnered with the clatter of leather heels on a hardwood floor.

"Hullo—this must be Cousin Rachel, all grown up!" A tall, thin man appeared in the kitchen doorway. His black cape streamed raindrops on the floor. He swept his stovepipe hat low with his bow.

Rachel stared at the man standing in the doorway like a dripping totem pole. He seemed to stretch as high as the door, with arms and legs going on forever. His hair was long and glistening black, combed straight back in flowing waves. Dark blue eyes probed like an eagle's from deep sockets. But they were dancing eyes, and as familiar to Rachel as the memories of her dolls. For she had been a small girl when this same man had tossed her high into the rafters, and her laughter had almost been as loud as his.

"Welcome to Washington, Rachel!" he boomed as he shrugged out of his sodden outer garment. He wore a black, broadcloth suit over a white shirt. His cravat was neatly tied beneath a beardless lantern chin. "I trust you had a safe and cheerful trip from the frontier!"

"Safe and cheerful, yes," Rachel said, her eyes sparkling.

This man's presence was like an elixir. "Restful, though, it was not!"

"We shall rectify that sad condition as soon as we can, or my name is not Doctor Randall Carey!" He handed his cape to Rose, stepped forward, and took Rachel's hand. He bowed low over it, as if to place a kiss on her knuckles, but his genuflection stopped just short of that and instead his boot heels clicked together lightly. "We know from your mother's telegram that your friend is in prison and that fact is your main reason for this visit. We trust you will have no objection to the use of our good offices to effect his release, if possible." He stood up from his bow, withdrew his hand with a smile, then took a seat at the kitchen table.

Rose got up and hung his dripping cloak on a hook behind the stove, then bustled about getting him a cup of tea before she sat down again and cleared her throat. She said to her husband: "We were just about to hear Rachel's account of what happened to Joseph when you came in, Randall."

"Good—I haven't missed anything, yet," he said, "and you won't have to repeat yourself." His expression became one of waiting. It was also a kind look, and it disarmed Rachel, removing her desire to fib. She decided to report as straightforwardly as she could what she knew of Joseph's actions. "Go on, Rachel," Randall smiled. "We're listening."

She took a deep breath, then let it out, slowly. "I wish I knew more," she began, haltingly, "but we had so little time to talk before the guard—"

"The guard?" Randall interrupted, his eyebrows arched. "You have already been to Old Capitol?"

"She got Willie to take her directly there from the station," Rose put in.

"Yes," Rachel continued. "I was so worried about Joseph that I just had to see him, right away."

"Is he all right?" asked the doctor. "I mean, is he holding up, physically? That place is no bed of roses." His eyes were suddenly full of concern.

Rose added, "Leave it to a doctor to bring in his interest. But we all hope Joseph is holding up well."

Randall smiled tightly, and they gave their attention to Rachel, waiting for her reply.

"He's not in good shape, I fear. He has a bullet wound that's not been treated and he's weak. Even feverish. But"—and her eyes searched Randall's, sensing a strength in him she desperately needed—"but I'm concerned about his emotional state as well, maybe more so. When he gave me his reason for deserting, I had to wonder, at least a little, if his long imprisonment may be affecting his judgment."

"Deserting?" Rose and the doctor said it in unison. Hetty's eyes showed the strongest interest Rachel had detected since she'd arrived. "We thought," Rose went on, "from Isabel's wire that he must have been captured as a war prisoner."

Rachel gave a silent blessing to her mother, again. Here she'd expected her mother to have predisposed her cousin against the man she had apparently despised, for her daughter's choice. Yet it was becoming clear that Isabel had selected words which would allow Rachel to make her own case. How unfair I've been to her, thought Rachel.

"No," she said aloud. She bowed her head, suddenly reluctant to meet their eyes. "No, the telegram that came to Michigan from the War Office, almost a month ago, only stated that Joseph had been arrested and placed in Old Capitol Prison for desertion because he'd laid down his gun and walked away from the battle."

She raised her head and looked at her listeners. "This afternoon, though, he told me that the reason he had done it was his conscience, that he couldn't point a gun at another human being ever again." She hesitated, suddenly embarrassed because his words seemed odd, here in this place. "He said he felt as if . . . as if some One came to him, and after he felt that, he knew he had to leave."

The eyes of the three Careys were on her with a mix of expressions. Her embarrassment increased while at the same time she was ashamed of it. The Careys were not Mennonites so she could guess how Joseph's action might sound to them. It made her uncomfortable.

Hetty stared at her with an intense light in her eyes. Rose looked at her more with a mother's compassion at her obvious discomfort than merely a reaction to her words. Randall Carey, doctor as well as relative, studied her face with a mixture of professional interest, as if she were a case as well as kin. He was the first to speak.

"If I may be so presumptuous, Rachel, it seems to me that you may not fully agree with Joseph's deed or position. Am I right?"

His voice was kind, but suddenly her discomfort flared into temper. Immediately she repressed it, because she knew he was right. "Yes," she whispered, "that's probably true." Then she quickly added: "At least until I have heard him out."

"How well do you know Joseph?" Randall asked her.

"I have known him—I mean, we have known each other since we were children." Her heart beat faster. She suddenly felt vulnerable, even foolish. She realized how obvious her feelings for Joseph must be.

As if to confirm it, Randall's voice grew gentle. "You did not realize, until just a short while ago, how well you know him or how little you know him, I'll wager. Am I right?"

Rachel felt tears spring to her eyes. She only nodded, amazed at his perception.

"Is Joseph sincere?" It was Rose.

"I—I think so," she stammered, suddenly wondering, "but we really did not have enough time to talk, so I don't know. . . ." Rachel couldn't finish. She felt disloyal.

"He's a Mennonite, isn't he?" Randall asked, his tone more a statement than a question. "And your family attend his church?"

"Yes," she replied. "But I—I mean we—don't attend anymore."

"Oh?"

She stared at the backs of her folded hands, resting in her lap. "In the last year or so my father wouldn't attend anymore. Mother never did, very much. I—I didn't go much anymore because Joseph didn't either." She wondered why she had used past tense, then shook off the thought. "It was on the issue of nonresistance that Father differed. Quite drastically."

Hetty's chair scraped backward. The noise was loud in the kitchen. She stood and glared down at Rachel, then she strode out of the room, her shoulders and back rigid.

Randall gave a sad grimace, at no one in particular. Silence reigned, except for the loud ticking of a kitchen clock Rachel hadn't noticed before. It hung between the door to the front rooms and the side door through which she had entered. Suddenly it seemed a long time ago. She stifled a yawn.

"Rachel," Randall broke the quiet, "I'm going to visit Joseph with you. That is, if you will allow me." His eyebrows arched over his deep sockets. "You are planning to return there tomorrow?"

"Yes, I am, and I'd be delighted to have you along." She chuckled brightly as a burden seemed to roll off her shoulders. "If they will let me in, that is. Let *us* in, I mean." Dr. Carey seemed just the ticket to secure admission. He seemed like the sort of man that Major Wood would defer to.

"If they will let you in?" Rose queried. She had appeared troubled by Hetty's behavior, but her attention returned promptly to Rachel.

"Did you have trouble being admitted today?" Randall added his question. There was an edge of anger in his voice.

"Well, not exactly," Rachel said, "not until I was on my way out and I asked to be allowed to return tomorrow."

Randall studied her face, probing her words. "We'll not have any problem. I can guarantee you that much," he said, in a soft voice. It sounded gentle, but there was the ring of cold steel in it, too. "You said that Joseph is wounded. I am a doctor. That in itself is sufficient for me to gain entrance."

Rachel felt a warm wave of relief. Dr. Randall Carey certainly gave the impression of being a strong, decisive man, cloaked with an authority that sprang in large measure from his character. Then abruptly she recalled her mother's statement that Randall Carey knew the president. That should add a few more weights to his influence, she thought cheerfully, and warmth spread in her.

Then her brain teased her with the memory of her scheme, and she almost laughed aloud. Maybe there actually *was* a chance she might get in to see the president and enlist his help—but no, Rachel! She mentally slapped herself. Hang on to what you've got, and right now that is the support of a strong man who can also help heal the body of your dear boy in a cell.

Rachel tried to stifle a yawn, but it was too impulsive for her this time. With the feeling of relief came a physical relaxation that brought home to her in a rush the full weight of her exhaustion.

Rose jumped up, full of apologies. "I'm so sorry, child! It's near suppertime and you haven't even been shown to your room to bathe and change your clothes!"

Rachel blushed furiously. She had completely forgotten she was sitting in a strange kitchen in nothing but a blanket wrapped around her undergarments, talking with a man neither her brother, father, nor husband.

Randall noticed her embarrassment, threw back his head, and laughed. But his wife sailed in for the rescue. "Randall, you go tell Willie to draw some water and cut some more wood. I'll rustle up a meal that will send off this damp October chill."

Rose laid a hand gently on Rachel's shoulder as Randall scurried from the kitchen. "As for you, young miss, I'll show you to your room and before you can turn around twice we'll bring you hot water and soap. You must be dog-tired after your long trip. I should be flogged around the quarterdeck for keeping you sitting and talking so long!" She beamed at Rachel and led her out of the kitchen. "Come along, child."

After Rose left the bedroom, Rachel stood at one of the wide windows and stared down at the grass, touched here and there with the first rust of autumn. She remarked to herself how slow the seasons changed in the South compared to Michigan. Through the tawny gold and red of the fall tree branches she could catch glimpses of the unfinished Capitol dome, and she mused on the unfinished nature of this war and the nation itself. It was over a mile away and appeared to be itself a war casualty. It almost looked as if some large gun had blown away part of the capital city's highest, proudest structure.

Later, out of the clothes she had worn for what felt like a week, washed, and in a warm bathrobe, Rachel sat on the edge of the high, soft bed in her upstairs room. It was a bright place, in spite of the overcast late afternoon, freshly painted in shades of yellow and rose. Chintzy curtains hung tastefully at the two windows which overlooked the front lawn and the tree-bordered street.

Drowsy from her basin bath, she let her musings go on, reflecting on the damage the war had brought, and would still bring, to individual lives. When it had begun a year and a half ago, it had seemed a distant, impersonal thing, not unlike the countless wars in faraway lands, known from history books. It had struck too close, into her heart, when war had claimed Joseph.

She felt the prick of shame at that thought. At least she had not lost her man to the Grim Reaper, like her cousin Hetty. She supposed she really should try to get to know the girl better, as a woman now, not a girl. Perhaps she could comfort her.

Yet she was puzzled as she remembered Hetty's abrupt, haughty exodus from the kitchen. If that's what it had been—haughty. All she had done, Rachel thought, was use the word nonresistance, and her cousin had gone off like an insulted society queen. Or was it simple hurt? Rachel gave her head a puzzled toss. She couldn't remember saying anything that might have made Hetty behave as she did. She sighed. "All the more reason to have a talk with her, get to know her," she said aloud to herself.

Rachel's mind was suddenly full of Joseph's face, replacing her cousin in her consciousness. The suddenness of the transition surprised her, but she focused on his words and on the stand he had taken. She started. That word had not come to her before in connection with Joseph's act. But that is what he had done, taken a stand. Unexpectedly, without an effort, she felt her mind seem to reach out for his and enter it. Comprehension began to dawn on her. She should stop being selfish, if she really loved him. Instead, she would try to see the war as one who had been taught all his life that violence was wrong, who then found himself one day on a battlefield.

Love for him swept over her like a tidal wave. It was so sudden and so intense that a sob escaped from her chest. She turned and fell forward on the bed, burying her face in the pillow and letting the surprised tears flow. But they were tears of deep joy. She realized in a flash that she was happier than ever she could remember. It was as if the universe had been opened for her to gaze deeply into it. In her heart of hearts she knew Joseph was right.

Hardly realizing she did it, she slid off the bed and onto her knees.

16

Rachel woke the next morning feeling deliciously rested and at peace. The sun was streaming brightly into the room, as cheerful as a June day, and even the remembrance of Joseph in prison didn't dull her spirits. Deep inside her was a firm belief that all things would work together for good where he was concerned.

She stretched luxuriously and threw back the covers. As she laced herself into her undergarments, she hummed a lively melody and thought back over the last evening's supper and easy conversation. The ham steaks had been done to a turn and the recounting of family stories, filling in years of happenings between Rose and her mother, had made Rachel almost feel like a girl again. Rachel told of the good times she and Joseph had had over the years of their growing up. The topic of his current status hadn't come up again after the arrangements had been settled for today's trip to the prison. Even Hetty had smiled once or twice during the long evening of talk around the roaring fireplace.

Rose had offered to press out the wrinkles in her spare dress. Rachel had gone upstairs to get it before she went to bed, absolutely worn out but happy.

Now the knock on the door signified the garment was ready. Rachel opened it and Rose handed in the dress. "Good morning, Rachel, I hope you slept well," Rose said, with a huge smile.

"Oh, yes, I did. Thank you."

"Do you need any help getting into it?"

"If you would, please."

Rose entered and went to work, fastening buttons and looking for wrinkles to smooth. "There," she exclaimed, a moment later. "You're enough to knock the pennies off a dead man's eyes! Let's go downstairs and have some coffee cake."

Hetty had already eaten and gone to her volunteer nurse duty at one of the many impromptu hospitals spread across the district, Rose informed her. Randall put down the paper he was reading at the ends of his long arms, took a sip of coffee, and smiled at Rachel. "Good morning, cousin. I didn't know you western farm girls were such late sleepers! You'd better hurry or I'll have all this delicious chow consumed!" He took a huge wedge of the golden brown pastry. The crumbs on his plate announced that it wasn't his first.

As they sat and ate and drank coffee, Rachel learned more about these warm, friendly kinfolk. She'd already known her mother had grown up with Rose, in eastern Ohio, and that Rose had attended a woman's college in Philadelphia. Randall had met her while he was in college there. He had been a doctor in his home state of Iowa, when the family had lived there. But now she learned how he had met Abraham Lincoln. It came up obliquely, when Rose reminded her husband that the president was expecting him later today.

"Excuse me for asking," Rachel put in, "but how did you get to know Mr. Lincoln?"

Randall's mouth was full of coffee cake so Rose answered for him. "He had known the president's personal physician since college days, and one day Stone—that's Abe's doctor—called Randall in to consult on Willie's fever, and he and the president hit it off from the day they met."

Randall chuckled. "I guess he was relieved to find someone else who was awkwardly tall and bony! And when he learned I'd grown up on the frontier, too, I guess he figured I must feel as much a misfit here in the city as he." He chuckled again, disarming Rachel's awe-filled expression just as if he were accustomed—as he was—to meeting persons who were impressed with his connections.

His countenance sobered. "I just wish, fervently, that I had been able to save his little boy's life." He sighed. "But medical science just has not advanced far enough to banish typhoid fever to the dustbin of horrors."

"It certainly was a tragedy," Rose remarked. "Mrs. Lincoln is still not fully recovered, and I sometimes wonder if she'll ever be over her grief. The poor dear."

They fell silent, all three of them with their own memories of the sad vigil of the nation nearly a year ago, while Willie Lincoln's life faded away.

"Well," Randall sighed, pushing his chair back and rising. "I'll have Willie bring up the buggy and I'll get my bag. We'll go have a look at Joseph's wound and see whether there might be anything else we can do for him." He winked at Rachel and grinned. "I'm eagerly anticipating meeting this curious young man of yours."

As they made their way to the Old Capitol, Dr. Carey kept up a steady chatter. The brilliant warm sunshine was rapidly drying the mud of the streets. As Willie guided the carriage along, Randall pointed out landmarks, public buildings, and famous or notorious persons when they happened to show their faces. Passers-by frequently lifted a hand in greeting to the doctor.

Rachel was struck by the informal, almost disorganized, atmosphere in this capital city of a nation at war. Uniforms were everywhere, as well as wagons, mule teams, and rivers of human beings congesting the thoroughfares, sending up loud cries, laughter, and curses. Ramshackle, temporary-looking structures had been thrown up almost cheek by jowl with stone buildings full of the dignity of time and function. Looming over all the bustle and color, growing larger as they neared the prison, was the familiar profile of the Capitol. The "New Capitol." And then they were in sight of the Old Capitol.

"Not long ago," Randall said, pointing at it, "that building had a slightly more honorable occupation than holding prisoners. It was housing the nation's Congress."

"Really?"

"Yes, back when the Brits burned the current one." Randall chuckled. "There are those, I reckon, who'd allow that the current occupants are more honorable than the men who wrote our laws there, some fifty years ago."

"Well, I would be one of those, for certain," Rachel said. "At least about one of its current occupants."

He peered intently at her. "Do I detect a bit more commitment to your young man than I sensed in our conversations yesterday? Then you didn't seem to understand just what made him tick."

Rachel remembered afresh the certainty she had felt on her knees the night before. It had lain like bedrock beneath her mood since first waking. She could hardly wait to tell Joseph of her newfound faith, both in him and in God. And in the stand he had taken, even before he said another word in explanation of it.

Of course she was eager to hear him elaborate his decision and his deed, but she knew down deep that it would be "all of a piece." It could not contradict the spirit of his moral choice which she had understood, on her knees last night. Also, she was eager to hear Joseph explain himself to Dr. Carey. And for Dr. Carey to lend his influence in getting Joseph released. Although how that might be brought about, she had no clue.

Then her mind was occupied by their arrival at the front door of Old Capitol. Willie pulled the buggy to a stop where he had yesterday. Randall unfolded himself from the conveyance and told Willie to wait. He helped Rachel down to the boardwalk which led to the front door.

The sentries snapped to attention. Rachel received a surprise when one of them respectfully addressed Dr. Carey by name, wishing him a good morning. Obviously this wasn't her escort's first trip here, Rachel thought.

"I've come to examine a prisoner," the doctor stated. "Please inform Major Wood." Rachel was impressed by the quiet authority in his voice.

One of the soldiers disappeared inside, returning almost immediately with the supervisor of the prison. "Well, well, this is indeed a pleasure, Dr. Carey, I'm sure!" Major Wood's voice was hale and hearty, with more than a shade of obsequiousness. His glance flickered toward Rachel and registered surprise. She thought she also saw a flash of embarrassed anger before the luminous dark eyes swept back to the doctor. It was gone too quickly, though, for her to be sure.

"Major, I'd like to examine your prisoner Joseph King, please." There was no trace of humor or conviviality in his tone. His eyes were expressionless. Rachel shivered.

Uncertainty appeared in Wood's face, followed by what looked to Rachel like apprehension. Like his earlier lapse of control, it was quickly gone. But it sparked anxiety in Rachel. This man acted like someone with a dangerous secret, a threat to himself.

Had something happened to Joseph during the night? Had they done something to him? Or did Wood realize, and dread, that a doctor would quickly perceive the neglect of Joseph's wound and take the information to higher authority?

Wood assumed an air of resignation and shrugged. "Yes, sir, Dr. Carey. Please follow me." He glanced at Rachel once more, with a blank face. Then he turned and led them across the threshold, along the gloomy corridor and down the steps to Joseph's cell.

Dr. Carey and Rachel found the object of their visit sitting on the whiskey keg, his head in his hands and his elbows braced on his knees. The major left a burning lamp with the doctor, then promptly left. As the cell door thumped shut, Rachel wondered at the changeful moods of the jailer, and she strove to suppress her anxiety. If only she could get Joseph out of that man's charge, she thought. Then she pushed him from her thoughts.

Randall walked purposefully up to an amazed Joseph and stuck out his hand with a big smile. "Hello. My name is Randall Carey, my wife is Rachel's cousin, and I am a physician. How are you, Joseph King?"

Joseph's mouth sagged open as the tall, lanky man in his black broadcloth suit set the lamp Wood had given him on the keg beside Joseph.

"I would like to examine that wound of yours. No, just stay seated," he said, as Joseph started to get up. Joseph sat down again. He stared at the doctor, still too surprised even to greet Rachel. She almost laughed aloud at his puzzlement.

Randall knelt on the dirty floor and touched the back of his hand to Joseph's forehead. "Low-grade fever," he muttered, as if to himself. Then he had the boy peel off his filthy shirt. Rachel saw the doctor wince and his thin lips tighten at the sight of the dried matter as he gingerly stripped away the makeshift bandage she had applied the day before. Carefully he touched the inflamed tissues.

Joseph grimaced. Rachel suddenly felt a tightness in her abdomen and turned away. She could hear Randall open his bag, then the clink and rustle of small bottles being unstoppered. Next, she heard a piece of cloth being torn into long strips, then silence. For an eternity.

"Rachel." She jumped at the doctor's voice. "Please take

these and fold them into lengths of about eighteen inches." She turned back and took the strips of gauze he was holding toward her. In his other hand he held a square piece of white cloth liberally smeared with a yellowish ointment.

She did as instructed and passed the gauze back to him. He applied the cloth to Joseph's armpit with the paste next to the wound, then held it gently in place while he wrapped the strips around Joseph's shoulder, upper arm, and neck, again and again. He expertly fastened the two loose ends where the pins wouldn't chafe and helped Joseph back into his shirt. During the whole operation he was intently silent, his face a study in quiet concentration. Rachel watched his expression, trying to read his prognosis in the angle of his eyebrows, the curve of his lips.

When he was finished, he unlimbered his long legs and stood up. "Young man, that was a serious wound. In another few days or a week you might have lost your entire arm, even your life." His smile faded. "You should thank God you were born with a hardy constitution."

Joseph looked up at the tall doctor and grinned. He spoke for the first time. "Maybe I owe my life to a couple bottles of wine." He nodded toward the two bottles, now lying empty near the foot of the wine rack. "The Good Samaritan story reminded me of something, so I poured the old stuff over my wound when I thought my arm was falling off."

Dr. Carey guffawed. "Smart. Very smart! You just might owe your life to two bottles of the fruit of the vine. It's a well-known fact that the ancient practitioners of medicine used wine to cleanse wounds." He chuckled again, shaking his head at the wonder of coincidences.

Joseph was laughing, too. He looked at Rachel and she thought that in spite of the dirt and grime he had never looked so handsome. In her heart something light and airy seemed to take off and soar through the dungeon cell and out into the bright, blue day.

"Oh, Joseph!" She stepped up to him and touched his face with both her hands. He turned just enough to touch his lips to her fingertips.

Dr. Carey stood, stooped slightly in the low room, watching them with a wistful look on his face. "If you are feeling up to it, Joseph, I'd like to hear your story. I realize that you hardly know me, but it appears rather obvious that you are quite close to this relative of mine, so that makes me feel like we are family." He set the lamp on the floor, sat on the other keg, and gave Joseph a gaze of encouragement. "I'm curious about your reasons for what you did that caused you to end up in this hole." He cast his arm out to indicate the cellar. "Your lady friend here did not have many of the details. In fact, I think she's fairly much in the dark about your reasons, too."

"That wouldn't surprise me, Dr. Carey," said Joseph with a crooked grin at the doctor. He reached up with his unbandaged arm and took Rachel's hand in his. "Our conversation last evening was rather haphazard, and I'm afraid our topics changed a lot." He kept on grinning at both of them. They were struck by how relaxed and cheerful he appeared, and they later commented on it to each other, because his mood did not seem to fit his physical circumstances.

He filled the doctor in on the details of his experiences, covering ground now familiar to Rachel, but she listened just as closely as before, basking in the sound of his voice. He ended with his entry into this cell in Old Capitol some four weeks ago. Rachel noticed his almost flippant disregard for the gravity of the charge against him and for his own narrow escapes from death and injury more serious than what he'd received. But when he finished the report and tried to answer Dr. Carey's specific question about his reasons, his momentum faltered and he looked toward the floor.

The doctor and Rachel waited in silence. She felt her heart pound, as if it were expanding with love. She suddenly wanted to blurt out her newfound trust and faith in him. She yearned to speak to him of her support no matter why he had deserted. No matter where the consequences of that deed might take him.

Dr. Carey spoke first. His voice had an odd quality that sounded different to Rachel. "If I were to give you a Bible, son, could you point to chapter and verse to defend your desertion?" It wasn't exactly a challenge, Rachel decided. Instead, it almost seemed to be the plaintive query of an anxious scholar, eager to know and eager to please, rolled into one.

"I think I could at least give it a try," Joseph answered quietly, without looking up.

"Show me," Randall whispered, digging a small black Bible out of his doctor's bag. It was well worn. He handed it to him.

Joseph took the book, staring at it as if he'd never seen a Holy Bible before. He balanced it on his knees with his right hand. He opened it with care, flipping pages with his left hand until coming to what he appeared to be searching for.

His hand stilled and he looked up at the doctor. "Who are you, anyway, and why did you ask me that question?"

"He knows the president!" Rachel blurted out. "He can help, if you'll let him, Joseph. Please, Joseph!"

He continued to stare at Carey. "Why would you want to help me?"

The doctor returned Joseph's gaze silently for several moments. Finally he sighed and seemed to glare at the backs of his hands. They were trembling. Joseph and Rachel exchanged surprised glances. "Because I have learned, since my youth, that conscience is a tender flower," he said, his voice barely audible. "It has the strength of angels, sufficient to penetrate stone and break it, if the seed is firmly rooted in the soil of Christian faith."

His voice suddenly strengthened into a chuckle. "Forgive me," he said. "I'm letting myself get carried away on the subtle current of memory!" He laughed again, and somehow the sound of it made the cell seem brighter. "That's a story for another time. Especially since I eagerly anticipate hearing Joseph's apologia now."

He gave Joseph a warm smile. "Fear not; my motives are benign. Rachel has told the truth. I do want to assist you as I am able, but I need to hear you talk. The depth of your commitment will make a difference.

"I know you were reared a Mennonite and I know quite a lot about that sect because I attended college in the Philadelphia area." He gave a sudden grin which somehow came out impish. "In fact I even kept company with a Mennonite girl for a while, until my duties kept me away from her so much that she gave up on me!" He laughed heartily, but his two listeners wondered if they were also hearing ghosts of pain.

"So come now, Joseph, let me hear how you applied the beliefs according to Menno Simons in such a manner as to give birth to your treasonous behavior on the field of battle!" His broad smile robbed the words of any sting.

Joseph flipped over a page and took a deep breath, then turned the sheet back again. "This isn't easy for me to do," he said. "I have never been much for speechmaking."

Rachel smiled to herself. Except when you're caught up in a dream, she thought. He glanced up at her, as if reading her thoughts, and a smile traced itself on her lips. He gave her an answering one, tentatively though, as if his thoughts were already being marshaled.

"Ever since I was old enough to think," he began, "I was taught that killing human beings is wrong. Most people are, I suppose. But more than that, I was instructed that *any*

kind of violence is a sin, even strong language. Cussing."
He grinned. "I suppose you'd call that violence of the
tongue. I had it pumped into me that war is evil and no
Mennonite boy could go fight in a war and still keep his
membership in good standing. I bought that line of reason-
ing without thinking, until. . . ." He paused and stared
down at the open Bible on his knees.

"Go on," Randall urged. He was watching Joseph intently.

"Until *this* war came along," Joseph added. "I suppose
the Mennonite nonresistance talk was rather—how would
you say it?—academic to me and to others of my age because there was no actual war to test our beliefs while we
were in our teens. Until last year. Then all the sermons and
Bible talk seemed weak stuff. Not strong enough to affect
the way I respond to a crisis for my country."

Randall started to speak, but Joseph motioned him to silence. "Excuse me, Dr. Carey, but for the first time I'm beginning to feel some words moving in my head." He
grinned. "The last few weeks I've felt so mush-headed I
haven't done much thinking. Mostly just moping around in
self-pity. So I'd better not stop now or I'll lose momentum." His grin widened and his eyes took in both of his listeners. "Maybe I should do like old Mr. Lytle, my teacher,
and allow for questions after the lecture."

They all laughed and Randall gave a mock deferential
bow.

"Anyway," Joseph continued, "the odd thing about the
teachings I'd received was that although I took them for
granted all my life, they did not keep me from enlisting.
Yet at the height of battle they all seemed to . . . to clobber
me like . . . like an artillery shell. It wasn't a specific verse
in the Bible, or particular words I had heard my father say,
and others too. It was more of a sense that if I claimed to
believe in the Christian faith and follow Christ, how could

I kill another human being, or even to try to kill? That's what made me desert. That feeling. Not some Bible reference flashing into my memory."

Joseph was becoming animated. He stood up and started to pace back and forth in front of Rachel and Dr. Carey. "I now believe God led me to walk off the battlefield. However, I know that can look mighty peculiar to another person, even another believer, unless it is based on chapter and verse from the Bible. And that is why I am feeling a dilemma."

Joseph suddenly stopped his pacing and faced his two friends. He shook his head as if in dismay. "Pish! And that's what is so disgusting to me about my memory. I know Pop must have quoted definite Bible verses in the New Testament for nonresistance, turning the other cheek, time and again, but do you think I can recall more than one percent of them? Hah!" He threw his arms up in disgust and let them slap down to his sides again. He flinched and grabbed for his sore shoulder.

Rachel winced at the look of shocked pain the motion brought to his expression.

"But didn't you just leaf to a place in the Bible a few minutes ago?" Dr. Carey asked. He stooped to retrieve the book from where Joseph had laid it when he stood up. "It's open to Matthew, chapter 5."

Joseph gave a wry smile. "Congratulate me on remembering at least Jesus' Sermon on the Mount."

"Ahh . . ." Randall mused, "Those several pages of the most succinct rendering of Christian morality of any document in the religious writings."

Joseph gave the doctor an odd look. Then he shrugged. "It certainly is a good place to learn how Christians are to behave." He held out his hand and Randall gave him the book, still open to the page Joseph had selected. He sat down and read, in a quiet voice:

> Ye have heard that it hath been said, An eye for an eye, and a tooth for a tooth; but I say unto you, That ye resist not evil: but whosoever shall smite thee on thy right cheek, turn to him the other also.

"And further down, it says:"

> Love your enemies, bless them that curse you, do good to them that hate you, and pray for them which despitefully use you, and persecute you.

Joseph looked up. "I know I heard these verses a lot as I was growing up. As far as I am concerned, they are enough." His voice faded almost to a whisper and he went on. "When I was running across the meadow towards that stone wall, I knew those Johnny Rebs were boys and men just like me. Human beings created and loved by God. But all I could feel was hate. And was I full of rage! I was an animal, not human anymore."

His voice ceased. The cell was so quiet the silence seemed to echo.

"I could not go on believing in God," Joseph continued, "and stay where I was to fight again. And I couldn't go on, *not* believing in God!" His eyes dropped to the open Bible, but his voice was now strong. "Even if I became dirt in the eyes of my country, I knew that my citizenship in God's kingdom was secure." He looked up again and his eyes blazed with a fresh decision. "And I don't care what happens to me now."

Rachel felt her heart was about to burst. Tears came into her eyes. She'd never been so proud of him. War had made a man out of him, that was certain. She almost laughed aloud as she appreciated the irony of the thought. He had made a choice which took moral courage yet that very same choice, to the government he served, branded him a coward, a deserter, and a traitor. And all of it in a supposedly Christian nation!

She felt the pride in the smile on her lips, and she saw the fire in Joseph's eyes melt to surprise then pleasure as he looked at her and stood up. She took a step and his good arm went around her. She laid her head on his shoulder. "But *I* care what happens to you," she murmured.

Dr. Carey cleared his throat. "Joseph, I thank you," he said hoarsely. He paused and cleared his throat again. Even then, his voice quavered when he spoke. "You remind me of a long time ago, of a lost young man. . . ." Suddenly he was busy with the lamp, still sitting on the floor near Joseph's stool. He picked it up and fiddled with the wick wheel.

Joseph and Rachel looked into each other's faces.

As if sensing the lull in a stage play, Wood abruptly reappeared. The cell door squawked open and he stepped through, holding another lamp high.

"With all due respect, Dr. Carey, and you too, miss"—he bowed slightly toward Rachel—"I must request you to leave now. It's lunchtime for the prisoner. We prefer not to have guests disturb the inmates while they dine." An almost imperceptible smile tugged at his mouth.

"Very well, major," Dr. Carey said as he straightened up and lifted the other lamp higher. "But I want you to know that I intend to see that this prisoner receives better medical attention in the future." Randall's voice was cold, hardly the same man who had just exposed his soul.

Major Wood blanched. Joseph and Rachel, still standing shoulder to shoulder, glanced at each other in surprise.

The doctor turned directly toward Joseph. "Young man," he said with firmness, "you take care of that arm now, you hear? I'll be back again as soon as I can." He took Rachel's arm and moved to lead her out. He turned back to face Joseph again, his back to the officer. "And maybe I'll find some additional help." His left eyelid closed slowly, in an elaborate wink.

The doctor and Rachel followed Wood out the door. The lamps were gone. Dimness and silence fell as heavy as death. Joseph sat down on the stool, his head in his hands, to await his meal.

* * *

The familiar gloom and quiet that settled around him after his visitors left was more bearable than it had been in a long time. He could not, in fact, remember when he had felt better since his imprisonment had begun, weeks ago.

And no wonder. There was the unexpected arrival of a girl he had not realized he loved until he'd ended up in a dark cold cell. If he'd ever doubted her love for him, that had been erased by the simple fact of her coming. Then he had been given proper medical attention for the first time since he landed in this pit where his wound had been slowly poisoning him. He had forgotten what good health felt like. And now the breath of firm and humane authority had come into his dwelling place with the fragrance of hope.

He didn't know what form the "additional help" hinted by the doctor would take. The tall man's no-nonsense manner left him with a confidence that his life might improve significantly, and soon. It hadn't slipped his mind that Rachel had said Dr. Carey knew the president.

He grinned into the murk out of sheer exuberance. Feeling too lively to sit, he moved in a brisk step around in his tiny home. The best part of his good feeling came not from the kind company or even the medical care, however. He was satisfied that he finally had some listeners with whom he could further develop his thoughts. He remembered well the relief he had felt when nurse Campbell had listened to him and drawn him out. But in the intervening weeks his mind had seemed to go soft, and without someone to talk *to*, he hadn't been able to work out his ideas and his—what was that word Dr. Carey had used?—apologia. That was a good, big one!

His deed and all its meaning had sat in his mind like a big boulder. In his heart he had known it was right to turn and walk away from combat. How could he ever forget that spiritual euphoria! But in the prison cell since then he couldn't seem to chip away at that huge rock of his conviction, to break it down into smooth pebbles small enough to hold in his hands and turn over for scrutiny. That had troubled him. Now, thanks to love and kinship, his beliefs had been drawn out and framed in words.

Well, maybe not totally. He had only begun. He stopped his pacing and stared at the cobwebby wall. It struck him that both Rachel and Dr. Carey had been in sympathy with him. He hadn't had to shape responses to questions that might have been sharper had they been hostile. His exuberance receded just a mite. He hadn't had to convince Rachel because she loved him. (Bless her heart, he thought, with a soft twitch to his lips.) And he hadn't had to argue with the doctor because for some reason the man seemed to have remembered some old feelings in himself that Joseph's words sparked.

What, though, if the questions about his beliefs and his battlefield desertion were to come from neutrals? Even worse, from those who were opposed to his position and who also had the power either to free him or condemn him to further imprisonment?

Or worse.

Joseph shivered and sat down. He huddled into himself, suddenly fearful of his future again. It was fine and dandy to have visitors, girlfriends, doctors, and so forth. But he was still a prisoner, and Major Wood was certainly in charge. Rachel and Dr. Carey, after all was said and done, could leave.

Joseph could not.

A chill rippled through him and suddenly he was aware of his body. He was tired. So tired: of darkness, of dirt, of monotony. He wanted to feel sunshine again, walk in the rain, ride Prince. He wished he could simply lie down and stretch out on a soft, white bed again and watch the breeze fill out the curtains till they floated out over the polished footboard of the bed.

He wanted to eat something solid and substantial. With some taste to it.

The thought brought him to his feet again. He remembered that food was the thing that had driven his visitors away. Wood had made a bad joke about not disturbing the inmates while they dined, but where was that dinner? As if his belly was servant to his brain, it started to clamor for sustenance. Tasteless as it may be, prison fare at least was filling.

He grinned into the murk out of sheer exuberance. Feeling too lively to sit, he moved in a brisk step around in his tiny home. The best part of his good feeling came not from the kind company or even the medical care, however. He was satisfied that he finally had some listeners with whom he could further develop his thoughts. He remembered well the relief he had felt when nurse Campbell had listened to him and drawn him out. But in the intervening weeks his mind had seemed to go soft, and without someone to talk *to*, he hadn't been able to work out his ideas and his—what was that word Dr. Carey had used?— apologia. That was a good, big one!

17

Another quarter hour passed before his meal arrived. It was not brought by his usual nemesis, Zack, but by Major Wood himself. And it was not the routine swill but—his nose told him as soon as the door opened—beefsteak fried in butter and smothered with onions, accompanied by boiled potatoes and green beans. Joseph's nose practically dragged the rest of him toward his jailer.

"Here, hold this, King," Wood said. "I've got a nice surprise for you."

Joseph took the tray handed to him with the meal on it. He stood, gaping at it like a fool. He was dumbfounded. Wood put down on the floor the lamp he'd brought in with the meal, then disappeared through the doorway. Instantly he reappeared, carrying with both hands a large wooden chair, complete with carved arms and padded leather upholstering. He carried the heavy piece of furniture over to a spot alongside the whiskey keg, set it down on the uneven floor, and walked it around until it was moderately level.

"Set the tray on the keg, King," he said, straightening up and smiling as wide as a barn door. "Then come and help."

In a daze Joseph obeyed, following the man through the open door and up the steps to the room where he'd been processed that first day. There sat a solid-looking square, wood table, its four legs and feet as ornately carved as Aunt Bessie's parlor furniture. Squarely in the center of the top surface was a crisp white linen doily, looking as if it had just been laundered.

"Grab that end there," Wood said, pointing to the side nearest Joseph. "Don't worry 'bout your arm. It isn't as heavy as it looks. Now let's carry it down to your room."

Down they went, somehow managing to keep the linen cloth on the tabletop. Wood was right. The table wasn't heavy enough to hurt Joseph's arm, but it was a sufficiently clumsy load to cause him to back down the stairs carefully.

"Watch you don't kick over the lamp!' Wood cried out as they scuffed into the cell.

When the table was in place next to the chair, Wood retrieved the lamp and put it in the exact center of the snowy cloth. The polished surfaces of chair and table gleamed softly in the glow of the oil flame.

The major brushed his hands together as if to signify a good job well done. He beamed at Joseph. "Now eat up, Mr. Joseph King, if you can get your jaw up far enough off the floor to chew!" He threw back his head and guffawed.

Joseph swallowed. His hands were trembling. As if in a dream he moved himself to sit in the throne-like chair, almost sinking away in the soft seat cushion. Steam curled off the plate in front of him as he lifted it from the tray and put it on the table. He began to eat.

Wood stood in front of the table, his hands jacked nonchalantly into half-fists by thumbs behind his belt. He chuckled. "I gotta hand it to you, King, you know how to work the system."

Joseph looked up at the man without stopping his chewing. So far he felt it was a dream, all this elegant treatment, but he had no intention of risking a sudden awakening. He'd eat so long as the food was there.

"What do you mean?" he asked between bites. It was delicious.

"Why didn't you tell me you know Dr. Carey?" Major Wood's face held his smile and he was the soul of good fellowship, but Joseph thought he detected a false note in the man's voice. "Any friend of Mr. Lincoln is a friend of William Wood. You could have received better treatment from day one if you'd told me."

Joseph's chewing slowed and his mind raced, but no words came to him.

"Yessirree," Wood continued, "it's like I told the good doctor just a while ago. There just hadn't been time to get a doctor in to see you. And we have had so many prisoners in all the other parts of Old Capitol here, that we've had to keep you down here. Not to mention—"

"I see," Joseph cut in. "Never mind." He felt a rush of contempt for his jailer. It must have shown on his face, for Wood's smile faltered. He waited, but Joseph just kept eating, avoiding the man's eyes.

Joseph knew then, as if it were a revelation, that he could not allow his keeper to go on believing he was only a manipulator. Major Wood thought so, and indeed why shouldn't he, since he was doubtlessly such himself? But that would deny Joseph's reason for being in here. At least it would spoil his witness to this gatekeeper of the prison. Instead, he must convince Wood that he had taken a stand upon scruple and was here for no other reason. Furthermore, he had not tried and would not try to get the powers-that-be to intercede for him. If they did so, well and good. If not, then he would be granted the peace and fortitude to persevere.

With these thoughts his appetite seemed to be ebbing away. Or maybe his shrunken belly simply was no longer able to accept such unaccustomed fare. He pushed away the steak only half eaten and sipped the coffee. He wiped his mouth on his sleeve and took a breath. His eyes met Wood's and he saw curiosity there. Joseph sensed the moment as a God-given opening.

"I have no complaint about my treatment, Major Wood," he said. "I broke the laws of the land so I deserve the punishment. It would not be right if I didn't have to pay a penalty."

Wood's curiosity shaded into surprise. Joseph realized his words must have sounded pious but he also knew they were the unvarnished truth. He realized it even as the words came off his tongue. He stood up. "I don't believe that war is right, or that a soldier who lays down his weapon and quits the army is wrong. If he is forced to fight and violate his conscience, the damage is greater than the good of the cause he's supposed to be fighting for."

Joseph stopped. Something wasn't right. He felt like a soapbox orator. As if to confirm his unease, his jailer's eyes lost their surprise and acquired a sly grin.

"Sure thing, King, sure thing," he said to Joseph. "Now do you want the rest of that beefsteak or not?" He winked, as if to signify he understood the essential Joseph King, no matter the pretty words. After all, his many months of duty as a prison-keeper had taught him much about the mental processes of inmates, how they struggled to retain their self-respect, and keep away the trolls in the head.

"No matter, you can keep the furniture and the lamp," he said, still grinning smugly. "And, oh yeah. . . ." He dug in his tunic pockets and produced a handful of lucifers. "Keep these, too, and let me know when you run out of coal oil. I'll have Zack bring you more." He laid the matches on the table. "Now I've got to go. Is there anything else I can get you, Mr. King?" He picked up the food tray.

"No, sir," Joseph said, staring at the wall behind Wood's head. "Er, wait—yes, there is. Uh, would you mind cleaning off the window? It's got quite a film of mud from all the rain splashing up, and I wondered if you could—"

"Will do!" Wood said. His voice was cheerful. The smugness seemed to have gone. "As I said, any friend of Mr. Lincoln. . . ." With that he left, turning the key in the lock behind him.

Joseph slumped into the chair. He rested his head against the high, padded back and gazed into the flame. The kerosene burned steadily and clean with only a thin line of smoke climbing up the glistening glass chimney. He reached out and turned down the wick, then sagged back into the chair again. He noted the glass reservoir was over half full.

He felt ashamed and weak. He knew that Major Wood had left thinking him no different from any other prisoner so far as his beliefs and goals were concerned. He had done a miserable job of persuading Wood that he was here because of his conscience, not because of cowardice, or disloyalty, or any baser motive. Wood still thought of him as a typical Yankee conniver, trying to wriggle out of a tight spot by getting help from wherever he could find it. Of course, that was a logical thing to assume. Wood was not a fool and he would not believe for a minute that a prisoner would stay in prison a second longer than he had to.

And I wouldn't either, thought Joseph. With that admission he grinned. But I didn't know, either, that Rachel was coming, or that she would have a nearby relative who'd have pull, who even knows Lincoln! Or that Wood would defer to Dr. Carey the way he did. I knew none of this and if I had, I. . . .

"You'd what, King?" he asked aloud. "Tell yourself the truth. You want out of here so bad you'd eat your way out, come another three or four weeks, and you know it.

It was true. Before Rachel had dropped in, not half an hour before her surprise arrival, he had counted his calendar marks again and knew that Christmas was only about two months away. And the thought of spending that holiday in here. . . . Well, he'd been beginning to learn the meaning of desperation for the first time.

Now since Rachel had come and even more since the visit of Dr. Carey, hope had bubbled up through his entire being and had changed his outlook. Only now, as he sat here, was he realizing just how much that was true.

He took one of the matches lying on the table and idly began picking his teeth with it. He let his eyes stray around his cell, so different now with the soft lamplight, the easy chair, and the elegant table.

He saw Dr. Carey's Bible on the floor next to the keg where he'd laid it when his dinner came. He reached for it, realizing only after he had it on the table that he'd used his sore arm. It hadn't hurt nearly as much as before.

He smiled. That, too, had changed his outlook. The lessening of physical pain and mental anguish and fear that the untended wound would put him out of this world, even before Christmas. Yes, his mood was certainly improved. Which was why, he supposed, his imprisonment was no longer unbearable.

His mind wouldn't rest. Now it told him that his well-being came from his perception that Dr. Carey was sympathetic to his reasons for deserting and that he knew the president. The president might therefore listen to Dr. Carey when the doctor told him why Joseph should not be held in jail any longer. And certainly Mr. Lincoln could personally intervene in the system of military justice and release Joseph.

Just like that.

Joseph sighed and came to his feet. He began to pace again, around the perimeter of the room, his hands crossed at the wrists behind him. It had been in the back of his mind ever since he had first heard that Dr. Carey and Mr. Lincoln were on friendly terms. No president, no self-respecting human being in a position of authority over another human being, would make any decision about treatment of that person under his power without being mighty sure the reasons were good. And one could hardly expect that a wartime president, especially one whose armies could not seem to win a battle, would be in any mood to release a deserting soldier for "reasons of conscience"!

Joseph laughed. It was so ridiculous it was hilarious. "Imagine yourself, King," he said aloud again. "Imagine having an audience with a busy president, distracted by war, afflicted by personal grief, frustrated by timid generals, threatened by foreign intervention to help his enemies. Imagine him allowing time to listen to a soldier charged with desertion, let alone even considering a pardon!"

His laughter grew. It sounded harsh in the confined spaces of his cell. Startlingly loud. But it grew and slapped back at him in broken echoes from the rough rock of the walls. He remembered that other time of panicked levity, when he'd been just a newcomer here.

He felt weak as tears came to his eyes. He bent double in his mirth and staggered to the chair. Falling into it he threw back his head and the gusts of hilarity continued, long past the originating humor. On into the hurt that now lay exposed in his heart. The terror.

Then he was weeping. The tears which the laughter had brought were multiplied in the agony and Joseph did not know what was happening to him. Sobs wracked his chest. His hands shook when he pulled out his shirttail to wipe his eyes. Then he gripped the arms of the chair and gritted his teeth. He ground them against all feeling and he tried to tie off the thoughts that leaped unbidden to his brain. And he silently doused the hope that had sprung up in his soul.

It was cruel. They shouldn't have come. It wasn't fair. He had been getting used to the regimen. He had erased the awful sense of insult and degradation he'd known in those first days and weeks of his confinement. He'd achieved, if that was the word, a numbness that denied the loss of hope. He had just begun to learn how to live when there's no hope.

And now there had come the warmth and caring of hope-bearing friends and he was jerked back into life. For what was life but hope? And what was hope but the gift of caring persons?

But what was the point of hoping? Wasn't he, Joseph King, old enough to know that conscience, scruple, correct moral choice—call it whatever—was rarely prized or rewarded in this world? He was a fool to hope, a bloody fool!

Gradually his misery was dissipated by drowsiness. It must be the soft chair, he thought, a smile sneaking across his face as torpor muffled his senses. Maybe it was the steak and potatoes. His smile grew wider, his eyes closed. His head fell back across the upholstery. With an effort he raised his legs and dropped them across the keg.

"Ah luxury," he said to himself. He felt purged by his laughter and weeping. Almost pleasant. He even chuckled again when he thought of Major Wood. How amused he would be if he only knew how far Joseph really was from manipulating the powers that be.

Just before he fell asleep he thought of the burning lamp. "Must blow it out," he murmured. But his eyes would not come open again.

* * *

Joseph woke abruptly and sat up straight, straining to hear. An unfamiliar scratching noise came to his ears. The light in his cell was different, although the lamp was still burning steadily.

The scraping sound came again. Now he identified it as issuing from the far end of his cell, behind the wine rack. He sat back with a sigh and a grin. Someone was removing the accumulated grime from the windowpane. He would have a brighter contact with the world again. Wood was as good as his word, bless his heart.

Joseph stood up and stretched. He blew out the lamp and moved toward the rapidly growing rectangle of brightening sunshine. He stared out at the muddy boots of the man excavating his peephole. He recognized the footwear as belonging to his longtime keeper, Zack. Just then the man leaned over to scoop a spadeful of dirt away and he saw Joseph's face in a shaft of sunbeam. He gave an obsequious grin.

Joseph smiled back and mouthed "thank-you" through the glass. He shook his head in amusement at the change from Zack's usual grin of smug contempt. Another fruit of Dr. Carey's visit, Joseph decided.

He turned and walked back to the table and chair, his new cozy parlor. He stood for a moment, tapping his thumb against his teeth, lost in thought. Presently he struck a match to the still-warm lamp. Sunshine there might be aplenty now, but a single long shaft wasn't the best for concentrated study. For that's what he had just decided to do. He picked up the Bible as he sat down. Yes, it was a decision, but more than that. He would commit himself to study this holy book of Christianity as never before. All his life it seemed, he'd had biblical teachings shoved at him (he grinned at the word) and he had even memorized many verses, thanks to his parents. But now he wanted to understand, not just memorize.

His grandmother Kate had a knack for storytelling. She could keep his attention for hours on end with her ability to enter into characters and situations, practically acting out her tales. She had done this with countless stories both from the Old and New Testaments. Consequently, Joseph, almost in spite of himself and certainly with little effort on his part, had gained a significant fund of knowledge about the persons and places of the Bible.

Adding Grandma Kate's "yarning" to his father and mother's fervid teaching by precept and example, he had acquired more than a nodding acquaintance with many of the Scriptures. He had even read through the entire Bible once, as a twelve-year-old.

Joseph sighed and put the past away from him. It was painful now that he realized how little effect all that immersion in those holy writings had apparently had on his life. Virtually none of the memorized verses had stayed with him. All his life the teaching on the Mennonite version of pacifism had been drilled into him, yet he had left and enlisted in the army as if he'd been reared a Catholic, or nothing. Without a twinge of conscience, at least not until he'd got down to the bloodletting of battle itself.

Why was that? he asked himself, staring into the steady flame. Is that simply human nature, to take one's teachings from babyhood on up for granted, actually almost ignoring them until put under the gun? In his case quite literally? If I had not gone to war would I ever have discovered that I really do believe the things I was taught rather than just *thinking* I believe them?

"Whew!" Joseph muttered. "That's too much to know for sure." He laughed and moved his eyes to the Bible still in his hand. He pushed his thoughts back to the decision he had just made. Yes he would read it through, at least the New Testament, from Matthew to Revelation. And he would be doing it as an adult this time: pondering, questioning, praying. Yes, praying. As Joseph read, something different was in his soul now: a presence whose words could not be adequately perceived without constant openness. And prayer.

A warm, peaceful spirit filled him as he leafed to the first chapter of the Gospel written by Matthew. He could almost forget where he was and why he was here. As he began to read with this feeling, nothing else seemed to matter. Only one thought pushed away his resolve and that was the worry (he almost laughed at the irony of it) that he might be interrupted before he'd finished!

For the next day almost without a break, Joseph King read the Bible. He read in the lamplight until the afternoon sunshine pierced the gloom through his newly cleaned window. Then he blew out the lamp to conserve oil, out of habit, and pulled the throne-like chair to a spot where God's natural light could fall on the page. He read until his supper was brought, then he read after he had eaten and the sun had died away, until his oil ran out.

In the morning when his breakfast was brought, he requested more kerosene and it was brought with a smile. The breakfast meal was ham, eggs, and coffee, brought by a Zack who had obviously been given orders to be all things to Joseph. At noon, when his dinner was carried in, he asked for paper and pencils, with a knife for keeping a sharp writing point. All these things were brought, even the knife.

Zack at first seemed uncomfortable in his new role as a nice person. It was an obvious struggle for him to play the part of servant to a prisoner, but curiosity overcame his discomfort. He had the ghost of a typical smirk when he first saw it was a Bible which Joseph was reading. But later when he could see that Joseph had been reading for hours, page after page, his eyes were full of questions.

When Joseph requested paper and pencil, Zack could not contain his wonderings. "Whatcha need writin' paper fer . . . fer only readin' the Bible?" He wiped his sleeve across his mouth to remove the grease of the chicken he'd just devoured. It was Joseph's dinner, but his shrunken bodily needs hadn't been up to such a feast. He had offered it to Zack, who'd promptly accepted.

"I'm taking notes," Joseph replied, with a friendly smile. "There are lots of things I want to have written down so I don't forget them."

Zack looked at Joseph with an expression that told him to go on.

"Also, in some chapters I find things that seem to fall into place with things I read in other chapters. If I write them down I can connect them better in my mind.

"Oh," Zack said. A sudden hunger came into the man's face. Then his eyes dropped and he suddenly seemed embarrassed.

"Have you read the Bible, Zack?"

"I cain't read." The big work-roughened hands jerked awkwardly. A muddy boot scuffed at the dirt floor.

"Want me to read some of it to you?"

Zack's face jerked up and his eyes fastened on Joseph. They studied Joseph and a gamut of emotions trailed through them.

Joseph waited.

A shade seemed to lower across Zack's vulnerability. "Naw, I reckon not now." He stooped and picked up the now-empty dinner tray. "I'll bring them things now," he said and seemed almost to run from the cell. Minutes later when he returned with the items Joseph had requested, he set them inside the door and quickly left, without so much as another glance at Joseph.

So Joseph read on, now taking notes as he'd outlined to Zack. He finished Matthew and Mark, then decided to jump to the Acts of the Apostles. From his youth he recollected that the first four books of the New Testament, the Gospels, were similar in telling of the life of Jesus. Acts told the story of Jesus' followers after he had left them and ascended to heaven.

Joseph had always enjoyed these storybooks. As he read he smiled nostalgically, recognizing many of the accounts his grandmother had told. Only now, as he read thoughtfully and maturely, a deeper level of meaning came out of the words. He jotted down his reflections.

When he came to certain incidents in the lives of Paul and Peter, he arrested his reading of Acts and leafed ahead to related material in letters they had written. Especially those of Paul, the most prolific of the apostolic writers. He would read from their own words, then jump back to the story line in Acts. Hours passed unheeded as Joseph read, fascinated by the words as if seen for the first time.

Following his noon meal, twenty-four hours after he'd begun to read, he blew out the lamp and reverted to the use of natural daylight again. He continued to read in the afternoon sunshine, jotting page after page of notes. Joseph felt none of the boredom he used to experience back in school when he had been forced to read books and take notes. Now, on the contrary, he was almost breathless with the excitement of discovery and discernment.

All the stories and verses were so familiar-sounding. The teachings sounded full of the ring of authority because they had been preached at him for his whole life. Yet something was so different. Everything was fresh. Beneath all the numbers of chapters and verses, running like a silver thread through all the words, was a sense of purpose and direction, of meaning and importance. It was exciting!

At one point, somewhere in the doldrums of midafternoon, Joseph came down to earth. He'd stopped reading to yawn and stretch, putting down the pencil and rising to pace and get his blood moving again after hours of sitting. Then, for the first time since the previous afternoon, Joseph thought about Rachel.

He felt a sudden rush of warmth. It was surprising because a part of his mind wondered why he didn't feel guilt for neglecting to think of her and to anticipate her speedy return. The rest of his consciousness, however, was aware that his thoughts of her seemed to mesh beautifully with the well-being that the reading and meditation was producing in him. That was the unexpected part. His love of Rachel and his mood of worship (yes, that was the attitude his reading was inspiring in him) seemed like parts of a whole.

He sighed and sat down again. He would have to tell her about this remarkable feeling next time she came. A worm of longing wriggled inside him. "How I hope she returns today!" he said to himself. Then he went back to his reading and taking of notes. He knew she would be back soon.

18

The midafternoon sunshine had marched up his page, dropped off the top of it, and proceeded to slither along his leg toward the door. He had just gotten up to light the lamp again when the stairs clattered with footsteps.

"Put your homework away, King; it's Jubilee Day!" Major Wood cried as he flung open the heavy oaken door.

Joseph almost dropped the match he'd been holding. Wood's broad grin loomed over him. The light from the lamp he held made Joseph squint.

"C'mon, King, get your stuff together—you're getting out of here!"

"I am?" Joseph blinked. "Out of here? Out of Old Capitol?"

"You bet!"

"How come? Is there finally a trial or something?"

"It isn't a trial. It's a release, signed by the president!" Wood's smile grew even larger. There wasn't even a hint of guile or bitterness in it.

Joseph stood for a moment, hesitant and unbelieving, suspecting a cruel joke. He'd had his hopes raised before, only to have them dashed. He wasn't going to get carried away now.

"Is this Dr. Carey's doing?" he finally asked.

"I reckon so, since he's sitting out in his carriage right now!" Wood was almost dancing in his excitement. It seemed he hadn't been lying when he claimed that any friend of the president was a friend of Major William Wood.

Did he dare believe the jailer? Joseph gave his home for the past month a last, lingering look. Was it really possible that the president of the United States was freeing him? He looked at Wood's expectant, eager face again, then shrugged and picked up his tunic, notes, and Dr. Carey's Bible. "All right, lead the way." He followed the officer out the door without a backward glance.

Wood handed Joseph his pack as they passed through the room at the head of the stairs. From the cobwebs all over it, he guessed it had been there all the time. Wood gave him a pat on the back and a comradely farewell. As the superintendent of Old Capitol had said, Dr. Carey was waiting in the carriage at the end of the boardwalk.

The late afternoon sunshine hit Joseph like a solid wall as he emerged from his prison. He staggered under the almost physical blow of being in the fresh air again, bombarded by sights and sounds. Dr. Carey jumped down to guide him into the vehicle. "Here, let me help you," he laughed. "I guess I didn't think of the impact freedom can have on a fellow chained underground like a poor beast!" He laughed jovially as they situated themselves in the plush, padded seats. "I have been to the White House, Joseph." His laugh settled into a warm smile as he told Willie to start the horse. "Mr. Lincoln and I have had a chat about you and your case!"

"Where's Rachel?" Suddenly, Joseph cared more about seeing her than getting free or hearing about presidents. He had something to ask her.

"Oh, she's back at the house." He grinned, conspiratorially. "Packing."

"Packing? Is she going home?"

"Yes."

"Without coming to see me again?" It hadn't really sunk in that he was leaving his cell.

"But Joseph—" There was a twinkle in Dr. Carey's eyes.

"I'm taking you to her. Then you can have a meal, a bath, and get some fresh clothes on." He chuckled. "I don't think you will be going back to Old Capitol anymore. He's released you into my custody."

Joseph stared at the doctor. "Is this your doing, sir?"

Dr. Carey chuckled again, "Oh, I suppose I had something to do with it, but Rachel made quite an impression, too."

"Rachel—" Joseph swallowed. "You mean she went to see Mr. Lincoln—" He shook his head slowly, at a loss for words.

"Oh, sure," Dr. Carey laughed. "Ordinary citizens go to see him every day. Doesn't seem to matter there's a war on, Abe sees them all. Of course, the wait can get pretty long, unless you've got an inside track. That's where I came in. . . ." The doctor smiled modestly.

"But how—" Joseph began.

"How did the two of us get you released, you mean? Not so fast, Willie," he interrupted himself. "You'll splash the pedestrians!" he cried to his driver.

"Sorry, massuh." The round, grizzled black face appeared in the window to the front. Its sober, respectful mien was broken for a moment by a dazzling grin and a wink at Joseph. Both the doctor and his passenger burst out laughing.

"We told the president the things you said to us," Randall continued, as Willie obediently slowed the vehicle. "And Abe listened because much of what you told me—which I passed on to him—he has heard before, from his own heart. He's a sensitive man." The doctor looked steadily at Joseph. "He has a big heart, Joseph. It hurts him beyond our imaginings, I'd guess, to have to ask young men and even boys to march off to battle. I think he manages to accept their sacrifices and their service only because he is not faced day by day with their being individuals."

Dr. Carey suddenly grinned. "He asked some questions about you, after we'd filled him in on your recent experiences. Most of them were ones only Rachel could answer."

"He did? What sort of questions?"

"About your home, your parents and friends. He was quite curious about your father, and what the Mennonites stand for." Dr. Carey glowed with satisfaction. "Rachel outlined basic church beliefs, as she'd learned them from your father. Then Lincoln said in a wistful tone that he wishes he could meet more of these Mennonites if they all believe the way you do. He said he could find all sorts of uses for your type of person."

"*My* type?" Joseph laughed. "*I* don't even know what kind of person I am! Not to put into words, that is."

Randall gave him a shrewd look as the carriage turned off the street and into the doctor's driveway. "A lot of us don't until the chips are down, Joseph."

Willie pulled the vehicle to a stop, then got down, unhitched the horse, and led it away. Joseph moved to get out.

"Just a moment, Joseph," Randall said. He laid a restraining hand on the young man's arm. "Before you rush into the arms of your beloved, let me be more specific about the terms of your release."

Joseph relaxed back into the seat again. The doctor fixed him with a serious look. "I'm convinced it's nothing short of criminal, Joseph. This nation is throwing the lives of its young men into the greedy maw of war and making no provision for those whose conscience and scruples forbid their participation."

Joseph blinked. "You mean there are others, like me?"

Dr. Carey nodded. "Definitely. My daughter reports to me the conversations she has with wounded soldiers, and I myself frequently patrol the wards of the numerous hospital tents in and near the district." He broke off to give a wry grin. "It's understandable that battle wounds and moral doubts appear together in the same man. But"—and his face grew serious—"I'm convinced that many of these boys are genuine in their wishes to be of service to their nation in nonviolent, constructive ways."

His sober eyes gripped Joseph. "And I intend that you, Joseph, should be an object lesson, to prove my belief. I believe I've persuaded the president to allow you to be my guinea pig."

Just then he was interrupted by the sound of fingers tapping window glass. Without turning toward the signal, Randall waved a hand toward it. He went on. "Joseph, I want you to become an orderly in hospital tents. I want you to work alongside nurses and doctors and surgeons, wherever the need is greatest. It will be dirty and dangerous—we don't know why disease spreads, or how, but we certainly realize that being exposed to disease and corruption increases one's chance of being infected by it."

"But I know nothing about—" Joseph began.

Dr. Carey cut him off. "I know you're completely untrained. I will do as much to train you as I can, as will other medical personnel you get assigned to. It's not pretty work, but it's a thousand times more useful, and needed, than sitting and rotting in a cell." Randall's face broke into a smile. "Besides, even though you'll still technically be a ward of the government—a prisoner—you'll be helping your fellow human beings, instead of killing them. Doesn't that strike you as a worthwhile activity for a pacifist?"

Joseph laughed in delight. "It's certainly better than fighting. But when will I start?" He felt a blush spreading up his cheeks. "I have some business to handle with Rachel, and I . . . uh. . . ."

Randall threw back his head and roared out a laugh. "I'd have been disappointed if you hadn't said so! No, there's no hurry. I convinced Abe you are trustworthy. Take some time to go home to Michigan, with Rachel, of course, and take care of family business." On the last two words, the man winked at Joseph and laughed again. "Report back to me after your father's up and about and other matters are attended to. Say by . . . ah . . . the second week of January. How's that?"

Joseph couldn't believe his ears. "That's excellent, sir! That's—that's—" But Dr. Carey's laugh sounded again, drowning out his words.

"Now, young man," he said, slapping Joseph's knee. "Let's get inside and say hello to the home folks and maybe get you a bath and a nap, or whatever!"

"Amazing!" was all that came out of Joseph's throat as they climbed the porch steps. "Amazing," he said again, stopping and looking around him at the grass and leaves and sky. Then at Dr. Carey. "Two days ago, only forty-eight hours, I was sitting in a dungeon without hope, with a festering wound, thinking myself abandoned, and today I'm. . . ." It was so overwhelming he could only lift his arms and let them fall again. His throat was suddenly too thick to swallow.

"God moves in mysterious ways," Randall said softly, and he put an arm across Joseph's shoulders to usher him into the house. "By the way, let's have a look at that arm again."

Joseph smiled and nodded. He closed his eyes to pinch off their wetness, but a stray tear rolled down his bearded cheek as they stepped through the door.

Rachel took his hand and squeezed it, and the look in her eyes said they had volumes to speak to each other, once they were alone. Then she introduced him to Rose and Hetty. He was made to feel at home and given a hot tub to soak in. His body felt giddy at the sensations of cleanness. When Dr. Carey finished treating and rewrapping his wound, just before they ate supper, he was amazed at the rapidity of its healing. He felt as healthy and raring to go as a colt. He left his beard full, though, at Rachel's insistence. She claimed it gave him greater "presence," whatever that meant, but he humored her.

They all sat around the kitchen table and talked as they finished their coffee. Everyone was in high spirits as befitted the occasion, even Hetty. Her misery of spirit seemed to melt away in the cheer of Joseph's blessing. And she was quite taken, as Rachel couldn't help but notice, by Joseph's smiling charm.

Rachel herself certainly had never been more in love with him than on this day of his deliverance. She could hardly wait to get him off to herself and thought she would have time after the meal. But then the big silly fellow started yawning and remarking how he hadn't had a good *bed* sleep in a month. Would anyone mind if he took himself off for a bit of a nap?

Of course they wouldn't, they said. No one could begin to imagine sleeping in a filthy, dark dungeon for so long. If he'd not said so himself, they all would have *ordered* him to bed. So they let him go. Randall went off to make calls, and the three women returned to the table and had a second cup of coffee.

"When did you say the train leaves?" Rachel asked. She was so keyed up her cup almost spilled as she raised it to her lips.

Rose smiled. "At two-thirty-three, tomorrow afternoon, if it's on time. Do you need any help in your packing?"

Rachel shook her head. "No, I've been ready since dinnertime. I can hardly wait!" She grinned at her relatives. "Say, do you have anything for me to help with? I've got to do *something* while I wait or I'll go stark mad!"

They all laughed.

"Well, I suppose we could find something," Rose said, hoisting her bulk to a standing position. "There are the supper dishes to wash, and kindling wood to split so's I can start breakfast in the morning. Then the rugs need beating and the parlor floor wants a wax—"

"Whoa, Cousin Rose, I won't go *that* mad!" Rachel cried, laughing. "But I will be happy to start with the dishes. Not the wood, though. I'd likely chop my toes off. I'm so excited!"

They all laughed again. Rachel got up, reached for the water bucket, and poured out enough into the large kettles, one for scrubbing, one for rinsing. Then she started to gather up the dishes, stacking them in the sink.

"Let me help you with those," Hetty said, standing up.

"You two go ahead," Rose ordered. "I'll be down in the root cellar." She left.

"I'll wash, if that's fine with you," Hetty said.

"Sure," Rachel smiled. She took a towel from a drawer while Hetty poured steaming water over a cake of soap in the large copper washing pan.

They went about their respective chores in companionable silence. Since their first contact barely two days ago, when Hetty's bitterness at the loss of her fiancé made her seem almost rude, the two cousins had grown more friendly. Hetty was grieving the death of her lover and tended to envy Rachel the fact that *her* man was at least still alive. She was impressed by Rachel's courage in coming across four states when she didn't even know whether she was truly loved by the man she loved.

Seeing the way her older cousin had dealt with uncertainties and fears had stirred Hetty. Gradually she had warmed to Rachel. Now, incredibly to herself, she was even able, almost, to forget her own loss and feel hopeful for Rachel's future. Her question, now, revealed that quite abruptly.

"Will you and Joseph marry, Rachel?" she asked, a sly grin on her face.

Rachel almost let slip the plate she was wiping. "I—I don't know. I honestly don't know. It depends. . . ."

"But do you want to? Marry him, I mean?"

Rachel could feel the blood creeping up her neck and spreading around to her cheeks. She felt suddenly hot. "I've wanted that for years," she said in a low voice. She gave a little laugh which caught in her throat. "But I want it far more now, now that he has changed."

"Has he really changed?"

"Oh, yes."

"How?" Hetty paused in her washing and leaned her sudsy hands on the edge of the sink. Her look was penetrating.

"I'm not sure I can really put it into words, but—but he seems more at peace now. Calmer." She frowned slightly, deep in thought.

"Is he happier?"

"Yes," Rachel replied. "I think that's the main difference." She wiped the last dish Hetty had washed and set it down carefully. "Yes, he seems to be more like he used to be before we grew up. More like he was when he was around ten or twelve."

"Rachel, do you think he's sincere? You've been telling me the things he said to you and to Father." She picked up a coffee cup and submerged it. "Does Joseph really mean all he said? Is he really so opposed to war?"

"I have no doubt he means it all."

"Do you believe that way, too? Do you think that if a man refuses to fight for his country for whatever reason, that he should be allowed off, as free as the wind, while others fight and . . ."—Hetty's voice faltered—"maybe die?" She rinsed the cup and set it on the drain board, not looking at her cousin.

Rachel considered her response as she wiped the cup and hung it on its hook in the cupboard. "No, I don't,

Hetty." She folded her dish towel and hung it up to dry before continuing. "No, and I don't believe for a moment that Joseph feels that way either."

Hetty suddenly turned and looked directly into Rachel's eyes. She said nothing, for a long moment, then her eyes filled with tears and she almost fell into Rachel's arms. "Oh, Rachel—" Sobs cut off her words. Rachel held her. Over her shoulder she saw Rose coming in with her arms full of carrots and potatoes. Rachel smiled reassuringly at the worried questions on Rose's face.

Hetty sobbed and then finally pulled away. "Oh, Rachel. I hope Joseph marries you. I want you always to be happy. Always!" She turned and ran from the kitchen, almost colliding with her mother in the doorway. Rose stood awkwardly, with vegetables in her arms and grateful comprehension in her face.

PART THREE

THE HOMECOMING

19

By midafternoon the next day, the train bearing Rachel and Joseph was leaving behind the last of the defensive works ringing Washington, D.C., and beginning its long pull to the northwest. Until they were on the train, Joseph hadn't found time to tell Rachel about his "parole." Now he was finishing for the second time his account of what he and Dr. Carey had discussed last night over a cup of hot chocolate. Joseph had awakened late, after the house had stilled for the night. Unable to return to sleep, he'd gotten up and wandered into the doctor's library. He'd been browsing hungrily—his old love of reading sharpened by weeks of mental torpor—when a tired Randall had come home. Despite his obvious fatigue, Dr. Carey insisted upon spelling out some of the details of the terms of Joseph's upcoming alternate service, as he called it.

The next day the whole Carey family had seen them off at the station, necessitating use of the Sunday two-seater for the large party. Randall said they were extremely fortunate in finding an *almost* straight-through train, luckier than Rachel had been a few days before. He promised to send the wire Joseph had composed to Ben and Lovina so that someone would be in Kalamazoo to meet them when the train arrived tomorrow around noon.

The morning had been full of sunshine, bidding them fair traveling. It seemed to gather even more bright sky away from the October clouds as the day passed noon. Joseph had shaken Randall Carey's hand with a gratitude impossible to put into words. Rachel insisted they simply must all come out to Michigan to visit, as soon as possible. Hetty had winked at Rachel and Rose had smirked over that, while the doctor looked bemused. Joseph felt left out.

Then they were waving from their window in a coach which badly needed cleaning of soldiers' mud from countless days. Showers of cinders fell around the Careys as the train chuffed out. Rachel and Joseph tried to get comfortable in a seat they would share for many hours of clickety-clack traveling.

"Dr. Carey gave my duties no formal title," Joseph was saying, "but that's only because no one's ever before been assigned in just the same way. My position will amount to a sort of alternate service," he said, "as if I were still in the army, yet without the duty to take part in actual fighting." He paused and smiled at Rachel. The afternoon sunshine came through the crusted window and cast his profile into crisp outline. She sat next to the aisle and he by the glass, his still-tender, bandaged shoulder to the outside. Time and again the lurching of the car threw them together, each time leaving her shoulder and arm burning.

"I think it will be a good thing for me, Rache," he went on. "I never did want to turn my back on my country in its hour of need, and now I'll be able to do something far better, to my mind, than killing and destroying."

"But what do you know about nursing and . . . and whatever it is you'll be—"

"Oh," he laughed, "I'll not be doing the nursing myself. Not exactly. I asked Dr. Carey that when he suggested his plan. No, I'll be responsible to assist nurses and maybe help hire other kinds of helpers for hospital tents, like the one I was in in Frederick, and surgeons' assistants. That sort of thing."

"Will you have to leave Michigan to come back soon?" She was sure he could feel the beating of her heart through

272

the fabric of the seat they shared. When he had first told her his return home was only temporary, her heart had fallen. Even though she'd known it was silly to think he could just go home, scot-free.

"Dr. Carey said I should look after things at home, stay for the Christmas season, 'to take care of family business,' in his words, then report to him early in January."

She decided the seats were poor conductors of the deeper emotions. "That will be nice," she said.

He gave her a sharp look.

"When do you think you will be back home to Michigan, to stay?" she asked, staring straight in front of them, at the heads bobbing and swaying like cabbages on overlong stems.

"I'll likely remain there until the end of the war, whenever that is." He stared out the window.

"Don't you expect to get some time off, like a furlough, so you can come home? At least to visit your father?" She tried hard to achieve a nonchalant tone.

"Oh, I think Dad will understand if I don't get home too often."

"*He* certainly is a casualty of this war," Rachel said, with feeling. "If his only son hadn't run off to war, Ben King would be a healthier man today."

She faced him squarely, the force of her words pulling his eyes around. "Surely there must be some provision in your new job . . . alternate service or whatever you call it, to help your own father." There were tears of frustration in her voice. Why couldn't this big dumb man realize—

"By the way, Rachel." He was grinning. Yes, actually grinning at her! "I'm sure going to need help getting everything planned and operating. A lot of help." There was a twinkle in his blue eyes, and she felt a first inkling. "Would you, Rachel, come to Washington city with me, as my partner? Dr. Carey mentioned something about the

273

more hands in service, the more good could be done."

Their eyes locked. She felt the color seeping into her cheeks. Her ears were on fire. Her chest was as light as a cloud, except for that heart in there, pounding like a hammer.

"Just what are you saying, Mr. King?" She would make him speak the words, clearly. That grin was becoming infuriating!

"Well now, considering how you are not a very typical woman for this modern, nineteenth century, hiking up your skirts and marching off to see about getting a childhood friend out of prison, taking a train ride by yourself, in wartime, being party to the exertion of pressure on the president of the United States, and—why, my goodness, you seem to think you can accomplish anything you put your aggressive mind to, whether it's ladylike or—"

"Joseph King, I resent your slurs on my character!" But she did not resent them at all. Not when his eyes burned into hers as they did while he spoke. He could go on saying all those kinds of words as long as he had breath.

"I certainly could use you as my co-worker, Rachel." Now his voice was like velvet, his face inches from hers. "Don't you think it's about time we got married?"

She could only nod. The lump in her throat forbade speech. Then, right there in public, surrounded by all the quaking cabbages, they kissed. Her mind raced wildly through time and distance, sparking pictures of memory and of fantasy. It was not like his kiss on an ancient day on the riverbank, after a casual swim. It was as different as a summer's white cloud is from a thunderhead in autumn. There was lightning and crashing and tumult in her.

"Does that mean yes?" He smiled tenderly.

"Yes," she whispered.

Their hands found each other. Her shoulder came against his, and stayed there. Their eyes took in the outdoors but without seeing the shabbiness of dirt or dying of summer, as their train rushed northward and westward, higher into the hills. They sat that way for many minutes, too close to talk, suspended in time and joy. Feeling the smile of God upon them.

They stayed in close contact as the train rumbled through gorges, across trestle bridges, beside a sweep of cattle-dotted pastures beyond the mountains. They spoke but little as the daylight faded from sunny to gray, then to inky night.

In spite of being announced as a straight-through, their train from time to time stopped to disgorge passengers or take on more. But then in wartime changes were usual. Uniformed soldiers came aboard from time to time, usually traveling in pairs or threes, obviously on leave. Their eyes would randomly catch Joseph's and take in the bound arm beneath his tunic hung loosely across his shoulders. Then they would nod and smile, touch their fingers in their caps when their gaze fell on Rachel.

One bluff, middle-aged sergeant momentarily put Joseph in mind of Wilfred Hawkins, and his mind drifted back to recall the events of last month, now only a sad memory. He felt a pang as he remembered the man's pain over the loss of his son and of his officer friend, General Reno. He recalled nurse Hannah Campbell and began to wonder how he, as a medical assistant, could help her in her vital work. And that overworked doctor, too, who'd first attended him on the field.

The miles clicked away in the soothing monotony of wheel-on-rail music. At some isolated hamlet in eastern Ohio, after darkness had fallen, they got off to stretch and grab a bite to eat, while the engine took on water and coal. Joseph had no funds, having forfeited all wages when arrested and jailed, so Rachel paid for the sandwiches, coffee, and apples.

"It's all right, darling." She smiled up at him. "Soon all that's mine will be yours." Touched, he gave her hand a squeeze. He knew he would never be able to take advantage of such trust, as so many men did.

They climbed back on their coach and got comfortable for the night. Rachel dug a heavy woolen blanket from her copious bag and spread it over them. "Cousin Rose said I was to keep this as a wedding gift, in case they couldn't make it to the celebration." In the dim, eerie light from the swinging oil lamp a yard or two down the aisle, Joseph could just make out the sly smile on her features.

"Pretty sure of yourself, weren't you? Trapping a man like you did?" But he didn't feel trapped.

Their hands joined again beneath the blanket. "You wouldn't happen to have a couple of cushions in that carpetbag, too, would you?"

"No, but why not use the bag itself?" she said, handing it to him. "You prop it against the window and I'll prop me against you, okay?"

"Okay, sweet," he whispered. Again their lips met, in the near dark, where there was no embarrassment for spectators. "And tomorrow morning we'll plan the big day, all right?" He bunched the bag and made himself comfortable, favoring his shoulder till it felt as cozy as a kitten in a haymow.

"Hey!" she said, "the bride is supposed to choose the day."

"Point well taken," he chuckled. "Then we'll ask my dad when it suits him, when he is up and around again."

"Yes, my love," she whispered, "as soon as your father is well. I'll be ready." Then she was asleep against him. Her deep, regular breathing made her seem fragile and precious to him. Sleep eluded him, however, for a long time, and when it finally came, it was fitful and unsatisfying. He woke and dozed, awakened, then drifted off again. Their progress seemed snail-like and the intervals between hamlets longer, as they progressed further west, away from more populous regions.

Joseph's mind was too crowded to sleep soundly, too full of excitement, both good and fearsome. It was so good to be out of that private dungeon where he'd come to terms with himself for the first time in his adulthood. It was good, very good, to have faith and trust which freed his character to be truly itself. It was good to be going home, but most of all, right now anyway, it was good to be betrothed.

He smiled at his pale reflection in the dirty glass. Occasionally he could see *out* the window, in the dark, when the yellow glow of a farmhouse window flashed past. Then the seething firefly dances of a whole village or town shimmered briefly and were gone, and the outside was once again lost behind the sickly reflection of the smoking, swinging lamp.

The bad. That was keeping him awake, too. But there wasn't so much of that, not anymore. He had a wound, but that was healing, or so it felt since Randall's treatment. He was pale and weak from weeks without sunshine, exercise, and proper food. Then there was the subliminal guilt of being a soldier who had *quit,* and he had always been taught that a job worth doing was worth doing well. Dr. Carey had stressed that even though he was a medical assistant, he'd still officially be a soldier who had quit. Of course, his father would ask, was a soldier's job worth doing, in the first place?

His father. There was some of the worst of the bad that was costing him sleep. His father was older, more worn out than when his son had left. Three attacks had to make him so. There could be no gainsaying the fact that Joseph had contributed to that attack and so, as the train rattled and sighed homeward, his feelings grew heavy. How would he

277

face his father? How would his father be? He could not imagine Ben King being bitter; it wasn't like him. But, then, he'd never had three heart attacks either.

And Ben hadn't yet heard a word about Joseph's change. Joseph wrestled with his guilt and his grace. He was coming back a changed person and he hoped that would restore his father, as it had restored him. He hoped it would create a healthy relationship between them and with his entire family, and the neighbors. He silently vowed it would. And he prayed.

Rachel slept on, stirring now and then before dropping back into deep slumber. She barely woke even when they changed trains at some sleepy western Ohio town, exchanging a northerly bearing for their familiar westering. He led her like a zombie from one train to the other and steered her to an empty seat in the new, less-crowded coach. Then he himself, for the first time in the long night, found real sleep, in a more restful position. Before he nodded off, he momentarily recalled his premonition about the train ride to Frederick being his last ride. He smiled self-indulgently. So much for superstition, he thought.

* * *

They pulled into the Kalamazoo station shortly before noon on a beautifully crisp, autumn day. They had dozed on and off through much of the morning, and when the train briefly changed direction and allowed the sun to angle a bolt of light into Joseph's face, he woke thinking he was back in his cell. His heart plummeted toward his boots, until he saw Rachel's luxurious hair spread over his shoulder like a silken web.

He smiled in quiet pleasure, remembering the beauty of his present world. Gently he shook her awake. "We're home, sweetheart. Rise and greet a new life!"

She stretched and yawned and joined him in looking out the windows. The train, banging and jolting as it slowed, drew them along the station platform before lurching to a stop. No familiar face greeted their expectant stares.

"Hello, where's our ride?" Joseph asked of the pane. He turned to Rachel. "Do you suppose the telegram didn't get delivered? If Randall got it off right away, they've had nearly twenty-two hours to do something about it."

Rachel said nothing as her eyes searched the platform and station buildings. There was practically no one about. Her gaze continued on past the structures to the hitching area. Just then a large horse towing a familiar carriage galloped up in a cloud of dust.

Joseph's eye was caught by the movement. "That's Caesar!" he shouted. I'd recognize that bobbed tail and plowhorse gait anywhere! Wonder why they didn't use Nancy." He squinted. "Who's that driving? Couldn't be Pop."

"It's Rufe!" Rachel cried "He's come for us."

"What's he doing here, in Pop's hack?"

"Oh, I never told you," Rachel said, collecting her things. "He's been working for your family since the heart attack." She glanced at Joseph. "The Kings' only son ran off to war, you see, and—"

"All right!" Joseph said, playfully punching her. He took her large bag and stood up with it. "I'll apologize, I'll apologize. Now let's get out of here and home to tell everyone all our news. C'mon." And he led her off the train.

20

In what felt like the depths of the night, Benjamin King woke in his bedroom to the sound of Caesar's loud hooves clattering away down the lane. They turned left along the high road toward Kalamazoo. He mentally blessed Rufus for volunteering to make the long trip to the station, starting before daylight, then having to turn around and head right back. That's why Ben had insisted on his taking Caesar. The fourteen-year-old gelding didn't care much for towing buggies. He much preferred plows and disks and other, respectably tough work. But Ben knew a dozen hours of steady going on hard roads needed the strength of a work-toughened horse. Nancy had gone lame last week and she'd never survive such a long trip.

It was still a while until sunrise, Ben knew, but a new dawn had already come to his heart. He smiled into the dark around him with a smile that felt idiotic in its child-likeness. He had slept better so far tonight than he had in the weeks he'd been bedridden. Ever since the telegram had come at suppertime, saying that Joseph and Rachel were on their way home, he'd felt almost reborn. Years seemed to drop off his body and even the weakness of his heart wasn't as great a burden to bear.

It was a complete surprise to hear that Joseph was coming home. Rachel had gone to Washington city only a few days ago, but not even in his most hopeful dreams had Ben expected her to bring Joseph along home to Michigan. To fetch back some word about him, yes, but *this*?

He lifted his head and turned toward the window. There was still no dawn glow, but he couldn't wait. He closed his eyes and let his head drop again into its familiar hollow in the pillow. Yes, his heart was filled with thanksgiving. His son, who had been lost to him, was come back to life! It was an answer to his most earnest prayer. And, he admitted, he had not really expected it to be answered. He felt ashamed along with his gratitude.

True, he didn't know why Joseph was allowed to come home. It might be under a dark cloud of censure and humiliation. It might be only temporary release, perhaps under heavy guard. A last farewell to a dying father, then back to lifetime imprisonment.

Or execution.

Oh, why hadn't the telegram said more?

"Stop it, Ben," he said aloud.

He went back to musing. From the time since he had received that first wire, the one which had brought on his heart attack and pneumonia, until now, he had not heard a word either from or about his son. Not a word as to formal charges, trial, or what kind of jail he was in. Nothing.

He sighed, as deeply as he dared. He was pleased to realize he didn't feel more than the slightest twinge of pain, just a flutter, actually. It was still a mystery to him why his son had done the thing that had caused him to be thrown in prison. Why hadn't he written? But it didn't matter now. He was alive and he was on his way home. In less than a dozen hours he would be able to lay eyes again on his son, his only child.

He must have dozed off, he thought later, for the next thing he knew it was daylight and Kate was clumping up the steps. The rich aroma of coffee preceded her.

"Good morning, good morning, son!" His mother was beaming as she swept into the room, a tray in her hands bearing two steaming mugs and a bowl of oatmeal. "How is every little thing this fine morning?" Swinging into the month-old routine, she set the tray on the bureau. Then she bustled around the bedroom, lifting blinds, puffing pillows and stacking them behind Ben's back, laying the board across the bed, and pulling up a chair to the bedside. He had never seen her so cheerful and full of energy since his accident.

"D'ya think they'll be here soon?" he asked her.

"Pish! Rufus probably isn't even halfway to Kalamazoo!" She laughed. "Here, eat this oatmeal before it's cold." She set the steaming bowl on the board and handed him a spoon. "You're as impatient as when you were a little boy, I declare. Besides, don't expect the speed out of ol' Caesar that Prince would give."

Ben grinned around a mouthful of the hot cereal and held out his hand for the coffee. "I'm still surprised old Caesar let himself be hitched to the buggy without more fuss."

"Well, it's the 'old' that explains it," his mother said, handing him the mug. She took the other one and sipped at it a few times before continuing. "In his prime Caesar would not have gone close to the shafts of a buggy, but now—well, advancing age changes creatures."

"How does it change 'creatures,' Mother, as you term them?" His eyes twinkled through the steam as he drank.

"Now you don't go giving me any sass or disrespect, young man, or I'll maybe not change your sheets as I was going to!" But her eyes twinkled right back.

"I'll say this, though," she continued, "knowing Joey's near home again peels some fifty or sixty years off me like skin off an onion."

They both laughed, comfortable after several weeks in the roles that Ben's accident and illness had thrust them into, as if the past fifty years hadn't passed, and he was still a lad.

He finished his breakfast, then slowly and carefully hauled himself out of bed to the chair Kate had vacated as she stripped the bed. He'd been capable of this physical activity for a week now, but today, Ben realized, it was different. He felt significantly better.

"Mother," he said in a low voice, suddenly tense with excitement, "I think I can stand up. Maybe even walk about a little!" And before she could respond, he got slowly to his feet.

"Benjamin—you be careful!" Her voice was sharp, but she only stood, with her arms outstretched, as if her baby were learning to walk. He took a step. Then two.

"You know what Doctor Adams said, not to try getting up and about for at least six weeks!" But she only stood, breathless, as Ben moved to the window, then turned to smile at her.

"I think I'm all right, Mother," he said.

She let her breath out slowly, realizing her heart was thumping in her chest. "I don't think you should overdo it though, son." She took a step toward him, expecting at any moment to see his face grimace in pain. "Why don't you get back into bed while I take these breakfast things downstairs and get the scissors. You did say you wanted your beard trimmed, didn't you? All right?"

"Well, okay," he said, and took a step back toward the bed. He felt his heart hammering in his chest and his legs quivered as he moved. He was amazed at how weak a person could become after only a few weeks in bed. He took another step, and another. Then he was at the chair.

"Why don't I just sit here while you go down, Mother? I feel great. Just a bit weak."

Kate studied him as he sat down, joy and fear warring with each other in her breast. Then she clucked, "Very well, Benjamin, but I don't want you to try any funny business while I'm gone!"

"Go on now, Mother. And tell Lovina I'll be surprising her one of these days by coming downstairs for dinner!"

Kate left the room with the tray of dishes. Ben sat in the armless, hard chair and stared around at the walls, ceiling, and window. His face was wreathed in a silly, fatuous smile. How good it was to be out of a prone position! To be up on his feet and off his behind again, like a normal adult. Why, he felt great—just a mite shaky, that's all.

He heard Lovina's voice rise in excitement from the kitchen where she was no doubt already preparing the celebratory feast for Joseph's homecoming. Then there were two pairs of feet rushing up the steps. Ben grinned. He decided he'd be standing when his wife came in so he began to rise. The next thing he knew he was falling clumsily. His wife and mother came into the room just in time to see him sprawl awkwardly across the bed.

Minutes later his womenfolk had exhausted their shrieks and scoldings and had bossily restored him to his accustomed horizontal position beneath the bedcovers. Only then was he able to get them to hear him. No, it was *not* a pain in his chest that had made him slump. He had not collapsed at all. It's just that his leg muscles had gone flabby and when he'd tried to stand up too quickly, they had given out. And that was all.

It took nearly a quarter of an hour for them to be persuaded and for their anxiety to be soothed. Even then Kate insisted on staying with him while Lovina went back downstairs to prepare the roast chicken.

Ben was amused at her concern. "Mother, why don't you just bring me a good book to read? You don't have to stay and guard me." He chuckled. "But make it a light one. A novel would do fine. I am not inclined to do any heavy thinking today of all days."

Kate snorted. "That's a sure sign you're not yourself. A *novel*, of all things." She shook her head. "What's the world coming to if Mennonite preachers start dabbling in such nonsense!"

Her twinkling eyes belied her gruffness, however, and apparently she was convinced at last of Ben's essential health. She left and went down to the bookcases in the parlor. She hadn't given Ben her honest assessment of fiction. She was aware that he knew she loved to read good stories. She had not only had read all the Leatherstocking Tales as they came out, but had practically recited them to Joseph as he was growing up. And then when that English upstart had begun churning out his thick books, she'd read all of them, too. And guess who had received his delight with Charles Dickens from her? That's right—the big old-young man upstairs.

Before she returned up to the bedroom, she helped Lovina get the birds ready for the oven. The two women were in high spirits and grew nostalgic as they worked. Then the two big fowls were deposited in the stove and it was still too soon to start the potatoes. They sat down over a cup of coffee and let their happiness take them back in time, remarking on moments when such and so had happened, or an incident that triggered a train of experiences.

Kate was halfway through her second cup when she suddenly remembered her errand for Ben. "Must be getting old and forgetful," she muttered to herself as she labored up the steps.

Ben was sleeping peacefully when she strode into the room. She quieted her step and tiptoed over to the bureau, where she laid the book within his reach. She stood for a long moment and stared down at his still face. Suddenly a powerful wave of love and contentment swept through her. She felt as young as a child but simultaneously as old and wise as a sage. For the first time in her nearly fourscore years she felt as though her life were just beginning. She could hardly wait to share it with her whole family. For the time she had left.

* * *

"Where's Grandma?" Joseph called out as he helped Rachel down from the cramped buggy. His mother had swept from the house at the sound of the horse's hooves and was waiting for them, outside the woodshed by the hitching rail. "I thought she'd be glad to see me! Oh, thank you, Rufe," he said, turning to the hired hand who led Caesar away. "Much obliged for fetching us. I'll be out to chat with you about the farm later."

Rufe gave a huge grin and a mock salute. "My pleasure," he said, and disappeared into the barn with horse and carriage.

Lovina chuckled. "Your Granny's probably putting the finishing touches to some welcome-home surprise."

"Now, Lovina, you've just ruined the surprise," Rachel scolded.

They all laughed, and then Joseph threw his good arm around his mother and she gave him a hearty kiss on the cheek. She wrinkled her nose at his full beard, then smiled. His tunic slid off his right shoulder as he embraced her, and Lovina gasped when she saw the bandage supporting his arm and shoulder.

"It's nothing, Ma," Joseph assured her. "I'll tell you all about it, when Pop and Granny can hear, too." He changed the subject quickly. "Ma, I hope you don't mind if Rachel stays a while. There's a lot to tell you, and I need her around to coach me in case I forget any details." He winked at Rachel behind Lovina's back. She colored instantly.

"Heavens no!" Lovina cried. "There's plenty of food for all of us, her too." She sobered and looked at Rachel in jesting horror. "Got to give her something to fatten her up."

They all giggled again as Joseph shepherded the two

women toward the back door. He felt fond affection for his mother. She had never been especially demonstrative in her feelings. But today she was smiling and joking, carrying on like a schoolgirl at a picnic. He grinned inwardly. He would indulge her, for he could imagine her gratification at having her only child at home again, alive and well. He didn't doubt she'd be amazed at the president's intervention. And proud of it as well. They all would, he hoped.

As for his and Rachel's secret, that would be fun to spring on them right away. He assisted her and his mother up the steps to the woodshed door, grinning in anticipation of his family's surprise and delight, he hoped, when he made the announcement.

Rachel had told him how her frequent visits to the King farm after Ben's accident had thawed much of the frostiness between the two families. He and Rachel had decided on the train that they would try to melt the last lingering coolness, if there still was any, by traveling together to the Kings first. Then they would take their good news to the Miller homestead. Maybe the joining of their two families would be a start toward bringing the church back together again. He fervently hoped so, because with his personal turnaround had come a new and growing love for his father's work and witness.

Lovina opened the door and led them through the shed to the kitchen. Joseph felt his taste buds stand up and quiver at the cloud of food smells that hit them. He was suddenly twice as happy, at least, to be home again.

"Yoohoo!" Lovina sang out. "Company's come!" It sounded like a prearranged signal.

"Upstairs!" Kate's voice rang down the steps, full of girlish excitement. "Come on up and see what you shall see!"

"Well, she certainly sounds happy." Lovina beamed and took their wraps to the closet, saying to Joseph: "Probably be better not to shock your father too much with the sight of that soldier's coat in this house." Her face became uncertain for an instant, then glowed again. "Let's go see why your grandma wouldn't come to greet you at the door!"

They had gone about halfway up the staircase, Lovina leading Joseph and Rachel, when Ben's voice boomed down over them. "Hello, everyone!"

He stood erect at the landing in the stairs, grinning like a naughty ten-year-old, leaning on his mother's arm.

Lovina turned and grinned at Joseph and Rachel. "Your surprise, son!"

"Father!" he exclaimed, "I thought you were sick in bed!" He became aware of Rachel making small sounds of surprise behind him.

"Not anymore, praise the Lord!" thundered Ben. His smile was as wide as an ocean. He spread his arms to match it, like Moses holding back the Red Sea. "Welcome home, son!" He took a slow step forward, preparing to descend.

"Be careful, Benjamin," Kate cried. "Your muscles aren't used to your weight! Remember this morning." She tightened her grip on his arm.

Joseph stared at his father. He couldn't believe it was the same man. Ben King was at least thirty pounds lighter. His hair and beard were as gray as the head of an old man. Joseph suddenly felt tears of anguish burn his eyes. "Here, Father, let me help!" He rushed up the last few steps to stand beside his father. "Better sit down, Pa." Together, he and his grandmother urged Ben back into his bedroom and helped him sit on the side of his bed. Rachel and Lovina followed. Kate sat on the chair.

"It sure is wonderful to see you up and around again, my dear," Lovina said, moving to her husband and stroking his hair. She faced Joseph and Rachel. "Just this morning he did it for the first time—got up and walked." She almost snickered. "Claims it's because today's special occasion makes him feel years younger!"

"It certainly is wonderful, and about time!" Kate chimed in.

"Yes, it surely is, Grandma," Rachel added. Then she realized what she'd said and met Joseph's eyes with a look that made him burst into laughter.

Before Kate could register more than a raised eyebrow at Rachel's choice of word, Ben King's best preacher voice rolled up over them: "Look at you all, standing around fussing over this old man as if *he* were the guest of honor. Shame on you all! No, I propose we divert our attention to this young man with the beard"—he gestured grandly at Joseph—"and allow him to give an accounting of himself." His voice was peremptory but the twinkle in his eye belied it.

"Now we all know the story of the prodigal son who ran away and squandered his inheritance, then was accepted home by his father in full sonship and with undying love. Well, there really isn't any match between that son and mine, except that I extend that same kind of love and family acceptance to you, Joseph. And I say that even before I know what happened to you."

Some of the preacher tone left Ben's voice and a gamut of emotions played in his eyes. "However, son, even though you have our faithful love, before we feed you the fatted calf—or plumped chicken, as the case may be—you have a price to pay. We all want to know, so you must tell us, just what happened to you since you left on that march out of Frederick."

He scowled mightily at his son. "You never wrote us a word after that, do you realize? And that's been more than a month ago." He pointed at Joseph's bandage. "And I'd wager your mother would like to know how you got that, too. I know I would!" Then Ben's voice broke, and he quickly looked down at his lap.

Joseph suddenly felt shy. He looked out the window.

The morning sunshine had stayed bright into the late afternoon and he could just see the edge of the barn roof from where he stood. It was a sight that brought home to him forcefully that his long ordeal was over, and he truly was home. Then his eyes met his father's. He took a step toward him and gripped Ben's hand with both of his own.

"Father, forgive me." Sudden tears filled his eyes. "I failed you miserably. I would not have had the courage— make that gall—to face you again if it hadn't been for what overtook me first on the battlefield, then in prison.

"I can't even imagine you ill, inactive, and flat on your back for days or weeks. To me you are now just the way I remember you." He smiled sadly. "Except for the loss of weight and the gray hair. But I know I caused you great heartache and physical torment, and I hope you will . . . will. . . ." He felt himself losing control.

His father struggled to his feet and threw his arms around Joseph. "Hush now," he whispered. Joseph could hear Ben's throat working loudly and feel the arms thumping his back. "You just hush now, y'hear?"

They stood thus for a long moment. The room was still. A robin sang in the October sunshine. Downstairs, the parlor pendulum clock ticktocked loudly.

Kate grunted and stood up. She sniffed and said, "I reckon we could all use some food."

"Yes, of course," Lovina chimed in. "Almost forgot. It must be 'bout ready."

"Let me help," Rachel said. The three women left the room, Rachel taking Kate's arm, Lovina going on ahead.

When they'd gone, Ben pushed Joseph to arm's length. "Here, let me take a better look at you, Son." His eyes glistened as they surveyed him. "And I want to hear the whole story, as I said, from the day you left here to the day you left for home." He raised a hand as Joseph opened his mouth to speak. "Everything, even the days of training, marching, and fighting, or whatever it was you did. Even the parts you know I would never approve of." He playfully punched Joseph in the chest. "After all, you left us so much in the dark we had only our imaginations to fill in the details."

"Of course, Pa," Joseph agreed, "but suppose I wait until we're at table so Grandma and Ma can hear it, too?" He found he was eager to tell all, to relate his change of heart and his penitence for rejecting his father's teachings. He realized he was not fearful of being honest because he believed his father already knew or at least sensed the remarkable change Joseph had undergone.

"Well, then, let's get down there!" Ben said, and started toward the top of the stairs. Joseph followed, but was startled when his father grabbed hold of him for quick support after they had gone a few steps.

"Sorry, Pa," Joseph said, gripping Ben's arm tightly, "I still don't think of you as a walking wounded, even though Rachel told me about your fall and heart attack. Here, grab hold with your free arm and let me go ahead of you on the stairs."

So hand in hand, arms intertwined, father and son got to the kitchen and sat in their places at the table. The women bustled about, Kate pouring coffee, Lovina making last-minute adjustments to the fragrant platters and carrying them to the table, Rachel setting the dishes and cutlery. The three of them frequently stopped and stared at Ben as if his presence at the table again was quite amazing, as indeed it was. It all seemed rather comical to Joseph.

"Serve it up, ladies!" thundered the object of their looks. "Someone has to feed this hardworking farmer. And don't give me any bother about this silly diet I'm about to break!"

"Coming right up, our banquet of celebration," Lovina almost chirped. Then the dishes were served and the women were seated. All heads turned expectantly toward Ben.

"Let us return thanks," he said. The heads all bowed.

"Our kind and merciful Father," he began, in a soft voice from which all bombast had vanished. "Please accept our humble and earnest thanksgiving for thy manifold blessings. In particular on this brilliant autumn day, Lord God, we return our gratitude for the restoration of our son to his rightful place in our home, and for the bestowal of renewed health to thy servant. Accept, also, our thanks for the fruits of thy creation, whereof we are about to partake. In the name of the Savior and our Christ, the Lord Jesus. Amen."

The heads came up and the steaming bowls and platters of food began their rounds.

"All right, now," Ben said, serving himself a large helping of mashed potatoes, "we are waiting to hear the story from our soldier boy." He glanced expectantly at Joseph.

"Uh . . . Ma and Pa," Joseph said, taking the bowl from his father. He shot a glance at Rachel across the table. "There's something I want to say, first, that is . . . uh . . . a part of the story, really, but . . . uh—" He suddenly busied himself with a spoonful of potatoes. "But it's a separate story I—I guess. . . ."

"Land's sake, son, what are you trying to say?" Kate beamed at him. "Does it have something to do with why Rachel has stayed for dinner instead of whisking off home right away to see her folks she's been away from for almost a week?"

Joseph blushed furiously. "Yes, I suppose it does." He fastened his gaze on Rachel and said, "We are going to be married. That is," he hurried on, "if it's all right with her folks."

"Hah—I knew it!" Kate cackled. Her grin was too broad to permit eating, so she just sat and glowed. Joseph was struck by his grandmother's attitude. He clearly remembered her antipathy toward Rachel. Obviously, some changes had been going on here at home, too.

The smiles on the faces of Ben and Lovina were wide, too, but Joseph sensed some hesitancy in his father. He was sure he knew the reason, that his father simply did not know the new man in his son's skin.

"Praise God," his mother said, simply and sincerely.

"Have you thought this decision through carefully?" Ben asked. "Is there a chance your father will not approve, Rachel?"

There was a wide river of significance to the question, as everyone at the table was well aware. Isaac Miller's parting of the ways with Ben's congregation had not been either silent or subtle.

"Yes, we have, Mr. King," Rachel said, softly but with firm conviction. "We are confident that the Lord's will is for Joseph and me to be together, as husband and wife."

Ben's eyebrows shot up. He forgot to eat.

"Pa, I think it's time for all of you to hear about everything that has happened since I left here," Joseph put in. "It's part of our decision to marry." He looked around the table, meeting the eyes of everyone in turn. "I'm not the same boy who went off to war." He glanced at Rachel again. "I'm not sure Rachel would have consented to marry the person who went away in my shoes. I'm not certain I would ever have considered asking her to be my wife, if I had not felt some changes in my life since I went."

"Felt changes?" Ben asked. He looked at Joseph with curiosity, then he remembered the forkful of carrots he'd started to convey toward his mouth a moment earlier. "Go on, son, I'm listening." He shoveled the vegetables into his face.

Joseph sipped his coffee, then wiped his mouth on his napkin. "It's a long story, longer actually than the month I spent in prison." He gave a wry smile. "First, I want to apologize for not keeping in touch after leaving for battle." His face turned sheepish. "After I deserted—yes, that's what it was I did—I know you got a telegram. They told me at Old Capitol they'd be sending it. So you knew that." He stared at the table, his fingers toying with his cup. "I guess I was too confused, too ashamed to write."

"But you couldn't write," Rachel protested, "with that wound—"

"Yes, what's this wound, anyway?" It was his mother. "You haven't told us about it and I've been remiss. As soon as we're done eating, I want to have a look at—"

"It's okay now, Ma," Joseph interrupted. "I took a musket ball between my side and my upper arm, but Rachel's cousin's husband is a good doctor. He fixed it up." He laughed, reassuringly. "It'll heal up perfectly in another couple of days."

"It was bad, though, when I first saw him," Rachel said. "He had a fever, and no one had treated the wound, after he got to prison. It was badly infected."

"That's criminal!" Kate sputtered. "Someone ought to be shot!"

They all burst out laughing. Kate looked indignant for a moment, then her unconscious witticism dawned on her and she joined in the merriment.

"Anyway," Joseph went on, "I could have gotten someone to write a letter for me, I suppose, if I'd really demanded it."

"I wonder," Ben said, almost to himself. He looked at his son with fresh sympathy and understanding.

"Tell your story, Joey," Kate said. "We are all listening."

Joseph did. He told of his enlistment, of the endless but nonetheless inadequate military drill. He spoke of the march from Frederick to South Mountain. He struggled to put the awful violence into words, and all of this he related as if it had happened to someone else. As if the chain of happenings were too evil to dwell on but needed to be told because of what it led to, the change in his life.

Joseph read the shock and horror in his parents' faces. And the excitement in Kate's. But then he described his flight and capture, the stay that night in the hospital tent, and Hannah Campbell's kind assistance. He remarked on Sergeant Hawkins's agony, the interminable, painful trip to the capital city, and how his conflicting emotions tore at him like a headache and stomach pain all rolled into one.

He told of his cell in the Old Capitol Prison and the endless days and nights of aloneness. This was the first part of his story that anyone could grasp. Rachel looked at him with eyes so full of love and pain that his heart thumped wildly in his chest.

His mouth got dry and he asked her to tell the story from where she came in. He drank his coffee, now gone cold, and finished his chicken. He watched his family's eyes on their future daughter-in-law as she spoke. Then he took back telling the story to describe the things that happened to him after Dr. Carey left his Bible behind in the cell. How he grew in the knowledge that he was not alone, would never be alone again, even if he had to spend the rest of his life in that cell.

"Praise the Father!" Ben breathed.

Kate was the first to ask the obvious question: "Well, Joey, my boy, aren't you going to tell us how come you're sitting here now, and not still back there in that cell, reading the Bible and making finger marks in the dust?"

"Yes," Lovina said. "I was about to ask that myself."

Joseph and Rachel exchanged looks.

"Mr. Lincoln freed me," Joseph said, nonchalantly.

Silence.

Benjamin was the first to find his tongue. "The president?"

"*Abe* Lincoln?" Kate's mouth hung open.

Lovina clapped her hands to her mouth. Her eyes became orbs.

Rachel giggled. "That's right!" she cried. "The president of the United States personally intervened in your son's case, and commuted his imprisonment."

The three older folks burst out in a babble of excited remarks and jumbled questions.

"Whoa!" Joseph shouted joyfully. "We saved that until last just to see your reactions. Ha ha, it was worth it! Seriously, though, I was as amazed as you all are, if not more. But it so happens that Rachel's cousin's husband, Dr. Randall Carey, is a physician friend of Mr. Lincoln, and apparently he thought my new stand was unique enough to tell the president about. Next thing I knew Dr. Carey had me released, into his custody."

"Wait a minute," his mother interrupted. "How about more coffee, anyone? I need to *do* something!"

They all joyously assented. She poured, as Joseph went on. "I can't take any credit for my release because nothing about me and my desertion merited anything in the eyes of the world but scorn and continuing in prison. But Mr. Lincoln was evidently impressed enough with my beliefs and convictions that he told Dr. Carey he was willing to let me serve out the war in a peacemaking capacity. I only have to answer to Dr. Carey."

Ben King's eyes held his son's. "Has he spelled out your duties already?" he asked Joseph.

"He appointed me as an orderly and general assistant in military hospitals, for the duration."

"What does that mean?" Kate demanded.

Joseph smiled at her. "I'm not really sure yet myself. But I will visit hospital tents wherever there are wounded and dying soldiers and try to get better care to them. Give them comfort and whatever help I can."

"Does that mean you'll go away again?" Lovina asked. Her voice was plaintive.

Joseph nodded regretfully. "Right after the new year

comes in." He swallowed and looked away. "I'll still officially be a deserter—a traitor—so after the war is over . . . I don't know what will happen. . . ."

"Oh," his mother said.

"Joseph." His father's voice was strange. " Look at me."

He obeyed. Ben's eyes brimmed with unshed tears.

"Today my prayers have been answered, my son." His smile quavered. "I am proud of you and profoundly grateful to God not only that you were spared, but also that you came to grips with your faith. And now in his infinite wisdom and mercy the Lord is giving you an opportunity for service."

Ben's voice strengthened as he spoke. "I don't know what specific tasks you will be engaged in. But I sense that in your new faith you are willing to be a vessel for him, to help bring healing instead of destruction. That is sufficient for me!"

He did not comment on Joseph's last sentence, about what might happen after the war. Those words had pierced Ben's chest like an icy dagger. Yet he thought of the stories of the martyrs in the Mennonite heritage of faith and understood that Joseph was in an honorable line.

Joseph felt fluttering in his chest. He glanced at Rachel with a lump in his throat. Her eyes were shining.

Ben spoke again. "I sense that there will be an important order of business to take care of before you leave." He was grinning now and strength seemed to flow from him. "Is it your wish to take a new wife along with you in your coming assignment?"

"Yes, Father, it is."

"Well then, son, and daughter, it is best that we begin plans for that happy event now. Don't you agree?"

Rachel and Joseph both nodded vigorously, like small children.

"And you, Mother and sweetheart?"

Kate and Lovina both nodded, vigorously. Then they looked at each other in surprise and burst out laughing.

"Excellent!" Ben started to stand up, but faltered. "Shucks! I must concentrate on getting my strength back."

"You just stay right there in your chair, Benjamin King!" Lovina cried, "while I help you start on that, right now!" She got up, hurried to the stove, and brought him another plateful of chicken and potatoes.

"Here, Ma," Joseph sang out, lifting his empty plate. "I'll have more, too, if you please."

She served him, then gave more to everyone else, topping up the coffee cups again, too. For the next few minutes the only sounds in the sun-drenched kitchen were those of happy people enjoying the appetites of cheerful spirits. Ben was the first to push back his empty plate, with a sigh.

"So," he boomed, sounding full of renewed strength already. "When shall this wedding take place?"

"Not so fast, Pa," Joseph laughed. He got up and walked around Rachel. He placed his hands on her shoulders. "First we have to go and get her parents' approval."

"You do that right now, children!" Ben thundered. "And we will expect you back here with the answer just as fast as ol' Caesar can move!"

"Pa, he must be exhausted!"

"Well then . . . ah . . . take Prince!" Ben responded. "He'll carry you both. And he's fast. Just ask someone who should know!"

In the general merriment, Rachel stood up and Joseph brought their wraps. He helped her into hers, then shrugged into his own tunic. He caught his father's grimace as the older man noted the military cut and ornament of the garment. Or was it merely its seedy, tattered appearance?

"It'll be the last time you'll see it, Father," Joseph said, in a quiet voice. "That I promise." He turned to Rachel. "Ready, my dear?"

She nodded and, smiling happily, said to the three still at table, "Thank you for the kind of son you made, my dear people. I know this coming Christmas will be the best I've ever had."

"Good-bye, all," Joseph said as they moved to the wood-shed doorway. "We'll be back in a jiffy!" Then they were gone.

* * *

"Here, Lov, help me to the window!" Ben ordered. His wife and his mother gave him their arms and the three of them watched their children leave on Prince's back, a few minutes later. Clouds were racing across the sky from the west and the wind was kicking up puffs of road dust and blowing through the last few dried-out cornstalks still standing in the front field. But there was only brightness and warmth in their hearts. Ben refused to worry about his son's future, how his military status might follow him like a devilish phantom.

"Let them learn war no more," he mused, almost to himself.

"Wouldn't it be something," he went on, "if the government of these United States would start a regular program to allow the sons of conscience to channel their beliefs into constructive work instead of making war? That would be better than causing poor, peace-loving fathers to have heart attacks."

They all laughed. Then Lovina and Kate King turned from the window to take the dirty dishes off the table.

The Author

Robert Koch was born in Kitchener, Ontario, in 1943. Since 1957, when his pastor father answered a call to Ohio, Koch has lived in the USA. For years he taught in high schools in Michigan. Since 1981 he has been teaching history and literature at the high school in Craig, Colorado, with a year off as a Fulbright teacher in England. He has written articles for church periodicals and for newspapers.

Koch attended Eastern Mennonite College, Harrisonburg, Virginia, and in 1965 earned his B.A. in history at Goshen (Indiana) College. In 1972 he was awarded an M.A. in humanities from Wayne State University (Detroit), and in 1976 another M.A., in social studies, from Western State College of Colorado. He also did some predoctoral studies in history at the University of Michigan in Ann Arbor.

Koch is married to Linda Epp and has three children: Andrew, a student at the University of Colorado in Boulder; and preschoolers Derek and Amanda. For want of a Mennonite congregation within a hundred miles, the Kochs attend Faith Lutheran Church of Craig.